House Blood

Also by Mike Lawson

The Inside Ring
The Second Perimeter
House Rules
House Secrets
House Justice
House Divided

House Blood

A Joe DeMarco Thriller

Mike Lawson

Atlantic Monthly Press
New York

Published simultaneously in Canada
Printed in the United States of America

FIRST EDITION

ISBN-13: 978-0-8021-1994-0

Atlantic Monthly Press
an imprint of Grove/Atlantic, Inc.
841 Broadway
New York, NY 10003

Distributed by Publishers Group West

www.groveatlantic.com

12 13 14   10 9 8 7 6 5 4 3 2 1

Prologue

Kelly and Nelson began by reviewing Brian Kincaid's phone records and credit card statements and immediately saw the pattern—a pattern that had not changed in over a year. On the first Wednesday of the first week, they followed Kincaid and confirmed what the data had shown.

They spent several days analyzing the security procedures for the office building on K Street. It was an older building—built in the fifties—and only seven stories high. It didn't have its own parking garage. Until a year ago, there was no general security for the building and if tenants wanted to protect their office spaces, they contracted with a private security company. But in 2008, two floors of the building were vacated by a law firm and temporarily leased by the Treasury Department to house federal employees displaced while a portion of the massive Treasury Department building on Pennsylvania Avenue was being renovated. The remaining five floors continued to be leased by private companies.

Because of whatever function the Treasury Department workers performed, there was now a metal detector in the lobby—something that had become almost a standard fixture in government buildings post 9/11—and during the day, two security guards screened people entering the building. Another requirement was that all the building's tenants were required to wear security badges so the guards could distinguish tenants from visitors, and doors were secured in such a way that everyone one was forced to enter and exit the building via the lobby.

The building had three stairwells. The center stairwell exited onto a small loading dock, and the loading dock door was always kept locked when not in use. The two outer stairwells exited into the lobby. There was a security camera in the lobby and cameras in the elevators, but there were no cameras monitoring the loading dock behind the building or the stairwells. None of the doors that permitted access to the building were alarmed. Apparently protecting whatever Treasury was doing wasn't worth the additional expense of wiring the building for alarms and adding more cameras.

At six P.M., the two day-shift security guards were replaced by a single guard, and at eight o'clock, well after most of the building's tenants had left for the day, the night-shift guard locked the lobby doors so he could use the restroom and go to other parts of the building if necessary. At midnight, for probably no good reason other than to keep himself awake, the guard made a floor-by-floor tour of the building that took approximately an hour. If a tenant needed to enter the building after eight P.M. he would buzz the guard and be required to show his security badge before being allowed to enter. Visitors were not allowed to enter after eight P.M. unless accompanied by a tenant.

It was hardly an airtight security system—not the type you'd see for a defense facility—but it was good enough to keep street people from wandering into the building and there were probably safes in the Treasury Department offices to further protect whatever documents were kept there. Kelly and Nelson, however, didn't care about the Treasury Department. They concluded that the building's security measures presented them no insurmountable problems, and the fact that there was a camera in the lobby actually worked to their advantage.

———◆◆◆———

The background information provided on Brian Kincaid showed that he had a .38-caliber Smith & Wesson revolver registered in his name. He didn't have a carry permit or a concealed-weapons permit, and Kelly assumed that Kincaid kept the gun in his house. One day, after Kincaid left for work, Kelly put on gloves, picked the lock on the back door of Kincaid's house, and entered to search for his pistol. Kincaid's financial records had shown that he didn't have a home security system and, since he didn't have children, Kelly figured the gun would not be locked in a gun safe but would most likely be in the master bedroom on the second floor or in the den on the first floor. He searched the bedroom first and found the gun almost immediately in the nightstand on the right-hand side of Kincaid's bed. He confirmed the gun was loaded, then placed it back in the nightstand and left the house.

On the following Wednesday, Kelly and Nelson followed Kincaid again to confirm he stuck to his routine. After Kincaid returned home, they went back to the building on K Street and, at approximately one A.M.—after the security guard had made his rounds—they went into the alley behind the building and Kelly picked the lock on the loading dock door. He then picked the lock three more times to make sure he could open the door quickly.

They jogged up the stairs to the sixth floor—both men proud they weren't the least bit winded by the climb—entered the hallway, and walked down the hall until they reached a door labeled *Downing and Kincaid, LLP.* Kelly picked the lock on the door, but had a hard time with it; it took him almost two minutes. He picked it several more times but couldn't open the door in less than a minute—and that wouldn't do. He needed to be able to enter the office quickly, and if someone was inside the office—which there would be on the night of the operation—an occupant was likely to hear him picking the lock. They were going to have to make or steal a key.

For the next two days they observed Kincaid, his business partner, Phil Downing, and the secretary they shared. They noticed that the secretary wore a cloth lanyard around her neck like a necklace, and that on the lanyard was her security badge and two keys. They figured one of the keys was for the office and that the secretary kept it on the lanyard because she frequently ran errands for her bosses and was probably worried about forgetting her key and locking herself out. The other might be for a file cabinet or a safe, which they didn't care about.

They followed the secretary that day when she left work and saw that she went immediately to a nearby bar. The next two days, she went to the same bar and each time had at least two drinks before she caught the Metro home. The secretary appeared to be a bit of a lush. As soon as she arrived at the bar, she would remove the security badge lanyard, drop it into her large purse, and plop the purse down on the floor on the right-hand side of her bar stool.

Kelly and Nelson had a brief, good-natured debate regarding which of them would be more appealing to the secretary. The next night when the woman went to the bar, Nelson approached her, standing on her left-hand side, and began talking to her. Kelly took a seat on the bar stool on her right, and when the woman appeared to be giving Nelson her full attention, he dropped his car keys on the floor. While picking them up, he used his big body to conceal what he was doing and plucked the lanyard from the secretary's purse, then immediately went to the men's room where he made a wax impression of the two keys on the lanyard. When he returned to the bar, the secretary was laughing loudly at something Nelson had said and had a hand on one of his muscular forearms. Kelly had no problem returning the security badge and keys to the secretary's purse.

The next day Kelly went to a locksmith in a seedy part of Washington and placed the wax impressions of the keys on the counter. The locksmith looked down at the impressions, then into Kelly's eyes. He didn't say anything. Kelly placed four hundred-dollar bills on the counter and the locksmith picked up the money, put it in his pocket, and started making the keys. It was a completely wordless transaction.

That night, again at approximately one A.M., Kelly picked the lock on the loading dock door for the fifth time. He could now open the door in less than thirty seconds. He jogged up to the sixth floor, walked down the hallway to the offices of *Downing and Kincaid, LLP,* and tried the keys. The first key opened the door.

The next day, Kelly and Nelson wrote down on a large white board every action they would take and then analyzed the plan. What would they do if Kincaid deviated from his schedule? What if the guard left his post unexpectedly? What if there were other tenants in the building at nine o'clock at night? This was their biggest concern—that one of the tenants might decide to work late.

The building's janitors left before seven P.M. each day except Friday, when they mopped and waxed the floors, and the Treasury Department's civil servants poured out of the building at exactly five P.M., like somebody had set off a fire alarm. There were no law firms in the building, therefore no lawyers likely to be pulling all-nighters preparing for a case. There was an accounting firm on one floor but, as it wasn't tax season, these folks wouldn't likely be working late, and all the other tenants had occupations that typically allowed them to leave at the end of a normal workday. Kelly and Nelson finally concluded they would simply have to take the risk of one or two tenants staying late, but that the risk was small.

Their preparations were now complete.

They were ready to kill Phil Downing.

The next Wednesday, at approximately five-thirty P.M., they followed Kincaid from his office to his home in Arlington. As he had done every other Wednesday, Kincaid spent an hour inside the house, where they assumed he showered, shaved, and changed clothes. At seven P.M., he left his house and drove to a restaurant in Rosslyn—the same restaurant where, according to his credit card statements, he dined almost every Wednesday. As soon as Kincaid entered the restaurant, they drove back to his house. Kelly picked the lock on the back door, removed the .38 from the nightstand next to Kincaid's bed, and then rejoined Nelson in the car.

At eight forty-five P.M., they were parked in front of a small parking lot a block from Kincaid's office. The lot was where Kincaid parked every day and he had a sticker on his windshield that showed he paid monthly. The lot had no attendant. Customers who didn't have monthly passes put their money in a box at the entrance and the money was collected twice a day.

At eight-fifty P.M., Kincaid drove into the parking lot. He exited his car, locked it, and headed in the direction of his building, and while Kelly followed Kincaid, Nelson parked their car in the lot where Kincaid had parked. Kelly watched as Kincaid buzzed the security guard, showed his security badge, and entered the building. Kelly looked at his watch. It was eight fifty-five P.M.

Nelson joined Kelly on the sidewalk in front of the building, and at nine-ten P.M. they watched Phil Downing buzz the security guard and enter the building. As soon as Downing was in the elevator, Kelly walked to the alley behind the building, picked the lock on the loading dock door, jogged up to the sixth floor, and cracked the stairwell door open so he could see down the hallway.

At nine twenty-six P.M., Kincaid exited his office. On all three Wednesdays that Kelly and Nelson had observed him, he'd left the building just a little before nine-thirty. Two minutes after Kincaid caught the elevator, Nelson called Kelly's cell phone. The cell phone vibrated once, then stopped, and Kelly didn't answer the phone. The phone call meant that Kincaid had left the building.

Now, unless Kincaid changed his routine, he would leave his car in the parking lot and walk to a nearby bar on M Street, where he would drink single-malt Scotch for approximately two hours and try to pick up a woman. If he did meet a woman it would not be ideal, but there wasn't anything that could be done about that. Nelson would follow Kincaid to make sure he went to the bar and didn't move his car. If Kincaid did remove his car from the parking lot and drove home or to some other establishment, Nelson would follow him. They needed to be able to gain access to Kincaid's car after Kelly accomplished his task.

Kelly looked at his watch. It was nine thirty-two P.M. He had eight minutes. He walked down the hallway and used his key to open the door to the offices of *Downing and Kincaid, LLP*. Downing was, as expected, sitting at his desk. When he saw Kelly, he rose and said, "What the hell? Who are—"

Kelly shot Downing in the heart with Kincaid's revolver. The gun wasn't silenced and the shot was alarmingly loud within the confines of Downing's office, but Kelly was confident the security guard in the lobby six floors below wouldn't hear the shot.

Kelly knelt next to Downing's body and checked for a pulse. Downing's heart was still beating, but just barely. Kelly wouldn't leave until he was dead. He knelt there looking down impassively at Downing, waiting for the man to die, and as he was waiting the phone on Downing's desk began to ring. Kelly looked at his watch. Nine-forty P.M. The call was right on time. Kelly checked Downing again for a pulse and this time didn't find one. Phil Downing was dead.

Kelly left Downing's office and took the stairs down to the loading dock and left the building. He walked to the parking lot where Kincaid's car was parked, checked to make sure no one was watching, and used a slim jim to open the driver's-side door. It took him less than five seconds. He then popped the trunk latch, placed Kincaid's gun beneath the spare tire, closed the trunk, and relocked the driver's-side door.

Kelly pulled out his cell phone and called Nelson—who was still watching Kincaid to make sure he didn't leave the bar—and five minutes later Nelson joined him in the parking lot.

"Everything go okay?" Nelson asked.

"Yep," Kelly said.

They entered their car and pulled out of the parking lot.

"Are you hungry?" Nelson said.

"Starving," Kelly said.

"You wanna go to Morton's for a steak?" Three years ago they couldn't have afforded a steak at Morton's.

"You think they'll serve us the way we're dressed?" They were both neatly attired but wearing casual clothes: jeans, polo shirts, and tennis shoes.

"And who's gonna refuse to serve us?" Nelson said.

Kelly laughed and high-fived Nelson. "Hooah!" he said.

Hooah is the phonetic spelling of the military acronym HUA, which stands for: Heard. Understood. Acknowledged. It's a word particularly favored by U.S. Army Rangers. When a Ranger is told to march, to fight, to kill—the response is: *Hooah!*

The only thing was, Kelly and Nelson were no longer in the military. They worked for a pharmaceutical company.

1

———◆———

Three years earlier
Wilmington, Delaware~March 2006

Orson Mulray was fifty-three years old. He stood six foot two and
weighed two hundred and fifty pounds, but thanks to a broad chest
and wide shoulders he carried the weight well and appeared powerful
rather than obese. He had a full head of gray hair that was trimmed
weekly by a stylist, a large, fleshy nose, and a blunt, determined chin.
He was not a handsome man, but he looked confident, competent,
and prosperous. One could envision him playing a corporate executive
in a movie—CEO or Chairman of the Board—and he would have
been perfect for the role because that's exactly who he was.

Orson sat in a dark blue suit in one of half a dozen graveside chairs.
Delaware's governor sat on his right-hand side, and next to the governor was her husband and next to him was a retired Delaware senator.
The senator had been one of his father's oldest friends. On Orson's
left were his son and daughter—his father's only grandchildren—two
sullen-looking teenagers whom Orson had barely spoken to since
divorcing his wife four years ago. The crowd standing behind the
graveside seats consisted of over two hundred people, mostly wealthy

businessmen and community leaders who had known his father and claimed to have admired him.

As his father's coffin was lowered into the ground, the governor reached over and took Orson's hand to convey her sympathy and support. He glanced over at her, gave her hand a small squeeze to let her know that he appreciated her being there, then looked straight ahead, his face appropriately solemn, as his father's casket descended slowly into the grave.

What he wanted to do was leap to his feet and cheer.

He didn't think the old bastard would ever die. There had been times when he had wondered, as illogical as it sounded, if Clayton Mulray had discovered an elixir for immortality. But *finally*, he was gone. Finally, at the age of eighty-four, his father's small, hard heart stopped beating—and, as soon as this farce of mourning was over, Orson Mulray would move forward with his plan to become, quite possibly, the richest man on the planet.

Clayton Mulray founded Mulray Pharma in 1953, the same year Orson was born. He worked eighteen-hour days. He developed an effective sales force, established a research division, and bought patents on promising drugs with money borrowed from greedy lenders. He learned how to bribe doctors to push his products on their patients, he manipulated the FDA to get his drugs approved, and he hired lobbyists to influence Congress. He contributed handsomely to those politicians favorable to his endeavors, like the retired senator who attended his funeral. At the time of his death, Mulray Pharma was the twelfth-largest pharmaceutical company in the world, the eighth-largest in the United States, and number 435 on the Fortune 500 list. Its revenues in 2006 were eighteen billion, its net income four billion, and it spent three point six billion on research. It was a solid company.

The problem—at least from his son's perspective—was that in the last five years of his life, the old man decided he wanted a *legacy*. After a lifetime of self-centered overindulgence, Clayton Mulray wanted to do something to help his fellow man, and he tasked Mulray Pharma's R&D division to concentrate their efforts on cost-effective drugs for diseases that affect third world countries: malaria, tuberculosis, measles, sleeping sickness caused by tsetse flies. Orson attempted to get his father to work on drugs that were more profitable—and on one drug in particular.

"Who gets bitten by tsetse flies?" he screamed at the old man. Then he answered his own question: "Fucking Africans, that's who! They don't have any money, you old fool!" But his father could not be deterred, and Orson didn't have the power to overrule him.

But now, Clayton Mulray was rotting in a fifty-thousand-dollar casket six feet beneath the ground.

———— ◆◆◆ ————

Following the funeral, Orson, his ex-wife, his children, his ex-wife's lawyer, and a few of his father's oldest servants—the chauffeur, cooks, gardeners, and maids—went to the office of his father's attorney to listen to a reading of the will.

Orson sat there stoically as the will was read, showing no emotion. His father had informed him a year earlier of his intentions and, of course, the company's board of directors and the SEC had to be informed as well. The will left small amounts to the servants—a hundred thousand to each individual—and established a two-hundred-million-dollar trust fund for Clayton's grandchildren. The trust would be controlled by his father's lawyer so that neither Orson nor his ex-wife could get their hands on the money. And all this was fine by Orson.

The bell ringer in the will—and the reason why the board and the SEC had to be notified in advance—was that half of Clayton Mulray's stock in the company would be sold and the money used to establish a philanthropic organization. At the time of his death, Clayton Mulray owned one hundred and four million shares of Mulray Pharma stock, currently trading at twenty-seven dollars a share—and the value of half those shares was one point four billion dollars. The philanthropy would be called the Clayton Mulray Foundation.

The only good news from Orson Mulray's perspective was that even after his father's insane act of generosity, Orson would still be the largest shareholder in Mulray Pharma. And because he was CEO and chairman of the board—and because the board was a rubber stamp—this meant he had total control of the company. And control of the company was the only thing that really mattered.

Another condition of the will was that in order for Orson to inherit his father's remaining stock, he had to agree to cap his salary as CEO at one million a year for the next five years. His father had wanted his only son to remain in charge of the company—he just didn't feel that Orson needed to be as rich as he had been. Fortunately, even though Orson's salary was capped at a million, his bonus was tied to the company's stock price and, if his plan succeeded, the price was going to jump dramatically. In fact, *dramatically* was an understatement.

So Orson Mulray was still a wealthy man. His father had been number 147 on the Forbes 400 list but, because of the will, Orson was now 355. He was still a member of America's most exclusive club—but just barely. He also inherited from his father a seventeen-thousand-square-foot mansion in the exclusive Montchanin section of Wilmington, a ski lodge in Vail, and a yacht worth two point five million.

The problem, at least temporarily, was his salary as CEO of Mulray Pharma. Half his salary went to his ex-wife, his taxes were mind-boggling, and there was no way he could get by on a mere five hundred thousand a year. If he needed cash he could, of course, always sell some of his stock—but the last thing he was going to do was sell stock. Not only didn't he want to jeopardize his position as largest shareholder in the company, but more important, if his plan succeeded, the more stock he had the richer he'd be in the long run. So, thanks to his father, he was going to have to sell the yacht and the place in Vail to maintain his lifestyle for a few years.

What his father had done to him was cruel and humiliating, and if he hadn't made his own funeral arrangements, Orson would have buried the old bastard in a cardboard box.

Orson went from the lawyer's office to the luxurious Green Room in the Hotel du Pont, where Fiona West was waiting. On the table was a bottle of Dom Pérignon Oenotheque Rose in an ice bucket, the champagne purchased by Fiona to celebrate his father's long-awaited demise.

Fiona raised her champagne flute in a toast as Orson sat. "Congratulations," she said. "You're now officially an orphan." Then, seeing that he was still brooding over the will, Fiona said, "Oh, cheer up, Orson. Five years from now you'll have more money than you can count."

And that was true. But what Fiona didn't understand was that he wasn't really motivated by money or the things money could buy. Money was just a way of keeping score. What motivated him was Mulray Pharma being the *twelfth* largest pharmaceutical company in the world, and not the first. Being *any* number on the Forbes 400 list but No. 1. And, most important, that if he succeeded, people would no longer say: *Orson Mulray? Oh! You mean Clayton's boy.* There was no point, however, in explaining any of this to Fiona.

He poured himself some champagne, and he and Fiona touched glasses. "To the future," he said.

To execute his plan, Orson needed someone to help him. For one thing, he couldn't do it all by himself and still manage the company. But the other reason he needed a partner was that he wanted to be at least one step removed from the crimes he planned to commit so that in the unlikely event those crimes ever came to light, there would be someone to blame. In Fiona West, he'd found the person he needed.

Fiona was a striking woman, almost six feet tall. She had a generous bosom, narrow hips, and shapely, mile-long legs. Her eyes were almond-shaped, the irises green, flecked with yellow. Her dark hair was cut short on top, close on the sides, and parted on the left. The hairstyle didn't make her look mannish, however—just edgy. In fact, *edgy* may have been the best way to describe Fiona both physically and emotionally. And although she was striking, she wasn't truly beautiful. Her face—a mirror to her personality—was too angular, too sharp, too severe. It reflected her coldness and her arrogance.

Fiona was Mulray Pharma's chief in-house legal counsel. She had five lawyers working for her and managed the work that was farmed out to any outside law firms the company retained. Orson's father had hired her—one of the few good decisions he'd made in his waning years—because she came with a well-deserved reputation for representing her clients in an absolutely feral manner: she ripped her opponents to shreds, using any tactic, ethical or otherwise, to win.

She became Orson's mistress a year after coming to work for the company, but Orson ended the affair after only two months. For some reason, she was just *awful* in bed. She would lie there with her eyes tightly shut, barely moving, clearly relieved when the act was over. Copulating with a corpse would have been more satisfying. Orson suspected the only reason she went to bed with him in the first place was to help her career—and he actually admired her for this.

Fiona was bright, determined, relentless, and ruthless—and flawed in a number of ways. She was extremely paranoid, childishly vindictive, and absolutely vicious when she didn't get her way. Orson suspected she was some variety of sociopath—and from his perspective, this wasn't a bad thing. She was *his* sociopath. His main concern was that she was going to be difficult to control—but Orson's job was controlling people.

He'd first approached her about his plan two years before his father's death. The initial discussions were very general, very cautious—almost philosophical in nature—but once he explained the financial upside, he found that caution wasn't necessary. For the amount of money he was talking about, Fiona, like himself, was willing to accept the risks. She finally decided she wanted to be paid one billion dollars if they were successful—and Orson agreed, because a billion was going to be a small percentage of what he expected to make. Had she asked for two or three billion he would have agreed, and the fact that she asked for only one meant that she didn't really understand the potential payoff. They didn't have a written contract, however, because Orson knew that if he reneged on his part of the deal Fiona would make sure that he served the remainder of his life in prison. As he came to know Fiona better, he realized she was more likely to just have him killed.

"When are you going to Princeton?" Fiona asked.

"Tomorrow morning," Orson said. "There's no reason to delay."

Since they had been discussing the plan the last two years while they waited for his father to die, there really wasn't anything more to discuss at this point. Orson would take care of the doctor-scientist while the rest of the preliminary actions would be Fiona's responsibility: arranging security for the research facility, obtaining a doctor to administer field testing of the drug, invading the Warwick Foundation, and hiring the security specialists.

Security specialists sounded better than *killers*.

2

———◆———

Princeton, New Jersey~March 2006

Orson Mulray drove himself to Princeton to meet Dr. Simon Ballard for
the first time. Ballard was Orson's Sir Galahad—he was going to bring
him the Holy Grail of medicine. And although this would be the first
time he would lay eyes on Ballard in the flesh, Orson knew everything
there was to know about the man. He had hired a private investigator to
delve into Ballard's past, to see if he had any nasty habits, any skeletons
in his closet. He didn't. Ballard was an open book, a very boring open
book. The only thing he cared about was his research.

Orson became aware of Simon Ballard when he asked himself the
following question: What kind of drug could he produce that every
civilized person in the world would buy and continue to buy, whether
they needed it or not? When he answered that question to his satisfac-
tion, he tasked Mulray Pharma's R&D division to look for scientists
who appeared to be taking the most unique approach to solving the
problem—and they discovered Simon Ballard.

Ballard had written a grant proposal that was rejected when Clayton
Mulray ran the company. In part, the proposal was rejected because
it was so poorly written that it was almost incomprehensible. It was

also rejected because even if Ballard's theories were correct, it was going to take a decade for him to get the data he needed to prove his theories and, after that, at least another decade to get the FDA to approve the drug. But his approach to curing the disease was radically different from other cures being tried, and this is what appealed to Orson Mulray.

The other good thing about Ballard was that rival drug companies had chosen to ignore him. Not only were his theories unorthodox, but Ballard was horrible at self-promotion—he had the personality of a fence post—and, as Orson had seen from his grant proposal, the man had almost no communication skills. But were the other companies right? Was Ballard a man who should be ignored?

Orson had learned from his father that a successful CEO had to rely on his instincts. You listened to your advisers, you looked at the data, but in the end you had to go with your gut—and Orson's gut told him to go with Ballard. He didn't rely totally on instinct, however. He took all of Ballard's research he could lay his hands on—including unpublished data hacked directly from Ballard's personal computer—and parceled it out to scientists who were the best in their fields of study. He didn't allow any of them to see the complete picture and he paid them an outrageous amount of money to confirm Ballard's conclusions, but only after they had signed nondisclosure agreements that would turn them into homeless paupers if they ever violated them. In the end, he decided to gamble on Ballard. And it wasn't a small gamble. Not only would he be risking a substantial percentage of Mulray Pharma's R&D budget—he could end up in jail if things went wrong.

———◆◆◆———

When Orson entered the laboratory, Simon Ballard was sitting in front of a computer monitor, squinting at the screen. Other than the two classes he taught, the man was almost always in the lab, and usually until one or two in the morning because he had virtually no social life. Every Tuesday he played chess with a colleague, and every Friday he had dinner with a woman who taught creative writing and spent the night at the woman's house.

Orson had his private detective plant listening devices in the woman's house because he was curious about her relationship with Ballard. Their conversations were mostly one-sided, with the woman either backstabbing her colleagues or going on for hours about a novel she'd been trying to get published for ten years. The two of them didn't sound particularly intimate and they never discussed any sort of future together. When they had sex, the act was brief and mostly silent. Orson concluded they were just two lonely, un-attractive people using each other for sex, and that Ballard had no deep feelings for the woman.

The man who was to be Orson Mulray's salvation was forty-four years old and he was wearing what he wore almost every day: baggy, wrinkled khaki pants, a white short-sleeved shirt, and running shoes. During the winter he added a ratty blue sweater to his ensemble. He was six foot three, weighed one hundred and fifty-two pounds, and had long spindly legs, a short torso, and long tubular arms. He looked like an ungainly, unsymmetrical, four-legged spider. His wire-rimmed glasses were so smudged with fingerprints it was a wonder he could see, and he needed a haircut. He was as physically imposing as dirt.

But what a brain.

Orson walked over to Ballard and introduced himself, and he could tell that Ballard didn't like being disturbed while he was working but was too meek to say so.

"Uh, what can I do for you?" Ballard asked.

Orson answered the question with a question. "Doctor, what do you want more than anything else in the world?"

"Why, I don't know," Ballard said, shaking his head, both irritated and confused. "I suppose I have everything I want. I make a decent salary and the university allows me to pursue my research."

"No, Doctor, you don't have everything you want. The first thing you want is unlimited funding for your research and the time to pursue it without interruption. Last year you were only able to obtain two hundred thousand in federal grants, and half the money went to the university to pay for its overhead instead of your research." Orson didn't bother to add that the reason he hadn't received more funding was because his grant proposals were so poorly written that no one could understand what the hell he was talking about.

"How do you know . . ."

"And the university wastes your valuable time by making you teach two classes that could be taught by someone with half your intelligence, and the salary you're paid is an insult."

"What do you want?" Ballard asked again.

"Doctor, I'm the CEO of Mulray Pharma. Last year we spent almost four *billion* on research and if you come to work for me, I'll quadruple your current salary."

Although Orson's salary as CEO was limited to a mere million, he could spend Mulray Pharma's money however he pleased on anything directly related to the company.

"What?" Ballard said. He had heard Orson—he just couldn't believe what he had heard.

"Obviously, the results of your research, if they come to fruition, would become the property of Mulray Pharma, but I'm also willing to structure your contract so that you'll get a percentage of any profits the company makes on the drug."

A different sort of man would have asked: How big a percentage? But Ballard didn't ask that question. Instead he asked, "How much will you commit to my research?"

"Doctor, I will give you a laboratory designed to your specifications, but the lab needs to be in Delaware where Mulray Pharma is headquartered. And I'll let you have as large a staff as you think you need but, for security reasons, we need to hold the number to the minimum required. Furthermore, I'll let you pick your staff and I'll throw enough money at the people you want to ensure they accept the job. However, and again for security reasons, I'll need to approve and do background checks on every person you hire."

Ballard just stood there with his mouth open. Judging by the expression on his face, one would have thought that he had just spoken to God.

"This . . . this . . . this is extraordinary," he stammered. "Why are you doing this?"

"For the obvious reason, Doctor. For money. I think you're going to produce one of the most valuable drugs ever manufactured."

"It will help so many people," Ballard said.

"Yes, that too," Orson said.

"You understand, don't you, that it will take years to get this drug approved. I mean, with the FDA's procedures . . ."

"Doctor, you let me worry about the FDA."

Before Ballard could say anything else, Orson said, "I asked what you wanted more than anything else in the world, and one of those things is the time and resources to pursue your research, as we've already discussed. But you want one other thing, Doctor. You want a certain prize for medicine, and I guarantee that if you produce the results I expect, I'll get you the prize. I'll *buy* you the prize."

"The Nobel?" Ballard said.

"I guarantee it.

Dr. Simon Ballard was his.

3

Paris, France~April 2006

Fiona's first task was obtaining the services of the right doctor to manage the field testing of Ballard's drug. This person had to be extremely charismatic and had to be an English-speaking foreigner—a doctor who was a U.S. citizen could complicate some of the legal issues Fiona might encounter in the future. After working her way through the dossiers of eight likely candidates—dossiers compiled by a rather unique firm of headhunters she employed—she decided a French physician named René Lambert was the best choice.

Lambert was a general practitioner based in Paris. Judging by his scholastic records he was most likely a mediocre doctor, but his medical skills were irrelevant. He knew enough medicine to do what Orson Mulray needed done. He came from old money, but the money had evaporated in the last decade due to a global recession and the fact that Lambert spent far more than he earned. He was up to his neck in debt and would soon be in over his head.

René Lambert was thirty-eight years old and had a beautiful Swedish wife and two beautiful daughters. He also had a mistress; the mistress would have to go. But the fact that he was appealing to women was one of the reasons Fiona selected him. He was dark-haired, tall, slender, and well muscled. His face was lean, his jaw strong, his chin dimpled. His eyes were a startling shade of blue. The only feature he had that wasn't perfect was his nose, which had a slight bump in the middle. The bump had been caused by a bicycling accident, but rather than detracting from his appearance the nose-bump actually enhanced it, making him appear more rugged and less pretty. Even Fiona—who had no interest in sex whatsoever—found his looks distracting.

She met Lambert in a suite at the Ritz Paris that cost twenty-two hundred euros a night. She wanted to impress upon him immediately that money was of no concern to his future employer. She poured him a glass of Johnnie Walker Blue without asking if that's what he wanted; she already knew his favorite drink. She began by saying, "Doctor, my name is Fiona West and I represent Orson Mulray, CEO of Mulray Pharma. Mr. Mulray is willing to pay you one million dollars a year for a job that we expect will take four or five years."

A million was a number that always got a prospective employee's immediate attention, and for a company that measured its profits in billions, a million really wasn't all that much. Lambert was shocked by the offer, but not as shocked as Simon Ballard had been. The expression on René Lambert's handsome face indicated that he was a man who had always expected that grand things would happen to him—and it looked as if they finally had.

"And, may I ask," Lambert said in wonderfully accented English— he was a TV producer's dream—"what I have to do to be compensated so generously?"

"I wasn't finished discussing your compensation," Fiona said, and then told him that in addition to his annual salary, Mulray Pharma would purchase back for him the mountain chalet in Grenoble he had been forced to sell to stay ahead of his creditors.

"But you need to dump your mistress here in Paris. Having a mistress may be acceptable to your wife, but it won't be to a number of other people. You need to have an untarnished image."

Lambert made a face that only a Frenchman could make, his expression saying: *C'est la vie.* Fiona knew, however, that Lambert was incapable of remaining faithful to his wife, and that she'd have to deal with his rampant libido at some future date.

"When are you going to tell me what you expect me to do?" Lambert said.

"Now," Fiona said.

First, she explained, he would have to convince Lizzie Warwick, founder of the Warwick Foundation, to partner with him. Fiona figured with his looks and his charm—and the secret and substantial financial backing of Mulray Pharma—that wouldn't be hard to do. Lizzie Warwick was not to know about his association with Mulray Pharma, of course. She would assume the money that Lambert brought to her foundation came from his wealthy European friends.

"I don't believe Lizzie will be a problem," Lambert said.

Second, he would have to spend at least six months of every year for the next four or five years in the godforsaken places where Lizzie Warwick went. He would be living in miserable and sometimes dangerous conditions. Fiona could tell this didn't appeal to him at all but, after a moment, he nodded his acceptance.

"Third," she said, "it will be your job to select appropriate subjects for certain clinical trials, establish facilities to house those subjects for as long as necessary, and hire appropriate local talent to administer drugs and obtain biological samples."

Before Lambert could respond, Fiona said, "And there's one more thing." After she told him what that was, Lambert emptied his Scotch glass in one swallow and said, "I don't think I can . . ."

"You realize," Fiona said, "that this drug will help millions of people. It will be a historic medical achievement, and you will have been part of that achievement."

"That may be but . . ."

23

It took Fiona almost an hour to convince Lambert, during which time he had two more Scotches—they were going to have to watch his drinking —but he finally agreed to become an employee of Mulray Pharma after Fiona agreed to increase his annual salary by another quarter million.

And at that moment, Fiona knew exactly how the Devil must have felt when he shook hands with Dr. Faust.

———◆◆◆———

Eastern Indonesia∼May 2006

Orson Mulray needed human subjects in order to test Dr. Ballard's drug, and the ideal subject was a person too poor and too ignorant to refuse anything supposedly being done for his or her benefit. Furthermore, these people would be required to sign documents stating that they consented to the testing, and it would be good if they were illiterate. Finally, the countries in which the test subjects resided had to have governments susceptible to bribery and without the resources to waste on issues as nebulous as drug testing. Lizzie Warwick and her foundation would provide subjects who met these criteria.

Now, almost all pharmaceutical companies do some clinical trials in third world countries these days, and although the practice may be frowned upon in some circles, it isn't illegal. So Orson didn't really need the Warwick Foundation to test Ballard's drug, but he wanted it for two reasons. First, by using Warwick for cover, there was less chance that another pharmaceutical company would discover that Mulray Pharma was developing a new product. The second reason was that Lizzie Warwick, like Fiona West, would provide a barrier between Orson Mulray and his crimes.

Lizzie Warwick came from a Philadelphia family that made its fortune producing weapons for any country with the means to buy them. Land mines were a particularly profitable product line. In 2003, in her thirties, unmarried and childless and having no idea what to do with her life, Lizzie accompanied a church group as a volunteer to help rebuild homes destroyed by a hurricane—and found her calling. She turned the family fortune into the Warwick Foundation and thereafter took it upon herself to go to places afflicted by war and natural disaster to do what she could.

Lizzie was a brave, bighearted woman, but the relief business is a complicated one, dealing with the logistics of moving supplies to distant shores, negotiating with foreign governments, raising money, then accounting for the money raised. Organizations like the Red Cross hire professionals to deal with these complex issues—and pay them well—but Lizzie, a person with absolutely no managerial ability, relied primarily on people like herself, people who didn't necessarily have the requisite skills but who were dedicated and willing to volunteer. This also made her and her foundation perfect for Orson Mulray.

———◆◆◆———

Lizzie met Dr. René Lambert for the first time on an Indonesian island that had been struck by torrential rains and mud slides, and as if God wasn't satisfied that these poor islanders had been sufficiently tested, a small earthquake demolished the few structures not swept away by the floods and slides. Ten villages were wiped out, hundreds died, and thousands were left homeless, starving, and dying of thirst and dysentery.

The night they met, Lizzie was sitting in her tent, so fatigued she could barely lift her thin arms. Her pale face was streaked with mud and sweat; her wiry red hair was plastered to her skull. Earlier that day, while passing out bottles of water to victims, she had heard a child crying, the sound coming from a hut so buried by mud that only the top of its tin roof was visible. Lizzie had joined the villagers' frantic efforts to save the child, but when they'd reached her an hour later, the little girl was dead.

René Lambert patted Lizzie sympathetically on the shoulder and then told her about himself. He said he had been blessed with so much that he could no longer sit idly by watching others suffer while he did nothing, so he'd brought a planeful of medical supplies to Indonesia and was tending to the unfortunate as best he could. But, he told her, he could see that he had grossly underestimated the enormity of the task.

"Oh, I know what you mean," Lizzie said.

Lambert worked with Lizzie for two weeks and, to impress her, he worked just as hard as she did—which was very hard indeed. One night, after a particularly long and frustrating day—a day when supplies Lizzie was expecting failed to arrive—Lambert proposed that they join forces. He would provide a medical arm for the Warwick Foundation. He would get other doctors and nurses to join him, à la Doctors Without Borders. More important, if they joined forces they could double their fund-raising efforts—and he was, he said with a self-deprecating smile, an excellent fund-raiser.

René Lambert bedazzled Lizzie Warwick.

"I can see, however, that we need a good administrator," Lambert said. "You know, an experienced person to deal with all the logistical problems of getting things to places like this. And it would be good if this person was able to manage the money as well. I don't know about you, but accounting is not one of my skills."

Lizzie admitted it wasn't one of hers, either. In fact, Lizzie rarely paid any attention to the money end of the business, and the accountant she used was a nice man who volunteered his time but really wasn't in the best of health.

"We're going to need some sort of security as well," Lambert said. "We have to make sure the things we bring to help these poor people actually get to them. Half the drugs I brought with me have been stolen."

"Do you know anyone who can do these jobs?" Lizzie asked.

"I believe I can find the right men," Dr. Lambert said.

4

Leavenworth, Kansas~June 2006

Bill Hobson was sixty-one years old. He was five foot eight, wore a hearing aid in his right ear, and had a small paunch. His gray hair was cut short, the way he'd always worn it, and wire-rimmed bifocals covered weak blue eyes. He did not cut an imposing figure. He was currently residing in a thirty-eight-dollar-per-night motel room. He had been in the room for three days—contemplating suicide.

William Benedict Hobson had attended the United States Military Academy at West Point, New York. Like most young men who graduate from that fine institution, he envisioned himself heroically leading battalions into battle, having four stars on his shoulders, maybe one day becoming chairman of the Joint Chiefs of Staff. It was not to be. The army needed warriors but it also needed men to help the army run like the well-oiled machine it was. *Somebody* had to be responsible for getting the food, ammunition, and boots to the front lines; somebody had to make sure there were spare parts to maintain the tanks, helicopters, and personnel carriers. And Bill Hobson, over his strenuous objections, became that somebody.

He was a maniac for detail and could juggle numbers and complex schedules in his head when other men needed computers to assist them. He also had that rare ability to anticipate all the things that could possibly go wrong and develop contingency plans to address those things. He became, almost from the day he left the Point, the man his bosses turned to to handle the complex logistics of military operations. And, as is often the case in bureaucracies, Hobson soon found that excelling could actually become a hindrance to advancement: he filled a vital niche and was too good at what he did to be allowed to transfer to the war-fighting side of the service.

He advanced, of course, and ultimately reached the rank of colonel, but when it came to selecting men for the general staff, he was passed over. At the level where stars are affixed to a soldier's uniform, the army has to consider the whole package and not just an individual's experience and ability. They have to consider if a man *looks* like a general, whether or not he will be an appropriate poster boy for the service. They need to gauge his political skills. Will he be able to swim with the sharks at the Pentagon and the even bigger sharks on Capitol Hill? Can he communicate? Can he give a speech that will not only rouse the troops but will provide the necessary sound bite for the evening news? And William Hobson, to his great dismay—dismay that eventually turned to boiling rage—was found lacking in these more esoteric qualities of generalship.

The army gave Hobson the opportunity to serve three more years as a colonel before he would be forced to retire, and his initial reaction was to tell the army to shove its opportunity up its ass. Then he had another idea. He decided that since the army wouldn't give him the star he deserved—and, more important, the pension that came with that star—he would steal enough to make up the difference.

Hobson waited until he was alone one night, then sat down at the desk of a staff sergeant who worked for him, entered the sergeant's password into his computer, and modified the payment information for a certain vendor the army used. This particular vendor sold tires for certain army vehicles—and the army has a *lot* of vehicles.

On subsequent nights, and over a three-month period, Hobson did other things on the staff sergeant's computer. He prepared a purchase order for four hundred and eighty thousand dollars' worth of tires. (He had wanted to order half a million dollars' worth but was worried about using such a round number.) The vendor never received the purchase order but, thanks to Hobson, all the required forms were electronically filed by the vendor, showing that the tires had been manufactured and inspected and would be sent to a dozen army bases around the globe upon receipt of payment. Then Hobson, as he was required to do in his position, authorized payment to the vendor, and the money was electronically sent on its way—it just didn't end up in the tire vendor's bank account, just as the tires never showed up in the supply system inventory.

Now, the Pentagon has a number of elaborate controls to prevent the type of crime Bill Hobson committed. There are checks and double checks, procedures to be followed that are subject to audit and review. But Hobson was intimately familiar with these procedures; he had, in fact, developed many of them. Also, an integral part of the army's fraud protection program was that supervisors of a certain rank had to approve procurements above a certain dollar value. But in this particular case, Hobson *was* that supervisor.

And although half a million dollars might sound like a lot to ordinary folk, in terms of the Pentagon's budget it was an amount that could literally be written off as a rounding error. That particular year, DOD's budget was four hundred and one *billion* dollars, and half a million was .000124% of that budget. It would be a miracle if an auditor noticed that half a million had disappeared, and if an auditor did notice, the chances of him tracing the loss back to Hobson was so small that . . . Well, put it this way: the auditor would be more likely to win the multistate mega-lotto with a single ticket than catch Bill Hobson.

The day four hundred and eighty thousand dollars was deposited into Hobson's bank account, he treated himself to dinner at the most expensive steakhouse in Washington. He was arrested two days after his steak dinner.

What Hobson didn't realize was that the night he changed the payment information in the tire vendor's file, the Pentagon's IT guys were doing one of their frequent, random security audits. They weren't looking for anything specific, just *funny business*. Funny business like folks stealing identity information, or viewing pornography online, or, the biggie, someone e-mailing classified documents to places they weren't supposed to go. The night Hobson replaced the tire vendor's bank account number with his own, a bright-eyed sergeant from Clinton, Iowa, named Millie Cooper, sitting in front of a computer on the B ring of the Pentagon, saw the changes being made on her screen. And Millie said: *Hmmm? I wonder what that's all about? Why are these numbers being changed at nine o'clock at night?* Millie noted that the person logged onto the computer was, per the password used, Staff Sergeant Henry Main, but when she checked the security guys' computer, it showed that Sergeant Main had swiped his badge through a bar-code reader when he left the Pentagon at 1630 hours. *Hmmm?* Millie said again.

Millie called her boss and the next day her boss called the lawyers and the army's Criminal Investigation Division. The lawyers obtained a warrant to find out whom the bank account belonged to and discovered it was one Colonel William Hobson and then everybody—cops, lawyers, and Millie—just sat back and watched until Hobson completed his crime. And then they arrested him.

Hobson was dishonorably discharged, stripped of his pension, and given ten years in Leavenworth, of which he served six. His wife divorced him, took his house and what little savings they had, and his children wouldn't speak to him. Maybe the worst thing that happened was that his dog died while he was in jail; Hobson had loved that dog more than he did his wife. On the day he left Leavenworth, his net worth, not counting his shoes and the clothes on his back, was three hundred and fourteen dollars. Considering his criminal record, Hobson figured he had two choices: he could get a job at a car wash or he could commit suicide—and suicide seemed more appealing.

As he sat there in his cheap, depressing motel room, there was a knock on the door, which puzzled him because he couldn't imagine who would want to talk to him. He was certain it wasn't a maid bringing him fresh towels. He opened the door, and standing there was a stunning woman. Her face was somewhat harsh and he didn't like her punkish haircut, but she had the kind of body he'd fantasized about when he masturbated in prison.

"Bill," she said, "my name is Fiona West and I have a job for you. May I come in?"

Hobson, too stunned to speak, stepped aside and allowed Fiona into his room, where she explained that the job entailed getting relief supplies to various third world countries and shipping biological samples to a lab in Delaware.

"I could do that with my eyes shut," Hobson said.

"You don't need to sell yourself, Bill. I know what you used to do and I know you were good at it. Until you decided to become a thief, that is." She held up a silencing hand when Hobson attempted to explain his career-ending decision. "I don't care why you did it," Fiona said.

"How much does the job pay?" Hobson asked, although he knew he was in no position to negotiate and would accept whatever salary she offered.

"Mulray Pharma is willing to pay you two hundred and fifty thousand dollars a year."

"Jesus!" Hobson said, before he could stop himself. As a retired one-star general he would have made less than a hundred thousand a year.

"In return, you will volunteer your services to the Warwick Foundation, but you won't tell them that Mulray Pharma is paying you to work there."

"Okay," Hobson said. He had no idea what the Warwick Foundation was. He was also bright enough to know that Fiona was hiring him to commit some sort of crime—and he didn't give a shit. Whatever crime he was about to commit was preferable to suicide.

Two weeks later, René Lambert introduced Bill Hobson to Lizzie Warwick. Lambert told Lizzie about the fine job Hobson had done for the army and how he was the perfect man to manage the Warwick Foundation. Dr. Lambert then pulled out a copy of Hobson's army personnel record—one that stopped at the point where he was arrested—and showed Lizzie the wide and varied experience he had. Then Hobson chimed in. He said he was willing to volunteer his time, as his army pension provided all the money he needed. He just wanted to do something meaningful, he said, for the good of his fellow man—and Lizzie had tears in her eyes as she hugged Bill and welcomed him to the Warwick Foundation.

Hobson now had a number of urgent things to do. He needed to find a place to live in Philadelphia and purchase a car. He needed to make himself intimately familiar with the Warwick Foundation's accounts and methods of operation, and he needed to start working with Lambert to establish the facilities needed for conducting Mulray Pharma's clinical trials. But the very first thing he was going to do was go out and buy a puppy to replace the dog he'd lost while he was in prison.

5

Paktika Province, Afghanistan~June 2006

The final item on Fiona's to-do list was hiring the killers.

About the time she recruited Hobson, she read a story on page six of the *New York Times* about two men who worked for a private security firm in Afghanistan called Romar-Slade Inc., the firm having been named after its founders, both former U.S. Army generals. According to the article, the two men—whose names were Kelly and Nelson—were protecting a duly elected Afghani provincial governor who was rumored to be an opium grower and, per the *Times,* the second most corrupt official in the country. (In 2006, the honor of first place went to the brother of the American-backed and questionably elected Afghani president.)

The article stated that the governor had been driving through a village in his province when Taliban assassins, hiding in a roadside house, fired upon the governor's car with automatic weapons. Kelly and Nelson responded to the attack immediately and in an overwhelming manner, and they turned the house into a mound of smoldering rubble in about ten minutes. No Taliban were found inside the house, however—they must have run out the back door when

Kelly and Nelson opened fire—but five bodies were found, three of whom were children.

It was not clear, however, if the children were killed by the Taliban or by the governor's bodyguards. This was unclear because the bodies were badly burned and partially dismembered—and this wasn't a place where forensic specialists sorted out the facts. The governor's rivals claimed his bodyguards were nothing more than cold-blooded killers and that their complete disregard for the lives of Afghani civilians was typical of the American invaders. Politicians—both Afghani and American—jumped up and down and made speeches. Congress held hearings regarding the abuses—financial and moral—perpetuated by private security firms. And, while all this was going on, Kelly and Nelson sat in a cell guarded by disinterested Afghani policemen as they waited to hear their fate.

Once upon a time, there were gunfighters in the Old West, men with Colt .45 six-shooters and lever-action Winchester rifles who hired themselves out to cattle kings, mining barons, and railroad magnates. Gunslingers no longer existed in the American West—or at least not in great numbers—but they did exist elsewhere. Today such men worked as mercenaries for private security firms in places like Iraq and Afghanistan—but they were much better armed.

Fiona's headhunters discovered that Kelly and Nelson both enlisted in the army at age eighteen and met each other in boot camp at Fort Polk, Louisiana. They attended Ranger training together at Fort Benning, spent two tours in Iraq in the same unit, and then were selected for Delta Force—the Department of Defense's elite, covert-action response team. If DOD, for whatever reason, needed facilities demolished or enemies captured or killed in places where the U.S. was not officially at war, Delta Force soldiers were sent in to do the job. And these were extraordinary soldiers. Eighty percent of the men who begin Delta training wash out, but those who don't are the most effective killers the army has.

Fiona's headhunters—and this was one of the reasons she used the firm—were also able to gain access to psychological exams Kelly and Nelson had taken to get into Delta Force. The army wanted capable killers—but not psychopaths. The two men's psych files contained the same phrase: *Judged to be capable of successfully suppressing counterproductive emotions following combat operations.* This was army-speak. It meant: killing people didn't bother Kelly and Nelson all that much.

Kelly and Nelson worked for Delta Force for five years—in Somalia, the Philippines, Pakistan, and Iran—but even Fiona's headhunters, with all their government connections, couldn't find out what they did there. The likely guess was that they had been inserted into these hostile places to kill terrorists—and that was good enough for Fiona. She had no doubt that these two men were the gunfighters she wanted.

Fiona flew to Afghanistan with ten heavily armed professional bodyguards. She had no intention of being killed or kidnapped while recruiting Kelly and Nelson. She paid a small bribe to the men who were guarding them—a bribe equal to what they made in a year—and entered the cell where they were being detained. They were lying on their cots, reading novels, when she walked in—which surprised her. She figured that if they read at all it would be pornographic magazines.

They were both brutes: six foot four, small waists, big chests, muscles on top of muscles. Kelly was black and Nelson was white, but aside from their skin coloring, they were actually quite similar in appearance: short, broad noses; brown eyes; thin lips; ears set close to their skulls. Fiona bet if their faces were completely covered with that black and green camo paint that soldiers use, they would have looked like frightening twins.

"What can we do for you?" Kelly said.

That was good: no boneheaded cracks about the fact that she was a good-looking woman and that they hadn't been with a woman in quite a while.

Without any sort of preamble, Fiona said, "If you agree to work for me, I'll bribe the right people and get you out of the mess you're currently in. Second, I'll pay you ten million dollars—five million each—for an assignment that will last approximately five years. You'll be given one third of the money up front and the rest in annual payments."

Kelly laughed. "What do you want us to do? Kill the president?"

"What if I said that's exactly what I wanted you to do?"

Kelly looked over at Nelson, and Fiona could tell that these two men had been together for so long they didn't need words to communicate.

Kelly, a smile still playing on his lips, said, "For that kind of money, we'd think about it."

He may have been smiling, but she knew he was serious. For ten million, he and his partner really might be willing to assassinate the president.

"Well," she said, "I don't want you to do anything that difficult."

"Okay," Kelly said. "So what do you want us to do?"

"My company has a laboratory in Delaware, and everything that happens inside that lab must remain secret. Right now we have a corporate security firm that's protecting the lab and monitoring everyone who works there, but if anyone attempts to pass information to a rival company, that person needs to be dealt with."

"You mean killed," Kelly said.

"Yes, if it comes to that."

"Go on. You're not offering us ten million to kill some lab rat that talks to the competition."

"The second thing you'll be asked to do is make sure that certain medical supplies reach certain places in the world. The places where we're sending these supplies are often in war zones or have just suffered some large-scale natural disaster. These supplies must reach their destination no matter what."

"Okay," Kelly said, "you want us to kill anybody who tries to get your supplies. The medical ones, that is."

"Yes. Furthermore, there is a man and a woman who will be in these disaster areas, and they must to be protected. This is just basic security work like you've been doing for Romar-Slade and you two won't personally handle the protection detail. What you'll do is hire competent people to protect them, and you'll supervise those people."

Kelly nodded. "When are you going to get to the part that makes us worth ten million?"

"Right now," Fiona said.

When she finished speaking, Kelly asked a couple of questions, then told Fiona, "We need to talk this over alone."

Fiona paced outside the jail, wondering how long it would take them to make up their minds. Unlike with René Lambert, she knew there was nothing else she could say or offer to convince them; they'd either agree or they wouldn't. If they didn't, considering all she'd told them, she was going to have to hire someone to kill them—and she knew it was going to be very hard to kill Kelly and Nelson.

But it took them only ten minutes to decide to accept her offer. Their freedom, plus ten million dollars for five years' work, was quite an incentive. She also suspected they had killed enough people during their careers that their consciences had become completely numb when it came to the act of murder. She was actually wrong about this, but it didn't matter.

Before she left Afghanistan, she flung money at local politicians like it was wedding rice and Kelly and Nelson were released from jail, charges against them were dismissed, and they promptly left the country.

Six months after Clayton Mulray's funeral, everything was in place.

Dr. Ballard's laboratory was fully staffed, his experiments were under way, and the lab was as well guarded as any top-secret government facility. Nothing left the building that wasn't supposed to leave. Nobody entered the building who wasn't supposed to enter. All phone calls and e-mails going in and out of the lab were monitored and, although they didn't know it, the home phones, home computers, and cell phones of the people who worked at the lab were also monitored. Five months after the facility opened—approximately one year after Clayton Mulray's death—Simon Ballard was ready to commence clinical trials.

Thanks to ex-Colonel William Hobson, the Warwick Foundation was running like a Swiss watch. Lizzie Warwick and the charming Dr. Lambert jetted off to awful places struck by man or nature and administered to those who suffered. While in these places, Dr. Lambert selected test subjects meeting Dr. Ballard's criteria. He housed these people in special facilities, ironically called Warwick Care Centers. He also hired local nurses or medical technicians— never doctors—to care for the people, administer the drug, and take biological samples. None of the nurses knew the exact nature of the drug.

Periodically, Lizzie and Lambert would go on a globe-trotting tour to raise money for the Warwick Foundation. They would speak to church groups and fraternal organizations and civic leaders; they were invited to banquets with generous rich people in attendance. And Lambert charmed the audiences the same way he charmed Lizzie Warwick when he met her, and donations increased substantially due to his efforts.

Kelly and Nelson hired a team of ex-soldiers to provide protection for Lizzie and Lambert. They supervised the delivery of supplies to places where Lizzie and the French doctor went and, in particular, they made sure that Simon Ballard's drugs reached those places.

They had only one security issue during the first three years. A molecular biologist who worked for Ballard discovered the casinos in Atlantic City and—after he lost thirty-seven thousand dollars on one incredibly unlucky weekend—decided to sell Ballard's research. Not knowing that his cell phone was being monitored, he called a man he knew at Pfizer and asked if he might be interested. Fortunately, the biologist was very vague about exactly what Ballard was doing, stating only that he was light-years ahead of anybody else in the field and that the potential payoff was mind-boggling. The guy at Pfizer said, "Sure. Let's get together and talk."

The biologist died in a car accident shortly after he made the phone call. The accident investigators couldn't explain why his car erupted into flames after it went off the road. Some sort of manufacturer's defect related to the fuel system, they supposed.

Then, in 2009, a more significant security issue arose in the form of Phil Downing—and Kelly and Nelson were dispatched to Washington, D.C.

That issue was resolved when Kelly put a bullet into Phil Downing's heart.

6

Washington, D.C. ~June 2011

As DeMarco walked into Mahoney's office, he heard his boss say, "Yes, Mr. President, I'll do what I can. Thank you for calling."

Mahoney hung up the phone and shook his head. "You know, I like that young guy but . . ."

DeMarco assumed he was referring to the president.

". . . but one of these days I'm gonna have to explain to him that I don't work for him."

DeMarco didn't know what Mahoney was talking about—and he didn't care.

"Mavis said you wanted to see me," DeMarco said, but Mahoney ignored him as he filled his coffee cup from a carafe on his desk, and then added a shot of bourbon.

John Fitzpatrick Mahoney—dressed in a gray suit and wearing a Kelly green tie in tribute to his shanty Irish ancestors—was a handsome man with a large hard gut, a broad back, and a wide butt. His most distinctive feature was a full head of snow-white hair. He had been Speaker of the United States House of Representatives for so long that people had a hard time remembering who the previous Speaker was—but he was no longer the Speaker. The year before, he had lost his job when the Republicans took control of the House.

Some Democrats urged Mahoney to fall upon his sword and resign for the sake of the party. To these folks Mahoney's response had been: *Go fuck yourselves*. He figured it wasn't his fault the economy was in the toilet and other Democrats didn't know how to run a decent campaign. He'd been a U.S. congressman for so long he didn't know how to do anything else and, at his age, he wasn't about to get a real job. So he'd bullied the Democrats into making him the minority leader, and he planned to stay in that position until his party could retake the House. And if they didn't . . . Well, he was confident he'd continue to be reelected from his district in Boston. His biggest regret—other than the loss of his title and the power and prestige that went with it—was that he had to give up the Speaker's office in the Capitol, a space he'd occupied for so long he thought of it as belonging to him and not the republic.

DeMarco had been extremely upset when Mahoney lost the Speaker's gavel—he may have been even more upset than Mahoney. Now, DeMarco didn't care about John Mahoney, and he didn't care about the Democratic Party. Having been exposed to politicians and their self-serving antics for so many years, he knew the country was in bad hands regardless of which party controlled the House. The reason he was upset was because he was afraid that when Mahoney lost his job, he would lose his.

Joe DeMarco's employment had always been tenuous. Mahoney had an official staff he used for day-to-day political shenanigans—but DeMarco wasn't a member of his official staff. DeMarco was the guy Mahoney turned to when there was some shitty job to be done he didn't want his staff wasting their time on—or, more important, that Mahoney didn't want traced back to him and his office. DeMarco was not, therefore, a vital cog in the machinery of government, and he had been terrified that when the Republicans took power, budget and staffing cuts would ensue and he'd be one of the cuts. But the budget axe never descended—and Mahoney continued to give him shitty jobs.

After Mahoney took a swig of his bourbon-laced coffee, he continued to ignore DeMarco. He picked up the phone again and punched a single button, which meant he was calling somebody on his staff. "The president just called," he said. "He wants to see if we can get another five hundred million added to the bill." He listened for a moment, then said, "Yeah, yeah, I know. He thinks there's a tree we shake over here. Anyway, figure something out."

DeMarco assumed Mahoney was talking to his chief of staff, a man named Perry Wallace. Wallace—unlike DeMarco or Mahoney—was a genius. He also had the same ethical DNA as Mahoney, which meant that he would lie, cheat, and steal to do his boss's bidding.

Mahoney listened to Wallace for a couple minutes, grunted a few times in some code that only Wallace could understand, and said, "Yeah, that might work. Get back to me by the end of the day."

Mahoney put the phone down and finally focused his watery, red-veined blue eyes on DeMarco. Mahoney's eyes may or may not have been the gateway to his soul, but they provided sure evidence of the amount of bourbon he consumed on a daily basis. Mahoney was the only high-functioning alcoholic DeMarco knew.

"A couple years ago," Mahoney said, "a lobbyist named Brian Kincaid was arrested for killing his partner, another lobbyist named Downing. You remember that?"

"No," DeMarco said. One lobbyist killing another may not have been a typical D.C. crime, but he didn't recall the event.

"Anyway," Mahoney said, "the evidence against Kincaid was overwhelming and he was convicted and given twenty-five to life."

DeMarco just stood there, waiting for Mahoney to get to the point.

"Well, Kincaid's mother went to school with Mary Pat."

Aw shit. DeMarco could now see where this was going. Mary Pat was Mahoney's wife—and possibly the nicest person on planet Earth—and she probably wanted to help her friend's son. And sure enough . . .

"Kincaid, of course, claims he's innocent," Mahoney said. "He appealed the verdict and just lost his appeal, and since this ain't the kind of case that's gonna go to the Supreme Court, his ass is cooked. He also spent every dime he had on lawyers and private detectives, and at this point there isn't anybody willing to help him. So his mother, who doesn't have any money either, came over to the house the other day, bawling her eyes out, and asked if there was anything I could do. Mary Pat explained to the dimwit that I can't overturn a verdict in a criminal case, but she said that she knew a guy who could do some investigating on her son's behalf, free of charge. Meaning you."

"But what in the hell am I supposed to do?" DeMarco whined. "I mean, especially if this guy has already had private detectives on the case?"

"I don't know and I don't care," Mahoney responded. "All I want is Mary Pat off my back. Go see Kincaid, spend a few days dinking around, then call up his mom and tell her that in spite of your herculean efforts, her son's gonna spend the rest of his life making license plates—or whatever the hell they make in prisons these days."

"But—"

"Mavis will tell you where they're keeping Kincaid, give you his mother's phone number, all that shit."

"Yeah, but—"

Mahoney picked up his phone again and called another politician —somebody whose opinion he actually cared about.

43

7

The District of Columbia—having no desire to have a large, unsightly penitentiary situated within its historic borders—exports its home-grown felons to various prisons around the country. Fortunately for DeMarco, Brian Kincaid was incarcerated at the maximum-security prison in Hazelton, West Virginia, only a three-hour drive from Washington.

Kincaid was forty-six years old, of medium height, and slightly built. A former lobbyist who once dressed in nice suits and ties, he now wore a soiled white T-shirt and baggy blue jeans that were too long. On his feet were flip-flops. His unwashed, dark hair was rapidly turning gray and there were charcoal-colored half-moons staining the pale skin beneath his eyes. Brian Kincaid looked like a man who had had the rug pulled out from under his feet—and it seemed doubtful that he would ever fully recover from the hard landing.

DeMarco lied to the authorities at Hazelton, claiming to be Kincaid's lawyer. Since DeMarco actually was a lawyer, it wasn't much of a lie. The lie, however, earned him the privilege of meeting Kincaid in a small conference room instead of having to talk to him on a phone while looking at him through a scarred sheet of bullet-proof glass. The room they were in contained two metal chairs and a small metal table; all the furniture was bolted firmly to the floor. So was Kincaid—he was connected by a chain that went from a wide leather belt on his waist to an eyebolt anchored in concrete.

When Kincaid met DeMarco, he grasped DeMarco's hand like a drowning man clutching a life preserver. "I can't tell you how grateful I am," he said. "When my mother told me you were a lawyer who worked for Congress . . . Well, I'm not embarrassed to tell you I cried."

Aw geez, DeMarco thought. That was the last thing he wanted to hear.

"I was thinking that maybe you could start with the appeal my last lawyer filed. I don't think he—"

DeMarco held up a hand to silence Kincaid. "Brian," DeMarco said, "let me explain a couple things to you. I'm a lawyer, but I don't practice law."

"What? What do you do?"

"I normally . . ."

DeMarco realized that he couldn't tell Kincaid what he normally did for Mahoney. He started over.

"I'm sort of an odd-jobs guy," he said. "If a congressman needs a little help with something—some sort of investigative work, some legwork his staff is too busy to handle—I sometimes get the job. So . . ."

When DeMarco was among strangers—and particularly if one of the strangers was a good-looking woman he wanted to impress—he'd say that he was a *political troubleshooter,* that job description sounding more glamorous than *odd-jobs guy.* But he didn't want to impress Brian Kincaid. He didn't want to give him any reason to get his hopes up.

". . . so the best thing I can do for you," DeMarco said, "is go back over the evidence they used to convict you and see if maybe I can find something the police overlooked."

Kincaid shook his head. "I don't think—"

"But the first thing I need is for you to just tell me what happened."

DeMarco needed Kincaid to tell him because he'd been too lazy to wade through two years' worth of court documents, depositions, pretrial motions, and appeals before coming to the prison.

Kincaid closed his eyes, inhaled, then slowly exhaled, like a man about to start down a path he'd been down too many times before. He opened his eyes and looked directly into DeMarco's and said, "I was framed."

"Okay," DeMarco said, but he wondered how often those three words were spoken by Hazelton's inmates. "Tell my why you think that."

"First, I need to give you a little background on Phil and me."

"Phil is Downing? Your ex-partner?"

"Yeah. When we met, we were both working for one of the big K Street outfits. We spent a little time on the Hill schmoozing junior staffers, but mostly we did research on upcoming bills, crunched numbers to see how much the bills would hurt or help a client, wrote position papers, that sort of thing. We weren't major players and we could tell if we stayed with this firm, we were never gonna be. But Phil and I were never friends. We didn't hang out together, we didn't socialize after work. One day, though, and I don't know why, we got to talking and I told him I wanted to start my own firm but I couldn't afford the overhead. You know, the money to lease an office, hire a secretary, that sort of thing. What I didn't tell him was that I had an opportunity to steal a client away from the outfit we were currently working for. Well, it turned out that Phil wanted to do the same thing. He had managed to convince a client with money that she needed a lobbyist and he wanted to go out on his own, but he couldn't afford an office either."

Kincaid lit a cigarette and exhaled the smoke through his nose. "Two years ago the only thing I smoked was the occasional cigar, but now I'm a pack-a-day man. Cancer, at this point, would almost be a blessing. Anyway, we started Downing and Kincaid. I took out a second mortgage on my house and Phil borrowed some money from his dad. We leased an office, rented some furniture, and hired a secretary. We each had one client. As time went on, I managed to get four more and Phil did the same, but when the economy tanked, Phil lost all his clients except for the one he started with. He was barely able to pay his share of the rent."

"Who were your clients?"

Kincaid waved the question away. "It doesn't matter. What you need to understand is Phil and I hated each other. We were like two teenagers who get married before they really get to know each other, and we fought over everything. We fought about the kind of furniture to lease for the office because Phil was a cheap son of a bitch and didn't understand that appearances mattered. We fought over the goddamn secretary and how much time she spent working for each of us. And if I liked a secretary, Phil hated her, but if I wanted to fire one, Phil loved the bitch. We fought over the fucking Internet provider, our cell phone plan, the answering service we used. There didn't seem to be anything we could agree on."

"So why didn't you split up?"

"We couldn't afford to. To pay the overhead, we needed each other. Plus, we were lobbyists; it wasn't like we worked as a team. He did his thing and I did mine. The only time we talked to each other was when there was some pissant issue we had to deal with, which was almost always something related to expenses or the secretary. We became this old married couple that sticks together because they can't afford to get divorced."

"Okay," DeMarco said, "but what does this have to do with Downing's murder?"

"It has to do with motive. The prosecutor had all kinds of evidence against me, but the weakest part of his case was motive. Why would I kill Phil? Well, they get our last secretary on the stand—a gal Phil was poking, by the way—and she testifies that Phil and I fought like cats and dogs. And she wasn't lying. There were times when we stood in front of her desk just screaming at each other. We never actually came to blows, but a couple of times it got close to that. And they got one of our previous secretaries to say the same thing. So the prosecutor argued that the night Phil was killed, we had some big blowup that pushed me over the edge and I shot him. He couldn't prove this, of course, but it didn't matter because of the evidence he had."

"Like what?"

"Phil was shot with my gun. To make matters worse, the cops found the gun hidden beneath the spare tire in my car. I always kept the gun in my house, in the nightstand next to my bed, and I couldn't explain how the gun got into the trunk of my car."

"So how did it get there?"

"I told you: I was framed. But the worst thing about the case was the timing."

"The timing?"

"I lobbied for foreign companies, companies that wanted to make sure that laws didn't get passed that would screw them selling stuff in the U.S. One of my clients was an association of four small businesses in Hong Kong, and because of the time difference, and because these particular clients were a complete pain in the ass, every Wednesday night I'd have a short conference call with them. They wanted to know what I'd done that week to earn my money, and since I couldn't afford to lose them, I called them every fucking Wednesday at nine P.M., which meant it was ten A.M. on Thursday in Hong Kong. And I'd been doing this for over a year. No matter where I was, I'd call these Chinese shits, and if I was in D.C. I'd call them from my office so if I had to refer to something, I'd have the paperwork available. The point I'm making is that if somebody wanted to frame me for Phil's murder, they'd know right where I was going to be every Wednesday night."

"I see," DeMarco said, but he really had no idea what Kincaid was talking about.

"The night it happened, I went to my office like I always did. I made my nine o'clock call to Hong Kong, which took about fifteen minutes, and then I spent a couple minutes after the call jotting down things I had to do before I talked to the Chinese guys again. And phone records confirmed I was on the phone to Hong Kong from nine until nine-fifteen.

"But that night, Phil shows up. He was never in the office at that time of night. Never. So when I finished my conference call, I asked him what he was doing there and, because we had such a warm relationship, all he told me was that he was waiting for a call. We talked for maybe two minutes, then I left. But the relevant thing here is that between nine-fifteen and about nine-thirty, I was in the office with Phil, and the cops could prove it."

"How?"

"For one thing, I admitted it when they first questioned me. I didn't have any reason to lie. But the other thing is our building has a night security guy and a camera in the lobby, and the timer on the camera showed when I arrived and when I left and when Phil got there. So there was no question that I was in the building with Phil between about nine-ten and nine-thirty, which means that Phil had to have been killed *after* I left, but the cops didn't believe me."

"Why not?"

"Because the security guy found his body only twenty minutes after I left. Phil's client called the guard, told him Phil was supposed to be in his office for an important conference call and that he wasn't answering either his cell or the phone in his office. The client told the guard that he needed to go check on Phil and make sure he hadn't had a heart attack or something, and the guard did and he finds Phil dead. And, according to the security guard and the camera, nobody entered the building after seven P.M., and when the cops talked to all the other tenants in the building, everybody said they left before seven P.M."

"So maybe one of the other tenants lied."

"Even if another tenant had been in the building, it wouldn't have mattered to the cops, because he was shot with my gun and I was the only tenant in the building who supposedly had any reason to kill him.

"At my trial we argued that somebody stole my gun from my house, snuck into the building without going through the lobby, shot Phil in the twenty-minute window between when I left and when the guard found his body, and then hid the gun in my car.

"It took the jury half an hour to find me guilty."

8

Kelly was in the first vehicle at the head of a convoy that consisted of Kelly's open-topped jeep, six two-and-a-half-ton cargo trucks, and Nelson's jeep bringing up the rear. The temperature was over a hundred degrees, Kelly's Ugandan driver smelled as if he hadn't bathed since the day he was born, and the road they were on was pockmarked with potholes—and artillery shell holes—and the ride was bone-jarring.

Conditions were even worse for Nelson. Being in the last vehicle in the convoy, he had been eating the dust churned up by the other seven vehicles for the last four hours and would be coated with grime by the time they reached the refugee camp. *Poor Nelson,* Kelly thought, and laughed. They had flipped a coin to see who would ride in the lead vehicle—the most dangerous position—and Nelson had lost.

The government of Uganda had been fighting the Lord's Resistance Army since 1987. The LRA—led by a madman with a Messiah complex named Joseph Kony—was so ruthless the international community had declared it a terrorist organization. Kony's soldiers had slaughtered entire villages, killing the old and helpless with machetes, bashing the heads of babies against trees, taking girls for sex slaves, and forcing boys as young as nine to become soldiers in their army. And when the Ugandan government wasn't fighting against Ugandans, it found reasons to fight the Sudanese and the Congolese. It seemed there was always somebody to fight, and this was the second time Lizzie Warwick had come to the country to aid people displaced by war.

The first time had been three years ago when the LRA overran a number of villages in northern Uganda and refugees fled to a camp near Ogur, a township in central Uganda. And while Lizzie was tending to the needs of several thousand refugees at Ogur, René Lambert found people suitable for Mulray Pharma's clinical trials and relocated them to a facility near Lake Victoria, which was safer as it was farther to the south than where the LRA typically roamed. The Ugandan army eventually pushed the LRA back into Sudan, and the refugees—except those Lambert relocated—returned to what remained of their homes. But war had broken out once again, and once again Lizzie had come to aid the refugees.

This time the refugee camp was near Moroto, about three hundred and fifty hard miles north of Kampala. Kelly and Nelson's mission, as far as Lizzie Warwick was concerned, was to make sure the convoy reached the camp with its lifesaving supplies. Their real mission was to deliver a cooler packed with dry ice and containing a single small box to René Lambert. Almost anyplace else in the world, the contents of the cooler could have been shipped to Lambert—but not even FedEx could guarantee delivery to this part of Uganda.

The good news was that Kelly and Nelson would leave the refugee camp in a helicopter. The chopper—which was secretly being paid for by Mulray Pharma—was at the camp so Lambert could commute safely between the camp and the care center near Lake Victoria, and so Lambert and Lizzie could be evacuated if the LRA overran the camp. In other words, the helicopter was there primarily to protect Mulray Pharma's investments, and Kelly and Nelson would be airlifted out of this particular corner of hell after they'd safely escorted the convoy to the camp.

The bad news was that they had to reach the refugee camp without being killed.

It was very likely that someplace along the dusty road to Moroto, the convoy would be attacked by LRA soldiers. The majority of the soldiers would be teenagers armed with machetes and old Russian AK-47s, and they were fearless and incredibly ruthless. Consequently, every person in the convoy was armed, although none of the others were armed as well as Kelly and Nelson. They would never allow themselves to be captured alive by these savage adolescents.

Kelly didn't understand the politics of Uganda. He didn't know why the LRA and its boy soldiers were so determined to exterminate people who looked just like them and who were just as poor. He didn't know—and he didn't care. All he cared about was reaching the refugee camp alive.

—————◆◆◆—————

Before leaving Kampala, Kelly had studied maps and Google Earth photos looking for spots where they might be ambushed, and one of those places was about twenty miles from the refugee camp where the road crossed a river. Thanks to a five-year drought, the river was now dry, but at one time a bridge had passed over it, and the bridge had been destroyed for God knows what reason by the warring factions. The remains of the bridge were now on what had become the right-hand side of the road, as vehicles were forced to drive down into a shallow gully to cross the dry riverbed. Just beyond the river crossing, the road turned sharply to the right. Kelly figured that the fallen bridge would be a good place for LRA troops to hide behind and that if they set up a roadblock right before the curve, the LRA would occupy the high ground in front of the convoy.

Half a mile from the river crossing, Kelly raised a hand to stop the convoy and studied the way ahead through his binoculars. He saw a flash of red near a twisted bridge trestle, focused on it, and smiled.

One of the attackers was wearing a red baseball cap on his head. Kelly then made what appeared to be a gesture for the convoy to proceed forward. The gesture was actually a signal for Nelson and the men in the trucks to expect an attack. Each of the six trucks contained a driver and a passenger, and the passenger was armed with a new M4 carbine that, on full automatic, fires approximately seven hundred rounds per minute. Kelly and Nelson had M4s as well, but their weapons were also equipped with grenade launchers that fired a 40mm grenade.

As Kelly's jeep crossed the riverbed, he dropped the front windshield down onto the jeep's hood so it wouldn't get in his way. Then, and just as he had expected, an ancient Range Rover rounded the curve ahead of him. The top had been chopped off the Rover with a cutting torch, turning the vehicle into a crude-looking convertible, and it was filled with teenagers. It looked like a circus Volkswagen overloaded with homicidal clowns. Kelly counted eight people crowded into the Rover, and all but the driver were armed with automatic rifles.

The boys in the Rover stood up and fired their weapons into the air. At the same time, a dozen more boys popped up from behind the fallen bridge and aimed their weapons at the convoy. But Kelly knew they wouldn't fire immediately; they didn't want to shoot up the convoy if they didn't have to. They wanted the trucks intact so they could move them off the road and later sell them, and they didn't want to damage whatever goods might be in the trucks. They expected that the men in the convoy, once they saw what they were up against, would offer a bribe to pass or simply run away and abandon the trucks.

Kelly had no intention of running. He raised the short-barreled M4 and fired a grenade at the Range Rover. Then, in rapid succession, he fired two more—and the Rover was turned into a mass of twisted metal and flame and screaming human beings. At the same time, Nelson began launching grenades at middle of the fallen bridge, immediately killing half a dozen teenagers hiding behind that portion of the structure, and the armed passengers in the convoy also opened fire, spraying down everyone who was visible. Some of the boys returned fire but most ducked down behind the fallen bridge trestles—and Kelly and Nelson fired more grenades at the bridge. Ten minutes after the attack began, five boys hiding behind the bridge ran off. Kelly assumed the others were all dead or wounded.

Kelly got out of his vehicle and walked back to each truck in the convoy. A passenger in one of the trucks had been killed, and one driver was slightly wounded, but that was the worst of it. More important, all the vehicles were still drivable. He ordered that the dead man's body be removed from the truck and tossed to the side of the road. When he reached Nelson's vehicle, Nelson—who looked like a six-foot-four-inch gingerbread man, he was so covered with red-brown dust—just shook his head and said, "That was pathetic."

Kelly returned to his jeep and directed the convoy forward. As his vehicle pushed aside the smoking wreckage that had once been the Range Rover, he noticed that one of the boys from the Rover was still alive but missing an arm. He turned to look behind him to make sure the trucks in the convoy were able to get past the wreckage and watched the driver in the lead truck deliberately run over the one-armed boy. This was a hard land.

———————◆◆◆———————

The refugee camp was surrounded by coiled razor wire and covered more than a hundred acres. It was teeming with people lying under makeshift shelters constructed of plastic tarps, blankets, and cardboard. That is, the *lucky* ones had cardboard; half the refugees just sat with the sun beating down mercilessly on their heads. Kelly doubted the supplies the convoy had brought would feed them for more than a few days.

There were a few uniformed soldiers walking the perimeter of the camp. Kelly didn't know if they were African Union or United Nations, but whoever they were, their charter was to protect the camp. He also knew they were useless and that if the camp was attacked, they'd run.

Lizzie Warwick was waiting near the main gate when the convoy arrived, and standing next to her was Earl Lee and two other armed men. These men were Ms. Warwick's personal security detail and they worked for Kelly and Nelson. Lizzie waved gaily when she saw Kelly, and Kelly smiled and waved back.

Lizzie was forty-two years old, although she looked younger, and she was dressed as she typically was on these missions of mercy: well-worn boots, khaki pants, and a long-sleeved shirt. Because she always wore a large-brimmed hat when she was outdoors to protect her delicate skin, her complexion was unnaturally pale, and where her flesh stretched over her cheekbones it seemed almost transparent.

She was about five foot six, and slender thanks to a vegetarian diet and the fact that she was in constant motion. She had curly red hair that was normally tied back in a practical ponytail, blue eyes, a cute upturned nose sprinkled with freckles, and full lips. She was an attractive woman in a wholesome, little sister way, but Kelly had always thought that if she ever wore makeup and tarted herself up a bit, she could be a stunner.

He jumped down from the jeep and approached her with a genuine smile. She was a flake, but a nice flake, and her commitment to the unfortunate was certainly genuine. Nelson, on the other hand, found her naïveté and her perpetual bubbliness annoying, so consequently Kelly was the one charged with talking to her whenever they encountered her on an assignment.

She hugged Kelly and said, "How was the trip? Any problems?"

"None at all," Kelly said, and that was true—or at least true on the scale that he and Nelson measured problems. The convoy had arrived intact and she didn't need to know that one of the people in the convoy had been killed. Nor would he tell her that they had slaughtered more than a dozen teenagers—and this is what annoyed

Nelson about Lizzie Warwick. She knew their job was to protect the convoy, and she must have known that the convoy might be attacked by the same people who had slaughtered the relatives of those in the camp and raped half the women there, but Lizzie believed that all Kelly and Nelson had to do was show that they were ferocious and heavily armed and they'd make it through without a fight.

Lizzie directed men to begin removing the supplies from the trucks and, as this was happening, the inhabitants of the camp—those who were still ambulatory, mostly women and children who looked like walking skeletons—started moving toward the trucks. Kelly watched for a moment to make sure Lizzie wasn't going to be trampled by the hungry refugees, and when he was satisfied she was safe, he made a motion for Earl Lee to join him and Nelson.

Neither Kelly nor Nelson liked Earl Lee, and they'd had a long discussion between themselves before they hired him. Like them, Lee was a former Army Ranger, and like them, he was a big-muscled man who was good at killing people. He was also a braggart, a boor, and a bigot but if you needed a man to protect a client, he wasn't a bad choice—just a disagreeable one.

"Kelly," Lee said, nodding his head. Then he looked over at Nelson and grinned. "You look like a pig my daddy had that liked to roll in the mud." Nelson didn't say anything, but his eyes, looking out through his dust-covered face, seemed unusually bright. Kelly knew that Nelson was dying to kick Lee's redneck ass and that if Lee ever gave him the slightest reason to, he would. And Lee was always doing what he had just done: making some snide comment that could have been an insult but wasn't quite one.

"How's it going here?" Kelly asked.

Lee shrugged. "Fine. The good darkies ain't misbehaving and we haven't seen any sign of the bad darkies."

Kelly, who was black, didn't react to Lee's language. He knew Lee had served with a lot of black men and got along okay with them, although he wasn't a friend to any of them. He just liked to say things like that in front of Kelly, hoping to get a rise out of him.

"Okay," Kelly said. "You need anything?"

"Yeah. A bottle of JD and some pussy."

"What an asshole," Nelson said as they walked away.

"He does his job."

"Yeah, but one of these days . . ."

———————◆◆◆———————

Kelly looked around for René Lambert but didn't see him and hoped that he wasn't going to have to walk all around the foul-smelling refugee camp to find the doctor. Finally he saw him, not more than fifty yards away, squatting on the ground next to an old man. The man looked like he was in his seventies—but maybe not. In this place, a man in his fifties could look like he was in his seventies. A few minutes later, the doctor finished his examination and waved to two of his African assistants. The assistants helped the old man to his feet, and Kelly could see that his left foot and ankle were grossly swollen from elephantiasis.

"Doctor," Kelly called out, and Lambert turned and treated Kelly to that marvelous smile of his.

"Ah, Kelly," he said. "Any problems?"

"No. I've brought the latest batch from Dr. Ballard. You'll get an e-mail tomorrow explaining what needs to be done. Where do you want me to put the drugs?"

"In my tent," Lambert said, and pointed to a tent that had been erected just inside the main gate of the camp.

The small box in the cooler containing fifty ten-milliliter clear glass vials was in fact the only thing that really mattered. It was the reason that Kelly and Nelson had accompanied the convoy and killed a score of African boys.

Everything else was window dressing.

———◆◆◆———

The chopper took them to Nairobi, Kenya; a long-range jet chartered by Hobson would be there tomorrow to fly them out of Africa. It was a long trip from the refugee camp to Nairobi—about three hundred miles—and they slept the whole way, and were feeling somewhat refreshed by the time they checked into a large suite at the Hilton.

Nelson came out of the shower with a towel wrapped round his waist, and when he turned to reach into his duffel bag for something to wear to dinner, Kelly looked, as he always did, at the scars on Nelson's broad back: three puckered, circular scars the size of dimes that were starkly white against Nelson's tanned skin. Nelson had saved Kelly's life three times, once in Somalia and once in Iran, but the first time was in Iraq, and the scars were a permanent, vivid reminder of that occasion.

They'd been in a Ranger unit then—this was before they were selected for Delta—and members of a six-man squad patrolling an al-Qaeda-infested section of Fallujah. At one point, the patrol passed a teenaged girl sitting on a sidewalk selling flowers, but because they'd seen the girl on previous patrols, they dismissed her as a threat. She was wearing a *hijab* on her head, blue jeans, and a long-sleeved blouse; she had no flowing robes or anything else to conceal a weapon. They concluded later that she'd been sitting on the Uzi.

Nelson and Kelly were at the tail end of the squad, bullshitting about something as their eyes continually and automatically scanned nearby buildings for threats. When Nelson glanced to his right at a curtain fluttering in an open second-story window, he saw, with his

59

peripheral vision, that the girl had a weapon in her hands. Nelson had better peripheral vision than any man Kelly had ever known; there were times when it seemed as if he literally had eyes in the back of his head. A second before the girl pulled the Uzi's trigger, Nelson shoved Kelly so hard he fell to the ground, and the girl's first volley hit Nelson. She stitched three bullets in a line across the middle of his back; fortunately, none of the bullets hit his spine. Before she had a chance to shoot anyone else, Kelly punched a hole through the flower girl's chest with his M4, pulverizing her brave young heart.

The investigation into why the Uzi rounds had been able to penetrate Nelson's body armor like it was made of crepe paper took eighteen months to come to the conclusion that the vendor generally made a good product and Nelson just had the bad luck to get armor that was defective.

They both ordered fish for dinner because they knew it would be fresh, most likely caught in Lake Victoria that day. They also ordered predinner gin martinis and were not surprised that the bartender made them perfectly; Kenya, after all, had once been part of the British Empire. They toasted each other silently for a mission well done, and just as Kelly was about to take a sip from his drink, his cell phone rang.

"Hello," he said.

"Is this Mr. Shaw?"

Shaw was the name Kelly gave to people when he didn't want those people to know his real name.

"Yes," he said. "Who is this?"

"It's Bob Ryan, Mr. Shaw."

Kelly had no idea who Bob Ryan was.

"What can I do for you, Mr. Ryan?"

"You told me to call you if Brian Kincaid received any visitors other than his mother or his trial lawyer, and that you'd pay me five hundred bucks to tell you if he did."

It was no wonder he couldn't remember Ryan. Ryan was a guard at the prison in West Virginia where Brian Kincaid was incarcerated, and Kelly hadn't spoken to the man in almost two years.

"Who visited him, Mr. Ryan?"

"Are you going to send me the money if I tell you?"

"Sir, my word is my bond," Kelly said—and he wasn't being facetious. "I'm out of the country right now, but you'll get the money by the end of next week. In cash. I promise. Now, who visited Kincaid?"

Kelly closed the phone.

"Do we have a problem?" Nelson asked.

"I don't know," he said, and told Nelson what Ryan had told him.

Kelly sat there, trying to decide if he should do something right away or wait until they returned to the States, and thinking about Ryan's phone call became a distraction to what would have otherwise been a pleasant dinner. Finally, he muttered, "Goddamnit," took out his phone, and made a call. He had no idea what time it was back in the U.S.—and he didn't give a shit. Hobson answered on the fourth ring.

The relationship that Kelly and Nelson had with Bill Hobson was odd. Technically—and as far as Lizzie Warwick was concerned —the ex-soldiers worked for Hobson. The reality was that Hobson worked directly for Fiona West, but often took his orders from Kelly.

"This is Kelly. Do you have a pen?"

"Uh, yeah," Hobson said. It sounded as if Hobson had been sleeping.

"A man named Joseph DeMarco visited Brian Kincaid in prison. He's a lawyer," Kelly said. When DeMarco had checked into the prison to see Kincaid he had to log in, and the log-in procedure required that he show identification and provide an address and phone number, and Kelly now gave those numbers to Hobson.

"I want you to hire a private detective named Dave Unger. He has an office someplace in the D.C. area, Arlington or Alexandria, I can't remember which. I've met Unger, and I served with his son in Iraq. Tell him I want him to find out everything he can about DeMarco and to follow him until we get back to the States. I also want him to bug the guy's home phone. I don't think he has the capability to monitor cell phone calls, but if he does, tell him to monitor DeMarco's cell phone as well."

"That sounds like overkill," Hobson said. "I mean, just because this guy visited Kincaid in prison—"

"Hobson, shut up. I didn't call to ask your opinion. Tell Unger you want daily reports from him, including tapes of any calls DeMarco makes. Nelson and I will be back in a few days, but if Unger turns up something important, call me. Do you understand?"

"Yeah," Hobson said.

Kelly closed the phone, feeling better because he'd taken some action. Tomorrow he'd call Fiona and tell her what he'd done—something he hated to do because Fiona had a tendency to overreact. But he'd worry about that tomorrow. Right now he was going to enjoy his meal with Nelson, have a good bottle of wine with dinner, and while they ate and drank they'd talk about the house in Montana—without a doubt, their favorite topic of discussion.

9

The D.C. Beltway had turned into a parking lot because of a three-car pileup, but DeMarco didn't really mind; he was in no hurry to meet Brian Kincaid's mother. As he sat there looking at four lanes of stationary vehicles ahead of him, he wondered, as he often did, what it would be like to have a normal job—or simply a job he liked.

When he'd graduated from law school, his father had just been killed—and his father, according to large-font headlines in the *New York Post,* had been a hit man for the mob. And the *Post* wasn't wrong. Young DeMarco quickly discovered that most respectable law firms had no desire to employ a lawyer with relatives in the Mafia. Unfortunately, DeMarco also looked like his father—like a guy you could imagine working as a leg breaker for a loan shark in Queens.

Then DeMarco got lucky—or at least, at the time he thought it was luck. One of his aunts had worked in D.C. when she was young and, like many other young women, she'd had an affair with John Mahoney. When she heard about her favorite nephew's employment problems, she convinced—or maybe blackmailed—Mahoney to give him a job. And Mahoney did. He stuck DeMarco in a closet-sized office in the subbasement of the Capitol and then introduced him to the rank underbelly of American politics.

DeMarco was hardly unique. There were a lot of guys like him in D.C.—guys who worked in almost invisible positions to keep their political masters in power. Most of these people resided in the private sector. They were employed by political action groups and so-called consulting firms, and passed out business cards with job titles that gave no clue as to what they actually did. Then there were those like DeMarco who held government positions with equally vague titles and no clearly defined role in any organization. DeMarco's title was "Counsel Pro Tem for Liaison Affairs"—and it was absolutely meaningless.

DeMarco was often used as a conduit, passing messages to and obtaining money from people who wanted Mahoney's help but whom Mahoney couldn't always acknowledge as supporters. Some of these folks were Democrats who desired to contribute more than the amount allowed by campaign finance laws; they knew that John Mahoney's price was much, much steeper. Some were registered Republican businessmen trying to prosper in a predominately blue congressional district. One was a woman who operated the most profitable escort service in Boston. Another secret contributor to Mahoney's coffers was the Archdiocese of Boston. But DeMarco's activities weren't limited to . . . well, Mahoney liked to call it *fund-raising*.

DeMarco's most recent assignment had involved a Massachusetts state legislator and the renovation of a low-income housing project in Boston. Mahoney wanted the job to go to a general contractor who contributed to him, but the state legislator was accepting bribes from a different contractor. When Mahoney called the state guy and told him to back off, the legislator, apparently thinking the ex-Speaker was no longer the powerhouse he'd once been, told Mahoney to go to hell—and Mahoney dispatched DeMarco. It took DeMarco three weeks to determine that the churchgoing family man was having an affair with a twenty-year-old intern, a strapping young fellow named Jeremy.

When it comes to being gay, the State of Massachusetts is considered fairly liberal. Two gay people can get married there; a gay man can certainly hold political office there. What's not okay is being a gay politician while claiming to be happily married to a woman—now we're talking *integrity,* not sexual orientation—and the state legislator decided that Mahoney's contractor was the best man for the job.

DeMarco learned that there were moral and legal lines, however, that not even Mahoney would cross, and the arbitrary placement of those lines had something to do with Mahoney's interpretation of the word *patriotism.* There were even more lines that DeMarco would not cross, and more than a few times he had come close to being fired for refusing to follow Mahoney's orders. So given a choice between working for a corrupt politician and being a normal lawyer who sued whoever was suable, DeMarco would have opted for *normal lawyer.* Unfortunately, he didn't have any experience doing whatever normal lawyers did.

Brian Kincaid's mother was a frail, gray-haired widow in her late sixties who lived alone in a small house badly in need of a gardener and a coat of paint. Her fingers were swollen and gnarled with rheumatoid arthritis. She gave DeMarco the same reception her son had given him: she hugged him with all the strength in her thin arms, telling him he was an "absolute godsend" for helping her boy—and, naturally, DeMarco felt guilty. He was about 50 percent certain that Brian Kincaid was a liar and a murderer—and 100 percent certain that he wasn't going to be able to get him out of jail.

DeMarco had gone to Mrs. Kincaid's house because that's where all of Kincaid's records were stored—everything related to his trial, motions and appeals filed by his lawyer, and reports from the private detective he'd hired. Kincaid's mom led him down to her basement and showed him four cardboard boxes stacked next to her washing machine. DeMarco thought for a moment about taking the boxes back to his house to review the paperwork—and instantly rejected that idea. First, he didn't want the boxes cluttering up his house. Second, he'd have to lug the boxes up Mrs. Kincaid's basement stairs and out to his car, and then repeat the lugging procedure at his place. But the main reason he decided not to take the boxes was because if he took them, he'd have to return them—and that meant he'd have to face Kincaid's mother again, which was something he didn't want to do.

He asked Mrs. Kincaid if it would be okay to review the records there in the basement, and she showed him a dusty, folding card table and folding chairs stacked in a corner. Next, she brought him a Coke and a ham sandwich; if he'd asked her to, she would have stood over him waving a fan to keep him cool.

DeMarco, cynic that he was, believed that this was the most important part of his assignment. His job was not to free Brian Kincaid; his job was to get Mary Pat Mahoney off her husband's back. The best way to do this, he figured, was to let Mrs. Kincaid see him sitting there for several hours poring diligently over her son's case. She would be an eyewitness to his earnest toil, and she would then pass this testimony on to Mary Pat.

The trial transcript and police reports matched what Kincaid had already told him: that the case had been a slam dunk for the prosecutor. Downing's body had been discovered at nine-fifty and Kincaid had left the building, per the security guard, at nine-thirty. Unfortunately, forensic medicine couldn't determine if Downing had been killed between nine-fifteen and nine-thirty, when Kincaid and Downing were in the building together, or if he'd been killed between nine-thirty and nine-fifty, as Kincaid claimed. The prosecutor didn't really have to determine the exact time of death, however, because he could establish that Kincaid hated Downing, that Downing had been killed with Kincaid's gun, and, most important, that no one else had been in the building other than the security guard when Downing was killed. Regarding Kincaid's defense—that someone else had killed Downing and framed Kincaid—there was no physical evidence or witnesses to support the theory that some unknown person had snuck into the building and shot Downing after Kincaid left.

An interesting twist to the case was that after Kincaid allegedly killed Downing, he went to a bar a block from his office and drank for two hours before going home. Kincaid's attorney argued that this proved that Kincaid was innocent, because no sane person would kill a man and then calmly go to a nearby bar and have a drink. The prosecutor countered by saying that Kincaid was so rattled by what he had done that after he stashed the murder weapon in the trunk of his car, he had *needed* a drink. The jury liked the prosecutor's explanation better.

The burning question—a question that Brian Kincaid had spent the last two years considering—was this: *Why would someone want to frame him for Phil Downing's murder?* There were only two plausible explanations. The first was that somebody hated Brian Kincaid, wanted him to spend twenty-five years in prison, and shot Downing and framed Kincaid with this end in mind. The problem with this theory was that Kincaid couldn't think of anybody who hated him that much, not even his ex-wife. And if somebody did hate him that much, why not just kill *him* instead of framing him for Downing's murder?

The second explanation, which Kincaid favored, was that somebody wanted Phil Downing dead but didn't want to give the police the opportunity to find the real murderer, so Brian Kincaid was framed to give the cops an immediate and perfect suspect. And that's pretty much what happened. Once the police were convinced that Kincaid was their guy, they spent no time at all looking for another suspect—and DeMarco didn't blame them.

Prior to his arrest, Kincaid had earned about ninety thousand dollars a year, and spent most of what he earned. To pay for his defense he exhausted his meager savings, sold his house and all his furnishings. To pay for the private detective, he sold his car. The private detective then spent a hundred hours—at a hundred and twenty bucks per hour—trying to find an alternative suspect for Phil Downing's murder or evidence to force a retrial. He failed.

Two and a half hours after descending into Mrs. Kincaid's basement, DeMarco emerged, carrying a single sheet of paper on which he'd made a few notes—and the complete conviction that Brian Kincaid was totally screwed. As he was leaving, Mrs. Kincaid hugged him and thanked him again for everything he was doing—which made DeMarco feel just awful.

1 0

——◆◆◆——

The private detective that Brian Kincaid had hired was a retired cop named Colin Gordon. He was a burly, bald-headed man with hound dog eyes and enormous ears, and he had a habit of tugging on his big right ear as he talked. His office was in a strip mall in Fairfax and there was a bail bondsman on one side and a personal injury lawyer on the other, guys who probably provided Gordon most of his business.

"I never could make up my mind whether Kincaid killed Downing or not," Gordon said. "You look at the evidence, and you just have to believe he did it. But if you talk to the guy, you tend to believe he's innocent. What about you, DeMarco? Do you think he's innocent?"

"I don't know," DeMarco said, "but you're right. He doesn't seem like the type who would kill somebody, but maybe he's just a good actor. And I'm probably wasting my time and yours, but I wanted to see if there was anything you didn't put in the reports you gave Kincaid."

Gordon frowned. "You think I held out on a client?"

"No, no. I'm not suggesting you did anything improper. What I'm asking is if there were things you didn't report because they were just impressions, things you couldn't verify. You know, a gut feeling you had but couldn't prove."

Gordon relaxed, satisfied DeMarco wasn't impugning him. "Nah," he said, "there wasn't anything like that. I told Kincaid everything, but I never came close to finding something that could help him." Gordon gave his big right ear another tug. "Kincaid probably told you, but my main job was to find somebody who had a reason to frame him for Downing's murder. But there just wasn't anybody like that. No one.

"When I was cop I worked robbery-homicide and never had a case involving a lobbyist, but based on what I read in the papers about people like Jack Abramoff, I was under the impression they were these slick-talking, evil guys that bribed congressmen and took them out on their yachts and hooked 'em up with beautiful babes. Well, if Downing or Kincaid did anything like that, I didn't see any evidence of it. Mostly all they did was stay on top of laws that Congress was working on, see how the laws would affect their clients, and pass on what they learned. And Kincaid and Downing were about as ordinary as you could get. Neither one was rich, so stealing their money wasn't a motive for murder or for framing Kincaid. They'd both been divorced, Downing twice, but their ex-wives had moved on and weren't interested in some big vendetta. They didn't have any enemies that I could find. They weren't suing anybody. They weren't screwing women who were with other men. They weren't going to be federal witnesses against some slimeball congressman."

"What about their clients?" DeMarco asked. "Maybe one of them was blackmailing a client because he discovered the client was doing something illegal, and the client decided to take care of the blackmailer."

"Dumb as that idea is," Gordon said, "I considered it."

DeMarco was offended; he didn't think it was such a dumb idea.

"In the case of Kincaid's clients," Gordon said, "I just asked Kincaid if he was doing anything like that. Since the guy had already been arrested for murder when he hired me, I figured he wasn't going to lie to me if he was blackmailing someone. Well, Kincaid said that not only wasn't he a blackmailer, he didn't know anything his clients did that would make them targets for blackmail. All of them were these dink-ass European and Asian companies, he never visited any of their operations, and if they were using slave labor or dumping toxic chemicals, he wouldn't have known a thing about it. So I'm pretty sure that one of Kincaid's clients didn't kill Phil Downing and frame him for murder because he was trying to extort money from them."

"What about Downing's clients?" DeMarco asked.

"At the time of his death, Downing only had one client. He'd lost the others when the economy turned to shit."

DeMarco now remembered that Kincaid had told him this—that Phil Downing was just barely making ends meet before he was killed.

"And his client was the Warwick Foundation," Gordon continued. "Do you know what the Warwick Foundation does, DeMarco?"

"No."

"It's a nonprofit that sends relief supplies and doctors and medicine to places that get hit by natural disasters. Or if there's a war going on someplace like Lebanon or Darfur, Warwick tries to get supplies to the losers. As near as I can tell, Lizzie Warwick is the closest thing this country has to Mother Teresa."

"That still doesn't mean—"

Gordon silenced DeMarco by raising one of his big paws. "Even though I didn't think it very likely that Lizzie Warwick had Downing killed, I still did some digging. The main thing I did was look to see if Downing had recently gotten rich. I mean, if you're black-mailing someone it's usually for money, so I checked Downing's bank accounts, but I didn't see any evidence of a large deposit or periodic payments from some strange source. I also looked to see if he'd bought any big-ticket items—a boat, a fancy new car, any-thing like that. He hadn't. I even—and if you tell anybody I said this, I'll call you a liar—I even broke into Downing's house and searched it for a bagful of cash. I didn't find one. The other thing I did was ask a lot of people about Warwick to see if anybody had heard anything funny about her—some kind of scandal, legal problems, boyfriend problems, anything off-color. Naturally, everybody I talked to thought I was nuts. And you know what I concluded after I did all this digging, DeMarco?"

"No. What?"

"I concluded that the only person who hated Phil Downing enough to kill him was Brian Kincaid."

It sounded to DeMarco like Gordon had been pretty thorough. "What about this secretary they shared? Kincaid told me Downing was having an affair with her."

"Strictly speaking, it wasn't an affair, because Downing wasn't married when he was dating her and she was single, too. I talked to her a couple of times to see if she knew anything that would help, but she wasn't all that helpful. For one thing, she was convinced Kincaid had killed her boyfriend and she knew I was trying to help Kincaid. But it's been over a year since I talked to her. Maybe she's through grieving and will open up to you."

⸺⸻◆⸻⸺

DeMarco got the impression that Sharon Palmer spent a lot of time, effort, and money to make herself attractive to men, just as a skilled hunter takes care baiting a trap. Her clothes were fashionable; her dyed ash-blonde hair was nicely styled; her makeup was perfectly applied. Unfortunately, nature had conspired against her. Her eyes were small and set too close to a sharp nose, her lips were thin, and the lines bracketing her mouth were evident through her makeup. Her breasts, however, were outstanding. They were large, well formed, and very noticeable—and DeMarco was willing to bet that Sharon had taken out a loan to have them made just that way.

She worked for a trade association that represented scrap metal recyclers. Her office was near Dupont Circle, and DeMarco was fortunate to arrive there just as she was about to leave work for the day. This was fortunate because when he asked Sharon if he could buy her a drink while he asked a few questions about Kincaid and Downing, he could tell that the idea of a free after-work drink appealed to her even if the subject matter didn't. He could also tell that *he* appealed to her.

They walked to a bar a block from her office. Sharon had a company security badge and a key card on a lanyard around her neck, and as soon as they arrived at the bar, she took off the lanyard and dumped the badge and key card into her purse, then dropped the purse on the floor at her feet. She ordered a Manhattan and, because that sounded good, DeMarco ordered one, too. He couldn't help but notice that she looked better in the dim lighting in the bar and, with the body she had, he could understand why Phil Downing had been attracted to her.

"What did you do for Downing and Kincaid?" DeMarco asked. He already knew she'd been their secretary, but he wanted to get her to start talking. He also wanted to get enough booze into her to get her to *keep* talking.

"Not much," she said. "I'd mail stuff to their clients, print off articles from the Internet, get copies of bills making their way through the House and the Senate, make appointments for them. That sort of thing. Mostly what they wanted was for me to answer the phone and say, 'I'm sorry, but Mr. Downing is having lunch with Senator McCain and won't be back until two.' Not that either one of them ever met with McCain or anybody else that important."

"Did you handle their billing?"

"No, they billed the clients themselves and kept their own books. They had a joint account they put money into for office expenses—you know, the rent, the phone bill, my salary, that sort of thing. I'd pay the office expenses out of the joint account, keep track of the expenses, and about every two months they'd have a giant fight because something cost too much or one of them didn't like the copy machine we leased or something stupid like that."

"I heard that you and Phil Downing dated."

She shrugged. "I'm an unmarried forty-year-old woman"—

DeMarco guessed she was closer to forty-five—"with a seventeen-year-old daughter who's a complete bitch. Phil wasn't totally unattractive, he wasn't married, and he asked me out. I never figured he was going to marry me and take care of me for the rest of my life, but being with him was better than spending every night alone with my daughter."

It didn't sound like Sharon Palmer was going to win any awards for Mother of the Year. Nor did it sound like Phil Downing had been the man of her dreams, and whatever grief she'd experienced upon his passing had certainly diminished over time.

"Why do you think Kincaid killed him?"

She shook her head. "I have no idea, but they probably got into one of their screaming matches over some dumb thing, and Phil . . . Well, he could be *nasty* when they argued, real insulting. Or maybe Phil shoved Brian or took a swing at him. He outweighed Brian by at least thirty pounds and maybe Brian got scared, got his gun, and shot him. Although I never knew Brian kept a gun in the office."

"Huh," DeMarco said, unable to think of anything more intelligent to say. Seeing that her glass was empty, he asked if she wanted another Manhattan. She looked at him for a moment, and he got the impression she might be thinking the same thing about him that she'd thought about Phil Downing: that he wasn't completely unattractive and that spending the night with him would be better than spending it with her daughter.

"Sure," she said. "Maybe just one more."

"Were either of them having any trouble with their clients before Phil died?"

"Brian wasn't, at least not that I ever heard him say. But a few weeks before Phil was killed, he was all down in the mouth one night, and when I asked him what was wrong, he said Warwick was thinking about switching to another firm."

"Really?" DeMarco said. This was new information. There hadn't been anything about this in Gordon's reports.

"Yeah, and if they'd dropped Phil, he would have been screwed, because Warwick was the only client he had left. In the end, Warwick decided to stick with him—but then the poor guy goes and gets killed."

"Did you tell anybody about this during Brian's trial or when the police were investigating?"

"You mean about Warwick thinking about switching firms?"

"Yeah."

"No one ever asked. And all this happened more than a month before Phil was killed and it didn't seem relevant."

"Did you ever get the impression that Phil had something on Warwick?"

"Had something on them? What do you mean?"

"Could he have known something about the foundation that he might have held over their head, something he could have used to force them to continue to retain him?" DeMarco didn't want to use the word *blackmail.*

"Geez, if he did, I don't know what it could have been."

"What exactly did he do for Warwick?"

"He lobbied for anything having to do with foreign aid or the government funding NGOs to help out during catastrophes. He'd even pay attention to real general stuff, like tax laws affecting nonprofits and charitable donations."

She reached out and gave DeMarco's hand a little pat. "I think we've talked enough about Brian and Phil, don't you, Joe? Tell me about yourself. Do you have a girlfriend?"

Until two months ago, DeMarco did indeed have a girlfriend, but she was gone now and her departure was still somewhat of an open wound. And he hadn't had sex since she left. He thought for a moment about making the effort—and he knew it wouldn't take all that much effort—to get Sharon Palmer to spend the night with him. It would be an uncomplicated one-night stand. Fortunately, his willpower was able to get a grip on his panting libido.

The fact was that, aside from the sex, DeMarco didn't like one-night stands. He always felt like some sort of greasy lounge lizard, sneaking out of a woman's bedroom at dawn knowing he had no intention of ever returning. He'd been married once, and he'd actually liked being married until his wife started cheating on him, and he wouldn't have minded getting married again if the right woman came along. Consequently, he preferred to go to bed with women who at least had *some* possibility of being the next Mrs. DeMarco. He could tell, after less than a half hour with her, that Sharon Palmer wasn't even a remote possibility.

There was no point saying this, however, as he might need her cooperation in the future. Instead, being a gallant gentleman, he lied. "I don't have a girlfriend but, unfortunately, I have to get going. I have to meet a guy for dinner. You know, a business thing."

Then he ran for the door before he could change his mind.

DeMarco lived in Georgetown, on P Street, in a narrow, two-story town house made of white-painted brick. It wasn't a large place, and when he was living with a woman, there were times when it seemed too small for two people. But now that he was alone again, there were some nights when the place seemed cavernous and the silence felt like it was crushing him. This was one of those nights—so he decided to have dinner in a noisy Georgetown bar where he'd be surrounded by others of his species.

He walked to a place in Georgetown called The Guards. He liked The Guards because it wasn't a college kid hangout and adults his age tended to gather there after work. He took a seat at the bar, a couple stools away from two good-looking women dressed in suits with short hemlines. They were drinking some kind of cobalt-blue drink served in a martini glass, and he thought about asking them what they were drinking just to start a conversation—and then realized he didn't really want to start a conversation. It suddenly seemed like too much work to be sociable and charming; he should have stayed at home.

He ordered a steak and a salad for dinner, preceded by a Grey Goose martini. As he sipped his martini, he thought about the fact that it hadn't been a very good year for him or anyone associated with him. He had lost his lover. Mahoney had lost the Speaker's job. And then there was his friend Emma's problem—a problem he didn't fully understand but which he knew was significantly larger than his and Mahoney's problems combined.

Angela DiCapria, DeMarco's lover for the past two years, worked for the CIA. He met her on a case where an agent was killed because one of Mahoney's cronies in Congress had leaked the identity of the agent to the press. When he met Angela she was married to an asshole; six months later she was living part-time with DeMarco and, three months after that, moved in completely. DeMarco wanted to marry her; but Angela, too recently stung by a bad marriage, wasn't ready to take that step.

All was going well until her employer sent her to Afghanistan. When she returned, she was different. She couldn't tell DeMarco what she had done over there, but whatever it was, it affected her significantly. She couldn't sleep, would often just sit in the dark for hours, and eventually began seeing a psychiatrist. DeMarco didn't know anything about post-traumatic stress disorder—but he suspected that's what his girlfriend had.

Angela eventually stopped seeing the shrink, but she became obsessive about her work—or, to be accurate, *more* obsessive. She did something terrorist-related at Langley—something classified in such a manner that she couldn't tell DeMarco exactly what she did—but after returning from Afghanistan, she didn't spend a mere ten or twelve hours a day at work; she began spending sixteen or eighteen hours there, and some nights she didn't come home and slept on the couch in her office. Or maybe she slept at her office because she didn't want to sleep with him. Whatever the case, she came home one evening and told him she was being transferred back to Afghanistan. When he asked her if there was anything she could do to get out of the assignment, she told him she'd asked for the transfer.

11

Kelly and Nelson had wanted to fly from Nairobi directly to their ranch in Montana—they had a lot of things to get done on the place before winter—but Fiona ordered them to take a small detour. To Peru. They were dreading the trip because what they had to do in Peru was, without a doubt, the most difficult part of their job. Given a choice between going to Peru and battling bloodthirsty teenagers in Africa armed with machetes and AK-47s, they would have chosen the teenagers.

Knowing what lay ahead of them, they barely spoke on the long flight to Arequipa, a city in southern Peru and the second-largest in the country.

They took a taxi to a private garage a few miles from the airport. Inside the garage was a four-wheel-drive Jeep Cherokee packed with a tent, sleeping bags, a satellite phone, food, spare gas cans, binoculars, night vision goggles, and gas masks. Kelly had to admit that when it came to pulling together what they needed for their missions, Hobson did a good job.

The drive from Arequipa to their destination took several hours, and the journey was unremarkable except for the occasional vehicle that came speeding down the narrow mountain road giving no thought to the possibility that another vehicle might be coming the other way. The scenery, which they had seen several times before, was magnificent, although neither man commented on it.

Approximately ten miles from the small town of Pinchollo, they pulled the Cherokee off the main road and into a picturesque mountain meadow. A small, fast-moving stream ran through the meadow, and they had an unobstructed view of the mountains. They didn't select the meadow because of the view or the stream, however; they picked it because it was large enough and flat enough to accommodate a helicopter.

While Kelly erected the tent and rolled out their sleeping bags, Nelson filled a pot with water from the stream and made a fire. The area was so sparsely populated they doubted they would encounter anyone, and if they did they'd just say they were a couple of crazy American tourists. If anyone tried to rob them, which was unlikely, the robbers would be in for a surprise. Even without automatic weapons and grenade launchers, Kelly and Nelson were extraordinarily lethal.

Nelson made them a quick meal, boiling freeze-dried food that came in pouches. Then they had some time to kill, because they couldn't start their mission until approximately midnight and it was only seven p.m. They were both tired from the long flight from Nairobi, followed by the drive from Arequipa to their campsite, so Kelly set his wristwatch alarm for eleven thirty p.m. and they went inside the tent and took naps so they'd be fresh for the work ahead.

At midnight, they filled knapsacks with the equipment they would need, then took off in the Jeep, with Nelson driving; he had better night vision than Kelly. Their camp was ten miles from the village of Pinchollo and the Warwick Care Center was twenty miles beyond the village, situated about a mile off the main road. There were no streetlights in Pinchollo and the town's inhabitants were early-to-bed, early-to-rise types, and consequently the town was completely dark when they drove through it and they saw no one on the streets. Nonetheless, they drove through the town with the headlights off.

Forty minutes after leaving the meadow, they took the turnoff for the Warwick Care Center and drove until they were within half a mile of the facility, then proceeded the rest of the way on foot, Nelson leading the way. They had flashlights and night vision goggles in their knapsacks, but didn't use either. The half-moon and stars provided light and they were careful treading across the rocky ground. If one of them sprained an ankle, it would complicate the mission.

The Warwick Care Center consisted of two large Quonset huts and several smaller enclosures. The two large huts were the sleeping quarters for the residents—one hut for the males, the other for females—and these huts were equipped with heating and ventilation systems. In between the two large huts was a smaller hut where the nurse lived. Two Honda generators were in a third enclosure and supplied electricity for the facility, and they could hear one of the generators running.

Kelly went to the small hut where the nurse lived. He put on night vision goggles and took a pistol from his knapsack. He slowly turned the doorknob and found it unlocked as he'd expected; in this part of the world, people rarely felt the need to lock their doors. He cracked open the door and listened, and when he could hear the nurse snoring, he stepped into the hut and shot the nurse in the back with a tranquilizer dart. He waited two minutes, then pulled the dart out of the man's back. Tomorrow the nurse would wonder about the sore spot on his back but would otherwise suffer no ill effects from the tranquilizer—or so Kelly had been told.

While Kelly was darting the nurse, Nelson shut off the generator that provided power for the ventilation system in the Quonset huts. When Nelson returned, Kelly made a hand signal and proceeded to the large Quonset hut where the male subjects slept while Nelson went to the females' hut. Kelly took a quart-sized metal canister from his knapsack, opened the door to the hut, placed the canister on the floor, turned a small valve on it, and shut the door. Nelson did the same thing in the women's hut.

Although the people inside the two huts had most likely been sleeping when Kelly and Nelson released the gas, some might have been awake. The subjects often slept poorly and woke frequently during the night, and the gas would render them all unconscious in about fifteen minutes; it was an effective anesthetic but not fast-acting. The best thing about the gas was that the side effects were minimal—mild headache, dizziness, slight nausea. Or so Kelly had been told.

After half an hour passed, Kelly turned to Nelson and said, "Let's get this done."

Kelly took a device out of his knapsack and they entered the Quonset hut where the males slept, then Kelly walked down the aisle between the cots looking down at the device in his hand. He was holding an RFID reader.

Radio-frequency identification uses radio waves to communicate between a reader and an electronic "tag" or "chip." Similar to bar-code systems, the technology is used for managing inventories and keeping track of parts; it's used in E-Z Pass systems to charge drivers on toll roads; casinos install RFID transmitters in poker chips to prevent counterfeiting; and when mad cow disease was discovered, RFID tags were attached to cows' ears so individual animals could be tracked from birth to slaughterhouse. Incredible amounts of information can be stored on RFID chips and, as is usually the case with electronics, the chips had gotten smaller over time and the amount of information that could be stored on them had increased dramatically.

When René Lambert selected the test subjects, there had to be a foolproof way of tying the subjects to the drugs and subsequent tests and biological samples. Therefore, each subject—with the subject's consent—had a microchip a bit bigger than a grain of rice inserted into his or her upper arm. The chip contained all the relevant information—age, race, sex, medical history, et cetera; it contained everything but the subject's name. Instead of a name each subject was given an alpha-numeric code number. The names of these people were—on so many levels—completely irrelevant.

Holding the RFID reader in his hand, Kelly pointed it at each sleeping patient, and when he was about halfway down the aisle the reader emitted a soft beep—indicating that he had located a subject who met certain criteria established by Dr. Ballard. Kelly stood there looking down at the sleeping man for a moment, for no other reason than to delay what he needed to do. He and Nelson had flipped a coin before they left their campsite—and this time Kelly had lost the coin toss.

Knowing he couldn't stall any longer, Kelly took out of his knapsack a small plastic bottle marked with the brand name of a popular nasal spray. He inserted the tip of the container into the man's right nostril and squeezed. And that was it. The man would be dead in less than five minutes.

Kelly continued down the aisle pointing the RFID reader at the sleeping, snoring men until the reader beeped again, then he repeated the procedure with the nasal spray dispenser, this time with no hesitation. Kelly didn't hesitate when he killed the third subject, either—a female in the second Quonset hut—but it was harder for him than killing the two males.

Kelly and Nelson walked in silence back to their vehicle and didn't speak during the drive back to their campsite. Had they been different men, they might have tried to rationalize what they had just done. They might have said: *Well, at least they didn't suffer. They were going to die pretty soon anyway.* But they didn't say those things—nor did they think them.

When they met Fiona for the first time in Afghanistan and she told them why Mulray Pharma was willing to pay them so much, Kelly had asked, "Are any of these people kids?"

"No," Fiona said.

"And how many people are we talking about?"

"I don't know," Fiona said, "and what difference does it make? If you're willing to kill a couple of people, why not a dozen, why not ten dozen? All you need to understand is that the risk of being caught is virtually nil. These people will die in medical facilities, their deaths will be attributed to natural causes, and the local authorities won't investigate."

And that's when Kelly had told her that he and Nelson needed to be alone to talk things over—but they really didn't talk that much.

Although Kelly was black and Nelson was white, they came from similar backgrounds. Kelly had been raised by his grandmother in a mining town in Kentucky. His father had been killed in a mining accident when he was two, and when he was four his mother went out to dinner one night with a tool-and-die salesman and never came back. His grandmother was a stern, unemotional woman and Kelly couldn't remember her ever hugging him, even the day he left to join the army; he did remember her beating him with a belt when he misbehaved. From the time he was ten, he fished and hunted to provide additional food for their table; he ate a lot of squirrel, possum, and coon when he was growing up.

Nelson was also a hunter. He'd been raised on a farm in South Dakota that produced no crops, and his family's only source of income was a government disability check his father received. Both his parents were beer-guzzling alcoholics. They didn't abuse him; they were just completely indifferent toward him. Nelson recalled a day when he was thirteen and it was twenty degrees below zero—thirty below when the windchill factor was taken into account—and the school bus broke down. The other kids called their parents to come pick them up, but

Nelson's family didn't have a functioning automobile at the time, so he decided to walk home, and was lucky he didn't lose his fingers and toes to frostbite. But his parents' only reaction when he entered the house—his skin blue, his teeth chattering so hard he couldn't speak—was to complain that because he was late and hadn't been there to knock the snow off the satellite dish, they'd missed one of their favorite TV shows.·

When they were of age, Kelly and Nelson joined the army for the same reason: the army, economically and socially, was a step up. They discovered each other in boot camp, and a lifelong bond was formed—a bond forged in the heat of combat, shared hardship, and pain.

They sat for a few minutes in silence after Fiona left their Afghani jail cell, until Nelson finally said what they were both thinking. "We could get the ranch."

Four months before they met Fiona, they had taken some time off from Romar-Slade to go fly-fishing in Montana. While they were there they saw the ranch—a hundred and fifty acres of paradise on the Bitterroot River with a view of Trapper Peak that was literally priceless. It was for sale, and when they asked the old woman selling it how much she wanted and she told them the price, they didn't say it was too much—it was simply beyond their reach, and always would be.

The ranch became their fantasy. If they ever won the lotto; if they ever came upon that buried pot of gold . . . They talked, and not idly, about stealing heroin from the Afghani politician they had been hired to protect. It would have been difficult but doable—but they had no idea how to turn heroin into money after they had it, and they knew the drug business was even more dangerous than the Taliban.

If they accepted Fiona's offer, however, fantasy could become reality. They could retire before the age of forty, rich for the first time in their lives. But they didn't really care about money, per se. They didn't want luxury cars or yachts or designer clothes or a spacious, palatial home. They didn't want to travel the world as pampered tourists; they'd already seen most of the world. What they wanted was a plot of land to call their own, a plot large enough to feel like they were living in a world of their own. They wanted space. They wanted a place where they didn't have to see other people on a daily basis, a place where they could fish and hunt and walk their dogs, a place where eagles soared and wolves still roamed and where they could sit on their front porch and gaze upon a mountain peak and pretend it was theirs alone. And all they had to do to get what they wanted was become assassins—though the word *assassin* was, quite frankly, too glamorous for what Fiona wanted them to do.

Kelly and Nelson had killed a lot of people during their army careers, and some of those people had been noncombatants—*collateral damage,* in military parlance. And on a couple of missions they performed while they were in Delta Force, they'd been sent in to execute terrorists and had been told not to leave witnesses, no matter how innocent those witnesses might appear to be—and they followed their orders. They could rationalize those killings, however; they were soldiers and it was the politicians who chose the targets and set the agenda.

When they left Delta and became mercenaries for a private security company, they did it for money, pure and simple. They knew if they stayed in the army—assuming they weren't killed—they'd end up training other soldiers before they were pensioned out, and the pensions would be adequate, but no more than adequate. So they signed on with Romar-Slade, who tripled their army salaries, and in return, they protected a corrupt, opium-growing Afghani politician. And when they killed to defend the politician, they knew they were often killing his business and political rivals and not enemies of the state. And they could live with that.

They did regret killing the three children in the roadside house— but they didn't weep, they didn't get drunk to dull the pain, they didn't toss and turn in their sleep. Their emotions had been cauterized by their childhoods, and they had seen and caused so much death during their careers that a dead human being made no more of an impression on them than a decaying log lying on the forest floor. And, from their perspective, it was the Taliban who were to blame for the children's deaths; it was the Taliban who had been callous enough to start a firefight in a house containing kids.

But they didn't kill for the sake of killing; they took no pleasure from the act. They weren't bullies; they didn't torment the weak. And they didn't kill innocents unless the innocents just happened to be in the wrong place at the wrong time—like the three children in the roadside house. They knew, however, that if they went to work for Fiona, they would be crossing a line they'd never crossed before. They would go from being hard and sometimes brutal men to truly bad men. More important, they knew they would be . . . diminished.

On the other hand, if they didn't accept Fiona's offer they knew they might spend years in an Afghani prison. Their employer was ready to sacrifice them as a matter of political expediency and for the sake of the bottom line. They also knew that the only marketable skill they had was killing, and that if they didn't take Fiona's deal they would spend the rest of their lives working for paramilitary organizations— assuming they ever got out of jail—and the ranch in Montana would continue to be nothing more than a dream.

Yes, they knew all these things, and they thought all these things, but didn't speak to any of them. So when Nelson said, "We could get the ranch," Kelly's response had been, "It's the only way we'll ever get it."

"Then I guess we do it," Nelson said.

"Yeah, I guess we do." Then Kelly held out his fist and Nelson tapped Kelly's fist with his own and said, "Hooah."

"Yeah, hooah," Kelly had said, the word no louder than a whisper.

The morning after they visited the Warwick Care Center outside Pinchollo, Kelly and Nelson slept in late and had a leisurely breakfast as they waited for the nurse to wake up from his tranquilizer-induced sleep and discover the three dead bodies in the Quonset huts. At nine-fifteen, the satellite phone rang and the nurse, following prescribed procedures, told Kelly that three of the residents had passed away during the night. One death wouldn't have surprised him, but three. . . . Well, mother of God, what a shock.

Yes, what a shock, Kelly said. Kelly told the man that a helicopter would arrive sometime that morning, and the nurse wasn't surprised by this. He had no idea where the helicopter was coming from or how fast it could fly; all he knew was that he worked for a wealthy American company and they could do marvelous things. Kelly told the nurse to place the bodies in the body bags provided for this situation, and then called the helicopter pilot that Hobson had hired.

Kelly gave the pilot the GPS coordinates of their campsite, then went back to reading while Nelson made a halfhearted effort to catch a fish he'd seen in the stream. Two hours later, the chopper arrived and picked up Kelly—there was no need for Nelson to go—and flew to the Warwick facility. While the bodies were being loaded into the helicopter, Kelly spent some time talking to the nurse, a short, brown, moon-faced man named Juan Carlos. His last name was unpronounceable.

"I don't understand how this could have happened," Juan Carlos said.

"I know," Kelly said, shaking his head sadly. "Are any of the other people presenting symptoms?"

"Some have headaches. Some say their stomachs are upset."

"Hmm," Kelly said. "You could have a carbon monoxide leak coming from the generators. Let's go take a look at them."

They did.

"Everything looks fine," Kelly said, "but carbon monoxide's the only thing I can think of. I better have somebody come out and inspect the generators and the ventilation systems. In the meantime, keep the windows in the Quonset huts open."

"But we've never had a problem with the generators in the past," Juan Carlos said.

"Well," Kelly said, "it may have nothing to do with the generators. These people have issues or they wouldn't be here. And they've been through a lot; they've suffered a lot. The people that died were probably just weaker than the others—weaker immune systems or something. Or maybe they had some sort of preexisting condition we didn't know about. Things like this happen, so don't beat yourself up, and, for God's sake, don't talk about this to anyone. If some sort of investigation was started . . . Well, you know, that could be the end of this operation here."

Juan Carlos wasn't the sharpest knife in the drawer. René Lambert must not have been able to find anyone else in the region with the medical background needed to manage the facility. And it wasn't good to hire folks that were *too* bright. But even Juan Carlos was smart enough to understand that he could lose his cushy fuckin' job if anybody made a fuss about the deaths that had occurred. Fortunately, there wasn't anyone likely to investigate, and the people who died didn't have relatives who would ask questions.

"I'll pray for them," Juan Carlos said, crossing himself.

"Yeah, me too," Kelly said.

The chopper dropped Kelly back off at the campsite. He and Nelson would now drive to Arequipa, catch a charter flight back to the states, and then proceed to their place in Montana. The three bodies would be taken to a mortuary in Lima, placed in vacuum-sealed aluminum coffins, then flown to Thailand; it was easier to bring corpses into Thailand than the U.S. After the autopsies were performed, certain tissue samples would be sent on to Dr. Ballard's lab.

Unless there was a security issue of some sort, or they had to get medical supplies to Lambert or perform the function they had just performed in Peru, there really wasn't much more for them to do, and Fiona had no problem with their remaining in Montana until she had another task for them. With any luck at all, they wouldn't have to leave their ranch for a few months.

Kelly just hoped that this DeMarco character, and whatever the hell he was doing with Brian Kincaid, didn't screw things up.

12

The oncologist was a small, dark-haired woman about Emma's age, and Emma imagined that during the course of her career she had told a lot of people they were going to die.

She wondered if she was going to be one of them.

Emma had always been extraordinarily healthy. In part, this was due to her lifestyle. She exercised fanatically, and always had. She was naturally slim but ate in such a manner as to stay that way. She also had good genes: the people on both her mother's and her father's side of her family tended to live long lives. She had been wounded twice during her career, once critically, but had never had a major illness. The only noncombat-related operation she ever had was when she was six and they removed her tonsils. She had low cholesterol, low blood pressure, and no sign of osteoporosis. Menopause had been a bitch, but then it was for every woman.

And then, out of the blue, came the cancer.

When she heard the prognosis, she told herself that she had lived a marvelous life, a meaningful life. She had been loved and had known the joys of love. She had done things few women ever have the opportunity to do, and she had served her country well and honorably. She had no regrets; there was nothing she felt had been left undone.

She had expected to live much longer, at least another twenty years, but if she died this year . . . well, she could accept that. What she could not accept was being an invalid—being shackled to a bed, filled with narcotics, too weak to think, much less move. She would never allow herself to get to the point where living was nothing more than one labored, pain-filled breath followed by another. If she couldn't live her life as she had always lived it—vigorously and independently and uncompromisingly—she would end it.

After she was diagnosed, she had the first operation, followed by a second, and then all the drugs. The side effects of the drugs had seemed worse than the disease. And now it was time to hear the verdict.

"I think we got it all," the oncologist said. "I think you're going to be all right. It could come back and if it does . . . Well, you know. I want to see you again in six months, but for now . . . you're a lucky woman."

She hadn't cried when she heard she had cancer, and she wouldn't cry now that she was being told she was cancer-free. She simply exhaled and said, "Thank you, Doctor."

But when she stepped outside the hospital, it hit her. She felt lightheaded and her knees almost buckled. She sat down on a bench next to a little white-haired, bright-eyed bird of a woman, a woman who was ninety if she was a day.

Everything suddenly seemed so vivid: the sky was an incredible shade of blue; the trees were greener than she remembered green ever being. She could hear a child laughing somewhere behind her, and the sound was like something an angel would make.

Then, for some reason that couldn't be explained in any rational way, the old lady sitting next to her reached out and took Emma's hand in her small frail one and said, "Isn't it a glorious day."

Then she cried.

DeMarco knew that she'd been sick but he had no idea what was wrong with her and, being Emma, she refused to tell him—and that really pissed him off.

He found out when he went to see her one day, and Christine answered the door. Christine was Emma's lover, and she and DeMarco had nothing in common and they didn't particularly like each other. Christine was that odd combination of ditz and genius; she had a master's degree in mathematics but earned her living as a cellist with the National Symphony. She was *cultured*—just ask her, she'd tell you—and considered DeMarco to be a Neanderthal: he was boorishly heterosexual, and given a choice between a good book and a baseball game, he'd pick the baseball game. She also considered him dangerous, because he would periodically drag Emma into his cases, and once Emma had been tortured and almost killed when she helped him.

What all this meant was that he and Christine rarely talked and certainly never confided in each other. So when he went to Emma's house that day and saw Christine's eyes swollen from crying, he almost didn't ask what was bothering her. He figured she and Emma had probably had a fight—Emma couldn't be easy to live with—or that maybe something related to her snooty orchestra job had gone awry. But his intuition told him that whatever she'd been bawling about was more significant than a lovers' spat. "What's wrong?" he asked.

And she told him: Emma was in the hospital and it was serious. Really serious.

"Well, what's wrong with her, for Christ's sake? What hospital is she in?"

"I can't tell you, Joe." She rarely called him Joe. "You know how she is. She wouldn't want me to." And he didn't argue with her, or not for long, because he knew she was right: no one protected her privacy more than Emma.

He'd met Emma when he just happened to be in the right place at the right time and saved her life—which was why she was his friend and often helped him—but although he had known her for more than a decade, he still knew very little about her. He knew that she had worked for the DIA—the Defense Intelligence Agency—and, at the time she retired, she had been very high up in the intelligence community. He knew she was gay but had a daughter, but never knew if she gave birth to her daughter or if she was adopted. She was wealthy—she had to be to afford her home in McLean—but she would never disclose the source of her wealth. She was an enigma in so many ways, and delighted in being so.

So it wasn't hard for him to understand that Emma wouldn't want him to know about her illness. After that day, he called periodically and spoke to Christine; he never spoke to Emma but at least he knew she was still alive. But today when he called, Christine sounded different.

"How's she doing?" he asked, and Christine gushed out the answer: "She's doing great. She's going to be okay." And then Christine started crying and couldn't stop, so DeMarco hung up and drove to Emma's place.

She was out in her backyard when he arrived. (Emma was fanatical about her yard.) She had just cut a red rose from a bush and was standing there looking at the flower. DeMarco thought there was something odd about her posture, her attitude, something—it was like she was seeing a rose for the first time in her life.

But she looked fine. She looked like she always had: tall and slim, though maybe a little paler than normal. Her gray-blonde hair was cut short, feathered the way she usually wore it. Her features had always struck him as aristocratic: a perfect straight nose, thin lips, a high brow. She looked like who she was: intelligent, competent, and aloof. She had the lightest blue eyes he'd ever seen.

"Well, you look okay," he said.

"I am okay."

"Are you going to tell me what's been wrong with you?"

"No. It's none of your business."

"Yes, it is, goddamnit! It *is* my business. I'm your friend. I care about you. "

"Well, too bad. I'm fine. Why are you here?"

"To see you and . . ."

"And what?"

"Do you know anything about an outfit called the Warwick Foundation?"

"Isn't this rose just perfect," she said, gazing at the flower in her hand. Before DeMarco could respond, she said, "Of course I've heard of Warwick, but . . ."

She said this like any intelligent, well-informed person would know about the foundation—and thus it was understandable that DeMarco didn't.

". . . but I'm not intimately familiar with the operation."

"Do you know anybody who is?" DeMarco asked.

"Yes," she said—and that's all she said.

God, she was exasperating. "Well, do you think maybe you could call this person and get me an appointment?"

"Has it ever occurred to you that you can probably find whatever you need on the Internet and without having to bother my friends?"

"Aw, gimme a break. I just need a little background, and I don't feel like spending a hundred hours on a computer."

"Why do you want to know about the foundation?" she asked— so he told her about Phil Downing and Brian Kincaid. And, as she always did, Emma listened intently as he spoke. Her concentration and attention to detail had always impressed him.

"Why was Downing making a conference call so late at night?" she asked. "And who was he calling?"

"According to the trial transcript, the conference call was set up by a guy named Hobson who works for Lizzie Warwick. It was supposed to have included Hobson, Downing, and the chief of staff to a congressman. Hobson was the guy who called the security guard when Downing didn't answer the phone. But I don't know why the call was being held so late."

"Well, you need to find out more, because that call is what placed Downing in the office the same time as Kincaid, and . . ."

"I realize that," DeMarco said, "but . . ."

". . . and when the body was discovered only fifteen minutes after Kincaid left the building, then Kincaid became the only suspect. So if you believe Brian Kincaid is innocent, you need to find out more about that call and the people involved in it."

"The thing is," DeMarco said, "it's kind of hard to believe he's innocent. The cops had a plausible motive, they had the murder weapon, and there was no evidence anyone else was in the building when Downing died. If I'd been on the jury, I would have voted to convict him, too."

"What's wrong with you!" Emma snapped. "You're either trying to help the man or you're not. You're either his advocate or you're not. If all you're doing is going through the motions, you should just quit right now and tell his poor mother that nothing can be done for her son."

Sheesh. "Look, can you just give me the name of somebody to talk to about Warwick?"

"Oh, for God's sake," she said.

Whatever had been wrong with her, neither the disease nor the cure had improved her disposition.

He followed her into the kitchen and could hear Christine at the other end of the house playing her cello, the kind of classical crap she always played. Maybe it was his imagination, but the music sounded like . . . like a joyous, grateful prayer. But what did he know? Emma picked up the phone in the kitchen and punched in a number. "Clive, it's Emma. I'm fine. How are you?"

Clive? What the hell kind of name was Clive? The guy was probably British.

After a few minutes of mundane chitchat, Emma said, "I have a friend . . ."

She rolled her eyes when she said *friend.*

". . . who needs some information about the Warwick Foundation. Could we come over and talk to you? Great. We'll be there in fifteen minutes."

Emma said that Clive lived about a mile a way. "We'll just walk," she told DeMarco.

"Why don't we drive? It'll be quicker."

"Because I want to walk."

A lot of smart, distinguished people lived in Emma's neighborhood in McLean. DeMarco was willing to bet that if he had a question about astrophysics, ancient Chinese religions, or Lyme disease, Emma would know a neighbor who could provide the answer.

As they were walking, Emma said, "Clive worked for the State Department for a number of years and now he volunteers for several charities. He's a wonderful man."

"The State Department? He's not British?"

"No. Why do you think he would be?"

"Well, the only guy I know named Clive is British."

"Who's that?"

"Clive Owen, the actor."

Emma looked over at him, and shook her head as if she felt sorry for him. It was sometimes rather hard to be Emma's friend.

Clive Standish—DeMarco thought *Standish* sounded British too—turned out to be a tall, stoop-shouldered man in his seventies with hair that looked like fluffy, white cotton candy. And, like a skinny Santa, he had twinkly blue eyes that looked out at the world benignly through wire-rimmed glasses. He was dressed casually in slacks, a short-sleeved shirt, and loafers, but the clothes looked expensive, particularly the shoes. DeMarco was guessing that Clive had been very high up the ladder at the State Department, though he came across as a modest fellow who would never brag about his accomplishments.

After Clive had poured glasses of iced tea for everyone, he said, "So. The Warwick Foundation. What would you like to know?"

Before DeMarco could answer, Emma said, "Start at the beginning. Tell us how it was established, about the family, what they currently do, et cetera."

This was typical of Emma. It may have been DeMarco's case, but she was effectively taking charge of the conversation. It was also typical that her curiosity was wide and far-ranging; she wanted to know everything. By comparison, DeMarco just wanted to know enough to get the job done.

"Well, let's see," Clive said. "Lizzie Warwick comes from an enormously wealthy Philadelphia family. Her grandfather and her father were defense contractors and made grenades, artillery shells, land mines—those sorts of nasty things. They were, by all accounts, very clever and extremely ruthless and made buckets of money. When Lizzie's parents died she inherited all the money, but for whatever reason—her education, her religion, who knows—she didn't have a deep avaricious streak running through her."

That's probably, DeMarco thought, because she was already so fucking rich.

"A couple of months after she inherited the family fortune, a hurricane occurred somewhere—I can't remember where—and thousands were made homeless. Lizzie decided she wanted to do something to help, but instead of just giving money as she'd done in the past, she joined a church group and went with them to rebuild homes and provide aid. Well, she found the experience so exhilarating that she decided to make this her life's work. She divested herself completely of the family businesses, established the Warwick Foundation, and when the next disaster came along, she jumped in with both feet. And someplace along the way, she ran into a French doctor named Lambert and they joined forces. And because Lambert is a very charming fellow, Warwick's fund-raising efforts have improved dramatically and the foundation has become much better organized and well-known. I believe she and Lambert are in Uganda right now helping people displaced by one of their never-ending wars."

Clive paused, sipped his tea, and wiped his mouth delicately with a small napkin. "Let's see, what else can I tell you? Oh, one other thing. Most relief organizations tend to operate fairly short-term. What I mean is, they'll fly in, do the best they can to help the local population for a few months by providing immediate aid, but then they move on to the next catastrophe and leave it to the local government to deal with the long-term ramifications of the disaster. Warwick is different. What I've been told, though I don't know anything about it personally, is that she'll find people who have no one—the very young, the very old, and those with crippling medical conditions—and she sets up facilities called Warwick Care Centers that become orphanages and assisted living places. She can't help everyone, of course, so she'll select a couple hundred people and provide for them. She does what she can."

"Having heard all that," DeMarco said, "I guess the question I'm going to ask is going to sound pretty stupid, but could Warwick or anyone working for her be doing anything illegal?"

Then DeMarco explained what he meant, how the possibility existed—although the odds were low—that Phil Downing had discovered something he could use to force Lizzie Warwick to continue to employ him as her lobbyist, and then somebody killed Downing because of what he knew and framed Kincaid for his murder.

Clive Standish surprised him. DeMarco expected him to say that Lizzie Warwick and the people who work for her are the saints who walk among us and would never do anything illegal. But that's not what Clive said. "Actually," he said, "there's a good possibility that someone working for Lizzie might be stealing money intended for the victims. That's a fairly common problem with relief organizations." Clive laughed. "The Red Cross, for example, has had a peck of problems."

Now DeMarco was positive the guy was a closet Limey. Who but a Brit would use the work *peck*?

"I remember a Red Cross manager in Pennsylvania," Clive said, "who was embezzling to support her crack cocaine habit, and another fellow in New Jersey who stole over a million in Red Cross funds. One reason why it's easy to steal from charities is because people don't expect the folks who volunteer to be thieves. Money intended for purchasing relief supplies will be embezzled, or the supplies will be stolen before they reach the disaster area and sold on the black market. Or money will be spent to bribe foreign officials, and the amount of the bribe will be exaggerated and the briber will keep some for himself. There are dozens of ways to strip money from charities both at home and abroad, and it happens all the time."

"Bribes?" DeMarco said.

"Of course," Clive said. "Governments in some countries are extremely corrupt. Now, you can be an idealist and refuse to abet the corruption, but if you want to get things done, you need the local government on your side. They can either help you get aid to a disaster area or they can become an enormous impediment. They'll insist that relief supplies be inspected, a task which can take weeks if they desire. You won't be able to hire local labor and for so-called national security reasons, you'll be prevented from going to wherever it is you need to go. So when your job is to get food, water, and medicine to people who are dying, you pay the bribes and get on with what you need to do. But sometimes, as I said, the person who is doing the bribing keeps a portion of the money for his services and no one is the wiser."

Bribes, DeMarco thought. He wondered if Phil Downing discovered that Warwick was giving money to some guy like Idi Amin or

Charles Taylor, and decided to use that information to squeeze the foundation.

"Have you ever heard anything negative about Warwick?" Emma asked. "Any past problems with employees embezzling money or doing anything else illegal?"

"No, I haven't," Clive said. "But if somebody was embezzling from Lizzie, I'm not sure she'd even know it. The woman's not stupid, but she focuses almost exclusively on the work in the field and leaves the financial management to other people. And I don't know if she brings in outside auditors like the big organizations do."

"Why would she need a lobbyist?" DeMarco asked.

"For the same reason everyone else does," Clive said. "Lobbyists tend to have bad reputations. People hear stories about banks and insurance companies having more lobbyists than we have members of Congress, and how these lobbyists corrupt our politicians. And many of these stories are true. On the other hand, Washington is enormously complex and every industry and special interest group—be they charities or environmental groups or profit-making corporations—are trying to make their voices heard, and for that they need lobbyists who understand the system and know the players. Are some lobbyists corrupt? Of course. But is there anything wrong with a charitable organization like Warwick lobbying to get what it needs? Of course not."

Since DeMarco knew one corrupt congressman very well and also knew several lobbyists who abetted his corruption, he didn't say what he thought about the fundamental nature of lobbyists. Instead he thanked Clive and Emma for their help and went home to his empty house.

13

It was Saturday, the day of the week that DeMarco accomplished those domestic chores he couldn't put off until another Saturday. He paid bills and washed clothes. If his lawn was higher than his ankles, he might mow it. If something in the house needed fixing, he would fix it—but only if it was absolutely necessary to do so. The clogged drain in the bathroom sink came dangerously close to falling into this category. It was taking about five minutes for water to drain out of the sink, which meant that hair and other nasty gunk was clogging the p-trap beneath the sink. The sink, however, wasn't overflowing—it was just taking a little too long to drain— and, consequently, this problem wasn't in the absolutely-must-fix category and would be postponed until it was.

This particular Saturday, DeMarco woke up with a slight hangover. The night before, he had dinner at a sports bar in Georgetown where he had onion rings and a cheeseburger the size of a Frisbee and watched the Washington Nationals get their asses kicked by the Florida Marlins. While he watched, he also drank a couple beers—and beer, even in small quantities, always gave him a hangover.

Stoically nursing the pain caused by self-inflicted alcohol poisoning, he sat at the desk in his den and paid the bills that were almost overdue and ignored those that weren't. He threw a load of clothes into the wash and vacuumed those rooms he occupied most frequently, but only the parts of the rooms that appeared to truly need vacuuming. He looked out his front window and saw that his grass was only an inch higher than the neighbor's on his right but three inches higher than the manicured lawn of the anal retentive neatnik on his left, and said: Fuck it. Chores complete, he flopped down on the couch wearing the same clothes he'd worn to bed the night before: a New York Knicks T-shirt and blue boxer shorts.

So what should he do about Brian Kincaid? Emma, as usual, was right. He should either pursue the case with something approaching real vigor or he should call up Mrs. Kincaid and lie that he'd done everything humanly possible. But the only thing he could think to pursue—with or without vigor—was, as Emma had said, the conference call that had so conveniently placed Downing in the office with Kincaid at the time of the murder.

And at that moment, the phone rang. It was Emma. "Well?" she said. "What are you going to do about Brian Kincaid?"

Sheesh. It was like she was psychic. "I don't know. I was just thinking about that when you called."

"You need to find out more about that conference call. Take another look at the trial transcript and go see that private detective again to see if he knows anything else about it."

"May I ask why you're taking such an interest in this?"

"Because I don't like coincidences," Emma said, "and it's possible that an innocent man has been convicted for a crime he didn't commit."

Bullshit. She was bored. She didn't have anything better to occupy her big brain at the moment and, after all her medical problems, Kincaid's troubles might provide an interesting diversion. But DeMarco didn't say this. Instead, coward that he was, he said, "Yeah, I might do that."

"And what about Downing's records? What happened to them after he died? Go talk to his secretary again and see where they are and take a look at them."

The words *Who the hell put you in charge of my life?* were on the tip of his tongue, but since he too often relied on Emma for help, he decided to keep that response to himself. "You know, it's Saturday," he said instead.

"So what?" she said. "And see if you can follow the money trail."

"What money trail?"

"You heard what Clive said, about how money is always being stolen from charities."

"Yeah, but he also said he hadn't heard anything like that about Warwick."

"Just because he hasn't heard it doesn't mean it isn't happening."

"But how would I do that, follow the money?"

"I don't know," Emma said, her tone saying: *Do I have to do all the thinking?* "And you should also find out how Downing's client knew the security guard's phone number at the building where Downing was killed. It seems odd to me that he would know the number."

Christ! He'd just gone from sitting on his ass, happily doing nothing, to a multi-item to-do list that would take hours to complete.

"And one other thing," Emma said.

Was there no end to this?

"You said Downing told his secretary that Warwick was thinking about hiring another lobbyist, but then he ended up keeping the account. Find out who replaced Downing after he died and see what he knows. And maybe you ought to talk to Lizzie Warwick and ask her if she really was thinking about replacing Downing and if she was, why she changed her mind."

DeMarco squeezed the phone in his hand hard enough to turn his knuckles white. She was, without a doubt, the most exasperating woman he'd ever known, including his ex-wife. To keep her from giving him anything more to do, he said, "How are you feeling today?"

Emma hung up.

———— ◆◆◆ ————

The small voice-activated tape recorder connected to DeMarco's phone line and hidden behind the electric meter outside his house stopped recording.

14

Sharon Palmer lived in a brick rambler in Vienna, Virginia, and DeMarco concluded that she was no more compulsive about yard work than he was. The doorbell was answered by a tall, dark-haired, teenaged girl, and DeMarco could see her resemblance to Sharon. The girl was barefoot, wearing a T-shirt that showed a slice of flat stomach, camo-colored cargo pants, and a scowl on her face that looked as if it might be a permanent fixture. She was holding a cell phone in her hand, and she pressed the phone against her chest and said to DeMarco, "Yeah?"

What a charmer.

"Is your mother here?" he asked.

The girl turned and yelled, "Mom, there's some guy here to see you." Then she walked away, leaving DeMarco standing in the open doorway.

Sharon came to the door. She was wearing a tank top and shorts that showed off good legs and, like her daughter, she was barefoot. Her hair was uncombed, she wore no makeup, and in the harsh light of day, she looked every bit her age. It also appeared, judging by her pallor and her red-veined eyes, that she'd had way too much to drink the night before.

"What do you want?" she said.

It appeared that DeMarco had quickly gone from potential boy toy to an annoyance.

"I just need to ask you a couple more things about Phil Downing." He paused to see if she would ask him in, but when she didn't, he continued. "I was wondering what happened to his records."

"His records?"

"Yeah. He must have had client files, billing records, that sort of thing."

"Oh. A couple days after Phil was killed, two guys came to the office. One of them said he represented the Warwick Foundation and had the authority to take Phil's files."

"And you just gave them to him?"

"Sure. Why not? One of my bosses was dead, the other one was in jail, and I was out of a job. I didn't give a shit what happened to Phil's records. The only reason I was even there that morning was to clean out my desk. And I have no idea what happened to all the rest of the crap in the office—the furniture, the phones, the copy machine, or Brian's files. None of that stuff was my problem at that point."

"Was there anyplace other than his office where Phil might have stored an important document?"

"Hell, I don't know," she said. "He probably had a safe deposit box at his bank, but I imagine that's been cleaned out by now." She started to swing the door shut, saying as she did, "Now I gotta go. I don't feel good."

"Wait. Just one more thing. Were you able to remember anything else about why Warwick was thinking about dropping Downing and later changed her mind?"

"No. Now listen to me. I'm hungover, I feel like shit, I'm tired, and I don't wanna talk anymore."

She shut the door in DeMarco's face.

DeMarco was surprised to find Doug Vale, of Vale, White, and Cohen, in his office on a Saturday. But maybe that's why he had such a big, fancy office—because he worked on Saturdays.

Vale was a good-looking guy in his early forties and was the lobbyist of record for the Warwick Foundation. He was dressed informally: a navy-blue sports jacket, a button-down oxford shirt, designer jeans, and Top-Siders without socks. He was the ultimate preppie, and DeMarco would've bet that he'd gone to a fancy boarding school like Choate, followed by one of the Ivy League colleges. He sipped bottled water as he talked to DeMarco.

DeMarco had gained entry to Vale's office by saying that he worked for Congress. The lobbyist was naturally surprised when DeMarco said he wanted to talk about Phil Downing, but being a good lobbyist, and thinking DeMarco might have some future potential value, he agreed to talk to him.

"How'd you end up getting Warwick as a client?" DeMarco asked.

"You mean other than the fact that Downing was killed?"

"Yeah," DeMarco said, "other than that."

"I represent a number of nonprofits and charitable organizations, and I met Lizzie Warwick at a function one night. I wasn't trying to steal her away from Downing—or at least I wasn't trying very hard—but we got to talking about what I could do for her that Phil couldn't. I pointed out that Downing was a one-man operation and he had no experience in Congress. I was a congressional aide for five years and several people on my staff have extensive experience on the Hill. I also told her about some things I had done for other clients, and she seemed impressed.

"The problem with Lizzie, though, is that I don't think she's ever fired anyone in her life. She'd consider that sort of thing mean. But she must have passed my name on to Hobson and . . . Do you know who Hobson is?"

"I know he works for Lizzie Warwick," DeMarco said.

"Actually, he's the guy who really runs the Warwick Foundation. I heard he was an officer in the army, and he's probably had a lot of experience firing people. Anyway, he called and we chatted, and I got the impression that he'd never given a lot of thought to what Downing did and whether he was worth the money Lizzie was paying him. He called back a couple of days later and said Lizzie was going to hire me, but then, about a week after that, he called again and said she'd decided to stick with Downing. And then Downing was killed and I got the job."

"What made her change her mind about not firing Downing?"

"I have no idea. You'll have to ask her."

As DeMarco was leaving, Vale said, "What exactly do you do in the House, Mr. DeMarco? When you called and said you wanted to talk to me, I looked at a House directory, but I couldn't find your name on anyone's staff."

"Mr. Vale, I don't work for any specific member. I have an office in the basement of the Capitol, next to the janitors. Believe me when I tell you that I'm not a man with a lot of influence."

———◆———

DeMarco called Kincaid's detective, Colin Gordon, and he too was in his office. What the hell was wrong with these people? Was the economy so bad that no one took the weekend off anymore? When he arrived at Gordon's office it was almost one P.M., and Gordon was eating a Reuben sandwich the size of a brick, reminding DeMarco that he'd skipped breakfast and was starving.

DeMarco told the detective he wanted to talk about the conference call that Phil Downing was supposed to have participated in the night he died. "What I'm curious about," DeMarco said, "is why this call was scheduled for so late—and just when Kincaid happened to be in his office making his own call to Hong Kong."

"Did you read the trial transcript?" Gordon asked.

"I sorta skimmed it," DeMarco admitted.

"Well, if you'd *read* it, you would have seen that the conference call was between Hobson and . . . You know who Hobson is, don't you?" His tone implied that maybe if DeMarco had done his homework he wouldn't be bugging him.

"Sure. He manages things for Lizzie Warwick."

"That's right. He keeps the foundation's books, gets supplies to the places she goes, hires people, handles her security, travel arrangements, things like that. I got the impression that Lizzie Warwick's completely consumed by the work in the field while Hobson takes care of everything else. Anyway, the call was between Hobson—who lives in Philadelphia—Phil Downing here in D.C., and Stephen Linger, chief of staff to Congressman Edward Talbot."

"What was the conference call about?" DeMarco asked.

"Some foreign aid bill. That's all I remember. The number of the bill is in the transcript. Anyway, Hobson, to make Lizzie Warwick happy, wanted to schmooze with Linger about the bill because Congressman Talbot was going to vote against it. And, naturally, Hobson wanted the foundation's lobbyist in on the call and he wanted Downing in his office in Washington so Downing could refer to data related to the bill."

"But why was the conference call held so late at night?"

"There's no big conspiracy here, DeMarco. Downing was killed in August. What does Congress do in August?"

DeMarco felt like saying, *Congress doesn't do anything regardless of the month of the year,* but he knew what Gordon was getting at. "Congress is in recess."

"That's right. And since Congressman Talbot is from California, he and his chief of staff were back home. The time of the conference call was set for nine forty-five East Coast time to suit Linger's schedule, but it would have only been six forty-five in California. Not that late, in other words. The night Downing was killed, Hobson initiated the conference call about nine-forty from his office in Philly and tried to get Downing on the line, but Downing didn't answer his phone. So Hobson got Linger on the line, called Downing again, but again, Downing didn't answer the phone. Hobson was positive Downing had to be in his office because the conference call with Linger was a semi–big deal, and when he couldn't reach Downing, he called the security guard, asked him to check on Downing, and the guard finds him dead. End of story."

"How did Hobson know the security guard's number?"

Gordon frowned. Apparently that wasn't a question that had occurred to him. Then he just shook his head as if it didn't matter and said, "I don't know. Maybe he looked it up. All I know is this conspiracy theory you're trying to develop—that the phone call was set up to get Downing in the office the same time as Kincaid—would have to include the willing participation of a man who works for a highly respected member of Congress."

DeMarco thought the phrase *highly respected member of Congress* was an oxymoron, but didn't say so.

Gordon took another bite of his sandwich; DeMarco noticed the man had a mouth that looked like the entry to the Holland Tunnel. After he swallowed, Gordon said, "And then, of course, you have the issue of motive. *Why* would the Warwick Foundation or Bill Hobson or Congressman Ed Talbot want to kill Phil Downing?"

"I don't know," DeMarco said, "but why would Hobson and Downing want to talk to Linger when Congress wasn't in session?"

"Because the bill was going to be voted on in the House as soon as the next session started," Gordon said. "All this information was either in the trial transcript or in the deposition Kincaid's lawyer took from Linger."

DeMarco sat there for a moment trying to come up with another astute question to ask—and finally one occurred to him.

"Where did you buy that sandwich?"

———◆———

The deli was a block from Gordon's office. DeMarco ordered a Reuben, a side of potato salad, and a glass of milk. As he waited impatiently for his sandwich, he thought about his discussion with the detective.

Unlike Gordon, DeMarco didn't immediately exclude the possibility that a congressman or his chief of staff could be involved in a criminal conspiracy with the Warwick Foundation. He had worked in Congress a long time and knew its members were capable of any crime, including murder. His long association with John Mahoney had strongly reinforced this opinion.

So let's run with that, he said to himself. Downing's about to get fired but then he discovers some nasty secret that will cause Congressman Talbot or his chief of staff major problems if the secret is revealed. But what could the secret possibly be? Well, Clive Standish said that a lot of money provided to charities never reached the intended victims. So maybe Talbot had helped steer federal funds to Warwick and Hobson siphoned off some of the money and gave a kickback to Talbot—and Downing somehow discovered this. Then, to keep from going to the hoosegow, Talbot or Linger conspire with Hobson, develop the bright idea for the conference call and the plan to frame Brian Kincaid for Downing's murder, and then hire a professional killer to whack Downing.

Hmm. Maybe—but pretty damn unlikely.

To go any further with this far-fetched notion, DeMarco would have to find out if Congress actually had provided any funds to Warwick and if Talbot had been involved—and this, in turn, meant one hell of a lot of work for DeMarco. The Government Accountability Office—which employs over three thousand people—can't figure out where all the government's money goes. DeMarco's chances of success working on his own were practically nil.

About the time his Reuben arrived, DeMarco decided that rather than spend the next decade trying to follow a murky congressional money trail, he'd try instead to find some rational explanation for why Lizzie Warwick was going to dump Phil Downing and later changed her mind. Unfortunately, the only people who could tell him what he needed to know were Lizzie Warwick, who was in Africa, or Bill Hobson, who was in Philly—and DeMarco definitely wasn't flying to Africa to talk to Lizzie.

He finished his lunch, called directory assistance, got a number for the Warwick Foundation, and called the number. No one answered. It appeared that at least one person on the eastern seaboard didn't work the weekend—and for this he was extremely grateful. He'd done enough work on a day that was supposed to be his day off and he was going home to enjoy what remained of his Saturday.

One more day in prison wouldn't matter that much to Brian Kincaid.

15

Bill Hobson read the report provided by the private detective that Kelly had forced him to hire, and listened to the wiretap tapes of DeMarco's phone calls. Goddamnit, now he was going to have to call Kelly and Nelson, which he hated to do. It wasn't just that they scared him, although they did. It was their lack of respect that bothered him. He'd been a full bird colonel in the United States Army, and those two thugs had never risen beyond the rank of sergeant.

When Hobson called, Kelly was hand-sanding a beautiful piece of maple that had been drying in a kiln for months.

When he and Nelson bought their place in Montana, the first thing they did was demolish the house that already existed on the land. What they wanted was the land and the view, not the house. Then they worked with an architect to design a new house—a classic log house—and hired a contractor who had a reputation for charging too much but finishing on time. And he did both those things: he charged them too much and he completed the work on schedule. They had the contractor do most of the work—the painting, the plumbing and wiring, installation of hardwood and slate tile floors—but they saved a lot of the work for themselves. They both liked to work with their hands and they needed something to do between missions.

They did the landscaping together, avoiding grass and any other plants requiring extensive maintenance. Nelson even bought a small John Deere dozer to move the dirt around because he loved operating the thing. He also built the rock wall bordering the driveway and was now working on building a fire pit and installing a flagstone patio.

Nelson liked working with stone and cement. Kelly liked working with wood. He'd built the mantel for the fireplace and bookshelves for the den, and was currently replicating a maple dining room table he saw in a shop in Missoula selling for almost four grand. A couple more days of sanding and he'd be ready to apply the varnish. But then Hobson called.

Nelson was sitting on a chaise longue on the half-finished patio drinking a beer. He was wearing only shorts and steel-toed work boots, and his broad chest was covered with powdery white dust and sweat. He had made good progress on installing the flagstones.

Kelly pulled over a deck chair and took a seat next to him. The day was clear, with not a cloud in the sky and the Bitterroot Mountains looked close enough to touch. Nelson offered him the beer bottle and Kelly took a sip and handed it back.

"Hobson just called," Kelly said. "We may have a problem."

"Aw, shit," Nelson said. "Are we gonna have to leave?"

"I don't know, but it's possible Fiona will want a meeting."

"What's going on?"

Kelly told him. This lawyer, DeMarco, after meeting with Kincaid in prison, was talking to other people: Downing's ex-girlfriend, the lobbyist who replaced Downing, and the detective Kincaid hired after he was convicted.

"And he seems to be working with a woman who lives in McLean, Virginia, a gal named Emma something," Kelly said, "but Unger—"

"Who's Unger?" Nelson said.

"The detective keeping tabs on DeMarco. Remember I told Hobson to hire him when we were in Nairobi."

"Oh, yeah," Nelson said.

"Anyway, Unger hasn't been able to get a handle on the woman, which is odd. He has a contact who works for the D.C. Metro police and the guy can normally get into any database, but the only thing he could find out is that she's retired civil service. Anyway, whoever she is, she seems to be spurring DeMarco on."

"Spurring him on to do what?"

"To clear Kincaid."

"Ah, goddamnit. Do we—"

Kelly held up a hand. "Relax. As near as I can tell, DeMarco hasn't found anything new—except maybe one thing. Downing's secretary apparently told DeMarco that Downing was about to lose his job as Warwick's lobbyist, and then a week later something changed and he kept the account."

"Son of a bitch!" Nelson said.

"Yeah, I know, that doesn't sound good. But based on the recording, it's pretty clear DeMarco doesn't know what Downing did to keep his job, which means that he really doesn't know anything, and that means we really don't have a problem."

"Well maybe you don't think it's a problem, but I'll bet you my left nut that Fiona will think it's a great, *big* fuckin' problem. I'm never gonna get this patio finished."

Kelly went back into the house and called Fiona and told her about DeMarco and the phone call that Unger had recorded. Naturally, she was pissed—but being pissed was a chronic condition for Fiona.

She concluded the call with, "Keep that detective on DeMarco. I want to think this over and talk with Orson."

"And we need to get more information on this woman who called DeMarco," Kelly said.

"I know. I'll get my headhunters working on that."

16

Having spent his Saturday working, DeMarco decided to devote Sunday to nothing but leisure. He slept in late, had brunch in Georgetown and read the *Washington Post* and then, because it was such a beautiful June day—warm but not muggy—he went to a driving range and hit a couple buckets of balls. When he returned home, he thought about mowing his lawn but again convinced himself that the grass wasn't really *that* high. He took a shower, put on shorts, a T-shirt, and tennis shoes without socks, and went out to the small patio in his backyard and lifted the lid on the Weber. He was going to barbecue a great big rib eye for dinner.

The Weber used propane, not charcoal, which DeMarco liked because charcoal was a pain in the ass. He'd heard barbecue fanatics claim that propane didn't give food the flavor of a good charcoal fire, but he always figured that was a load of crap and the people who believed this—people like Emma—were culinary snobs with no common sense.

The last time he'd used the grill had been a month ago when he'd cooked some salmon, and the grill was encrusted with burnt salmon skin and various other nasty, greasy things. So he took out his wire barbecue brush and scraped it a few times across the grill. Good enough. He had this theory: any nasty germs clinging to the rusty metal of the grill would be incinerated as soon as the barbecue got hot and, therefore, he was safe. He had no idea if his theory dovetailed with medical science; all he knew for sure was that he'd never become ill after using his barbecue.

He turned on the barbecue and while it was getting hot, he made a vodka martini. As he was in a celebratory mood—although he had nothing in particular to celebrate—he made the martini with the Grey Goose he normally reserved for guests instead of the cheaper vodka he usually drank when he was by himself. When the thermometer on the barbecue said the temperature was five hundred degrees, he plopped his steak down on the grill and put a potato in the microwave. Experience had shown that four minutes on each side would result in the perfect steak, and about eight minutes in the microwave was about the right time for a big potato. While his dinner was cooking, he checked the TV schedule: the Yankees were playing the Red Sox. He hated the fucking Yankees; if they lost that would be the perfect dessert to complement his meal. He turned on the television in his den, saw it was only the second inning and that neither team had scored. For all practical purposes, the game was just starting.

What more could a man ask for? A steak, a baked potato slathered with butter and sour cream, a martini, and a baseball game.

And then the phone rang.

"Hi, cutie," the caller said.

Cutie? No one called him *cutie*. His own mother didn't call him *cutie*.

"Uh, who's this?"

"It's Sharon."

"Sharon?"

"Sharon Palmer, silly."

"Oh, Sharon," he said. She sounded drunk. "Uh, what can I do for you?"

"Well, I was just sitting here having a Manhattan—that's my drink, you know—and I got to thinking about that question you asked me."

"What question was that?"

"When you came to my house the other day, you asked if I remembered anything more about Phil almost losing the Warwick account."

"Well, did you?"

"Not so fast, big boy. You'll need to buy me a drink to find out."

Aw, shit. Shit, shit, shit.

"Uh, sure. Where are you?"

"Georgetown. Didn't you tell me you lived in Georgetown?"

"Yeah," DeMarco said.

"Well, I'm here at Clyde's. You know Clyde's?"

"Yeah. I can be there in ten minutes."

Shit. He went outside and took his steak off the grill. It was cooked on one side, exactly half done. He shut off the microwave; his potato was half done. He put the steak and his martini in the refrigerator. *Shit.*

He considered the way he was dressed, in shorts and a T-shirt, and thought about changing before he met Sharon. Then he said to hell with it, and left the house and headed toward M Street. It would take him ten minutes to walk to Clyde's. He could have driven there in two minutes and then spent fifteen minutes trying to find a place to park, so walking was the better choice.

As he walked, he cursed Sharon Palmer, Emma, and Brian Kincaid —in no particular order.

The tape recorder connected to DeMarco's phone line waited for another call.

"Ooh, look at you," Sharon said when DeMarco walked over to her table in Clyde's. "I like you in shorts. You have strong thighs. And those shoulders . . . Well, you look just yummy."

He wondered how many drinks she'd had.

"Uh," he said, "you look nice yourself."

And she did. She was wearing a short jean skirt that stopped at mid-thigh and a tank top, no bra. Once again he had the thought that whoever built her boobs was a superb craftsman.

He ordered her another Manhattan and a beer for himself. He noticed that the game was playing on the television behind the bar so he took a seat where he could see it while they talked. Just to make his agony complete, the fucking Yankees had managed to score three runs while he was walking to the bar.

"So," he said after their drinks arrived, "what did you want to tell me about Downing?"

"Um, this is good," she said, sipping her Manhattan.

"Sharon. What were you going to tell me about Downing?"

"Well, they were showing this soccer game on TV over at this other bar, Brazil playing somebody, and they showed that big Jesus statue on the hill in Rio."

"Yeah?" DeMarco said. He had no idea what she was talking about.

"Anyway, the Jesus statue made me think about how it'd be fun to go there someday, and that's when I remembered."

"Remembered what?"

"The day after Phil told me Warwick was thinking about dumping him, he goes to see Hobson . . . You know who Hobson is, don't you?"

"Yeah," he said, wishing she'd just get to the point.

"Well, Phil goes to see Hobson, to beg for his job I guess, and when he comes back he locks himself in his office for a couple of hours and then has me book him a flight to Lima and another flight to someplace else I can't remember."

"Lima?"

"Right. Lima, Peru. Anyway, he leaves the next day and he comes back three or four days later, and when he comes back he's in a good mood and not all grumpy like he was before he left. And two days later, he takes me out to dinner and tells me that Warwick has decided to keep him on."

"Why'd he go to Peru?"

"I don't know. I don't know why he went or what he did there. He wouldn't tell me and when I asked, he just acted all smug. Phil could be kind of an asshole at times."

"But was his reason for going there connected to the Warwick Foundation?"

"I told you, I don't know, but I'm pretty sure it wasn't a vacation. Phil was a smoker and he'd just about go crazy every time he had to take a flight that lasted more than a couple of hours. Like I found this great package for Vegas one time—flight, hotel, everything super cheap—but the son of a bitch wouldn't take me because he didn't want to fly that far. Well, I wouldn't give him any you-know-what for a week so he finally took me to Atlantic City. It cost twice as much to go there because I couldn't find a good deal for hotel rooms on a weekend and we had to drive four hours to get there, but that was Phil. He'd rather drive to Atlantic City and pay twice as much than fly to Vegas and get stuck on a plane. What I'm telling you is, I can't imagine he went to Peru for a vacation."

"Why the hell didn't you tell me this the last time we talked?" DeMarco asked.

"Hey! Don't you get all pissy with me, buster. The other day when you stopped by my house, without calling first or anything, I was so hungover I thought I was going to die. I could barely remember my own name. Plus Phil was killed over two years ago. *You* try remembering shit that happened two years ago. The only reason I even remembered today was because of the Jesus statue and that's when I called you—which I didn't have to do, you know."

It occurred to DeMarco, given how much the woman appeared to drink, her not being able to remember something probably wasn't unusual. And, like she said, the event happened two years ago. "Did you mention this trip to Peru to the cops or to Brian's lawyer before the trial?" he asked.

"No. The only thing the cops wanted to know was if Brian had some motive for killing Phil. They were already convinced he killed him and they just wanted to know why, and when I told them about Phil and Brian fighting all the time, they didn't ask about anything else. And it was the same at the trial. I was just asked to testify about how they argued all the time and hated each other. And, like I told you before, this thing with Phil going to Peru happened a *month* before Brian killed him. I didn't see how it was relevant then, and I don't see how it's relevant now."

She raised her empty Manhattan glass to let DeMarco know she was ready for another.

"Uh, did you drive here?"

"Are you kidding? Do you know how hard it is to find parking in Georgetown? I had my bitchy daughter drop me off so I could do some shopping."

All DeMarco wanted to do was go home and finish his dinner, but he bought her another drink, as it seemed impolite not to. As she was drinking, she rambled on about how Georgetown wasn't as classy as it used to be, but DeMarco noticed she wasn't looking at him as she talked. She and a heavyset guy at the bar—a guy whose shirt was unbuttoned too far, revealing a nest of gray chest-hair—were making google-eyes at each other, and when DeMarco said he had to leave, she didn't make any attempt to stop him. As he was leaving Clyde's, he saw the guy get off his bar stool and begin talking to Sharon.

Somebody was going to get lucky tonight—and it wasn't going to be DeMarco.

17

The phone on Bill Hobson's desk rang, the short, single ring that meant the call was from his secretary.

"Yes?" he said.

"Bill, there's a man here from Congress, a Mr. DeMarco, and he says he'd like to speak with you."

Hobson was too shocked to respond.

"Bill," the secretary said, "would you like to see him now or should I schedule an appointment for later? You have a meeting in forty-five minutes."

It always irritated him that his secretary called him *Bill* instead of *Mr. Hobson,* but this was the kind of outfit that permitted crap like that.

"Uh, I'll see him now," he said.

The man who walked into his office was a broad-shouldered guy about five ten, maybe five eleven. A good-looking guy with a full head of dark hair, a prominent nose, blue eyes, and a cleft in his chin. Kind of hard-looking, too, Hobson thought, but from what he'd been told, DeMarco was just a lawyer who worked for Congress. Not too many hard cases in jobs like that.

"Mr. DeMarco, I'm Bill Hobson. What can I do for you?"

"I'm looking into Phil Downing's murder, and I just wanted to ask a couple of questions."

"Really!" Hobson said, pretending to be surprised. "Why would somebody who works for Congress be asking about that?"

"Brian Kincaid's mother is a friend of a member of the House and—"

"Which member?"

"I can't say. Anyway, when Kincaid's last appeal was bounced by the judge, his mother asked this congressman to see if anything could be done to help him."

"Help him how?"

DeMarco shrugged. "See if any errors were made with regard to his defense. See if the cops overlooked anything."

"I see," Hobson said. "Well, I feel sorry for Kincaid's mother, but he did it, DeMarco. The evidence against him was rock solid. He's not getting out of jail."

"I think you're right," DeMarco said, "but I was asked to look into things, so I'm looking."

"So how can I help you?"

"I was wondering what you could tell me about the conference call that took place—or was supposed to have taken place—the night Downing was killed. I'm talking about the call between you, Downing, and Congressman Talbot's chief of staff."

"What do you want to know about it?"

"I'm just curious why it was scheduled to begin so late at night, and at the same time that Brian Kincaid was in his office making a conference call himself."

DeMarco had heard Gordon's explanation for the conference call, but he wanted to see if Hobson would tell the same story.

"If I remember correctly, it was to suit Steve Linger's schedule. He was in California at the time with Congressman Talbot, and the time difference complicated things. As for Kincaid being there, that was just a coincidence. Until the trial, I had no idea why Kincaid was in his office at that time of night. I never met Kincaid."

"I see," DeMarco said, and Hobson thought he looked skeptical. But maybe he was just being paranoid.

"The other thing I wanted to ask about was the night Downing was killed, you called the security guard at his building and asked him to check on Downing, and that's why Downing's body was found so soon after Kincaid left the building. How did you know the security guard's phone number?"

"I called the Secret Service."

"Secret Service? Why would you—"

"Downing told me one time that a couple of the floors in his building were occupied by the Treasury Department and he was bitching because after they moved in, they ramped up the building's security. You know—metal detectors, badges, that sort of thing. Anyway, I worked in D.C. a long time before I retired and started volunteering for Lizzie Warwick, and I knew the Secret Service's Uniform Division handles security for Treasury Department assets. So I just looked online and called the D.C. number for the Secret Service—somebody's there twenty-four hours a day—and I told them that somebody in one of the buildings Treasury uses could be in trouble and they gave me the guard's number."

"I see," DeMarco said again. He hadn't known that Treasury had space in Downing's building—he'd verify that—but he knew that Hobson was right about the Secret Service providing security for their buildings.

"Is there anything else?" Hobson asked.

"Yeah, just one more thing. Do you have any idea why Phil Downing went to Peru about a month before he was killed?"

When DeMarco asked the question, Hobson was just beginning to take a sip of coffee—and the question startled him so much that he almost spit it out, but then he swallowed, started coughing, and couldn't seem to stop.

"Are you okay?" DeMarco asked.

"Yeah," Hobson said. "Sorry. That just went down the wrong way. What were you saying?"

"I was asking if you had any idea why Phil Downing went to Peru. His secretary told me you were thinking about firing him as Warwick's lobbyist, but then he went to Peru and afterward you decided to keep him on. So I was just wondering why he went. Was Lizzie Warwick in Peru at the time?"

There was no point lying about Lizzie's work in Peru. All DeMarco would have to do was spend ten minutes on the Internet to find out about that.

"Four years ago," Hobson said, "there was an earthquake in southern Peru. Three hundred people were killed and about five thousand were left homeless, so Lizzie decided to help out; that's what she does. But she didn't think about getting a new lobbyist until two years later. She met Doug Vale—that's the guy we use now—at a party and was impressed with him. But I didn't tell Phil I was going to fire him. What I did tell him was that Lizzie liked Vale and he seemed to be doing a lot of things that Phil wasn't. Well, Phil, I think just to impress me and Lizzie, took a trip to Peru to do a follow-up on the work she did there. When he came back he showed me a film he'd made of people giving testimonials about how Lizzie had helped them, but the real point of the film was to show how much Lizzie could do with the money she'd been given. Downing was planning to use the film to impress folks on the Hill. Anyway, when I told Lizzie what he'd done, we decided to stick with him. But then, a month later, his partner kills him."

"Do you have a copy of this film?"

"No. Downing had the only copy. I don't know what he did with it, and it wasn't with the rest of his files."

DeMarco left a few minutes later, and Hobson thought he went away happy with what he'd been told. But son of a bitch! He knew about Downing going to Peru. He was going to have to call Kelly again. And Fiona.

He was never sure who scared him more—Fiona or the two killers. Fiona was the most cold-blooded bitch Hobson had ever known and was the driving force behind everything Kelly and Nelson did. Kelly and Nelson might kill him—but she would give the order.

He made the calls, and Fiona's reaction was just what he expected— she went through the roof—and said she wanted to see him, Kelly, and Nelson tomorrow.

18

Fiona didn't want Kelly and Nelson anywhere near Mulray Pharma, so she reserved a suite at a hotel near the Philadelphia airport. Kelly and Nelson were so damn big that it was uncomfortable if the four of them met in a normal-sized room.

She didn't offer the three men coffee or drinks, and immediately directed Hobson to summarize everything he knew about DeMarco and what DeMarco seemed to know about Peru. While Hobson was talking, Nelson went over to the minibar, plucked out two Heinekens, and tossed one to Kelly; he ignored Hobson. After Hobson finished speaking, Fiona just sat for a moment staring at him, and then said, "All this . . . this *shit* because of you and your big mouth."

Before Hobson could say anything—not that there was anything he could say—Kelly said, "I don't think we oughta panic here. It sounds like all DeMarco knows is that Downing went to Peru, and Hobson gave him a rational explanation for why he went there. DeMarco may quit digging at this point."

"Maybe, but I wonder what Downing's old girlfriend knows about Peru," Fiona said.

"My guess is that she doesn't know anything," Kelly said. "If she knew something she would have told DeMarco. Or it would have come up during the trial or when DeMarco met with Hobson."

"Yeah," Fiona said, "but like you said, you're guessing."

Kelly shrugged.

No one said anything for a couple minutes, until Kelly finally said, "I recommend doing nothing at this point. There's no way DeMarco can piece together enough information to figure out what's going on."

"Well, Phil Downing sure as hell did," Fiona said.

"Yeah, but like you said, Downing had the benefit of Hobson's big mouth."

***

Hobson had never been able to figure out exactly what Downing heard that day.

During the time he'd been working for the Warwick Foundation, Hobson had never given a lot of thought to Phil Downing. Lizzie had hired Downing to keep her connected to the right people on the Hill, and as near as Hobson could tell, he did that—but it was hard for him to tell if Downing was really worth the money the foundation paid him. And since Downing didn't have any connection to what Mulray Pharma was secretly doing with Warwick, he didn't really give a shit whether Downing was worth the money or not. But then Lizzie goes to some party and meets Doug Vale, and Vale charms her—which wasn't all that hard to do—and she asked Hobson to see if Vale would be a better man for the job than Downing, and Hobson concluded that he would be. So he called up Downing and said they were going to replace him.

It just wasn't a big deal as far as he was concerned.

The day after he told Downing he was firing him, Downing came to his office, and he got there after Hobson's secretary had left for the day. And when Downing entered the office, he had been on the phone with René Lambert and he had the phone on the speaker because he was loading shit into his briefcase, getting ready to leave. But he couldn't remember *exactly* what he and Lambert had talked about. He remembered they talked briefly about Juan Carlos, the guy they had in Peru managing the facility, and Lambert complaining about some dumb thing Juan had done. They also talked about a bunch of other stuff—how things were going at the facility in Pakistan; how Simon Ballard wanted a different kind of container for shipping some samples, something with better temperature control; and how they needed a new propane-fueled refrigerator for storing drugs at the facility in Uganda—but he couldn't remember anything he said that could have tipped Downing off to exactly what they were doing. Whatever it was, though, it had been enough.

When he'd finished talking to Lambert that day, he was surprised to find Downing standing in the reception area, outside his office door. And he remembered wondering at the time about how much of his conversation with Lambert Downing had overheard. He talked with Downing for ten minutes after that, listening patiently while Downing begged him not to dump him, and him giving Downing some bullshit spiel about how it was time for a change. Then, five days later, Downing comes back, says he's been to Peru, and he's figured out what they're doing—and if they don't keep him on as their lobbyist, he's going to blow the whistle on everything. And, by the way, he doesn't think he's getting paid enough.

Phil Downing didn't know it, but he was a dead man walking after that.

Hobson had always thought that the way they killed Downing was too complicated, too . . . *elaborate*. He didn't say so at the time because Fiona didn't give a damn about his opinion, but if it had been up to him, he would have had Kelly just shoot the son of a bitch, take his wallet, and let the cops think that Downing had been killed in a mugging. But that's not what Fiona wanted. She said they were dealing with billions of dollars—she said that every time *any* issue came up—and that she wanted absolutely *no* investigation into Downing's death. She wanted to kill him and immediately give the cops his killer.

And it worked. Brian Kincaid was in the can thirty-six hours after Downing died and the cops never looked at another suspect. And two years later, it had looked like Kincaid was a closed book—until this cluck DeMarco comes along and starts asking questions.

———————

Fiona stood up, signaling that the meeting was over. "I need to talk to Orson," she said. Looking at Kelly, she added, "But I want you two to start personally watching DeMarco and this woman in McLean." She paused and muttered, "I wish you hadn't used that private detective."

"Hey, we were in Africa when this first came up, and then we had to go to Peru. It seemed prudent at the time," Kelly said.

"Yeah, I know," Fiona said. "But now the detective's a loose end. If it's necessary to take care of DeMarco, you may need to get rid of him, too."

"The detective's the father of a guy we served with," Nelson said.

"I guess you should have thought of that before you hired him," Fiona said.

"What about Downing's old secretary?" Kelly asked.

Fiona shrugged. "Maybe her, too."

"Jesus!" Hobson said. "You're overreacting. DeMarco doesn't know anything."

"Shut up!" Fiona said. "I don't want to hear another fucking word from you. You have no idea how close we are. Another three months, maybe less, we'll be ready to go public. So I don't care how many people have to die."

"What a surprise," Nelson muttered.

"Hey!" Fiona said, pointing a slim finger at Nelson. "I'm not in the mood for any of your crap, either."

Nelson just looked at her, a smile playing on his lips, probably thinking he could snap her neck with one hand.

"Anyway," Fiona said to Kelly, "I want you guys watching DeMarco and the woman. Based on that one phone call, it sounds as if she knows everything he does. And start thinking about ways to take these people out if we need to."

As Hobson left the hotel room a thought occurred to him, a thought that sent a shiver down his spine. When the project was complete— Orson Mulray's project, that is—Fiona would no longer need him, and he wondered if, when that day came, she would tell Kelly and Nelson to take *him* out.

Fiona had said that in less than three months Mulray would be ready to go public—which meant Bill Hobson had less than three months to make himself bullet-proof.

19

Fiona paced Orson Mulray's office, telling him about the meeting with Kelly, Nelson, and Hobson. As she paced, her right hand, with its long red-painted fingernails, moved up and down her left forearm—scratching, scratching, scratching like she was trying to plow furrows into her skin. Orson didn't recall her having that particular mannerism when he first met her, but in the last year—as they got closer to the finish line—he noticed that whenever she got upset, she'd start with the scratching, her right hand just *raking* her left forearm as she paced the room. He had never seen her draw blood, but he wouldn't be surprised if one day she did.

"Let's be logical about this," Orson said. "The likelihood of DeMarco discovering anything is small. The only reason Downing did was because he heard Hobson talking to Lambert and because he went to Peru to see for himself what was going on."

"But what if DeMarco *does* discover something?" Fiona said.

"Then we'll deal with the issue when the time comes. I mean, for God's sake, Fiona. You're talking about killing DeMarco, this woman in McLean, a private detective, and Downing's old secretary. The last thing we need is a pile of dead bodies that could lead back to us. For now, let's just watch these people. My guess is that DeMarco will give up pretty soon and tell Kincaid's mother that nothing can be done for her son."

"I don't know," Fiona said. "I've got a bad feeling about this. Maybe we should monitor these people the way we do the geeks in Ballard's lab. Cell phones, e-mails, everything."

"No. To do that would take a dozen people—and then you'd have a dozen more people who might discover something we don't want them to know. Just relax."

He said this knowing Fiona didn't know how to relax.

"When will we be ready to go public?" Fiona said.

"Now that's a problem," Orson said. "Ballard was ready to conclude that everything was finished, but then we got those anomalies from the Thai study and now we have to wait until he finishes analyzing the autopsy samples from Peru. The problem with Ballard is . . . well, it's like he's just looking for an excuse to do more research. If I leave it to him, he'll be conducting research until we're both dead."

"So what are you going to do?"

"Oh, I'll deal with Simon. You just make sure that DeMarco doesn't become a problem. But I don't want anyone killed, Fiona. Not without my authorization. Do you understand?"

———— ◆ ————

When Orson Mulray joined forces with Simon Ballard five years earlier, he had four major hurdles to overcome. The first was the scientific hurdle: Ballard had a theory on how to prevent the disease, but that's all it was—a *theory*. It was a sound theory, a logical theory, and Ballard had done an enormous amount of research to back it up, but in order to proceed from theory to marketable drug, Ballard needed to *test* his theory.

It was rather like the first folks who decided man could fly. It appeared reasonable to some that gluing feathers to their bodies and flapping their arms like wings might work. It worked for birds; why not for humans? After some daring person tested this particular theory—and ended up broken and bloody at the bottom of a cliff—other theories were developed.

Such was the case with Ballard's drug—until it was actually tested on human beings, he couldn't be sure it would fly.

Which led to the second problem. The conventional, safe, and legal way to conduct human trials was for Ballard to do all he possibly could to validate his theory in the laboratory, proceed to tests on mice, monkeys, and so forth, then develop an überconservative protocol for clinical trials and submit that protocol to the cautious, slow-moving bureaucrats at the FDA for their approval. And if Orson Mulray went that route it would take eight to twelve years to get the drug to the marketplace—and he had no intention of taking twelve years.

Then there was the third hurdle—the highest one of all. The only way to *really* prove that Ballard's drug was effective was via tissue samples—and in the case of the particular disease involved, one could only obtain those samples during an autopsy. With other drugs, a little blood, piss, and shit, a harmless biopsy or a CT scan, and doctors would be able to tell if a particular treatment worked. Not so with Simon Ballard's drug. To get to the part of the body he needed to examine, it was necessary to wait for the patient to die—and, once again, Orson had no intention of waiting. He was working to his own timetable—not God's.

The final hurdle was potential legal problems. In many countries, including the United States, there were many people willing to participate in risky drug trials provided the drug was their only salvation or if they were compensated in some way. It may have sounded ghoulishly mercenary, but it was a fact that people were often paid to be medical guinea pigs. Underlying all this, however, was the confidence that the doctors knew what they were doing and that the drugs being administered wouldn't actually kill them. And therein lay the rub: if a few patients died testing Simon Ballard's theory, then—no matter what medical waivers the test subjects had signed—the deaths would make the news, Mulray Pharma would be sued by rapacious lawyers, and it would be more difficult than ever to bring the drug to market.

Orson decided that rather than go *over* all these high hurdles, he would simply run around them. He would skip much of the tedious R&D phase and immediately inject Ballard's drug into people—people who would have no idea why they were being injected. Which was how Lizzie Warwick came into the picture. The people she cared for—trusting, ignorant, and helpless—were virtually invisible. And they dwelled in places where government officials could easily be bribed to look the other way, and if a few of them died during clinical trials, no one would really care—much less contact a lawyer.

Phase I testing of Ballard's drug was conducted in Peru on people whom Lizzie pulled from the rubble of an earthquake. This was the most critical of all the phases, because this was the first time Ballard would have definitive proof that his theory was viable. Fifty-five people meeting Ballard's criteria were selected by René Lambert and placed in a Warwick "care center," and a medical technician, the ever-cheerful Juan Carlos, was trained to administer the drug. For six months, the drug was given and appropriate, nonlethal biological samples were taken. At the end of six months, four people were killed—one per month—autopsies were performed, and the Phase I testing was determined to be an enormous success. Not only was Ballard's drug working as predicted, there was no evident damage to other healthy organs: liver, kidneys, lungs, et cetera.

Following Phase I, a second phase was needed, because early results showed that certain refinements could be made to improve the drug's effectiveness. Phase II testing would validate these refinements. Fifty unfortunates rendered homeless by another earthquake, in Pakistan, were chosen for Phase II. As was done in Peru, these people were isolated, a local nurse was hired, and the Phase II drug was administered for a six-month period. During this time, with a little assistance from Kelly and Nelson, three people perished—and Dr. Ballard's drug was declared to be completely effective; it even exceeded the good doctor's own expectations.

Phase III testing was required to enhance the delivery mechanism for the drug. In Phase I and II testing the drug was injected—and this was fine for test purposes. But, for economic rather than medical reasons, Orson wanted a delivery mechanism that didn't involve needles. People were squeamish about needles. Orson wanted a pill, a nasal spray, a gum, a patch—anything other than needles—and Ballard ultimately concluded that a nasal spray would work best. The nasal spray was tested on the folks in Uganda who had been dislocated due to war, but it did take three more corpses to validate the effectiveness of the spray. It was purely coincidental that a toxin-laden nasal spray was also used to euthanize the test subjects.

The last thing Orson Mulray needed to do was perform legitimate clinical trials—or at least *semi*legitimate trials. To do this, Ballard did a little thing known as *dry-labbing*, a term familiar to most engineers and scientists. In dry-labbing, a scientist already knows the results he wants and then designs tests that will produce exactly those results. And that's what Ballard did: based on all the human trials previously conducted in Peru, Pakistan, and Africa, he designed a series of laboratory experiments that proved exactly what he wanted to prove. The result of all these experiments was a *mountain* of data, and a report—filled with charts and graphs and images taken with electron microscopes—was issued. There were twenty-eight appendices to the report.

Now, had Orson Mulray chosen to do so, he could have given this document to the U.S. Food and Drug Administration to begin the long road to clinical trials in the United States. But Orson Mulray had no intention of dealing with the FDA. Instead he chose Thailand, where there was a medical institution run by a Harvard-educated Thai physician. The brother of this physician was—and not coincidentally—the Thai minister of health. So, in accordance with the laws of Thailand—laws bent somewhat, but not too much, by generous donations from Mulray Pharma—legitimate clinical trials commenced after the Phase III testing. The trials were expected to take approximately one year and would include one thousand people, some of whom would be given placebos. If any of these people died of natural causes, their bodies would be autopsied—and of the thousand patients selected, one hundred and fifty were chosen because the likelihood of them living less than a year was extraordinarily small. The test results and samples from the subjects in Africa, Pakistan, and Peru were mixed in with those from the Thailand trials.

After ten months, when the clinical trials in Thailand were nearing completion, a minor glitch occurred: a previously unseen test result raised some questions about the safety of the drug. Ballard decided he needed a bit more data, and he wanted the data obtained from the subjects in Peru—that is, from the subjects who had been receiving the drug the longest time.

This was the reason Kelly and Nelson had been rerouted from Africa to Peru to acquire three corpses.

———◆◆◆———

Orson Mulray called Ballard to his office the day after meeting with Fiona. He wanted to wrap up the trials in Thailand and go public— after which he would become extraordinarily rich.

Ballard, of course, didn't want to meet with him. He said he was too busy. So Orson sent a car to Ballard's lab and told the driver to throw Ballard into the trunk if that's what it took to get him to the meeting. The driver asked if he was joking; Orson told him he wasn't.

"Well?" Orson said as soon as Ballard stepped into his office.

Ballard looked like he always did, with his smudged glasses, wrinkled white shirt, wrinkled khaki pants, and scuffed running shoes. No one would ever guess this man was paid more than half a million dollars a year.

"Well, what?" Ballard responded, genuinely confused by the question.

"The autopsy results from the Peru subjects. What did they tell you?" Orson said.

Then Ballard did what he always did when Orson asked about the drug—he launched into a seemingly endless discussion filled with words that Orson didn't understand.

"Goddamnit, man!" Orson screamed. Even a person who prided himself on always remaining calm could be pushed over the edge by Simon Ballard. "I want to know if the results from the Peru autopsies show that the drug is still safe."

Once again, Ballard began to tell him about the relationship between the anomalous Thai test results and the other testing that had been done to date. Before he'd mumbled more than three sentences, Orson slammed his hand down on his desk.

"No! I don't want to hear any more scientific mumbo jumbo. I want you to answer a simple yes-or-no question. I want you to tell me if the weird test results we got in Thailand invalidate your previous conclusions regarding the safety of the drug. Yes or no?"

"Well, when you put it that way, no," Ballard said.

Orson closed his eyes—feeling both gratitude and relief—and the urge to throw Simon Ballard through a window somewhat abated.

"Then if that's the case," Orson said, "I'm going public next month. By then we'll have more than eleven months of data from the trials in Thailand, and that's enough."

"Well, I would like to do just a bit more testing on one aspect of—"

"No," Orson said. He didn't scream the word this time, he just said it very firmly. Then he added, "Dr. Ballard, you need to think about what you want to do with the rest of your life. You need to think about another disease to cure. And I will get you the Nobel as I promised, but that can't happen until we go public with the drug. You do understand that, don't you?"

The expression on Ballard's face indicated that he'd forgotten all about the Nobel.

"What I want you to do is go back to your lab and tie a bow around all your research. Then, like I said, I want you to apply that big brain of yours to some other problem."

"Well . . ." Ballard said.

Orson sighed. The man started every sentence with *well*.

". . . there is an aspect to cervical cancer that's always intrigued me. You see the cervix—"

"Good, that's good," Orson said. "I like diseases that affect women; they pay more attention to their health than men do." Orson laughed. "I heard this joke that if a man discovers blood in his stool, he's likely to shit in the dark for the rest of his life rather than go see a doctor."

Ballard gave him a confused look.

"Anyway," Orson said, irritated that Ballard didn't get it, "write up a proposal and we'll talk about it later."

Orson had never been sure how much Ballard understood about what happened at the Warwick Care Centers.

One of the things he discovered during his five-year association with Ballard was that the man had no interest in people whatsoever. The thing that interested him was the puzzle, and in order to solve this biological puzzle, Ballard needed data—and a few dead human beings provided the necessary data. But not once in the time they worked together did Ballard ask about the people in the human trials. He would give Orson the equivalent of a shopping list: *I need X number of subjects injected, Y number of samples taken to determine the effect on liver, kidney, and lungs, and, by the way, I need the results from three autopsies.*

He realized that Ballard was smart enough to not want to know about the clinical trials. Mulray Pharma was responsible for the trials—not Dr. Simon Ballard. Ballard might have thought that ignorance would provide some sort of defense if anyone ever discovered what Mulray Pharma had done—or maybe he just didn't care.

But he must have wondered how Orson could arrange for autopsy results to be provided in such a timely manner. Did he really believe that people died just to suit his research schedule?

Whatever the case, at this point it was irrelevant.

———◆◆◆———

As soon as Ballard left his office, Orson called Dr. Panyarachun in Thailand. "I want the trials completed by the end of the month. Tell your brother." He meant the minister of public health. "I'll send the money to your accounts as soon as I see something in writing."

Dr. Panyarachun—in his irritating, lilting Thai-accented English—thanked him profusely. Orson had learned that the doctor was building a vacation home on Maui, and the sooner he got his money from Mulray Pharma, the sooner he'd be able to complete it.

———◆◆◆———

Orson looked at his watch. It was almost noon—which meant it was almost time for a long, tedious afternoon with his board of directors.

Not only was Orson pleased with the way the clinical trials had gone, he was equally pleased with the way he'd handled the board. His board of directors had been specifically chosen because they didn't interfere with the way he managed the company. Some were men his father had selected and old pals from when Clayton Mulray ran the company, and most of these people were in their seventies and could barely stay awake during the meetings. A third of the board consisted of academics—professors at prestigious universities in some field related to medicine. Their resumes were impressive—but they weren't businessmen. The final third consisted of CEOs of other companies, and none of these companies were involved in the pharmaceutical industry and all these people were too busy worrying about their own operations to give much thought to Mulray Pharma.

The thing about the board members was that it wasn't in their best interest to rock the boat. They were given twenty-five thousand dollars to attend a board meeting, there were four meetings a year, they flew first class, and were put up in five-star hotels. And the board meetings always began with a long lunch during which the waiters made sure everyone's wineglass stayed full and, after lunch, when everyone was full, tipsy, and sleepy, the meeting would commence.

All the data provided to the board was, of course, prepared by Orson Mulray's people, and Ballard's drug was just one of thirty being developed by Mulray Pharma and one of half a dozen undergoing clinical trials. And Orson would tell them, without getting too specific, that the trials were progressing well. Naturally, he never discussed what was taking place at the Warwick Care Centers. Nor were the costs associated with developing the drug out of line compared with past development efforts, although a little creative accounting helped in this regard. When one of the board members—almost always one of the professors—asked for more detail on some scientific aspect of the drug, Orson would turn to Ballard and Ballard would begin to ramble on in his typically confusing, inarticulate way, and after a couple of minutes, the professor would wish that he'd never asked the question and would drop the subject. And all the board members knew, of course, that it was vital that they not discuss drugs under development outside the boardroom.

The upshot of all this was that in the five years it took to develop Simon Ballard's drug, Mulray Pharma performed well but not spectacularly. The company was still the eighth-largest pharmaceutical company in the United States, although its stock price had dropped slightly during the recession. More important, Orson Mulray had managed to keep his board of directors informed of what he was doing without telling them what he was *really* doing, and he fulfilled completely his legal obligations as CEO.

And now all he had to do was get through one final board meeting.

20

DeMarco parked in front of a narrow, four-story office building on the Washington side of the Potomac River. Across the river was the Pentagon. He'd always found the Pentagon ominous; it just looked like a place where conspiracies were hatched. And last year his paranoia about military cabals was proven valid when he was used as a sacrificial pawn in a lethal game being played by a superspy at the NSA and a four-star army general.

DeMarco wanted to know what Phil Downing had done in Peru, and there was a man in the office building who could help him. Yesterday he had concluded—with no facts to support his conclusion—that Hobson had lied to him. When he'd told Hobson that he knew Downing had been to Peru, Hobson wasn't surprised—he was *shocked.* He was so shocked he almost choked to death on his coffee. And although the story Hobson gave him for why Downing went to Peru made sense—that Downing, to keep his job and impress Hobson, had gone there to develop a pitch to showcase Lizzie Warwick's work—DeMarco had the feeling that Hobson was making up the story on the spot.

But why would Hobson lie? The answer to that question had to be because he was trying to cover up the real reason Downing went to South America. Remembering what Clive Standish had said about embezzlers working for charities, maybe Downing went to Peru to prove Hobson was pilfering money from Lizzie Warwick. Or drugs. Cocaine was South America's best-known export; maybe some of Lizzie's do-gooders were drug mules for a Peruvian cartel. Well, that was a stretch, but whatever the case, he needed some facts regarding Downing's trip across the equator.

DeMarco entered the lobby and proceeded to the elevator, where there was a reader-board that identified the building's occupants: four lawyers on the first floor, a PR firm on the second, and three more lawyers on the third. Washington was infested with lawyers. The sign in the lobby, however, gave no indication as to who worked on the fourth floor—and that's where DeMarco was headed.

The fourth floor was occupied by a man named Neil. He was also the owner of the building—although none of the building's tenants knew this. Neil didn't even want to talk to his tenants, much less listen to their complaints, so he used a property management firm to collect the rent and deal with maintenance issues. Another thing his tenants didn't know was that Neil bugged their offices.

Neil called himself an information broker. This meant that for a substantial fee he would gladly invade the privacy of his fellow citizens and tell you anything you wanted to know about them. To this end, he had people on retainer in places that warehouse privileged data—the IRS, Social Security, Google, credit card and cell phone companies; he even had a guy at Amazon—and if these people couldn't tell him what he needed to know, he and his small staff were adept at hacking, bugging, and spying. Neil did a lot of work for the U.S. government —including the people who resided in the five-sided building across the river—and it was most likely his federal clients who kept him from going to jail. DeMarco met Neil through Emma, and she knew him from her days at the DIA.

Neil was irritating, arrogant, obnoxious—and very smart. He was a balding, fat man who tied his remaining gray-blond hair into a small, thin ponytail that touched his collar, and he dressed— unless there was snow on the ground—in baggy shorts, Hawaiian shirts, and sandals. As it was June, DeMarco was likely to be treated to the sight of Neil's very stout, very hairy legs protruding from his shorts.

Neil was seated at his desk, flipping through a stack of black-and-white photographs, when DeMarco walked into his office. He turned the photos over as soon as he saw DeMarco, which made DeMarco wonder who Neil was planning to blackmail.

"Four years ago," DeMarco said, "there was an earthquake in Peru and the Warwick Foundation . . . Have you heard of them?"

"Of course," Neil said. "I donate to them."

Sheesh. "Anyway, after this earthquake, Warwick sent a team down there to help the victims. Two years after the quake, a guy named Phil Downing, who was Warwick's lobbyist, supposedly went to wherever this earthquake happened to do a follow-up on Warwick's work."

"Supposedly?" Neil said.

"Yeah. I'm not too sure about the guy who gave me the info. I do know from talking to Downing's secretary that he booked a flight to Lima, so I'm guessing he really made the trip. Anyway, a month after Downing gets back from Peru, he's allegedly killed by his partner, another lobbyist, named Kincaid."

"Allegedly?" Neil said.

"Yeah. That's a word us lawyers use. I want you to see if you can find out what Downing was really doing in Peru. Check his phone records and see—"

"Phone records for a dead guy from two years ago?"

"Yeah. See if you can figure out who he talked to down there. I'd be really interested if he was talking to somebody in the Peruvian government or somebody tied in with drugs. Check his banking transactions and see if he sent money to someone who lives there, maybe someone he paid to get information. I don't know. Just get me whatever you can on this trip he made."

"This might not be easy," Neil said, rubbing his meaty chin. "I'm guessing Peru isn't the sort of place where everybody has a computer that's connected to the Net."

"I don't need to hear all the reasons why you're gonna pad your bill, Neil. Just get me what you can."

Neil smiled—thinking, no doubt, about how much he was going to pad his bill.

DeMarco left Neil's office and drove to Alexandria to get a haircut. He'd been going to the same place for the last three years and he always used the same stylist: a blonde in her thirties with large, soft breasts that she pressed against DeMarco's back the whole time she was trimming his hair. She always cut his hair too short—and he always gave her a five-dollar tip.

While waiting his turn to have his hair cut, he read the *Washington Post*. The front-page story that morning was about a congressman who had been pulled over by a cop for driving erratically. The problem, however, wasn't just that the man failed the Breathalyzer test—the problem was that he was dressed in women's clothes. The *Post* speculated that the congressman's Jimmy Choos, with their four-inch stiletto heels, might have contributed to his demise, as they would have made it harder for him to maintain his balance when the cop administered the field sobriety test. The article also included the politician's mug shot. In the photo he wasn't wearing the blonde wig he had on when he was arrested but he did have mascara on his eyelashes.

Hoo-boy.

Neil called as he was leaving the barbershop.

"I got what I could on Downing's trip to Peru, but it's not much. Per his credit card statement, he charged a flight from Dulles to Lima, then another flight from Lima to someplace called Arequipa, and he rented a car at the Arequipa airport. There were no other credit card charges the whole time he was in Peru, so if he paid for a hotel or any other kind of service, he paid in cash. He made no calls from his cell phone to anyone in Peru while he was down there, and when he got back from Peru he made no calls from his home, office, or cell phones to Peru. He wrote no checks to anyone in Peru or, for that matter, to anyone outside the United States in the three-month period prior to his death. If he sent someone cash, I can't tell you that.

"I called the rental car company in Arequipa, talked to some lady, gave her a bullshit story, and she pulled the records for Downing's rental car. He rented a four-wheel-drive Honda SUV and put down on the form that his destination was a place called Pinchollo—I guess that's how you pronounce it—which I could barely find on a map. Pinchollo was one of the towns hit by the earthquake in 2007, so maybe he really did go there to see how things had improved after the quake. So I don't know what else to do, Joe. It looks like you may have to go down there if you want more."

"To Peru? Are you out of your fucking mind?"

"Hey, what can I tell you?"

Irritated, DeMarco asked, "So how much do I owe you?"

Neil told him.

"You gotta be shittin' me!" DeMarco screamed. "You spent less than an hour doing what you did."

"Hey, you know my rates. And send cash."

If DeMarco knew anyone else that could do what Neil did, he would have refused to pay him. And it wasn't like the money was coming out of his own pocket—the American taxpayer was footing the bill. Still, it pissed him off.

As might be expected, the minority leader of the United States House of Representatives wasn't immediately available to see his lowly subordinate. DeMarco told Mahoney's secretary that he needed to see the man, and then went to his office, put his feet up on his desk, and took a nap. An hour later, Mavis called and said he'd be granted an audience if he could get there in the next five minutes—but he'd better hurry because Master Mahoney was extremely busy.

When DeMarco entered his office, he could see that Mahoney was indeed busy. He had his suit jacket off and was standing in front of his desk putting golf balls into one of those office putting cups, the type that returns the ball to you. There was a glass filled with bourbon on his desk and in between putts, he would sip from it.

DeMarco waited impatiently for Mahoney to stroke the next ball. It missed the cup, but not by much. He had played golf with Mahoney once and the guy played well. He also cheated.

As Mahoney lined up his next putt, he said, "Got a game with the VP tomorrow and a couple of Japanese politicians we're trying to schmooze. The VP said we should let one of the Japs win but I say, fuck 'em."

And this was a guy the president called upon for advice on how to run the country.

"How much time and effort do you want me to spend on Brian Kincaid?" DeMarco asked.

"I already told you: not much. Just go through the motions, tell Kincaid's mom you worked your ass off, and be done with it. I just want Mary Pat to leave me alone. She asked me again last night if you'd found anything to help the guy."

"Well, in order for me to do anything more for Kincaid I may have to hire a detective in Peru."

"Peru? What in the hell are you talking about?"

DeMarco gave him the whole story: how Downing had been about to get fired as Warwick's lobbyist, took a trip to Peru, and maybe found something down there he used to blackmail Warwick to keep his job. Then a month later, he gets killed and Brian Kincaid is—maybe—framed for his murder.

Mahoney was only half listening as DeMarco spoke, more interested in his putting. At one point, while DeMarco was talking, he landed a ball in the cup and said, "Oh, yeah, I'm gonna kick some ass." When DeMarco finished, Mahoney said, "That's a whole bunch of fuckin' maybes. You don't really know anything."

"I *know* that," DeMarco said. "But I'm pretty sure Hobson lied to me. And if Kincaid was framed for killing Downing, then Ed Talbot's chief of staff might have been in on it."

"What do you mean?" Mahoney said, and he stopped putting. He was suddenly interested in what DeMarco had to say.

Since Mahoney hadn't been paying attention the first time he told the story, DeMarco had to explain again how the conference call that was supposed to have taken place between Hobson, Downing, and Congressman Talbot's chief of staff, Stephen Linger, put Downing in the office at the same time Kincaid was there—and how that was one of the main reasons Kincaid was convicted.

"But why would Talbot or Linger want Downing killed?" Mahoney asked.

"I don't know that they did," DeMarco said. "I'm just saying it's a possibility, but I haven't found anything that shows that Congressman Talbot is connected in any way to the Warwick Foundation other than voting against some bill that Lizzie Warwick wanted passed."

"The little prick's been busting my balls lately," Mahoney said. *Uh, oh. This wasn't good.*

Talbot was a Republican and Mahoney was a Democrat, so the fact that Talbot had been busting Mahoney's balls was understandable.

But now DeMarco had a problem. Until this moment, Mahoney hadn't given a rat's ass about Brian Kincaid, but if Kincaid's situation could be used to cause problems for a rival politician, then that was something Mahoney cared about.

"Anyway," DeMarco said, "in order for me to get more information on what Downing did in Peru, I'll have to hire someone local and see if the guy can retrace Downing's steps. And I wanted to check with you before I did that."

Mahoney stood there a moment sipping bourbon, mulling things over in his big white-haired head. Finally he said, "You don't need to hire anyone. Go yourself."

"To Peru?"

"Sure, why not? It's not like you got anything better to do."

"But I thought you wanted me to—"

"That'll wait. Go to Peru."

DeMarco left Mahoney's office, and as he walked down the hallway, he had an overwhelming urge to pound his head against a wall until he was unconscious. He did *not* want to go to Peru. He should never have said anything about Talbot until he had more information.

21

DeMarco, as a GS-13 civil servant, earned approximately four weeks of vacation time a year—and he used every bit of it. And when he took his vacations—if he had the money—he liked to travel to places like Key West, the Bahamas, and Hilton Head. Sunny places, places where he could golf. Occasionally, he'd make a trip out west to Las Vegas or Tahoe, where he could lose money at the craps tables after he played golf. And although he'd never been to Europe, the thought of going there had some appeal. But what he was not interested in doing, no matter how much money and time he had, was traveling to South America.

When he thought about South America, he imagined rotten roads and overcrowded buses filled with people who carried live chickens in crates on their laps. The water was unfit to drink, the cops were corrupt, and there were bandits on every corner. And kidnapping. Kidnapping was a cottage industry in South America. So he could just see it: He goes to Peru. He gets diarrhea, maybe malaria, too. He gets robbed and then he gets kidnapped—and the kidnappers whack off his ears and send them to his mother, who doesn't have enough money to pay the ransom.

The morning after meeting with Mahoney, DeMarco called a travel agent he'd used before and told the agent he had to go to a place called . . . Shit, he couldn't even pronounce it. He spelled it. P..i..n..c..h..o..l..l..o.

"Never heard of it," the travel agent said.

He waited while she tapped on a keyboard and thought about that book *Alive*—and the possibility of his plane going down in the Andes and him being the main course for a rugby team that turns into a tribe of cannibals.

"The best thing to do is to fly into Lima," the travel agent said. "They have a modern airport there and lots of flights into the airport. From there you can catch a flight to Arequipa, which is the closest major city to Pinchollo. Then, I guess, you can take a bus from Arequipa to Pinchollo but . . ."

"You *guess?*"

". . . but it would probably be better to rent a car, something with four-wheel drive. And maybe you oughta get spare gas cans because gas stations might be pretty far apart."

"Have you ever been to this place?"

"No. I'm looking at a Web site."

Great.

"Is there a hotel in Pinchollo?"

"I don't know. I don't see one on this Web site."

This just kept getting better and better.

"Tell you what," the travel agent said. "Give me an hour and I'll make some calls and see if I can get some more information."

She called back forty-five minutes later and said, "Yeah, you'll definitely need four-wheel drive. And maybe a sleeping bag and a tent."

"A tent! Are you shitting me!" DeMarco said.

"Joe, Pinchollo isn't a city. I'm not even sure it would be classified as a town. It's a *village.* And by the way, June in the southern hemisphere isn't the same as June here in D.C. It might get a little chilly down there."

He told the agent to make him plane and car reservations and to e-mail him everything she had on the region. Then, after cursing Mahoney, he set about making a list of what he would need if he had to go to a place that didn't have hotels. His idea of roughing it was a Hilton with slow room service—and he'd never been camping in his life. But the guy across the street—an IRS accountant who helped DeMarco with his taxes—was an outdoors nut. He and his wife—both in their sixties—did crazy things like white-water rafting and rock climbing, and one time they hiked a good portion of the Appalachian Trail. They were insane, but they were nice people, and probably had the gear he needed.

He walked across the street. The accountant wasn't home but his wife was. He told her he had to go to Peru, to some godforsaken place that was probably in the Andes Mountains.

"Oh, my God! Peru!" she said. "Geez, I wish I was going with you."

"I wish you were going instead of me," DeMarco said. "Anyway, I was wondering if I could borrow a sleeping bag from you and anything else you think I might need."

He decided not to take a tent. He could just seeing himself trying to erect the thing and then suffocating to death when it collapsed on him during the night. If he couldn't find lodging, he'd sleep in his rental car. But he figured a sleeping bag might be a good idea.

She poured him a cup of fruit juice—her husband would have given him a beer—then told him to wait while she went down to the basement to find the stuff he'd need. While he was waiting, he used his cell phone to call Emma and told her what was going on, concluding with, "So Mahoney wants me to go to Peru."

"Well, it's beautiful there," she said. "You should take a little extra time and see the country, particularly the Inca ruins."

Screw the Inca ruins! If he wanted to see the remnants of a once great civilization he'd go to Detroit.

It took him two trips to carry home all the things his neighbor's wife gave him: a sleeping bag, a little one-burner propane stove, some tin cooking utensils, dried food that came in pouches and that he had no intention of eating unless he was starving, and a set of her husband's rain gear. As he was leaving, she said, "I hope you have a pair of good hiking boots. If your car breaks down and you have to walk, you don't want to be wearing tennis shoes."

Of course he didn't have hiking boots. The farthest he normally hiked was from the lot where he parked to the stadium where the Nationals played. He also figured he'd better stock up on medicine, whatever you took to avoid diarrhea and malaria. And bug repellent. He wondered if they had snakes in Peru.

He finally decided to go to the shopping mall at Tysons Corner. There was a drug store there where he could get the medicine—he didn't know if they sold quinine over the counter—and a sporting goods store where he could buy boots. And he was going to use his government credit card and get the most expensive boots they had.

———◆◆◆———

Nelson sat in his car half a block from DeMarco's house and watched DeMarco lug camping equipment from a neighbor's house to his own. What the hell was going on? Was this guy going on vacation? A few minutes later, DeMarco backed his car out of his garage.

As he followed DeMarco, he pulled the cell phone off his belt and called the detective, Unger. "Go pick up the tape recorder at DeMarco's house. Call me as soon as you've listened to it."

When DeMarco went into a sporting goods store, Nelson stood outside the store and watched him try on a pair of hiking boots. Unger called back while DeMarco was trying on a third pair of boots.

"I listened to the tape," Unger said. "He called a travel agent and it looks like he's taking a trip to Peru. You want me to play the tape for you?"

Aw, shit. "Yeah," Nelson said, and listened to the tape. This was bad. DeMarco was a dead man. And Unger might be, too.

Nelson called Kelly. He would let Kelly deal with Fiona.

Emma sat at her kitchen table, sipping herbal tea, thinking about Peru.

She'd only been there once, but she'd loved it. Once you got away from Lima, a city of almost eight million, the country seemed pure, unspoiled. And the views of the Andes had been incredible. She went to her den and pulled out an atlas and saw that Pinchollo was located in the canyon country at the southern end of Peru—and these weren't ordinary canyons. These were the deepest canyons in the world; the Colca Canyon was twice the depth of the Grand Canyon in Arizona.

Her curiosity piqued, she went online and did a little more research, looking mostly at sites that showed photographs of the region. It was breathtaking. She wanted to see those canyons.

Kelly was in a rental car, parked on Emma's street, and knew he couldn't sit there for long. This wasn't like Georgetown where DeMarco lived, where you could barely find a parking space. This was a wealthy neighborhood; the houses were big, spaced far apart, and people parked in their garages. There were only three other vehicles parked on the street, and one of those belonged to a cable company. Plus, there was the fact that he was black. A lot of the folks in this neighborhood probably considered themselves liberals but he knew if he stayed where he was for very long, someone was bound to call the police.

As Fiona had expected, her headhunters had been able to find out more about Emma. Not only were the headhunters good—and extremely well connected because of their backgrounds—but they had gobs of Mulray Pharma's money to throw at problems, and one of the things they learned was that she was ex-DIA.

"This woman had an awesome career," one of the headhunters told Kelly. "I never heard of her when I worked at Langley because I was just too low on the totem pole to have any contact with her, but at the end of her career she was right up at the top in intelligence circles. I mean, talking to SecDef and the president's national security adviser. And not only that, I heard a rumor that she still works for the agency occasionally, even though she's supposed to be retired."

A Pentagon spook, Kelly thought. This wasn't good at all.

DeMarco, as near as he could tell, was just a low-level gofer on Capitol Hill. And although he was a lawyer, he'd apparently never practiced law, so he wasn't even much of a legal threat when it came to getting Brian Kincaid out of jail. But Emma . . . She sounded bright, competent, and connected. And based on her house, she was rich, too. If she was an adversary, she could be a significant problem.

Kelly's cell phone vibrated and he pulled it off his belt. It was Nelson.

"Aw, shit," Kelly said when Nelson told him DeMarco was going to Pinchollo.

He called Fiona and gave her the bad news.

"Goddamnit all to hell!" Fiona shouted. "I want you to . . ." Then she stopped speaking. "I'll call you back in a few minutes."

Fiona walked over to a window in her office and looked out—although she wasn't really looking at anything. She was trying to figure out what to do about DeMarco. She didn't realize it but she was scratching her left forearm furiously.

Orson had told her not to kill DeMarco because he was afraid that if DeMarco was murdered, his death could lead back to Mulray Pharma. He had also told her she was not permitted to kill the man unless he gave his authorization. She thought about this for a moment and concluded: *To hell with Orson and his authorization.*

Orson was her boss in name only. Because of what they had done together, they were equal partners as far as she was concerned. And what was he going to do? Fire her if she disobeyed an order? No way was that going to happen. All she knew was that they were too close to the finish line—too close to her billion-dollar payoff—to allow DeMarco or anyone else to stop them. It was possible that DeMarco would go to Peru and find nothing—but it was also possible he'd go there and fuck everything up. She was *not* going to let that happen. She picked up the phone and called Kelly back.

"Take him out," she said. "But you have to do it in such a way that it looks, I don't know, *random.*"

"Random?" Kelly said.

"Yeah, you can't make it look like he was singled out."

"What do you want me to do, Fiona? Arrange for a lightning strike?"

"I want you to use your fucking head!" Fiona screamed. "We're paying you and your no-neck partner ten million bucks, so *earn* it. Figure out a way to get rid of him where no one will suspect he was killed for any reason that can be connected to us."

Kelly called Nelson and passed on what Fiona had said, including the no-neck comment, which made Nelson laugh. "Okay," Nelson said, "I'll look for an opportunity. But this guy's leaving tomorrow, and I'm not sure we can set something up that fast. Maybe we should wait for him to get to Peru."

"I don't think Fiona would like that," Kelly said.

<hr />

After spending half an hour looking at Peruvian Web sites, Emma went back to the kitchen and poured another cup of tea.

As she sipped her tea, she thought about the last six months—and how they could have been the last six months of her life—and made up her mind. She picked up the phone and called DeMarco. He wasn't at home and she didn't bother to leave a message. She called his cell phone.

"Where are you?" she asked.

"I'm at a sporting goods store. I need to get some boots for the trip. But, Jesus, these damn things are heavy. I got a pair on now and they feel like they weigh ten pounds apiece."

"I'll go," Emma said.

"What?"

"I said, I'll go to Peru for you."

"Why would you do that?'

"Because I want to. Because I need to. I need to go someplace that's . . . I don't know. Pure. Wild. Untamed. Something."

"What about your health?"

"I'm *doing* this for my health—my mental health."

"Yeah, well, thanks, but I can't let you do it. I mean, what if you got kidnapped?"

"Why on earth would someone kidnap me?"

"Because that's what they do there."

"You're an idiot. I'm more likely to get kidnapped in Georgetown."

DeMarco was pretty sure that wasn't true, but he didn't say so. "No," he said. "I can't let you do it. Phil Downing got killed after he went there and you could get killed, too, and I'm not going to have that on my conscience."

"You don't have any idea why Downing was killed," Emma countered. "And if he was killed because he went to Peru, it's because somebody knew he went there and knew what he found. But nobody knows that I'm involved in this thing."

She was right about that, DeMarco thought, but before he could say anything, Emma said, "And let's face it. I've got a lot better chance of finding out what Downing did in Peru than you do. I've got contacts there, and I speak Spanish and you don't. What you need to do is check out Congressman Talbot and his chief of staff. You're in a better position to do that than I am."

"Yeah, I suppose," DeMarco said, "but . . ."

"Look," Emma snapped. "I'm going, and that's all there is to it, and there's no reason for both of us to go."

———◆◆◆———

DeMarco closed his cell phone. Should he or should he not go to Peru with Emma?

He finally concluded she was right. His time would be better spent trying to find a connection between the Warwick Foundation and Congressman Talbot, and she was more likely to learn something in Peru—and that was true whether she spoke Spanish or not. As for the danger of her going there, she was probably right about that, too.

Hobson knew that *he* was interested in Downing's trip to Peru, but no one knew that Emma was involved in his investigation.

He looked down at his feet, at the fourth pair of boots he'd tried on. He didn't really need the boots now that he wasn't going to Peru, but he kinda liked this pair. The other boots the salesman had shown him looked as if they'd been designed for nuts who wanted to scale Mount Everest—big, stiff, heavy clodhoppers. But these weren't so heavy, and they were lined with Gore-Tex and had rubber soles with some sort of tread that looked like you could walk up an ice wall. He decided to buy them. He had a pair of rubber boots he wore when it snowed, but these boots were much cooler than those.

Nelson watched DeMarco stomp around the sporting goods store in another pair of boots, the fourth pair the damn guy had tried on. It looked like he'd finally found a pair he liked, because he put the boots back in the box and took them to the sales counter.

When DeMarco left Tysons Corner, Nelson was a block behind him.

Christine's reaction when Emma said she was going to Peru was predictable—she became almost hysterical. She said there was no way Emma should be going after what she'd been through with the cancer, and Emma explained, as best she could, that she *needed* to go.

She called a couple of DIA people she knew who were familiar with southern Peru, then went down to the basement and found an old knapsack. She tossed a baseball cap, lightweight rain gear, a couple changes of clothes, a jacket, and a pair of battered hiking boots into the knapsack. She wouldn't take a tent or a sleeping bag; people in that region were hospitable and poor, and for a few dollars she'd find lodging. She went online to see about flights to Peru and saw that a United flight was departing for Lima in three hours. Damn. She had wanted to spend a little more time talking to Christine before she left, but now she'd have to hustle. She decided that rather than waste more time on the computer, she'd spend the time talking to Christine and buy her ticket at the airport.

She hugged Christine as she was leaving and told her not to worry. She said she'd call when she could but that cell phone coverage was bound to be spotty. Christine didn't answer. She just stood there with her arms crossed over her chest. She was angry. Well, she'd get over it.

A Mercedes backed out of Emma's garage, and Kelly looked at the woman driving and compared her with the photo Fiona's headhunters had e-mailed him. It was Emma. He let her get a couple blocks ahead of him, then followed her down Old Dominion Drive and onto the Dulles Airport access road. When she parked in the long-term parking lot at the airport, he thought: *This isn't good*.

Kelly kept gear in his car he might need when he was following a subject; Nelson did the same thing. In Kelly's trunk was a knapsack containing a Colt 9mm and two extra magazines, a folding knife with a four-inch serrated blade, lock picks, an LED flashlight, a ski mask, a couple hats, a lightweight jacket, duct tape, and a few other odds and ends. He also had his passports with him in case he might have to leave the country quickly. He dumped everything out of his knapsack except for his passports, the flashlight, the hats, and the jacket, and followed Emma to the terminal.

As DeMarco drove from Tysons Corner to his home in Georgetown, he grappled with a dilemma: Should he or should he not tell Mahoney that Emma was going to Peru for him?

DeMarco had involved Emma in some of his assignments in the past because she had connections in places where he had none, places like the Pentagon and the CIA. Or, as in this case, she knew people in the State Department like Clive Standish. And Mahoney understood why DeMarco involved her—but he didn't like it when he did. He didn't like it because Emma had a rigid moral code and a conscience, and if Mahoney told her to do something and she didn't want to do it, she'd tell Mahoney to go to hell. The fact was, no one told Emma what to do. The other reason DeMarco was reluctant to tell Mahoney that Emma was going to Peru for him was that Mahoney, just to prove that he was the guy in charge, might make DeMarco go to Peru anyway—and DeMarco didn't want to do that.

The more he thought about it, the more he realized there wasn't any dilemma. He wouldn't tell Mahoney, at least not right away. If Emma found something significant in Peru, then he might tell him that Emma had gone to Peru for him. Maybe. He'd grapple with that dilemma later. For the next couple days, he'd spend his time trying to find some nefarious connection between the Warwick Foundation and Congressman Talbot. He'd do most of the work from home, using the Internet and calling people who could help him, and stay away from Capitol Hill, where he might accidentally run into Mahoney —assuming Mahoney was even at the Capitol, actually doing his job, and not out playing golf.

All dilemmas having been grappled with and overcome, DeMarco's thoughts turned to his stomach. On his way home, he'd be passing close to a place in Arlington that made great ribs, so he'd stop there and pick up some ribs and corn bread for dinner. He was almost to the ribs place when he saw a liquor store and remembered he was low on vodka. Vodka was a staple—like butter and sugar and toilet paper. He pulled into the small parking lot in front of the liquor store.

Nelson watched DeMarco enter the liquor store—and an idea occurred to him. He pulled into a parking space near DeMarco's car, put on a baseball cap, and walked past the store, making sure to keep his head down so the bill of the cap obscured his face; there were almost certainly security cameras inside the liquor store. After glancing into the store, he walked back to his car and called Kelly.

"DeMarco just went into a liquor store. There're only two other people inside, the clerk and some kid. I'm gonna take out DeMarco right now—him and everybody else in the store. It'll look like a robbery gone bad and nobody will know DeMarco was the primary target."

"I don't know," Kelly said. "I'm at Dulles. That woman from McLean is taking a trip. I'm wondering if she's planning to meet DeMarco in Peru."

"Well, if I take care of him, she won't be meeting him."

"I don't know," Kelly said again. "I don't like doing things on the spur of the moment like this."

"I don't either," Nelson said, "but we may not get another chance."

"They got cameras in those stores."

"I've got a ski mask in my kit."

Kelly hesitated; he didn't have a good feeling about this. Nelson could take out three unarmed guys without even breaking a sweat, but something could always go wrong. A cop could drive by at the wrong moment. The liquor store might have some sort of alarm system to alert the cops. Kelly liked to do things the way they did when they took care of Phil Downing—lots of surveillance, research, and dry runs. But Nelson was right, too. Another opportunity like this might not come along again anytime soon, and Fiona had made it clear she wanted DeMarco taken care of as soon as possible.

"Okay," Kelly finally said. "I may have to follow this woman to wherever she's going, so I may be out of touch for a while."

"Hooah," Nelson said.

"Yeah, hooah," Kelly said. "You just watch your ass."

DeMarco reached for a bottle of Stoli, then noticed that Absolut was having some kind of promotion: attached to the 750-ml bottles of Absolut were little airline-sized bottles of vodka mixed with something, and you got the little bottle for free. He looked at the little bottle: raspberry vodka. That sounded awful, but what hell. The little bottle was free and the Absolut was about the same price as the Stoli.

Rich Bennallack stood in front of all the wine bottles, overwhelmed. He was a beer drinker and didn't know one wine from another—and there had to be two hundred bottles in the damn store to choose from. But a girl he'd met last week had invited him over to her place for dinner and he knew he should bring some wine, but what should he get? White, red? What the hell was Shiraz?

His mom had introduced him to the girl. She was dying to see him married so she could have grandkids, and she was always trying to hook him up with some girl. Most of the girls she introduced him to, although they weren't complete dogs, just weren't his type. But this one . . . Well, ol' mom picked a winner this time, and he wanted to make a good impression.

But what kind of wine should he buy? He thought you were supposed to get red for meat and white for fish, but he didn't know what she was cooking for dinner. And no way was he buying two bottles of wine. Maybe the clerk could help him.

Jesus Salvador was thinking this day was never gonna end. Some days were like that. You stood behind the counter and watched the clock creep by, like it took an hour for the minute hand to move a minute. And he had an exam tomorrow—a calculus test—that was going to be harder than shit. He'd been trying to study in between customers, but enough of them kept dribbling into the store that he wasn't able to focus. As soon as he got out of here, he was gonna go to some all-night café and drink a gallon of coffee to stay awake and study his ass off. It was a bitch trying to get an engineering degree while holding down a job.

Nelson took a 9mm semiauto and a ski mask from the gym bag in the trunk of his car, and slipped the mask over his head. He needed to move quickly, before DeMarco left the store. He'd go in, say gimme the money to the Hispanic guy behind the counter, grab whatever bills were in the register, and then shoot the clerk. He wanted the cameras to see that; he didn't want it to look like DeMarco had been singled out as a target. So one in the chest for the clerk, two for DeMarco to make sure he was dead, and then one for the kid lingering by the wine bottles.

———◆———

Rich Bennallack saw the guy come into the store, a big son of a bitch wearing a ski mask. And he had a gun in his hand. *Oh, shit.*

Jesus Salvador stood there unable to move as the man in the ski mask walked up to the counter and pointed the gun at his face. "Give me the money," the guy said. "You hesitate one fucking second, I'll kill you."

Jesus didn't hesitate. He opened the drawer to the cash register, yanked out all the bills as fast as he could, and placed the money on the counter in front of the guy. But the guy didn't pick up the money. He just stood there—his eyes all cold—looking at Jesus, pointing the gun at his head. *Aw, Jesus,* Jesus thought. *Please don't let this happen.*

Then Jesus heard a voice say, "Police! Drop the gun!"

It was the young guy who couldn't figure out what kind of wine to buy.

———◆———

What the fuck? Nelson thought. He slowly turned his head—he didn't want to move too quickly in case the kid was jittery—and saw he was holding a .40-caliber Glock. The young guy had to be an off-duty cop, a gung ho rookie most likely. Talk about rotten luck. But he hadn't heard him chamber a round, and it seemed unlikely that he would have a round chambered when he was off-duty. So the kid could be bluffing. His gun was pointed at Nelson, but for all practical purposes it was empty. On the other hand, he might carry the weapon with a round in the chamber, and since the weapon was a Glock, the safety was right on the trigger. But would he shoot right away? Probably not. And in a way, this was good. The cameras in the store would show him shooting the kid because the kid was pointing a gun at him, and then he'd have a motive for killing everybody else in the store because they were witnesses, including DeMarco.

"I said, 'Police! Drop the fucking gun!'"

He sounded scared. He'd probably never pulled his gun before. "Okay, okay," Nelson said, like he was intimidated. He knew how good he was and he knew how fast he was, and he knew the kid would hesitate for just a second before pulling the trigger—and he knew *he* wouldn't. He reached out, like he was about to put his gun on the counter in front of the cash register—then spun toward the kid and fired.

The first bullet hit him in the chest. So did the second one.

22

Kelly watched as Emma approached the United Airlines counter. Fortunately, there was a long line of people waiting to check in, which would give him some time to figure out what to do. But then, goddamnit, she bypassed the long line with all the poor slobs flying coach and went to the first-class line, where there was only one person ahead of her.

Kelly was fairly sure she was going to Peru, but he wasn't positive. He'd get a ticket for an international flight—it didn't matter where—and follow her to her departure gate. Then, once he was certain where she was going, he'd get a ticket on the same plane. She'd never seen him before. He glanced over at the Delta first-class counter and saw no one waiting there, and according to the departure board, Delta had a flight leaving for Nassau in an hour. That would do.

Kelly followed Emma through security and, just as he'd feared, saw she was flying to Lima—and that the flight was leaving in forty-five minutes. Making a point of not looking at her, he walked up to the United counter and asked for a coach ticket to Lima—and the lady told him the flight was full.

"What about first class?" he asked.

"Sorry," the lady said. "All seats are taken. We sold the last ticket just a few minutes ago. I can put you on standby, if you'd like."

Son of a bitch!

"Look," he said, "I need to get to Lima right away. It's a family emergency. Check all the other airlines and see when the next flight leaves for Lima."

It turned out the next flight from Dulles to Lima was another United flight leaving two hours after Emma's, and Kelly bought a first-class ticket. Since he was about 99 percent positive that Emma was headed for the Warwick Care Center near Pinchollo, the two-hour lead she had didn't really matter. He'd catch up with her in Pinchollo—and deal with her when he did.

He wondered how Nelson was doing.

<hr>

DeMarco couldn't believe it: he was alive.

When the robber spun toward the young cop to shoot him, the cop shot the robber twice, but the robber got off a shot, too, and the bullet shattered a bottle of Stoli about six inches from DeMarco's head. Jesus! If he hadn't decided to look at the Absolut promotion, he would have been standing right in front of that bottle when the robber fired.

He was going to buy Absolut for the rest of his life.

His ears still ringing from the gunshots, DeMarco brushed glass and vodka off his shoulders and walked over to look at the robber, who was bleeding from the chest and not moving. As he approached, the cop pointed a finger at him and said, "Just stand still, and don't even think about leaving. We'll need to get a statement from you."

The kid kicked the robber's gun a few feet away from his outstretched hand, then knelt down next to him. "Call 911," he yelled at the clerk. "This man's still alive." Then he pulled his cell phone off his belt and speed-dialed a number. "Lieutenant, it's Bennallack. I just shot a guy trying to rob a liquor store, the one on Harrison Street. The guy's still alive but I don't think he's going to make it. Yeah, an ambulance is on the way." The kid listened a moment, said, "Yes sir," and closed his phone.

DeMarco watched as the cop pulled the ski mask off the robber, who turned out to be a white guy in his thirties with short dark hair. Little bubbles of blood were escaping from his lips.

———◆———

There are a lot of places in the world where it's easy to obtain firearms, the United States arguably being one of the easiest of those places. In Peru, however, obtaining a gun was a real chore. Normally, Kelly would have called Hobson and told Hobson to obtain the weapons he needed and ship them to Peru, but there wasn't time for that. Kelly wanted the guns waiting for him when he arrived in Peru—and there was a man in Lima who could make that happen.

The first time Kelly and Nelson went to Peru on behalf of Mulray Pharma—and knowing that at some point in the future they might need items that couldn't be purchased in a typical department store—they spent some time in a few of Lima's low-class drinking establishments, until they finally made contact with a German piece of flotsam named Gustav Freytag. Gustav was wanted for various and sundry crimes in Europe, and had lived in Lima for twenty years. He was primarily a middleman and, for a price, he could direct you to people who provided any number of goods and services. If your predilections ran toward eleven-year-old girls or boys, Gustav knew the appropriate pimp. Drugs? Not a problem. A liver for a rich man dying of cirrhosis? Well, a liver was harder to obtain than cocaine, heroin, or boys, but one could be found for a price. Obtaining what

Kelly wanted—a semiautomatic pistol, a hunting rifle with a good scope, and a sat phone—wouldn't be difficult at all.

Kelly called Gustav from Dulles and told him what he needed.

"I want the guns, along with a four-wheel-drive vehicle, waiting for me at the airport in Arequipa," Kelly said. "And the vehicle and the guns had better be in excellent condition or I'll come looking for you."

"You need not threaten me, Mr. Shaw."

As far as Freytag knew, Kelly's name was Shaw.

"And I need one other thing," Kelly told the German. "I want you to send a man to the airport to meet United Flight 7599 from Dulles. There's an American woman on the flight. She's tall and slim, has short blonde hair, and she's wearing a blue sweater and jeans and carrying a tan-colored knapsack. The knapsack has a Sierra Club patch on it. Did you get all that? I want your man to confirm this woman is catching a flight to Arequipa."

"Do you want my man to follow her to Arequipa?" Gustav asked.

"No. This woman would spot the idiots you employ. I just want your guy waiting at the Lima arrival gate and to see if she catches a connecting flight to Arequipa. If she doesn't, call me. Do you understand?"

"Yes."

Kelly called Fiona next and told her what was going on—that Nelson was taking care of DeMarco at a liquor store and he was following Emma to Peru. Fiona wasn't too happy to hear that Emma was going to land two hours before him.

"Yeah, well there's nothing I can do about that, but since I'm pretty sure I know where she's headed, it's not a problem. What do you want me to do when I catch up with her?"

"What do you think?" Fiona said.

Kelly went to a restaurant in the terminal to get something to eat before his flight departed. While he ate, he wondered how Nelson was doing. He should have taken care of DeMarco by now. After he finished his meal, when he still hadn't heard from Nelson, he called him and the call went straight to voice mail. Kelly figured Nelson had probably turned off his phone before he went into the liquor store, but he should have turned it back on by now. And Nelson wasn't the type to forget to charge the battery.

Just before he boarded the flight to Lima, he called Nelson again, and again got his voice mail.

Something was wrong.

23

The city of Arequipa, Peru, has a population of almost a million. It lies in a valley in the western Andes at seven thousand, eight hundred feet above sea level, and nearby mountains, some still active volcanoes, rise as high as twenty thousand feet. Spanish conquistadors founded Arequipa in the sixteenth century, and within the modern city there's an old colonial district with cobblestone streets, splendid plazas, and magnificent white stone fountains. There's also a cathedral—*Catedral de Arequipa*—which was constructed in 1544 but which has been repeatedly damaged by earthquakes and fires and rebuilt several times. It was almost as if God didn't like the house of worship the Spaniards erected in His honor.

As much as Emma wanted to explore the city, it had been a long flight from Washington to Lima that had included a layover in Miami, then another two-hour flight from Lima to Arequipa. Consequently, the only thing she really wanted to see by the time she arrived was a bed. If she didn't learn anything alarming in Pinchollo, she might spend a day or two sightseeing in Arequipa before returning home.

The next morning she rented a four-wheel-drive Land Rover. It had forty thousand miles on it and reeked of cigarette smoke, but the tires were almost new and the engine sounded fine. She had the rental car company strap two five-gallon containers of gasoline to the back of the vehicle. She figured it would take six to eight hours to drive from Arequipa to her destination—which was fine by her. She'd come to Peru to see towering mountains, condors, and those magnificent canyons, and she was looking forward to the journey.

Leaving Arequipa, she passed a series of small townships built on the flanks of Chachani, one of the volcanic massifs towering over Arequipa. The road was a two-lane blacktop blasted out of the mountain's flanks, crowded with trucks and buses and winding ever upward. The first part of the journey was through country that was bone-dry, with only a few saguaro-like cactus plants to provide some relief from the rocks. About ninety minutes from Arequipa, she reached the boundary of a nature preserve, the Salinas-Aguada Blanca. Here, at twelve thousand feet, was the pampa, a grassy plain populated by vicuña, the wild cousin of the domestic alpaca. In the background was the perfect cone of the volcano El Misti.

The road continued to climb—she wondered if it would ever stop climbing—until she finally arrived at a mountain divide where a roadside sign said the elevation was four thousand, eight hundred meters. Almost sixteen thousand feet! She was lucky she wasn't feeling symptoms of altitude sickness; she suspected being a marathon runner was probably one reason why. And although the altitude didn't take her breath away, the scenery did. From where she stood, she could see Ampato and Hualca Hualca, each mountain twenty thousand feet high.

She was glad she had come to this place—it was everything she imagined. She was also glad that DeMarco had decided not to come with her. He would have complained the whole time and, being an off-and-on-again smoker, he would have wheezed himself to death at this elevation.

Finally, the road began to descend. When she reached the town of Chivay, she saw she was at a mere twelve thousand feet. Chivay was the largest town in the region, with a population of about four thousand, and overlooking it was Cotallaully, a sixteen-thousand-foot peak that is the city's *apu*—its guardian mountain spirit. At Chivay, she turned westward, heading into the region along the southern rim of the Colca Canyon, which had been struck by the quake—and the enormous landslides that followed—in 2007. The small towns of Yanque, Achoma, Maca, Cabanaconde, and Huambo had all suffered some damage, but Pinchollo had apparently been the hardest hit, as this was where Lizzie Warwick initially focused her relief efforts.

As she drove, she was amazed by the amount of terracing on the steep hillsides and awed by the tenacity of a people who had the determination to farm in such rugged country. At one point, she passed through a long, winding tunnel bored through the side of a mountain, a tunnel so long she couldn't see the light at the other end when she entered it. She was astounded the tunnel had survived the quake and couldn't imagine what it must have been like to have been inside it when the earthquake struck. She stopped again at another lookout point, and found herself looking thousands of feet upward at the mountains and thousands of feet downward into the Colca Canyon. The Colca River was just a thin ribbon of silver from where she stood.

Late in the afternoon, she reached Pinchollo and saw areas that had still not been rebuilt four years after the quake. Mounds of brick and stone dotted the landscape like untidy grave markers. She stopped when she came to an eighteenth-century Catholic church called San Sebastian. The church also appeared to have been damaged by the quake; there was scaffolding on one side but nobody was working. There was a small plaza near the church where people could sit and enjoy the sun on their faces. Today was sunny, if a bit cool. Emma grabbed a bag from her car containing food, a bottle of water, and a bottle of Peruvian wine, and took a seat on a stone bench on the northern edge of the plaza.

Two old women were sitting about twenty yards away from her, heads close together, speaking in low voices. A couple of gossipers Emma figured. The old women wore straw hats on their heads, alpaca jackets, and long, dark skirts with magnificent embroidery on the hem. Across the plaza were two young men, smoking and laughing about something. Emma nodded to the old women, then ignored them as she pulled a loaf of bread, fruit, and cheese from her bag. She could feel their eyes on her and she imagined they were wondering what she was doing by herself. Usually the tourists who came to this rugged region to look at the canyons and the condors came in groups.

Finally, and as Emma had expected, one of the two young men walked over. In heavily accented English, he asked if Emma spoke English. Emma said, "I do but I also speak Spanish," and the young man smiled in relief that she could speak his language. She guessed he was about nineteen or twenty. He was short and broad, wore jeans, ragged tennis shoes, a faded red sweater, and a fedora-like black hat. She could tell he was proud of his hat. He told her his name was Marco and said that if she needed a guide, he was her man.

Emma didn't respond to his offer. Instead she asked if he would like a glass of wine, a bit of cheese. He beamed again, a dazzling smile, his white teeth in brilliant contrast to his dark skin. She uncorked the wine bottle, took plastic cups out of her bag, and told him to call his friend over so he could have some wine, too. Marco made a motion with his arm and his friend, a man who turned out to be Marco's cousin and whose name was Arturo, joined them. Emma looked over and could see the old women staring, and she raised the bottle and motioned them over.

Emma wasn't a gregarious person, but this was different. This was a mission, and the mission required her to be sociable. She chatted with the young men and the old women for half an hour, asking questions about the town and the surrounding area. Eventually she steered the conversation to the earthquake that had occurred four years ago. The men and women all began to speak at once about the devastation, the horror of people being crushed by their own roofs as they slept, how some people had simply disappeared as if swallowed by the earth itself. Lizzie Warwick, they all agreed, was a saint. She and René Lambert had arrived with thirty people four days after the quake and had helped so many people. They tended tirelessly to the wounded, passed out food and water, helped dig for those trapped in the rubble, and set up temporary shelters for those who had lost their homes. One of the old women said that without Lizzie and the handsome French doctor the number of dead would have doubled or tripled; her sister was alive today only because of Dr. Lambert.

Emma asked if any of them remembered a man named Downing, a big man, an American. He worked for Lizzie Warwick, she said, and he came here two years ago to take pictures of how things had improved since the earthquake. Neither Marco nor the old women remembered Downing, but Arturo did.

"He didn't take pictures here, though," Arturo said. "He wanted to find Juan Carlos and the hospital."

"The hospital?" Emma said.

Arturo explained that it wasn't really a hospital. It was a camp, a . . . He groped for the right word. A *facility,* he finally said, unable to think of any other word to describe the place. Lizzie Warwick built it to house some people left homeless by the quake.

Emma figured Arturo had to be speaking about one of the long-term Warwick care facilities that her friend, Clive Standish, had mentioned.

"And that's where Mr. Downing went when he came here?" Emma asked.

Arturo shrugged. "I guess. As soon as I told him where it was, he drove off."

"And where is this place?" Emma asked.

Marco jumped in at this point. He said the facility was just off the main road about twenty miles west of Pinchollo. He then scratched a rough map in the dirt with his finger and described a landmark Emma could use to locate the road to the place.

"Why did they build this facility so far from here?" Emma asked.

Marco shrugged. "Maybe they were worried about another quake. I don't know."

That may have been true, Emma thought, but she was still surprised. If this facility had been constructed to help the local people, it would have made more sense to build it closer to Pinchollo so friends could visit more easily. She didn't say this, however, and reminded herself not to jump to conclusions until she had more information.

It was getting late and Emma was tired from the long drive from Arequipa. She decided she'd visit the Warwick facility tomorrow and talk to this man, Juan Carlos. She asked her new friends if there was a place she could sleep that night, saying she would pay in U.S. dollars for a bed. One of the old women said she could stay with her daughter, a recent widow, but that she didn't have to pay anything.

Emma slept on the floor in the widow's house that night, next to a fireplace. She had two rough blankets for a mattress, two rough blankets to keep her warm, and her knapsack for a pillow—and slept like a baby. She left a hundred dollars on the widow's table before she left; a hundred dollars was a small fortune in this part of the world.

The Warwick Care Center was located about twenty miles from Pinchollo and off the main road, but Emma would have driven right past the place if Marco hadn't told her to look for a rock formation that vaguely resembled the head of a dog. The road to the facility was nothing more than two deep ruts created by the tires of other vehicles.

She drove for a mile, going up a slight grade, until she crested a hill and could see the facility half a mile away. It was built on rocky but relatively flat ground, and behind it Emma could see a small stream. She wondered if the proximity of the stream was the reason for choosing this site.

As for the facility itself, Emma was impressed. There were two large, modern Quonset huts and four smaller enclosures. The buildings looked like the type that could be erected quickly by a team of men who knew what they were doing, but she wondered how they got building materials to this site four years ago; sections of the road to the east would have been impassable immediately after the earthquake. And again she wondered why the facility had been erected in such an isolated spot and not closer to Pinchollo or some population center like Chivay.

She parked her Land Rover in an open space in front of one of the large Quonset huts where she saw a few people sitting outside on benches, enjoying the late morning sun on their faces. They all stared at her as she exited her vehicle and a few of them smiled and waved their hands in greeting, but no one approached her. Everyone she saw appeared healthy, although one woman was holding a cane in her hands.

A man came out of one of the smaller huts and walked toward her with a smile on his face. He introduced himself as Juan Carlos, and like the men she had encountered in the village the day before, he was short and cheerful with a broad, round face. He was wearing jeans, a hooded gray sweatshirt, and a Colorado Rockies baseball cap.

As much as she hated to do it, Emma began with a lie. She told Juan Carlos that she worked for the Red Cross and had heard about the marvelous things the Warwick Foundation had done after the earthquake, particularly setting up this special facility. She said she'd spoken to a man named Phil Downing who worked for Warwick and he'd told her about this place.

"Do you remember Mr. Downing?" Emma asked. "He came here two years ago."

"Oh, yes," Juan Carlos said, and then made an expression that made it clear he hadn't been fond of Downing.

"Mr. Downing told me he took videos to show American politicians how the money Lizzie Warwick had been given was being used to help people."

"He didn't take videos while he was here," Juan Carlos said. "He just asked lots of questions and made me show him around." Juan Carlos hesitated. "He was a rude man, but because he worked for Señorita Warwick, I was respectful. I was glad when he left."

"Yes, I didn't particularly like him either," Emma said. "Anyway, I was visiting in Chivay and because of what Downing told me, I decided to come here to see for myself what Warwick had done. But first, I'd like to know more about you. The people in Pinchollo speak very highly of you."

Juan Carlos beamed at the false compliment. He said that eight years ago he went to Lima, stayed with a distant cousin, and took classes to become an emergency medical technician and an ambulance driver. He thought the work would be exciting, but he grew to hate it. Lima was too large, too crowded, too noisy, too smelly. And the job. . . . Well, mother of God, it was awful. Bodies mangled in car accidents; drug addicts who overdosed; people beaten, knifed, and shot. He couldn't stand it. He went back to his hometown, not sure what he was going to do next, and a couple of months after he returned, the earthquake happened.

He did what he could to care for the survivors, but he had no idea how to deal with such a large-scale disaster. Fortunately for him and everyone else in the area, Lizzie Warwick, Dr. Lambert, and their team showed up and took charge. When Dr. Lambert discovered that Juan Carlos had had medical training, he asked him if he wanted to manage a facility they were going to establish to care for some of the survivors.

"Why did they build this facility so far from Pinchollo?"

"Dr. Lambert said they would have to clear away all the rubble to build in Pinchollo. And maybe there were issues with whoever owned the land."

Emma thought that answer odd. There was a lot of uninhabited land near Pinchollo—it wasn't a densely populated area—and certainly Lambert could have found a spot just outside the town to build where it wouldn't have been necessary to clear away debris from damaged structures.

"How did they get building materials to this place? The roads must have been damaged by the quake."

"Helicopters," Juan Carlos said. "Big helicopters. They brought in everything you see here and a team of men, and they built the facility in just a few days. We have a pump to pump water from the spring, two generators that supply electricity, chemical toilets, and heat for the winter. Every couple of months I call Mr. Hobson and . . . Do you know who Mr. Hobson is?"

Emma nodded.

". . . and I tell him what supplies I need and he sends food, diesel for the generators, anything I want."

"How did Ms. Warwick and Dr. Lambert decide who should live here?" Emma asked.

Juan Carlos gestured toward the people sitting outside. "These people have no one. After the quake, if we didn't take care of them, they would have been all alone, without food and shelter. Many of them would have died."

"I see," Emma said. "But there must have been a *lot* of people after the quake that needed help."

"Oh, yes, there were so many. Children who lost their parents, people with horrible injuries."

"What happened to those people?"

"The children, Miss Warwick sent to Arequipa and Lima, some to Chivay. They have organizations in those cities to help with orphans. The badly injured, they sent to Arequipa, where they have hospitals."

"I see," Emma said again, although the picture still wasn't completely clear to her. "And what exactly do you do for the people who live here?"

"Feed them. Care for them. And I give them Dr. Lambert's medicine," Juan Carlos said. The pride in the job he was doing was evident on his broad face. "I also take samples and administer tests and mail them to Dr. Lambert so he can make sure they are okay."

"I don't understand," Emma said. "Are all these people sick?"

"Oh, not really. Just the usual things—arthritis, high blood pressure, digestion issues, but nothing too serious."

"So what is this medicine you give them?"

Juan Carlos shrugged. "Drugs that Dr. Lambert prescribes to keep them healthy. He gave them all exams before he admitted them to the facility."

"Would you mind giving me a tour?" Emma said.

The two large Quonset huts were like military barracks. There were beds for about twenty-five people in each hut and lockers at the foot of the beds for storing their belongings. Juan Carlos said the women lived in one of the huts and the men in the other. One of the small outbuildings housed two large generators and fuel for the generators. The second outbuilding was Juan Carlos's home and office. It contained his bed, a small desk, bookshelves, file cabinets, and a satellite phone. The third building was a kitchen with propane-fueled barbecues.

"Do you cook all the meals?"

"Oh, no. The men and women who live here take turns cooking," Juan Carlos said. "Some of the women are excellent cooks," he added, patting his small potbelly.

The fourth small hut was a miniature clinic. There was a bed, boxes of disposable syringes, containers for biological samples, a laptop, and a printer. Juan Carlos didn't object when Emma picked up a vial containing what appeared to be blood. The first thing she noticed was that the vial was marked only with an alphanumeric label and didn't identify the patient by name. When she asked about the label, Juan Carlos became quite animated and explained that each person living at the facility had a small electronic chip inserted in his or her upper arm.

"It just took a small incision," he said, "not really painful at all."

"You're kidding," Emma said.

"No, no. It's very, very important, Dr. Lambert said, to make sure we don't mix up the samples. So whenever a sample is taken, I use the RFID reader—Dr. Lambert taught me how to use it. I point the reader at the chip in the person, and the reader talks somehow to the computer and a label is generated, then the label is placed on any specimens taken from the person. It's a very good system and there are no mistakes—writing down the wrong name or something like that."

"Ah, I understand," Emma said, but she found what she had just heard chilling. They had *tagged* these people the way biologists do when they track animals in the wild. She could understand the logic of using the RFID chips, but her instincts told her something was wrong with this.

"Where do you send the samples?"

"A laboratory in Delaware, USA." Before Emma could ask another question, he added, "I also administer tests, and I send the test results to Delaware, too. I drive to Arequipa once a month and use the Federal Express to send them."

"What sort of tests?"

He explained, and Emma began to get a better understanding of what this was all about.

"Have there ever been any fatalities here?"

For the first time, Juan Carlos hesitated, and Emma didn't think he was going to answer the question, but then he said, "When we set up the facility, fifty-five people lived here. Now there are forty-six. Four died the first year, but this was understandable. It was a very hard winter that year and some were still traumatized by the earthquake and some had been injured. One man who died was buried beneath his own house for two days before he could be rescued."

"But what killed these people?"

"Dr. Lambert said it was most likely heart issues or some respiratory infection."

"Most likely?"

"Yes, that's what he said. The next year two people died. One was a woman who Dr. Lambert said had a weak heart; the man . . . Well, he just died. He missed his wife a lot. I think he wanted to die. The following year, thank God, everyone stayed healthy, but . . ."

Juan Carlos stopped speaking, so Emma prompted him. "But what?

Juan Carlos looked away, as if he felt guilty about something.

"Look," Emma said, "if you don't want to talk about this because it's too painful, I understand. And I'm sure if people died, it wasn't your fault. I'm only asking about fatalities because if the Red Cross sets up a place like this, we need to understand some of the problems we might encounter."

Juan Carlos nodded. "If you use generators, you need to be careful," he said. "A short time ago, three people died here one night and—"

"All on the same night?"

"Yes. Dr. Lambert's man said it was probably the generators. Carbon monoxide. The morning after the people died, everyone was nauseous and complaining of headaches. The Warwick Foundation sent a technician from Arequipa to look at the generators and he did some maintenance on them, and we haven't had any problems since. So be careful if you use generators."

"Were autopsies performed on the people who died?" Emma asked.

"I don't know. Mr. Hobson sent a helicopter for the bodies. To give them a proper burial, I was told, but maybe they did autopsies, too."

Emma found it astounding that they would send a helicopter for the dead and not bury them locally, but she didn't say this to Juan Carlos.

"Did anyone tell you not to talk about this place and the people who died?" Emma asked.

"Who is there to talk to?" Juan Carlos said. "But yes, Dr. Lambert said that if anyone from the media came here, I was to refer them to him. The same with anybody from the government, but the government doesn't care about these people. No one from the government has ever been here. Ever. Only Señorita Warwick and Doctor Lambert care. But I'm sure he wouldn't mind me talking to somebody from the Red Cross."

The man was so open and honest, Emma again felt guilty about duping him.

"Can I look at these drugs you give them?"

"If you want to, but there really isn't anything to see," Juan Carlos said, and walked over to a cabinet and removed a small vial from a cardboard box. The liquid in the vial was transparent, like water. As he handed it to Emma, he said, "There's no name on the bottle. Just numbers and letters and a bar code."

And that's all there was. The label said *A234XA,* and Emma had no idea what that meant.

Juan Carlos handed her another small container. This one was plastic and looked like a nasal spray dispenser. The label contained a bar code and the alphanumeric code *A234XC. Nasal spray,* Emma thought. She wondered if the drugs were for treating respiratory infections or sinus problems.

After the tour, she sat outside with a few of the patients, although she wasn't sure *patient* was the correct word. They all seemed to be in good health, and if they were ill, there was no common symptom she could see. She asked Juan Carlos if it would be okay for her to sleep at the facility that night and he said they had several empty beds and that would be fine.

She took a short walk, then ate dinner with a group of women, sitting on the lockers in the hut where they slept. She steered the conversation eventually to the fatalities, and learned one other thing. The first year, when four people died, they died in the second half of the year—not immediately after the facility opened, as Juan Carlos had implied—and they died about a month apart.

After dinner, she excused herself and walked down to the stream behind the facility. She took a seat on a rock, and as the sun and the temperature dropped, she thought about what she had learned. The first thing that occurred to her was that building and operating this facility had to be horrendously expensive. The Quonset huts weren't cheap, and Warwick had paid for a construction crew and heavy-lift helicopters to transport building materials from Arequipa or Lima. And Warwick continued to pay for fuel and food for approximately fifty people. It would have been much less expensive to have transported these people to Arequipa or Chivay after the quake and house them there; the money being spent on such a small number of people could have been used to provide for several hundred if this facility had been placed somewhere else. Which made her think about how the facility was so isolated. It wasn't exactly hidden, but to say that it was off the beaten path was an understatement.

Lastly she thought about the RFID chips inserted into people's arms, the drugs being administered, the samples taken—and she thought she knew what was going on and what Phil Downing had discovered by coming here.

If she was right, Lizzie Warwick was a monster.

Kelly lay on his belly and watched Emma through the scope of his rifle. It would be easy to kill her right where she sat, but he couldn't do that. He needed to know what she and DeMarco knew and what she had learned from that simpleton Juan Carlos. As soon as she left the care center, he'd take her and question her. And then he'd kill her.

There was only one good road leading from the care center back to Arequipa. In many places the road was barely wide enough for two cars to pass, and five miles from his current position was a blind curve—the sort of curve where a sensible driver would sound his horn to alert any vehicles coming from the opposite direction. When Emma left the facility, Kelly would get in his car, drive rapidly down the road, and park on the downhill side of the curve. When Emma rounded the curve, his car would be parked in the middle of the road, and she'd be forced to stop. Then he'd point a pistol at her face and take her. If she tried to back up, he'd shoot out her tires—or shoot her.

He'd make her tell him everything she and DeMarco had learned—and there was no doubt she would tell him—and then she would simply disappear. She was a woman who came on her own to the wilds of Peru, and her rental car would be found abandoned on the road. Maybe she had been attacked by robbers. Maybe she'd been kidnapped. If her car had a flat tire, they might think that she walked down the mountain road to find help and stumbled and fell into the steep ravine that ran alongside the road. Her death would be an unsolvable mystery.

She sat by the stream for an hour, then walked to her Land Rover, and Kelly thought she might be planning to leave. But she didn't leave; instead she reached into her car and pulled out her knapsack and entered the women's Quonset hut. It appeared she was planning to spend the night. He had no choice, however, but to stay where he was and continue watching in case she did decide to leave.

While he waited, he retrieved the satellite phone from his vehicle and called Nelson, and when Nelson again didn't answer his cell phone, he called Fiona. "I can't reach Nelson."

There was a long pause before Fiona spoke. "Nelson screwed up. He was shot and right now he's in a hospital and under arrest."

"He was shot?" Kelly said, unable to believe what he was hearing.

"Yeah," she said. She explained that when Nelson entered the liquor store to kill DeMarco, an off-duty cop was in the store and he shot Nelson. She concluded by saying, "Do you think he'll talk?"

"You cold-blooded cunt!" he screamed. "How bad is he hurt?"

"I don't know. I just found all this out a little while ago and I don't have all the details yet. I got a lawyer for him, and the lawyer will call me after he gets in to see him."

"Jesus," Kelly said.

"What's your status?" Fiona asked.

He was having a hard time concentrating, but he told her about Emma.

"You have to find out what she knows and then take care of her," Fiona said.

"I know that! I'll deal with her tomorrow and then I'm flying back. In the meantime, you damn well better figure out a way to help Nelson, or I'll beat you to a bloody pulp."

24

Emma forced herself to stay awake for two hours after going to bed, and then, when she was fairly sure everyone was sleeping, she rose from her cot. She pulled a small flashlight out of her knapsack but didn't turn it on until she was outside the Quonset hut.

She wanted to take one of the vials Juan Carlos had shown her. She didn't know if he kept an inventory of the drugs—she imagined he did—but if she stole one of the vials tonight, he wouldn't realize it was missing until after she was gone, and she doubted he would call the police; she wasn't even sure there were any police in the region he could call.

She used the flashlight to find her way back to the small hut used as a clinic, where Juan Carlos stored the drugs. The door to the hut wasn't locked, and she went immediately to the sheet metal cabinet where the drugs were stored—and discovered that the cabinet was locked, and with a good padlock manufactured by Master Lock. Emma tugged on the lock, but as she didn't have any lock picks, that was all she could do.

She returned to the women's Quonset hut and tried to fall asleep, but her mind was spinning.

Kelly spent a sleepless night.

An hour after dawn, he saw Emma come out of the women's Quonset hut. She used one of the portable toilets, then spent an hour sitting outside drinking coffee, eating fruit, and talking with a couple of the women—which infuriated Kelly. He wanted her to get going so he could deal with her and get back to D.C. and check on Nelson. Finally, she shook hands with Juan Carlos and got into her Land Rover.

Kelly immediately abandoned his position on the hillside and drove to the blind curve as fast as he could. He almost lost control of his vehicle at one point, and barely avoided going off the road and into the ravine that ran alongside it. He parked in the center of the narrow road, then took up a position near the rear bumper of his car, his Glock in his hand—and waited for Emma. Fifteen minutes later, he heard her honk her horn before she rounded the curve, and then watched calmly as she slammed on her brakes, stopping six feet from him.

Kelly pointed the Glock at her face and said, "Get out of the car."

He didn't know if she could hear him, but he could see her face through the windshield of the Land Rover, and he had no doubt she understood what he wanted. She didn't seem to be afraid, though. She just sat there looking at him, her face just as impassive as his, and then she pressed down on the gas pedal and drove directly at him.

He hadn't expected that at all.

He snapped off a shot, but he was trying to dodge out of the way at the same time and the shot went high—and then the hood of the Land Rover struck him a glancing blow, knocking him off the road and down into the ravine. He fell about ten feet before he hit the ground the first time and, when he hit, he heard a bone in his left arm snap. Then he just kept falling, bouncing and rolling, down the steep hillside. He hit his left shoulder hard on a boulder. Then his head struck something—and all was darkness.

━━◆◆◆━━

Emma closed her eyes for a moment, then exited the Land Rover. The man who had tried to kill her, kidnap her, or rob her—she wasn't sure which—was lying a hundred feet below her, on his back, on a narrow ledge, and he wasn't moving. She figured he was dead; he'd fallen a long way. If she'd had a rope, she might have climbed down to see if he was still alive, but since she didn't have one, she wasn't about to risk her life climbing down a steep hillside to check on the condition of a man who had just pointed a gun at her face.

When she had rounded the curve and saw him standing there, holding a gun, she'd hit the brakes. He'd obviously thought she'd step out of her vehicle because he was armed. He obviously didn't know her. The look on his face was almost comical as she drove straight at him. Her intent had been to crush him between her Land Rover and his Explorer, but the man had been too quick. He'd jumped out of the way and her car had only struck him a glancing blow—but that was enough to knock him off the road and down into the ravine.

You jumped the wrong way, amigo.

She looked at her car. Her bumper had a small dent in it from hitting the Explorer's bumper, but there appeared to be no other damage. Then she noticed there was a long, fresh scratch on the roof of her vehicle, and she figured the scratch had been caused by the shot he fired at her. She also noticed that if the bullet had been four inches lower, it wouldn't have scratched the roof—it would have gone through the windshield and hit her in the face. The guy had been pretty good, Emma thought. Even while diving out of the way, he'd almost managed to kill her.

She walked over to the man's Explorer. Lying on the front passenger seat was a satellite phone. On the backseat was a knapsack—and a rifle with a high-powered scope. She picked up the knapsack, and in one of the zippered side pockets she found two U.S. passports, one made out in the name of Kelly and the other made out in the name of Shaw. The two passports had the same photo of a good-looking black man. Folded up in one of the passports was an airline ticket for a flight from Dulles to Lima, and the ticket was made out to Shaw. He'd left Washington about two hours after she did.

She searched the Explorer and the rest of the knapsack and found a flashlight, an extra magazine for the pistol, and some clothes he had purchased in Lima, but nothing that gave her any idea as to why he had stopped her car at gunpoint. The logical assumption was that he had followed her from Washington and his mission had something to do with the Warwick Foundation and the facility she'd just visited—but that was just an assumption.

She looked down into the ravine again. The man, whoever he was, hadn't moved.

She had no regrets if she'd killed him. Nor did she have any intention of reporting the incident to the Peruvian authorities. There was no way she was going to get caught up in the investigation of a fatal accident in Peru, particularly since she had deliberately caused the fatality. The one thing she did regret was that she was going to have to leave Peru right away. There'd be no more sightseeing for her.

Her immediate problem was that the man's car was blocking her way and he hadn't left the keys in the car. Fortunately, the Explorer was pointed downhill, and the road was steep. Emma placed the satellite phone and the man's two passports in her Land Rover; she left the knapsack and the rifle on the backseat of the Explorer. Then she put the Explorer in neutral, turned the steering wheel sharply to the right—and pushed. The car crashed down into the ravine, starting a small landslide, and ended up on its top about a hundred yards below the man.

Good. If someone bothered to investigate, they'd conclude that the man had lost control of his car, the car had gone off the road and fallen into the ravine, and he'd been thrown from the car as it crashed down the hillside.

She returned to her car and used Shaw/Kelly's satellite phone to call DeMarco's cell phone. "A man just tried to kill me or kidnap me," she said.

"Aw, goddamnit," DeMarco said. "Didn't I tell you that would happen if you went down there? Are you all right?"

"I'm fine, but the man is dead. Or, I think he is."

"What?"

"And he wasn't a local. He followed me here from D.C."

"But how the hell did he even know you were going to Peru?"

"I don't know."

"Well, what did you find out down there?"

"I don't have time to go into that right now. We'll talk when I get back. But I need you to do a couple of things. Get a pen."

She gave DeMarco the names on the two passports and the passport ID numbers. "Tell Neil to find out who this guy is and everything about him. Let's hope one of the names he used is real. And write down these phone numbers and give them to Neil, too," she said, and gave him two numbers that were in the recent-calls directory of the satellite phone.

"The other thing I want you and Neil to do is see if there's a link between the Warwick Foundation and a pharmaceutical company."

"A pharmaceutical company?"

"Yes. I think there's something really ugly going on down here, Joe, and I think Phil Downing found out about it and that's why he was killed."

"But what—"

Emma hung up. She looked one last time at the body lying below her—the man still hadn't moved—then put the Land Rover in gear and drove away.

25

Fiona sat in front of Orson Mulray's desk, telling him what had happened with DeMarco and Emma—and as she spoke, Orson felt the anger welling up inside him like lava rising in a volcano. He had never struck a woman in his life, but right now he wanted to knock Fiona's arrogant head right off her shoulders. Nelson was in a hospital and under arrest, Kelly seemed to have disappeared, DeMarco was still alive, and Fiona had no idea where Emma was or what she had learned in Peru.

"God damn you!" Orson said. "Why in the hell didn't you talk to me before you ordered Kelly and Nelson to kill those people?"

"I, uh . . . It was a judgment call," Fiona muttered. Knowing the enormity of her failure, she actually sounded contrite and embarrassed —and Orson couldn't recall her ever having displayed either of those emotions in the past.

"When I found out DeMarco and his pal were going to Peru," Fiona said, "I felt I had to act. I mean, what would you have done? Did you want them going down there and poking around and screwing things up when we're so close to finishing what we started?"

"Don't you understand, Fiona? I wasn't worried about them finding anything in Peru, not at this point. The only concern I had was them finding some way to tie us directly to Downing's death."

"But if they went to Peru, they might have been able to figure out *why* we killed Downing."

Orson shook his head; she still didn't understand. "It doesn't matter if they figured out why we killed Downing, not unless they could actually prove we had him killed."

"But if they learned what Downing learned . . ."

"Fiona, we had to kill Downing because of *when* he learned what he did. If he had talked at that point, it could have interrupted the trials before we had the data we needed. But at this point . . . well, it just doesn't matter."

"I don't understand."

"I know you don't." Before she could say anything else, he said, "What's Nelson's status?"

"He's in bad shape, but unfortunately he's going to live. I wish that cop had killed him. I got him a good lawyer, but the lawyer says there's no doubt he'll be convicted. They have him on video trying to rob a liquor store, not to mention three eyewitnesses. If he talks, we have a major problem."

"He's not going to talk," Orson said. "Right now, the worst thing that will happen to him is he'll be convicted for attempted armed robbery, but if he tells what he did for us, he'll have to confess to multiple homicides. So he's not going to talk, but you need to get the word to him that as long as he keeps his mouth shut we'll do everything we can for him and we'll be there for him when he gets out of prison."

Fiona nodded.

"I wonder if DeMarco knows he was the target," Orson said.

"I don't see how he could," Fiona said. "He was just a customer in the store when someone tried to rob it, and he's never met Nelson."

"I hope you're right about that. What about Kelly?"

"He called me once from Peru and when I told him about Nelson, he about went nuts. But I haven't heard from him since and I don't have a clue what he's doing or where he's at."

"My God, you've fucked this up," Orson muttered. "Is Emma back from Peru?"

"I don't know. Kelly may have killed her."

"What about DeMarco?"

"After Nelson was shot, I told Hobson to put that private detective back on DeMarco. And we've still got the tap on DeMarco's landline. Anyway, according to Hobson, DeMarco's been mostly staying at home, making a lot of phone calls. It looks like he's trying to find out if Congressman Talbot is getting kickbacks from the Warwick Foundation."

"Then he's wasting his time," Orson said. He didn't say anything for a moment as he pondered everything. "Tell that detective to back off DeMarco and start watching Emma's house to see if she comes back from Peru. And keep trying to reach Kelly."

"I will, but I need to find somebody to replace Kelly and Nelson."

"Why?"

"Because right now Nelson's useless to us and Kelly's AWOL. And whether you want to or not, Orson, we may need to deal with DeMarco in the future, and right now I don't have anyone to do that."

"Do you have someone in mind?"

"There's a guy who provides on-site security for Lizzie Warwick. His name's Earl Lee. Lambert told me once that if we ever needed someone else like Kelly and Nelson, Lee would probably do. He's in Africa right now with Lizzie, and I'm going to fly him back here and talk to him."

Orson shook his head.

"What?" Fiona said. "Do you have a better idea?"

"No, unfortunately not." When he couldn't think of anything else to say—or anything else to do to make up for Fiona's debacle—he said, "Just leave, Fiona. And see if you can restrain yourself from trying to kill anyone else in the near future."

26

When DeMarco walked into Neil's high-tech sanctuary and saw Emma, he could see she was exhausted; she'd come straight from Dulles and obviously hadn't slept much on the long flight from Peru. At least he hoped she was just tired from the flight and that he wasn't seeing evidence of something related to her medical condition. Now he really did feel guilty for letting her take a trip he should have taken.

"Are you okay?" he asked. "You look beat."

Emma ignored the comment. "I think the Warwick Foundation is working with some pharmaceutical company to develop a new drug, and they're testing the drug on the people Lizzie Warwick is supposedly helping."

"You gotta be shittin' me," Neil said.

"How do you know that?" DeMarco said.

Emma explained that when Lizzie Warwick went to Peru four years ago to help the earthquake victims, René Lambert culled out of the population people without families and then relocated them to an area away from the disaster site. He set up a facility in which to house them and surgically implanted a small RFID chip in each person so test results could be tied unerringly to specific subjects; Emma found that particularly macabre. Then Lambert hired a medical technician—not a doctor—to administer the drugs and take samples and mail the samples back to a lab in the U.S. so the efficacy of the drug could be evaluated.

"Well, that sounds kind of . . . *slimy*, using people that way," DeMarco said, "but are they doing anything illegal?"

"I think they killed some of the test subjects," Emma said.

"Killed them? Do you mean with the drug they're testing?"

"I don't know. Nine people have died at the facility in Peru in the last four years, and the man running the place believes they died of natural causes. But the death rate seems high to me, and the deaths occurred in . . . in clusters. A short time ago three people died on the same night. And four years ago, six months after the testing started, one person died every month in a four-month period. That just seems too regular, like people dying to suit a schedule."

"Well, it seems to me you're jumping to a whole bunch of conclusions without any evidence," DeMarco said.

"I may be," Emma said, "but Phil Downing was killed for a reason. And that man followed me to Peru and aimed a gun at my head for a reason. And the only thing I can think of is that Warwick—or somebody—is trying to cover something up. Something serious, like murder."

"What drug are they testing?" DeMarco asked. "I mean, what are they trying to cure?"

"I don't know. The drugs are simply marked with a number. And the technician administering the drugs—he's a good man—doesn't have any idea what he's giving those people. He trusts Lambert. And you're right, Joe. Warwick may be doing something slimy, as you put it, but she may not actually be breaking any laws. I have no idea what the laws are for doing drug testing in a place like Peru. But I know *something* is wrong down there. I know it."

"From what I've heard about Lizzie Warwick," DeMarco said, "it's kind of hard to imagine she'd be involved in something like this."

"I know. I can't believe she'd do this either, but it appears as though she is. So we need facts. What did you get, Neil?"

Neil cleared his throat, usually an indicator that they were about to be treated to one of his long-winded, semidramatic presentations. "You asked me to find out if the Warwick Foundation is connected to a pharmaceutical company. The answer is . . . several."

"Several?" Emma said.

"Yes. The foundation's donation records were easy to access. Unlike contributions given to politicians, most people want it known that they're charitable folk giving money to help the unfortunate. And, of course, they get a tax break for their donations. Well, in the case of the Warwick Foundation, several pharmaceutical companies donate money and drugs to support Lizzie's overseas missions."

"What sort of drugs?"

"About what you'd expect. Painkillers, antibiotics, things to treat infection, dysentery, that sort of thing. And if the pharmaceutical company has ties to some company that makes bandages, splints, crutches, whatever, they donate those, too. Eight pharmaceutical companies have donated very generously to Warwick."

"Does one company appear to be more generous than the others?"

"Yes, Mulray Pharma. But they're not significantly more generous." Neil tapped his keyboard. "They donated ten percent more than Merck, five percent more than Pfizer. But other donors, like Gates and Buffett, have donated more than Mulray. Now, you have to keep in mind that these are the *recorded* donations. Somebody could have mailed Warwick a boxful of cash that wasn't reported. Or if a drug company is conducting legitimate trials, they could be funding the trials directly and the money wouldn't pass through Warwick."

Emma rubbed her hand over her face as if trying to scrub away her fatigue. "The man who runs the Warwick facility in Peru told me he mails bio samples to a lab in Delaware, and I saw a mailing label addressed to Delaware, to a company called Biomed something, Inc. I can't remember the second word."

The fact that Emma couldn't remember was an indicator of how tired she was.

Neil turned to his computer and tapped on a keyboard; Google made Neil's job even easier. "Biomed Futures, Inc.," he said, "is located in Smyrna, Delaware, not far from Mulray Pharma's headquarters in Wilmington. But Celgene, Incyte, Agilent, and AstraZeneca all have offices in Delaware, and since the state's the size of a postage stamp, they're all within a short drive of the lab. I'll do some more digging."

"What about you, Joe?" Emma said. "What did you find out about Congressman Talbot and his aide?"

"In the four days you've been gone, I've found zip," DeMarco said. "The bill that Hobson, Downing, and Linger were planning to talk about the night Downing died was a massive foreign aid bill, and it included aid for countries where Lizzie Warwick had operated in the past. But there wasn't anything in the bill that was Warwick-specific; it was just your generic foreign aid bill. And because the bill was initiated by the Democrats, naturally all the Republicans were going to vote against it. The only thing that made Talbot different from the other sixteen Republicans on the House Foreign Affairs Committee was that two years ago, he was the ranking Republican member."

"Great," Emma said. "Another dead end."

"Yeah, but that conference call still smells wrong," DeMarco said. "What I mean is, there was no reason for it. The bill was going to pass whether Talbot voted for it or not, so I still find it suspicious that Hobson would set up a call with Linger when Congress was out of session and at the exact time Kincaid was in the office with Downing. But the bottom line is, I didn't find anything to prove Linger or Talbot were involved in some kind of conspiracy with Hobson or Lizzie Warwick."

"Neil," Emma said, "when you figure out which pharmaceutical company runs that lab in Delaware, see if you can tie Congressman Talbot to the company."

Neil made a note on a Post-it sticker and pasted the note on one of the three monitors on his desk.

"And what about the man with two passports I encountered in Peru?" Emma asked. "What did you find out about him?"

"I haven't made a lot of progress on him yet," Neil said. "The two numbers he called from the sat phone went to untraceable, prepaid cell phones, so I don't know who owns the phones. I did call the numbers. One went to voice mail, but the voice mail didn't identify who received the call, not even a first name. The second number was answered by a woman, but she wouldn't identify herself. She just said I had called the wrong number and hung up. Maybe she's the guy's girlfriend, I don't know."

"But what did you find out about the man himself? Kelly, Shaw, whoever the hell he is."

"Well, nothing yet. I've been working mostly on the pharmaceutical company question."

"You need to get moving on this thing!" Emma snapped. "I need to know everything you can find out about everyone associated with Lizzie Warwick's foundation. I need to know what drug company is hooked in with Warwick, and I definitely need to know about the man I killed in Peru. So step up, Neil! Work all night if you have to."

Neil looked sheepish and said, "Okay, I'll get right on it."

DeMarco couldn't believe it. If he had told Neil to work all night, Neil would have laughed in his face. He was dying to know what kind of hold Emma had over the man.

Emma stood up. "I need to go home and get some sleep—I'm so tired I can't think straight. We'll regroup after Neil gets more data and then figure out the next step."

"Hold on," DeMarco said. "We've got another problem."

"What's that?" Emma said.

"You said the guy you killed in Peru left D.C. two hours after you did. How did he know where you were going?"

"I thought about that," Emma said. "You must have tripped an alarm when you went to see Kincaid in prison. Or maybe you tripped it when you went to see Hobson, and somebody started following you."

"And then what?" DeMarco said. "They started following every person I came in contact with? And if that guy followed you to the airport, the most he would have been able to figure out is that you were flying to Lima. How did he know you were going to Pinchollo?"

"My brain must be turning to mush," Emma said. "Neil, have Bobby see if my phones or Joe's are tapped or if we have bugs installed in our houses."

Bobby was a young man who worked for Neil. He had a black belt in computer hacking, but he also installed listening devices for Neil when Neil wanted to bug somebody, like the other tenants in his building. Bobby, consequently, had the skills and equipment to tell if anyone was monitoring DeMarco's and Emma's conversations.

"And you and I," Emma said to DeMarco, "need to start watching our backsides to see if we're being tailed."

———◆◆◆———

Emma and DeMarco left Neil's office together, and as they were walking back to their cars, DeMarco said, "By the way, you weren't the only one who was almost killed," and he told her about the attempted robbery in the liquor store and how the robber's bullet had missed his head by about six inches. He concluded with, "If I hadn't decided to go look at the Absolut, I would have been standing right in front of that bullet."

Emma stopped walking. "Who was the robber?"

"I don't know. Some guy in a ski mask. An ambulance carted him off, and he's probably dead by now."

"Where did this happen? Which liquor store?"

"The ABC store on Harrison in Arlington. Why are you . . .?"

Emma took her cell phone off her belt, called Neil, and told him to find out everything he could about the man who tried to rob the liquor store. She hung up before Neil could say anything.

"What?" DeMarco said. "You think that guy was in the store to kill me?"

"I don't know, but I don't like coincidences. And if you wanted to kill somebody who was poking into what happened to Phil Downing but you didn't want anybody to know *why* the person was killed, killing him in a liquor store robbery would provide pretty good cover."

"I can't believe the way your mind works sometimes," DeMarco said.

When Emma arrived home, Christine said, "Oh, my God. Look at you. You look awful."

"I'm just tired. I haven't slept in—"

"You've *got* to take care of yourself!" Christine said. "If you get run-down, you could . . ." Christine began to cry.

Emma took her into her arms and said, "Christine, you have to stop worrying about me. I'm all right. I'm the same as I was before."

And then a thought occurred to her. Would she have survived the cancer if some drug company hadn't experimented on human beings to develop the drugs? Most likely not.

27

---◆◆◆---

Keeping one hand on the hospital bed for support, Kelly took a few tentative steps. His right hip hurt like a bastard and there were bruises all over his torso, but at least he could walk. He also had a headache from the concussion he'd suffered when his head hit a rock, but the doctor said the headache would probably go away in a few days. The major problem was that his left arm was useless. His left ulna was broken, his forearm was in a soft cast, and his left shoulder had been dislocated.

He was one lucky son of a bitch.

He didn't know how long he'd remained unconscious after the fall, but when he first woke up, it felt like every bone in his body was broken. To make matters worse, the ledge he was lying on was so narrow that if he moved and lost his balance, he'd roll off and plummet into the ravine. He could see his car about a hundred yards below him—Emma must have pushed it off the road—but he couldn't see any way that he was going to be able to climb back up to the road in the condition he was in. He knew he had to do something, though; if he didn't, he'd die of exposure or internal injuries.

He lay there thinking about what to do next, thinking about Nelson, thinking about the pain, thinking how that bitch had completely surprised him. It was humiliating the way she took him out.

His eyes were closed when a rope hit his chest, and when he opened them he saw a little Peruvian guy climbing down the rope toward him. When the little guy reached him, Kelly couldn't understand him, but based on the way he gestured, Kelly understood he was going to leave him where he was and go for help. He gave Kelly some water and threw a blanket over him, then climbed back up the rope.

An hour later, half a dozen little Peruvian guys appeared on the road above the ravine. They climbed down, put him on a makeshift stretcher, and used ropes to pull him up to the roadway. He must have passed out after that because when he woke up again he found himself in a small clinic in Chivay, where he was pumped full of fluids and antibiotics and his left forearm was put in a cast. It wasn't until the following day that he recovered enough to get out of bed.

The good news was that he had his wallet and it was stuffed with cash. The bad news was he didn't have a passport. His passports—his real one and the one made out in the name of Shaw—had been in his knapsack and the knapsack had been in the Explorer, which was now a pile of scrap metal balanced precariously on a steep hillside hundreds of feet below the road. If his left arm had been functional, he would have paid someone to drive him back to the crash site and would have then rappelled down and retrieved his passports. With a broken arm and a dislocated shoulder, that was problematic. He could probably find some young guy willing to risk his life for money and get the guy to retrieve his knapsack for him. That could create another issue, however. If the guy saw the rifle in the Explorer and discovered that Kelly had two passports with the same photo but different names, he might decide to involve the Peruvian cops. Right now everyone assumed he was just a bad driver who had driven off the road, and he thought it best to leave things standing the way they were.

He paid a man to drive him to Arequipa and called Fiona, telling her what had happened and to get him a passport so he could fly out of the country. He suggested that Hobson throw money at the right bureaucrat and maybe somebody at the U.S. Consulate in Lima would be able to help. When he asked Fiona about Nelson's condition, she said that she didn't know any more than she'd told him the last time they talked: that Nelson had been shot and was recovering in a hospital. Kelly suspected she was lying and keeping things from him, and if she was, he was gonna bitch-slap her the next time he saw her. He only needed one arm to do that.

"I finally heard from Kelly," Fiona said. "He didn't contact me earlier because he was in a hospital."

"In a hospital?" Orson said.

"Yeah. Emma almost killed him."

Orson was astounded. "*She* almost killed *him*?" he said. "How in the world . . ."

"He said she ran him over with her car."

"How did he allow *that* to happen?"

"He didn't say."

Orson shook his head, still amazed that a woman had almost killed Kelly. "So what did she do in Peru? What did she learn?"

"I don't know. She took Kelly out before he could question her, and all Kelly knows is she stayed overnight at the care center."

"Is she back from Peru?"

"Yes. I pulled that private detective off DeMarco like you told me, and he's been watching her house."

Fiona started to say something else, but Orson raised a hand to silence her as he mulled over everything she had told him. Finally, he said, "I suppose the worst-case scenario is she figured out that we're doing clinical trials in Peru. That's regrettable, but at this point, not truly harmful."

"You don't know that," Fiona said.

"Yes I do," Orson said. "But when Kelly gets back I want him to watch her instead of that detective. And I mean *watch* her, Fiona, not kill her."

"I don't think Kelly's going to be much help. The only thing he cares about right now is Nelson."

"Did you talk to that man you mentioned, that fellow Lee?"

"Not yet. He's flying back from Uganda today. I'll see him tonight."

28

Emma slept for twelve hours after she returned home from Peru. When she woke up, Christine said that DeMarco had called while she was sleeping and wanted her to call him back as soon as possible.

"Bobby found something at my place," DeMarco said.

That meant that Neil's man Bobby had found a bug either in DeMarco's house or connected to his landline.

"He'll be at your place this morning," DeMarco added.

"I'll talk to you later," Emma said.

While waiting for Bobby, Emma ate a breakfast consisting of black coffee and plain yogurt mixed with strawberries and chatted briefly with Christine before Christine left for work. Emma was glad she was going to work; she wanted her out of the house when Bobby arrived to look for listening devices.

Bobby was a slim, intense young black man who wore his hair in dreadlocks; he was smart as a whip and he rarely spoke. He spent an hour walking through Emma's house with a couple of electronic gizmos and finally declared it bug-free. He told her DeMarco had a voice-activated recorder connected to his landline.

"Is his cell phone being monitored?" Emma asked.

"I don't think so," Bobby said. "I had him make a long call on his cell so I could see if anybody intercepted the call, and nobody did. So either his cell's not being monitored or it's not being monitored on a full-time basis."

"What did you do with the recorder connected to his landline?" Emma asked him.

"Joe told me to leave it where it was."

"Good," Emma said. They might want to say something on DeMarco's phone to intentionally mislead whoever was bugging it. For once, DeMarco was using his head.

She thanked Bobby, and after he left, she sent a text message to DeMarco's cell phone saying: *See U at N's.*

As she backed her car out of the garage, she noticed a gray sedan parked on her street, half a block away. A block later, she saw the same sedan in her rearview mirror. She made a couple of unnecessary turns to confirm the sedan was following her and then spent the next ten minutes losing whoever was shadowing her. She still arrived at Neil's place before DeMarco, even though he lived closer to Neil's than she did.

"Did anyone follow you here?" she asked DeMarco when he arrived.

"No. That's what took me so long. I drove around for quite a while to make sure I wasn't being tailed."

"Well, somebody was following me," Emma said.

"Ah, shit," Neil said. "Did they follow you here?"

"Of course not," Emma said.

"Well, that's good," Neil said. "I don't need—"

"Just get on with it, Neil," Emma said. "Tell us what you've learned."

"First," Neil said, "the lab in Delaware—Biomed Futures, Inc.—is owned by Mulray Pharma. I got that from property tax records but I don't have a clue what they do inside the place.

"I could find no connection between Mulray Pharma and the Warwick Foundation other than the fact that Mulray is one of several pharmaceutical companies that donates to Warwick. Nor did I learn anything about Lizzie Warwick to make me think she is anything other than what she appears to be. I did, however, discover a number of interesting things about the people who work for Lizzie."

Neil opened a file folder lying on his desk. "Let's start with the man who tried to rob the liquor store. He isn't your average crackhead stickup guy. His name is Randal Nelson and he's an ex-army Ranger. He's also ex-Delta."

"Delta?" Emma said.

"Yeah. Then he got out of the army and turned merc and went to work for a private security outfit called Romar-Slade. He made the news a few years ago when he was arrested in Afghanistan for killing some kids while he was protecting an Afghani politician, then all the charges against him were dismissed and he resigned from the security company. But that's not the big news. Before he decided to start robbing liquor stores, he was working for Lizzie Warwick. He and his partner, a guy named Kelly—"

"Kelly? Is he the man . . ."

"Yep," Neil said. "The guy you killed in Peru. His real name is James Kelly. Shaw must be an alias he uses. Anyway, Kelly and Nelson have a security company and provide security for Warwick. That's all aboveboard. Their company's legitimate, they pay their taxes, and they have half a dozen employees on their payroll, all involved in security work for Warwick. What's not aboveboard is that these two guys have a hundred-and-fifty-acre spread in Montana worth one point eight million. They bought it about the same time they signed on with Warwick and they don't have a mortgage on the place. Now, I suppose these two ex–army sergeants could have saved their pennies and invested wisely and that's how they were able to afford the property. A more likely scenario is somebody gave them a shopping bag full of greenbacks about the time they went to work for Saint Lizzie. Whatever the case, Nelson is not a guy who should have been robbing a liquor store, and he's definitely connected to Warwick and the guy you met in Peru."

"Excellent, Neil," Emma said—and DeMarco thought that sounded like *Good dog.*

"Next we have Monsieur René Lambert. By the way, it wasn't easy for me to get this information. Fortunately, I have a . . . What would you call it? A reciprocal arrangement with a gentleman in Marseille. He and I—"

"Get to the point, Neil," Emma said.

Bad dog.

"Six years ago, Dr. Lambert was in dire financial straits. He was forced to sell his chalet in Grenoble to pay down some of his debt, but that only covered about a third of what he owed. Now, I don't know how bankruptcy works in France, but it appears to me that he was headed in that direction. Then, voila, the same year he teams up with Lizzie Warwick, he's able to pay off all his creditors, buy back the place in Grenoble, and purchase a number of pricey things for his wife and daughters."

"So where's the money coming from?" Emma asked.

"An account in the French Antilles, but neither I nor my friend in Marseille could figure out who owns the Antilles account. Whoever's funding Dr. Lambert is very skillful at covering up the money trail— and to cover it up from *moi* . . . Well, they're good."

"Then there's Mr. Hobson," Neil said. "Well, Mr. Hobson is actually ex-*Colonel* Hobson. Eleven years ago, he was incarcerated at the federal penitentiary in Leavenworth for trying to steal approximately half a million dollars from the United States Army, but less than a month after he's released from prison, he's managing the Warwick Foundation for Lizzie Warwick."

"Lizzie hired an ex-con?" DeMarco said.

Neil nodded. "I don't know if she knew he was an ex-con but, yes, she did. I would have assumed that she would have done some sort

of background check on the man that's handling all the money passing through her foundation, but maybe not. Or maybe she figured
Hobson had paid his debt to society and she was willing to give him
another chance. I don't know. But, as in the case of Dr. Lambert, I
can't figure out where Hobson's money is coming from. He gets no
salary from Warwick—he apparently donates his time—yet this man,
who has no pension from the army, lives in a respectable apartment
building and drives a respectable car. He's not filthy rich like Lambert,
but he has some source of income and he's not paying taxes on it. You
could sic the IRS on him if you wanted to."

DeMarco wondered if he should sic the IRS on Neil; he was fairly
certain a large portion of his income wasn't reported to the taxman, either.

"What about Congressman Talbot?" Emma asked. "Could you
link him to Mulray Pharma?"

"In a way," Neil said. "You remember a few years ago when everybody was making a big stink about how you could get drugs cheaper
in Canada than in the U.S.? When that issue arose, drug companies,
including Mulray Pharma, began throwing money at politicians to
maintain the status quo, and Congressman Talbot was one of those
politicians. Talbot is not only on the House Foreign Affairs Committee, but he's also on the health subcommittee. Talbot wasn't singled
out, however. The pharmaceutical companies were throwing money
at everyone, Republicans and Democrats, and Talbot was just one of
them. What this means is that if somebody wanted Talbot's chief of
staff to participate in a conference call related to something Mulray
Pharma cared about, Talbot might agree to do a favor for a generous
contributor—but I didn't find anything that tied Talbot to Mulray
Pharma doing clinical trials in Peru, or anything else that makes me
think he conspired in Downing's death."

"This is a goddamn mess," DeMarco said. "We need to get somebody official investigating. Justice, FDA, FBI—somebody who can
unravel all this shit."

"And what would we tell them?" Emma snapped. "That the War-wick Foundation and Mulray Pharma are giving a few poor people drugs that appear to be keeping them healthy and, by the way, we have no proof they're doing anything illegal?"

"So what do you wanna do?"

No one followed Emma home from Neil's office, and there was no gray sedan parked on her block.

Emma decided to make a tour of her yard. She was fanati-cal about her yard. She hired gardeners, consulted with experts whenever her lawn and plants appeared unhealthy, and spent a lot of time on her hands and knees pulling noxious weeds. Most people looking at her yard considered it a botanical marvel; Emma's opinion was quite the opposite. Due to her illness, she hadn't been able to give her plants the attention they deserved the last six months, and she saw signs of neglect everywhere she looked.

As she walked about, turning over the occasional leaf to inspect for plant-nibbling pests, she made mental notes about all the work that needed to be done. She also thought about everything she had learned in Peru and what Neil had told her. She didn't know what it all meant, but one thing she knew for sure: she and DeMarco were lucky to be alive. But what should they do next? DeMarco, for once, was right. They needed to get some law enforcement agency engaged in this, somebody who could unsnarl the legal issues associated with doing clinical trials in foreign countries and who had the means to determine if murder had occurred in Peru as she believed. But how could she get a law enforcement agency involved?

She made a second tour of her yard as she pondered this question. My God! Was that moss in her lawn?

She went back inside the house and called the gardening service she used and rattled off a list of things she wanted accomplished in the next week. Then she made a second call.

———◆———

"Unger called me," Hobson said.

"Who the hell's Unger?" Fiona said. She was in no mood for Hobson.

"He's the private detective Kelly made me hire to watch DeMarco. And he was following Emma, like you told me to have him do. Anyway, Emma made him."

"Made him? What does that mean?"

"It means he was following her and she figured out he was following her, and then she lost him. But now she knows that somebody's watching her."

Fiona squeezed the phone so hard she was surprised she didn't leave indentations in the plastic. It seemed like everything she did lately turned to shit.

"What do you want me to do?" Hobson asked.

"I want you to shut up so I can think."

She really wanted to know what Emma was doing, but if she was capable of almost killing Kelly, she was probably good enough to catch the PI and make him tell her who he was working for. So what should she do? Hire somebody else to follow Emma? She could wait until Earl Lee arrived from Africa and have him start following Emma, but Lee hadn't agreed to work for her yet and she had no idea how capable he was. Maybe it was time to back off on Emma and DeMarco. Orson had said that Emma couldn't have learned anything in Peru that would disrupt their plans at this point. She wasn't sure why he was so confident; all she could do was hope that he was right.

"Tell Unger his services are no longer required," Fiona said. "Give him a fat bonus and then tell him if he ever talks about what he did for us, something bad will happen to him. Oh, and tell him to take the tap off DeMarco's phone, and to make sure he's not caught when he does."

29

Celia Montoya worked for the *Washington Post,* and six months ago she published a series of articles that shined a harsh light on government mismanagement and corporate greed.

The Department of Veterans Affairs had awarded a lucrative contract to a company that ran assisted living facilities for veterans throughout the country. Montoya discovered that while the company and its shareholders were making record profits, the veterans —most of whom had devastating, permanent injuries incurred in the line of duty—were receiving substandard care and living in abysmal conditions in understaffed facilities. The company claimed Montoya grossly exaggerated conditions in their facilities—although the veterans and their families backed up the reporter—and the VA was more interested in covering up its own incompetence than in correcting the situation. And then Congress did what it always did: the politicians held a few televised hearings so they could show how *outraged* they all were, but didn't pass new laws to prevent future abuses, as new laws might adversely affect the economy—meaning the income of those folks who contributed most heavily to the politicians' campaigns. In the end, the only thing that happened was that conditions in the facilities temporarily improved and a few low-level scapegoats lost their jobs, but had it not been for Montoya, not even that would have happened.

Celia Montoya jousted at windmills—and that's what Emma liked about her.

Emma called Montoya, but the reporter wasn't in her office so she left a message on her voice mail. "How would you like to earn a Pulitzer?" Emma said.

———————◆◆◆———————

Emma met Celia Montoya at an umbrella-covered table on the grounds of the U.S. Botanic Garden. The garden is adjacent to the U.S. Capitol and has a magnificent Lord and Burnham greenhouse containing over twenty thousand plants. The garden's Web site says it's operated and maintained by Congress—which, of course, it isn't. Congress couldn't operate and maintain a hot dog stand. The architect of the Capitol is actually the person responsible for the garden, and although Emma didn't know who the current architect was, she assumed this person was not a politician and therefore capable of performing some useful function. After she talked to the reporter, Emma planned to walk through the conservatory and see what new things were growing.

Montoya was in her early thirties. She was slim and pretty and seemed to vibrate with energy; her intelligence was palpable. Emma quickly told her about her trip to Peru and how Mulray Pharma appeared to be working in concert with the Warwick Foundation to test drugs on disaster victims.

"The care center in Peru," Emma said, "is located in an illogically remote place and being operated at great expense. Mulray is obviously trying to hide whatever they're doing there, and they don't care about the money they're spending because whatever they're doing is going to make them a lot more money."

Montoya shook her head. "Look. I know a couple journalists who have written about U.S. pharmaceutical companies doing clinical trials abroad. The companies go to places where the standard of living is deplorable and pay people a couple bucks a day to be guinea pigs, and the follow-up on what happens to these people is nonexistent. But the companies aren't doing anything illegal. Unethical maybe, but not illegal. So it sounds to me like what's going on in Peru is just more of the same except that Warwick is assisting the drug company, which isn't illegal either. Lizzie Warwick probably thinks Mulray Pharma is actually helping people, and maybe they are."

"Some of the people at the care center in Peru have been killed," Emma said.

"Killed!" Montoya said. "Do you mean by the drugs they were given?"

"I'm not sure," Emma said.

"Then what makes you think . . ."

Emma told Montoya the same thing she told DeMarco. "Nine out of fifty-five people have died at the Warwick Care Center in Peru since it was established four years ago, and that seems to me to be an abnormally high death rate. More startling is the fact that people have died at what appear to be regular intervals, and three people all died on the same night. Those deaths need to be explained."

She could see that Montoya was not convinced, but she plowed ahead.

"And I suspect that Warwick and Mulray Pharma may be doing the same thing in other countries. Lizzie Warwick teamed up with René Lambert five years ago, and in that time she's conducted relief operations in Uganda, Pakistan, and Indonesia as well as Peru. So what I would like you to do is confirm what I've told you about the care center in Peru and see if the same thing is going on in other places. I think if you wrote a story about an American drug company using a relief organization to help test their drugs on disaster victims *someone* will be compelled to investigate. Certainly the Peruvian government will feel some obligation, and based on what I discovered there, maybe a U.S. law enforcement agency will get involved as well. If nothing else, a story in the *Washington Post* will put Mulray Pharma and Warwick on the defensive and force them to explain what they're doing."

"I don't think so," Montoya said. "Like I told you, the story's been done before. If you had some evidence that they were doing something criminal . . ."

Emma didn't want to tell Montoya about Kelly—the fact that she had killed him in Peru—but she could see that she was going to have to.

"Celia, what I'm going to tell you next is off the record. It has to be off the record because if you write about this I could go to jail or, at a minimum, be in a lot of legal hot water."

"What are you talking about?"

"A man working for Warwick followed me when I went to Peru. He set up a roadblock on a remote mountain road, pulled a gun on me, and ordered me from my car. I think he was planning to kill me. I'm sure he was. And another man working for Warwick tried to kill an associate of mine."

"You can't be serious."

Emma then explained everything. How she had killed Kelly; how Nelson, Kelly's partner, tried to kill DeMarco in a fake liquor store robbery; and how Phil Downing was killed and Brian Kincaid most likely framed for his murder.

When she finished speaking, Montoya said, "I can understand how all those things would make you suspicious, but you don't have any hard evidence. I mean, you don't really know why Nelson was in that liquor store and . . ."

"He sure as hell didn't have any motive for committing robbery," Emma said.

". . . and all Kelly did was point a gun at you, and you don't really know why he did that either."

"He was going to kill me," Emma said. Still seeing that Montoya wasn't convinced, she added, "Look, I know I can't substantiate everything I suspect, and that's why I need your help. Something's wrong with Warwick. You must see that."

When Montoya shook her head, Emma placed her hand on the young woman's forearm. "Celia, the possibility is very real that Warwick and Mulray have killed to test a new drug. And there's no doubt in my mind that they're willing to kill people to cover up what they're doing. Don't you want to do something about that?"

"Okay," Montoya finally said. "Start over. I need names, dates—all the facts you have."

30

As soon as Kelly got off the plane from Peru, he called Fiona and asked about Nelson's condition and what she was doing to help him.

"Kelly, you need to understand that there really isn't much that can be done for Nelson," Fiona said. "I got him a good lawyer, but he's going to jail. He was taped during the commission of an armed robbery, he tried to shoot a cop, and there were three eyewitnesses, one of them being DeMarco. But the lawyer says that because of his condition, they probably won't keep him in jail for very long."

"What are you talking about? His condition?"

Fiona hesitated. "He's paralyzed from the waist down. One of the bullets damaged his spinal cord."

"Aw, Jesus," Kelly said. He felt like he was going to throw up.

"Yeah, I know," Fiona said, trying to sound sympathetic. "But like I said, the good news is that because he's paralyzed they'll probably give him a shorter prison sentence."

"The good news? Did you say *the good news*?" Kelly screamed.

"Calm down. We're on your side, and we want to help. And if Nelson keeps his mouth shut, we'll do everything we can for him. Special facilities, therapy, whatever. *If* he keeps his mouth shut."

Kelly, still reeling from the news of Nelson being paralyzed, said, "Fiona, if anything happens to Nelson while he's in the hospital—an infection, a blood clot, fucking anything—if he dies, I'm gonna kill you."

"Nothing's going to happen to him, but you have to get a grip on yourself because I may need you to deal with some of the fallout from all this. DeMarco's still alive and Emma has returned from Peru, and I don't know what the hell they're doing. So—"

"What hospital is Nelson in?"

"Arlington Hospital."

"Who's his lawyer?"

Fiona didn't respond immediately.

"Fiona, give me the name of his lawyer or I'm going to beat you so bad *you'll* need therapy."

"His name is Dennis Conroy. His office is on Connecticut Avenue in the District. But you should stay away from him."

Kelly hung up.

Kelly limped through the terminal as fast as he could and headed for the long-term parking lot, where he had parked his car when he'd followed Emma to the airport. He needed to get to the hospital right away and see how bad Nelson was hurt. Maybe Fiona was wrong about Nelson's condition—maybe the paralysis was temporary. Whatever the case, he needed to see Nelson and let him know that he was there for him.

He didn't know where Arlington Hospital was located, but he had a Garmin GPS in his car, and he impatiently tapped the screen on the Garmin until he found the address. It seemed to take forever for the annoying female voice to tell him to "drive to the highlighted route." He backed his car out of the parking space, his tires squealing, and headed toward the booth to pay his parking fee, and because he was driving so fast he almost hit another car. As he waited for the other car to get out of his way, he took a deep breath and closed his eyes for a moment. Fiona was right—he needed to get a grip on himself.

Fiona was probably right about something else, too: Nelson was going to be convicted for armed robbery and attempted murder. This meant that he might have to spring Nelson from the hospital, assuming Nelson was well enough to be moved. That being the case, he needed to take his time and get all the facts he could before going to the hospital. Being seen with Nelson wouldn't be smart until he had a plan.

He needed to talk to Nelson's lawyer.

Dennis Conroy was a partner in a law firm that employed forty other lawyers and paralegals, and Kelly learned from the firm's Web site that he had successfully defended a number of notorious people. Most of his clients were white-collar criminals, however; defending liquor store robbers was not something he normally did.

Conroy parked his Lexus in an underground garage in the same building that housed his law firm. His name was on the parking place; there was a red star next to his name. When he stepped from his car, Kelly could see that he was an unimpressive-looking white man with a balding head and a protruding belly, but he got the impression from the way Conroy carried himself that the lawyer was confident, arrogant, and normally quite pleased with himself. Kelly exited his vehicle and caught up to him before he reached the garage elevators.

"Mr. Conroy," Kelly said.

Conroy turned and looked at Kelly, and the sight of a large black man walking toward him seemed to make him nervous, even though Kelly had a cast on one arm and was limping. "Yes, what can I do for you?" Conroy said.

Kelly didn't answer until he was close enough to Conroy to touch him. "You're representing a man named Nelson. I'm Nelson's friend and business partner, and I need to know what kind of shape he's in, how he's being guarded, what his prospects are if he goes to court. All that sort of stuff."

"I can't talk to you about a client," Conroy said, "even if he is your business partner."

Kelly's right arm—his good arm—moved like a cobra striking as he hit Conroy in the throat with two fingers. Conroy dropped his expensive briefcase, fell to his knees, clutched his throat with both hands, and began to gag. Kelly hoped he hadn't crushed the man's larynx. It wouldn't be good for Nelson to have a lawyer who couldn't speak.

Kelly reached down and, with one arm, yanked Conroy to his feet and dragged him over to a stairwell, where there was less chance they'd be disturbed. He opened the stairwell door, shoved Conroy inside, then propped him up against a wall.

"Listen to me closely, Dennis," Kelly said. "You're going to tell me what I want to know and you're going to do whatever I tell you. If you don't, I'll kill you and then I'll deal with Nelson's *new* lawyer. Now, you're probably thinking that as soon as I leave, you'll call the cops and tell them I assaulted you. But you need to think very hard before you do that. I know you were given a lot of money to defend Nelson, and you must have known at the time you agreed to represent him that he wasn't your typical stickup guy. You must have known that you were dealing with serious people, serious people with serious problems, or they wouldn't have hired you. I represent those people, Dennis, and when I say I'll kill you, I'm not bluffing. Now tell me what I want to know."

Conroy told him that Nelson was paralyzed from the waist down and his condition was permanent—he would never walk again. Kelly momentarily closed his eyes when he heard this. Conroy went on to say that if Nelson hadn't been in such good physical shape he would never have survived the two gunshot wounds.

"His doctor told me that it'll be at least a month before he'll be able to use a wheelchair, and when he is, he'll be taken to court and arraigned. I've urged him to plead guilty, because there's no way he's going to be found innocent if he goes to trial. If he pleads guilty, he'll do less jail time than if he fights the system. And because he doesn't have any priors and with his injuries . . . Well, the fact is, the State of Virginia would prefer not to put a cripple in jail; it's a pain in the ass for the jailers, and expensive, too. So if he pleads guilty, I might even be able to get him a suspended sentence so he doesn't do any time in prison."

"What if he doesn't plead guilty?"

The lawyer shrugged. "I can probably get him out on bail, then he'll go to trial in five or six months and be found guilty."

"How's he being guarded?"

"Look, I can't be a party to an escape attempt. I could go to jail or be disbarred."

"Would you rather be dead or disbarred?"

"There's a cop outside his door, and one will remain there until he can be moved to a jail cell. That's the procedure."

"Just one cop?"

"Yes. I guess they figure that's all that's necessary since he can't walk."

"I want to talk to him on the phone. Can he talk?"

"Yes. He's weak but he can talk."

"Do they frisk you when you go in to see him?"

"Yes. To make sure I'm not bringing him a weapon."

"Do they take away your cell phone?"

"No."

"Good. Give me your cell phone number. I want you to go see Nelson now, and I'll call him on your cell phone in half an hour."

"I can't go today. My schedule's completely full."

Kelly shook his head. "I can see that you and I still aren't communicating," he said—and hit Conroy in the solar plexus.

A solid blow to the solar plexus makes it difficult to breathe—in fact, a person hit in that location as hard as Kelly hit Conroy thinks he'll never breathe again. As Conroy struggled to get air into his lungs, Kelly placed his right hand gently on the attorney's shoulder and said, "Dennis, Nelson has become your number one priority. It's like he's the only client you have and you will drop everything else you're doing and give his case your undivided attention. Now do we understand each other?"

———— ✦ ————

Kelly's phone call with Nelson was brief. Nelson was able to talk, but he was so traumatized by what had happened to him that he seemed unable to concentrate. At one point he started crying. Kelly had never seen Nelson cry in his life, and the sound of him sobbing almost broke his heart. He had no doubt Nelson was thinking about suicide. He would be if he were in Nelson's condition.

Kelly told him that somehow, someway, he was going to get him out. "Just get strong, strong enough so we can move if we need to."

Nelson was silent for a moment, then softly said, "Hooah."

"Hooah," Kelly said, his voice catching when he said the word.

31

Earl Lee had been ordered by Bill Hobson to come to Philadelphia, and that's whom Lee thought he'd be meeting. He was surprised when he opened his hotel room door and saw a woman standing there.

"May I come in, Earl?" Fiona said.

"I don't know. Who are you? And how do you know my name?"

"I'm the person who told Hobson to fly you here from Africa," Fiona said. "Now may I come in?"

Lee stepped aside, and Fiona entered the room.

"So what's going on?" Lee asked.

Fiona didn't answer as she examined him. He was a tall, muscular man wearing a tight-fitting olive-green T-shirt and blue jeans. He had blond stubble on his cheeks and chin, and more blond stubble on his closely shaved head. She noticed that unlike Kelly and Nelson, he hadn't kept himself in top shape; there was a ring of fat expanding his waistline. She also didn't see in his eyes the intelligence she saw in Kelly's—but maybe that was a good thing.

Fiona sat down in the only chair in the room and gestured for Lee to sit on the bed. He hesitated for a moment, then complied.

"Earl," she said, "let me explain a few things to you. Bill Hobson doesn't work for Lizzie Warwick; he works for me. Kelly and Nelson don't work for the Warwick Foundation, either. They also work for me. For that matter, the whole time you've been providing protection for Lizzie, you've really been working for me, too."

It took a few seconds for Lee to digest all that. "What do you want?"

"Kelly and Nelson have been doing special assignments for me for the last five years, but Nelson's been injured and Kelly's become a loose cannon. I need a man to replace them."

"What kind of special assignments?"

Fiona didn't have the time or the inclination to beat around the bush. "They kill people for me."

Lee, instead of being shocked, smiled. "I always knew those two pricks were doing more than just delivering supplies to Lizzie. So is that what you want me to do? Kill somebody for you?"

"Maybe. Right now things are kind of fluid, but I may need Kelly and Nelson taken out." Lee elevated an eyebrow in surprise when he heard that. "I may also need at least two other people killed—a man and a woman who have become a problem. Are you interested?"

"I don't know. What's in it for me?"

"You'll continue to receive your salary from Kelly's company, the same salary they've been paying you to protect Lizzie Warwick and René Lambert. In addition, I'll give you two hundred grand up front and I'll pay you fifty thousand for every person I need you to eliminate."

"You're shittin' me!" Lee said. Then, realizing he should be negotiating, he said, "Is that how much you've been paying Kelly and Nelson?"

"That's none of your business. Now, do you want the job or not?"

"How do I know this isn't some kind of setup?"

Fiona laughed. "A setup? What do you think, Earl? Do you think I'm a cop and I flew you all the way from Uganda so I could trap you in some kind of murder-for-hire sting?"

"I don't know," Lee said.

"Earl, you don't have to take the job. You can walk away, right now, no hard feelings. You can fly back to Africa tomorrow and continue to be Lizzie's bodyguard. But if you talk to anybody about the discussion we just had, I'll hire somebody to kill you. I have at my disposal an incredible amount of money—more money than you can possibly imagine—and I'm sure I can find somebody to take care of you if you become a problem."

Lee just looked at her for a moment, then stood up and walked over to a window. From the window, he could see planes landing at the Philadelphia airport, and when he looked down, he saw a guy park a Hummer in front of the hotel's entrance. He'd always wanted a Hummer; he thought they were the coolest cars ever made. He turned back to face Fiona.

"I want three hundred grand up front."

"Fine," Fiona said—like an extra hundred thousand dollars was nothing. He should have asked for half a million.

"But I gotta tell you that Kelly and Nelson aren't going to be easy to kill. I may need help."

"No. You're on your own. We—"

"Who's *we*?"

"Never mind that. *I* can't afford to have more people involved in this. And they won't be as hard to kill as you might think. Nelson's been shot and is paralyzed from the waist down, and Kelly's so worried about Nelson that his head isn't screwed on right."

"When do I get the money?"

"Stay in this room tonight and tomorrow morning Hobson will bring it to you—but he won't know why you're getting it. At some point in the future, you may need to take care of Hobson, too." She stood up to leave. "I want you in D.C. by tomorrow afternoon. If I need you to do something, that's probably where it'll happen. So get a room there and be prepared to move on a moment's notice."

"I don't have any weapons. I had to leave my gear in Africa when I flew here."

"Tell Hobson to get you whatever you need. Guns, a car, whatever."

"I was also the guy in charge of Warwick's protection deal. Don't you need to find somebody to replace me?"

"No. Tell one of the guys on your team that he's in charge now and that you won't be coming back. Providing protection for Lizzie and Lambert is not the priority it was when you were initially hired. In fact, at this point, we don't really need Lizzie and Lambert anymore, and if something were to happen to them, that might actually be a good thing."

"I don't understand," Lee said.

"You don't need to understand."

Fiona reached into her purse, took out a cell phone, and handed it to Lee. "When I need to talk to you, I'll call you on that cell phone, and you can use that phone if you need to talk to me, but I don't want you calling unless it's important. My number is the only number programmed into the contacts directory."

"I don't even know your name," Lee said.

"It's Fiona."

"Fiona. I never met a Fiona before."

"Whatever," Fiona said, and turned to leave.

"Hey, wait a minute," Lee said. "I've been out in the boondocks a long time. I could use a little company. How 'bout we go somewhere and have a couple of beers, maybe some dinner."

"A couple of *beers*?" Fiona said, and laughed. "Earl, just keep your mind on the job, keep your mouth shut, and don't forget that you're replaceable."

Emma sent a text message to DeMarco and told him to call her from a pay phone. Fifteen minutes later, DeMarco did.

"Do you have any idea how hard it is to find a working pay phone these days? Maybe it's time to get rid of that tap on my phone."

Emma ignored DeMarco's whining and told him about her discussion with Celia Montoya.

"That's good," DeMarco said when she finished. "Siccing the press on these guys is probably the best thing we can do at this point."

"I hope so," Emma said. "And now you and I need to find a place to hide out for a couple of weeks."

"Hide out? Why the hell would we do that?" DeMarco said.

"Joe, Kelly and Nelson were ex-Delta, the best killers money can buy. Nelson's in a hospital right now and Kelly's dead but—"

"So if Nelson's hurt and Kelly's dead, why do we have to go into hiding?"

"Because we're dealing with a company that has billions of dollars at its disposal. They hired Kelly, Nelson, Hobson, and Lambert. They funded facilities to warehouse people while they experimented on them. And if they could hire Kelly and Nelson, they can hire more people just like them. So I think we need to go underground for a while."

"For how long?"

"I don't know, but at least a couple of weeks. After Montoya publishes her story, everything we know will be out in the open and killing us won't make sense. In fact, at that point, it would be dangerous to kill us."

"I dunno," DeMarco said. "I don't like the idea of letting these people drive us out of our homes."

"I don't like it either, but it's the prudent thing to do."

"Yeah, maybe. I need to talk to Mahoney about this."

"No you don't."

"Yeah, I do. Where would we go?"

"I don't know yet. I'll figure something out. And I'm taking Christine with me."

Oh, great! Two weeks around Christine was gonna be a real treat—like a nonstop root canal.

"You know," DeMarco said, "there's one guy we've kind of lost sight of during this whole thing, and that's Brian Kincaid. So far we don't have anything that's going to help get him released from prison."

"I know, but there isn't anything we can do about that right now. Maybe we can make something happen after Montoya's story breaks."

But DeMarco wasn't really thinking about Brian Kincaid. He was really thinking: *Two weeks with Christine? God help me.*

Celia Montoya knew that in order to write the story, she needed to organize things like a military operation. She had to get reporters in four different countries to descend on Warwick's facilities simultaneously, and she had to interview Lizzie Warwick at the same time. If she tried to conduct the interviews in series, Warwick or Mulray Pharma would make sure nobody talked.

She called four reporters. She didn't know any of them personally, but she knew of their work, and after she talked to them, she came away with a good feeling. To cover Pakistan, she contacted an Oxford-educated Pakistani who worked for the BBC. In Africa there was a crazy Aussie who had covered wars over there for twenty years. He had a reputation for being a drunk when he wasn't working, but when he worked he stayed sober and was willing to take risks that most people wouldn't. In Peru, she found a woman who had gone to school at American University in Washington, D.C., and now worked as a stringer for a number of European papers. For Indonesia, she found another BBC stringer, a Dutchman who had married a local woman and had lived in the country for years.

After each reporter agreed to work with her, she set up a conference call to talk to all them at the same time. She told them the first thing they had to do before approaching anyone was find out if Warwick had set up other facilities like the one that Emma had discovered in Peru. The facilities would most likely be in an isolated location some distance away from the disaster area where Warwick had initially gone to deliver aid. Then they would have to identify the person managing the facility—most likely a local nurse or emergency medical technician like the guy in Peru. Once they had located the facilities and identified the facility manager, the reporters would go to each of the facilities at the same time and question the manager and the patients—the inmates, the guinea pigs—whatever the appropriate term was. She wanted the reporters to confirm that the patients had been administered drugs and that test samples had been sent to Mulray Pharma's lab in Delaware. They should attempt to find out what the drugs were intended to treat and, most important, they should try to determine if test subjects had died after being given the drugs. She was confident the reporters would succeed. These were talented, experienced journalists; they knew how to cajole, badger, and wheedle information out of people, and if the facility managers were as unsophisticated as the one in Peru, they'd find out what Montoya needed to know.

"And what are you going to be doing?" asked the Aussie reporter, the one who would visit the Warwick Care Center in Uganda.

"I'll be confronting Lizzie Warwick and René Lambert," Montoya responded.

"Well, then," the Aussie said, "we'll have to raise a pint together when you're done with that."

Emma decided they should hide out in a high-end resort on Hilton Head, which was fine by DeMarco since Emma was picking up the tab. She checked them in under phony names, paid in cash, and made sure no one followed them to the resort. She reminded Christine and DeMarco about ten times not to use their cell phones or credit cards. Once they arrived, she and Christine went for long walks on the beach and visited boutiques and antique stores. Christine played her cello. Emma visited gardens and greenhouses in the area and annoyed the staff with questions about how they grew their plants. DeMarco ate with them a few times, but most of the time he allowed them to dine alone, because he knew that they wanted to be alone.

So while Emma and Christine were enjoying a romantic getaway, DeMarco read mystery novels, played golf, and watched sports on ESPN. One day he went fishing, got sunburned, and caught two small sea bass. Considering what he'd paid to go on the charter boat, he figured those fish cost him about fifty bucks a pound—but they were worth it.

Earl Lee checked into a cheap motel in D.C. He could have afforded better, but he didn't feel comfortable in someplace swanky. He started working out every day at a local gym; if he had to take on Kelly, he needed to get back in shape. He also visited a gun club in Virginia and practiced with a .45 semiauto.

When he hadn't heard from Fiona in two weeks, Lee called her. "Uh, I'm just wondering if there's anything you need me to do. I'm just sittin' around here."

Fiona said, "Goddamnit, I told you I'd call you when I needed you. Don't call me again or I'll ship your ass back to Uganda."

Lee hung up, thinking: *Man, that is one nasty bitch.*

32

Celia Montoya hired a helicopter in Kampala to take her to the refugee camp in northern Uganda. Her editor hadn't been too happy about paying for the chopper but agreed that it was safer for Montoya to fly to the camp than drive there. He didn't want one of his best reporters to end up kidnapped—or dead.

Montoya didn't call Warwick and Lambert to tell them she was coming. She just showed up at the refugee camp, introduced herself as a reporter for the *Washington Post,* and said she wanted to interview them. They naturally assumed that she wanted to write a story about all the suffering refugees—man's inhumanity to man, that sort of thing. They also assumed she would take photos of emaciated African mothers holding their starving babies, babies with huge, bewildered eyes. And Montoya did nothing, initially, to dispel their assumptions.

She conducted the interview in Lizzie's tent, which was stifling even though the flaps were open. The only one sweating heavily, however, was Montoya. It appeared that Lambert and Lizzie had become acclimated to the climate—but no one could become acclimated to the smell of the refugee camp or to the sight of the poor people who lived there.

The tent contained a simple folding cot, two folding canvas camp chairs, and a collapsible table. On the table were a laptop computer, a satellite phone, and stacks of paper that looked to Montoya like they might be supply invoices. Lizzie offered Montoya one of the folding chairs and Lambert sat in the other. Lizzie sat on her cot.

Lizzie was wearing a long-sleeved white blouse and faded khaki pants. A straw hat covered her frizzy red hair. Lambert had on jeans and a blue shirt, the color of the shirt matching his eyes. They were a striking couple, although for different reasons. Lambert was as handsome as any Hollywood star, while Lizzie, with her pale face and tired, compassionate eyes . . . Well, there was something saintly about her. But what saint would ever do what she was doing? They smiled when Montoya took their photograph; she was sure they wouldn't be smiling by the time she left.

"Do you mind if I record this?" she said, taking a small digital recorder from her pocket.

"Not at all," Lambert said.

"I have information," Montoya said, "that the Warwick Foundation is testing drugs manufactured by Mulray Pharma on the people in your so-called care centers. That *is* what you call them, isn't it? Care centers?"

"What? What are you talking about?" Lizzie Warwick said, and Montoya had the impression she was genuinely confused.

Lambert didn't say anything.

"Approximately four hours ago, reporters working with me visited your care centers in Pakistan, Indonesia, Peru, and the one here in Uganda near Lake Victoria. I've been informed that in all these facilities, except for the one in Indonesia, people are being administered drugs and biological samples are being taken and sent to a Mulray lab in Delaware."

It appeared that the care center in Indonesia was either a control group or a group that Mulray Pharma was holding in reserve in case it needed to do more testing.

Turning her head to look directly at Lambert, Montoya said, "*You* selected the test subjects, Dr. Lambert, and you trained the people who administer the drugs and take the samples. You also inserted RFID chips into these people so that you're able to tie the samples to the subjects."

"What on earth are you talking about?" Lizzie said. Before Montoya could answer, she turned to Lambert and said, "Do you know what she's talking about, René?"

Lambert didn't respond. He didn't even look at Lizzie. He just continued to stare at Celia, his mouth set in a firm line.

"Ms. Warwick," Celia said, "can you explain to me why all the patients in your care centers are elderly people in good health? Why is it that none of these people have full-blown AIDS or tuberculosis or any of the other diseases commonly found in this part of the world? I saw an old man as I was coming to your tent. His legs were grossly swollen with elephantiasis. Why isn't he at your Lake Victoria care center? Are you afraid that people who have other significant diseases will invalidate the drug testing results?"

"I don't know what you're talking about!" Lizzie screamed, and struck her clenched fists on her thighs. "All I know is that the people René placed in the centers have no one to care for them, and if we didn't help them, they'd be dead by now. Isn't that right, René?"

"Well, Dr. Lambert?" Montoya said. "Would you care to comment?"

"I've done nothing illegal," Lambert said. "All the people in our facilities have consented to be part of the trials."

"What!" Lizzie said, rising to her feet.

Ignoring Lizzie, Montoya said to Lambert, "What you're doing may be legal, but it's unethical. It's immoral. You've taken advantage of these people."

"Exactly how have I taken advantage of them, Ms. Montoya?" Lambert responded. "If reporters have visited our facilities as you say, then they've seen people who are healthy and well cared for and suffering no ill effects from the drugs they've been given."

"René, I want to know what you and this woman are talking about!" Lizzie shrieked. There were two bright red spots on her pale cheeks and her small hands were clenched into fists.

"Dr. Lambert," Montoya continued, "we've discovered that a number of people in your care centers have died after being administered the drugs. In two places—in Peru and Pakistan—there have been multiple fatalities on the same day, and in all your facilities, fatalities have occurred at regular intervals, almost as if they're dying to suit some sort of schedule."

"That's true, people have died," Lambert said.

"Oh, my God," Lizzie said.

Lambert continued. "As you said, the people in our care centers are elderly. Old people die. And these old people have all suffered the trauma of a natural disaster or a war. But they didn't die to suit a schedule; I don't even know what that means. And we performed autopsies on those who died, and the autopsy results document the cause of death, which was most often cardiac arrest or respiratory illnesses that the elderly are particularly susceptible to."

"Who performed the autopsies?"

Before Lambert could respond, Lizzie said, "René, I want you to answer me! Are you saying that this woman is telling the truth, that you've been using my foundation to conduct testing for a pharmaceutical company?"

Lambert rose. He didn't even look at Lizzie Warwick. "Ms. Montoya, you need to be very careful. You're implying that Mulray Pharma and I have done something illegal and underhanded when that is in fact not the case. I won't hesitate to sue you and your newspaper if you impugn my reputation."

And with that, Lambert left the tent.

Lizzie Warwick just stood there for a moment looking thunderstruck, then she dropped back onto the cot where she'd been sitting as if her legs had suddenly turned to rubber.

"Are you all right, Ms. Warwick?" Celia said.

"No. I'm not. You have to tell me what's going on."

———————◆◆◆———————

After the reporter left, Lizzie went looking for Lambert. She was normally a tranquil person, often frustrated by the difficulty of the work she was doing, but rarely angry. As she walked toward Lambert's tent, though, she was so angry she was literally shaking. When she found that Lambert wasn't in his tent, she searched the camp for him, crying out his name. One of the United Nations soldiers protecting the refugee camp finally told her that Lambert and his security people had left the camp in a jeep, and that's when Lizzie sat down on the dry, red African dirt and cried as the people in the camp looked on. An old woman who was nothing more than skin and bones sat down next to her and put an arm around her shoulders as Lizzie sobbed.

"Don't cry, my daughter," the old woman said in Bantu. "Everything will be all right."

33

Orson Mulray looked at the page one headline on yesterday's *Washington Post*—MULRAY EXPERIMENTS ON DISASTER VICTIMS—and smiled.

Celia Montoya was a clever reporter—able to report the facts accurately yet twist them into something alarming and sinister—and Mulray Pharma was portrayed as this awful, evil corporate entity that would do anything to make a buck. She made it clear that Mulray Pharma was taking advantage of poor, uneducated people to test some unspecified new drug and that clinical trials were being conducted in "total secrecy" so no one would know if any of the test subjects had been adversely affected. She reported that a number of people had died in the Warwick Care Centers—"a statistically higher than normal number"—but was careful not to accuse Mulray Pharma of killing anyone. She made much ado—much ado about nothing—regarding the implantation of RFID chips in the subjects. The article concluded by saying that the Justice Department and the FDA had told the *Post* that they were "considering" investigating Mulray Pharma.

Orson also noted that Mulray Pharma's stock plunged after the story was released—and this made him smile too.

He looked at himself in the mirror and was pleased by what he saw. He knew he wasn't a handsome man—he was a bit heavy and there was more than a hint of German Bürgermeister about him—but he looked . . . *solid.* Yes, that was the word.

His barber had trimmed his hair that morning, after which he had a facial to make his skin tight and glowing. He was wearing a dark blue Savile Row suit, a plain white shirt, and a maroon silk tie. He had thought about conducting the press conference with his sleeves rolled up—like an executive who had been busy working and had just stopped for a moment to deal with the latest media nonsense—but decided against that. He didn't want to give the impression that he was the least bit harried.

He turned away from the mirror and asked Fiona, "How do I look?"

"Fine, you look fine," she said, her fingernails raking her left forearm.

"Is Ballard here?" Orson asked.

"He's waiting in your conference room, and I have someone watching him to make sure he doesn't wander off."

"And how does he look?" Orson asked.

"Like he always does. He needs a haircut and his pants are too short. Oh, and he's wearing white socks."

"Perfect," Orson said.

"Are you sure you want to address the media yourself?" Fiona asked. "As your lawyer, I advise you not to. Everything you're about to say can be said by a spokesman, and later on—if it's necessary—you can say the spokesman was confused and misrepresented your position."

"I'm sure, Fiona. I've been waiting for this moment for five years. By the way, I'd suggest you buy as much Mulray Pharma stock as you can afford this morning. I expect that after the press conference the price will double."

Orson Mulray looked out at the mob of reporters standing in front of him. There were at least fifty people in the room, and it seemed as if half of them were holding cameras. All the networks were present, as well as the major cable stations. He assumed the scruffy folk in the crowd were print media people.

The reporters were clearly astounded that Orson was addressing the media himself, and addressing them only twenty-four hours after the story broke in the *Post*. They had all expected that Mulray's PR flack would issue a bland written statement to the effect that while Mulray admitted to no wrongdoing, the company had no comment on Montoya's story due to the possibility of pending legal action. They were in for a surprise.

He glanced over at Simon Ballard, who was standing to his right and slightly behind him—in the background, where he belonged. Ballard seemed bewildered by the reporters and stood completely still, as if frozen in place, the proverbial deer caught in the headlights. After the press conference, Orson would have Ballard taken someplace where the media couldn't find him, and there he would be coached extensively on how to deal with the media in the future—not that Orson had any intention of allowing Ballard to ever be alone with a reporter.

Orson stepped up to the podium and tapped on the microphone to make sure it was working; four people in media relations would have been fired had it not been. He stared out at the crowd, unsmiling, his face serious, and waited until there was complete silence in the room.

"Let me begin by saying that Ms. Montoya's article in the *Washington Post* is essentially accurate."

A collective gasp issued from the crowd, and Orson glanced down and saw two reporters look at each other, the expressions on their faces saying: *Can you believe he just said that?*

"That is," Orson continued after the room was silent again, "Ms. Montoya has most of her *facts* correct, but the implication that Mulray

Pharma has done anything illegal or, for that matter, immoral, is incorrect."

He gestured toward Ballard. "Standing to my right is Dr. Simon Ballard. I approached Dr. Ballard approximately five years ago when I discovered he was pioneering a cure for one of the most horrible diseases affecting mankind. This disease affects some people in a devastating way, but it affects all people to some degree."

"What disease?" a reporter shouted out, one of the scruffy ones.

Orson ignored the question. "Dr. Ballard conducted all the necessary experimentation and laboratory testing to prove the efficacy and safety of a drug to treat this disease, and then Mulray Pharma set about doing clinical trials consistent with international law and sound medical practice. Because of the potential value of this drug, these clinical trials were conducted in such a manner as to prevent our competitors from learning of its existence. That is, we were secretive about what we were doing—as all drug companies are secretive when developing a new product. We were not secretive, however, because we were attempting to cover anything up. We also chose to perform clinical trials outside the United States because, quite frankly, this is a drug that mankind desperately needs, and if we had followed the FDA's procedures it would have taken approximately twice as long— maybe three times as long—to make the drug available."

"What is this drug used for?" a reporter cried out.

Orson acted as if he hadn't heard the reporter. "Our primary clinical trials were conducted in Thailand under the supervision of a Harvard-educated Thai doctor and in accordance with drug testing requirements in that country. Furthermore, as Ms. Montoya stated in her article, we selected a number of test subjects who were also victims of wars or natural disasters. We did this because we could help these people by providing them food and shelter while they participated in the clinical trials, and they were fully informed they would be taking part in the trials. We used interpreters to make sure they understood this, and all the participants signed documents stating that they agreed to participate, understood the risks, and were in no way coerced. In return for their participation, these people—who are poor and homeless and have no one to care for them—were placed in assisted living facilities."

The skeptics in the crowd began to grumble—and, being reporters, they were all skeptics. Orson held up his hands. "There is nothing unusual or immoral about paying people to participate in drug trials. We do that in the United States all the time, and we paid the people in Thailand to participate. And all test results have been fully and properly documented."

A number of questions were shouted out by the reporters, but Orson simply stood there until they stopped. He was not going to lose control of the news conference.

"Beginning this month, we are going to begin treating people for this disease in Thailand, where we've completed all required clinical trials. At the same time, we will begin submitting our test results to the FDA in the United States as well as to the equivalent of the FDA in other countries. I would urge Americans to write their congressmen and senators and tell them to do everything they can to ensure that the FDA acts in a timely manner. Every day we delay giving people the drug is one more day the disease will progress."

"Are you ever going to tell us what the damn disease is?" a reporter cried out, a man with a booming voice.

"Yes, sir," Orson said. He was enjoying this; he felt like a stripper peeling off her clothes at an agonizingly slow pace. "But first I wish to address a couple of points in Ms. Montoya's article. She notes that people had RFID chips implanted so we could positively tie test results to specific subjects. She said this was like 'tagging animals in the wild' and made it sound as if we were doing something cruel and unusual. Ms. Montoya chose to ignore the fact that implanting these small chips is a safe and painless procedure. More important, she also failed to mention that RFID technology is commonly used today in medical and biological applications because this technology prevents errors in record keeping which simply can not be tolerated when dealing with people's health.

"Second, Ms. Montoya noted that some of our test subjects died, and this is also true. The majority of our test subjects are elderly people, and these people were, in many cases, subjected to considerable trauma before we took them under our care. So the fact that a few elderly people died is tragic, but not really unusual or unexpected. All the people who did die were given autopsies to verify the cause of death and to prove their deaths had nothing to do with Dr. Ballard's drug, and all autopsy results have been documented, along with all other clinical data. And, by the way, these people were given funeral services in accordance with the customs of their religion and culture. Now, as to the disease."

"Finally," someone said.

"Dr. Ballard has developed a drug to prevent Alzheimer's. This drug will not, unfortunately, reverse the course of the disease for people who already have it, but what it will do is prevent the disease from progressing. More important, if administered early enough, Dr. Ballard's drug will keep people predisposed to Alzheimer's from getting the disease."

Orson paused for a long beat to let the reporters absorb the significance of what he had just said, then looked directly into one of the cameras—into the eyes of the TV viewing audience. "I'm only fifty-eight years old, and I'm already starting to experience those occasional moments when I can't put names to faces or can't remember if I've seen a movie or read a particular book. And that scares me. And I remember my father so often saying to me 'I don't think I've told you this story before' when in fact he'd told it a hundred times before, and I wonder if I'm doing the same thing. And that scares me. Most often, though, I think of my favorite uncle. He was a brilliant man—he taught international law at Cornell. But I remember the first time he went to a store a block from his house and couldn't find his way home, and how he cried when my aunt had to go pick him up. And I remember when he stopped bathing and would wear the same food-stained shirt for a week, and I remember him at the end, his eyes vacant, his mouth hanging open, literally being held prisoner in a vigorous body by a brain that had ceased to function. My memories of my uncle don't scare me—they terrify me. And I'm sure all of you, particularly if you're about my age, share my fear of the future, wondering if one day you will become like my uncle. Well, thanks to Simon Ballard, we no longer need to fear."

Orson stopped speaking and stood for a moment looking down at the podium, as if caught up in the emotion of his own recollections, then once again looked out at the reporters, who were finally silent.

"In conclusion, Mulray Pharma has developed a drug that billions of people will eventually take to prevent Alzheimer's, and, contrary to Ms. Montoya's wild accusations, the testing performed to develop this cure was done in a completely legal and ethical fashion and all test results and test protocols will be submitted to the FDA. And, as I said earlier, I urge all of you to contact your elected representatives to expedite the use of the drug in this country. Thank you."

* * *

Emma, DeMarco, and Christine had watched Mulray's press conference in Emma and Christine's suite at the resort in Hilton Head. Emma turned off the television as soon as it was over, then just sat there scowling.

DeMarco didn't know what to say, either.

But Christine did. "My God! A cure for Alzheimer's. My grandmother has Alzheimer's. It's horrible. She doesn't even know who I am when I visit her. And I've been worried about my mother, too. It seems like every time I call her, she mentions losing her glasses or house keys or something. I mean, what Mulray did is horrible, but if there's a drug . . ."

Emma said, "I'm going to get that smug son of a bitch. I'm going to get him if it takes the rest of my life."

When Emma called Celia Montoya, the reporter didn't sound particularly pleased to hear from her.

"Before the press conference, my editor ran around the office telling everybody I was the next Bob Woodward. Today, he won't look at me, and now all he can talk about is the possibility of the paper being sued by Mulray. Before we published, the paper's lawyers said that Mulray had no grounds for a suit, but now they're waffling."

"Your article was correct," Emma said. "Your editor needs to back you up."

"Yeah, well, I'll be sure to tell him you said that. You know, if you'd be willing to talk about that guy trying to kill you in Peru, it could help."

"I'll think about it," Emma said, "but I'm not sure it would help all that much. Although I'm certain Kelly was going to kill me, I can't prove it. I also can't prove Nelson was in that liquor store to kill DeMarco. And even if I had proof, Kelly and Nelson work for Lizzie Warwick, not Mulray Pharma."

"I'm positive Lizzie had no idea about the drug testing," Montoya said.

"How could that be? How could she not be aware of what was happening in those places?"

"I don't know what lies Lambert told her, but she told me she was never involved in the medical end of things, and I believed her.

After she hooked up with him, she focused totally on the nonmedical stuff—water, food, clothing, et cetera—while he handled the medical supplies and treating the victims. And the care centers were totally Lambert's bailiwick. She told me she was worried at one time about the cost of the centers because she could see it took a lot of money to operate them, but Hobson told her the centers were being funded by Lambert's European donors and that these same people were funding other things she was doing. In other words, Hobson basically told her not to rock the boat and she was satisfied with his explanation. In fact, she rarely visited the care centers. She'd been to the one in Peru but had never even seen the one in Uganda, near Lake Victoria. She didn't have time to go there, and she had no idea Mulray Pharma was subsidizing her foundation to the degree it was."

"I don't know," Emma said, still skeptical. "I find it hard to believe she could be so clueless."

"All I can say is that if you'd been with me when I interviewed her in Africa, I think you'd be convinced. Maybe she's the best actress since Meryl Streep, but I think she's just a sweet woman who put her trust completely in Lambert and Hobson, and they kept her in the dark."

Following the press conference, Orson Mulray took the elevator to the roof of the building and walked out and stood at the railing, looking eastward. He felt like the captain of a great sailing ship as he looked out toward the Atlantic, scanning the horizon, looking for his first glimpse of some New World. He wished he had someone to share this moment with—someone other than Fiona, that is. In an odd way, and as much as he had despised the man, he wished he could share it with his father.

He had taken an enormous risk—and it had paid off. And people had not even begun to grasp how much money the drug was worth. He did sincerely regret, however, that a few elderly people had to die—he wasn't a sociopath like Fiona—and if he had been able to produce the drug in a reasonable time frame following more traditional methods, he would have. But the fact was that people often died developing new cures for old diseases. That was one of the dirty little secrets of medicine that folks usually chose to ignore, and the number that died in this case was really quite small. He wasn't sure of the exact number, but it was certainly less than a score—and millions, if not billions, would reap the benefits. And not only would mankind benefit medically, his achievement would result in thousands of new jobs and a more vibrant global economy. Furthermore—and not far in the future—he would establish the *Orson* Mulray Foundation and would become known worldwide for his great generosity.

He looked skyward and said out loud, "What do you think about your boy now, Dad?"

34

Lizzie Warwick flew from Kampala to Philadelphia the same day Celia Montoya's story was released in the *Washington Post*. She wasn't aware of the article, however, until her plane landed and she saw the headlines on the papers in the terminal. She dropped her carry-on bag onto the ground and pulled a newspaper from a rack without paying for it and started to read. As she read, she muttered, "No, no, this can't be." The lady running the newsstand asked if she was going to buy the paper and muttered curses in Hindi as a dazed Lizzie dropped the paper on a stack of Philadelphia Eagles T-shirts and walked away.

Her lawyers were surprised when she showed up in their offices. Not just surprised that she was there, but also surprised by her appearance. She was still wearing the same white blouse, khaki pants, and scuffed boots that she'd been wearing when Montoya interviewed her in Uganda—except that now the blouse and pants looked as if she'd pulled them from the bottom of a laundry hamper. And it wasn't just her attire; she looked absolutely wild-eyed.

She was ushered into the senior partner's office.

"I assume," the senior partner said, "that this has to do with your involvement with Mulray Pharma."

"I wasn't involved with Mulray Pharma, goddamnit!" Lizzie shouted.

The lawyer had never heard Lizzie swear before. In fact, he couldn't recall her ever raising her voice before.

"I want you to sue those people," Lizzie said. "They've damaged my reputation and the reputation of my foundation. I want them to pay for what they did. I want them destroyed."

"I see," the lawyer said. Then he hemmed and hawed for a while—for a lawyer, he wasn't a very articulate man—before eventually telling her that suing Mulray Pharma was going to be extremely expensive.

"I don't care what it costs," Lizzie said.

"When I say it will be expensive, Lizzie. . . . Well, you're not as wealthy as you once were, and you don't have the resources to take on a long legal battle with a large corporation like Mulray Pharma." Before Lizzie could respond, he added, "The other thing is that, quite frankly, I don't think you can win."

"Why not?" Lizzie asked.

"Because I'm afraid it's going to be impossible to prove that you had no idea what Mulray Pharma and René Lambert were doing. I mean, *I* believe you," the lawyer added quickly, "but it sounds somewhat, uh, implausible that they could be doing this right under your nose, so to speak."

"But I didn't know what they were doing! I thought we were just helping those people. And René dealt with the care centers and the medical end of things. I never got involved in any of that."

"Lizzie, I suggest we wait a while before doing anything. I'm concerned that the government may discover that Orson Mulray has done something illegal—although it doesn't sound like he did—and you could possibly be indicted as an accomplice. I think we should wait until things shake out a bit."

"An accomplice?" Lizzie said.

"What I would like to do is issue a press release on your behalf. You have to tell the media something. The release will simply say that you had no involvement in Mulray Pharma's clinical trials—I prefer the words *no involvement* to being *unaware*—and that you have no further comment as you're considering legal action against the company. How does that sound for an opening salvo?"

"An accomplice?" Lizzie said again.

She rose from the chair where she'd been sitting and started toward the door. She staggered as if she were drunk, but the senior partner was sure that was due to her being tired after the long flight.

"Lizzie, shall I issue the press release?" the lawyer said to her back.

She waved a hand over her shoulder, a gesture that might have meant either *Go ahead* or *I don't care what you do.*

The lawyer picked up his phone as soon as she left his office and said, "Carol, have Matthew drive Ms. Warwick home and make sure she gets inside without being hounded by the press. Tell him not to leave until she's behind locked doors."

———◆◆◆———

Lizzie gradually became aware that she was sitting on the floor in her bedroom in front of an unlit gas fireplace. She was wearing a white terry-cloth robe and nothing else. She wondered how long she'd been sitting there—and why she was sitting there. On the floor of the fireplace hearth was an empty bottle, lying on its side. Next to it was another bottle, one that was upright and still a third full. The label on the bottle said: *Kammer Williams Fine Pear Brandy.*

She remembered that when she got home after meeting with her useless lawyer there had been a dozen reporters in her driveway. She remembered the nice young man who drove her home—although she didn't know who he was—and how he shooed away the reporters and helped her unlock the front door. After she was inside the house, she called a number of her friends, or people she *thought* were friends—people who had been big donors and supporters in the past. She had just wanted to tell them her side of the story, but she was surprised that many of them didn't return her phone calls and that those who did speak to her seemed unusually cool and guarded.

She hadn't felt so alone since the day her mother died.

She also remembered that the phones kept ringing and ringing and that every time she answered one, thinking it might be one of her so-called friends calling back, it turned out to be a reporter, so she had walked through the house yanking the cords out of the phone jacks. It was after that that she'd decided she wanted a drink. She rarely drank, and when she did she drank white wine, but the wine was down in the basement and the idea of going down all those steps, then struggling with a cork puller . . . Well, it was just too much. She went to the liquor cabinet in the formal dining room and pushed bottles aside, unable to decide what she wanted to drink, until she saw a bottle of pear brandy.

She remembered thinking as she grasped the bottle: *I have become my mother.*

Her mother had been like her: a small, quiet woman, delicate and frail. She played the piano and loved the poems of Emily Dickinson and held tea parties in the garden. But the last two years of her life, her mother had roamed the enormous house in a bathrobe, rarely bathed, and sipped sherry and fruit brandies all day long. She committed suicide at the age of forty-two—the same age Lizzie was now—with peach brandy and sleeping pills. Her father said her mother killed herself because she was bipolar and clinically depressed and refused to take her medication, but Lizzie had always known that was a lie. Her mother had indeed been depressed, but her condition had been caused by her father's cruelty and unfaithfulness and not a medical condition.

Her father. She adored him when she was a little girl. He called her Princess; she called him Big Bear Daddy. As she grew older, however, and saw what he was doing to her mother, she grew to hate him. He had been a huge, heavy, hairy man—aggressive, pushy, and loud—and when he ate, he was just like a bear, tearing into his food, taking huge bites, barely chewing before he swallowed. Whenever he was home—which wasn't all that often—he would get drunk and scream at her poor mother, and his big round face would become an angry red man-in-the-moon. She also realized something else: Orson Mulray looked very much like her father.

She started drinking the brandy after she made the phones stop ringing, but it wasn't just the phones she was trying to stop. She was really trying to stop the words that kept playing inside her head, like a needle stuck on an old phonograph record: *I didn't know. It wasn't my fault. What do I do? I didn't know. It wasn't my fault. What do I do?*

She thought brandy might make the words stop—but it didn't. The only time the chant stopped was when she slept—and she took a few sleeping pills to help with that. She didn't know how many hours she'd slept in the three days since she'd been back from Uganda, but she slept a lot. She was awake now, however—and the words were back.

I didn't know. It wasn't my fault. What do I do?

She reached for the brandy bottle on the hearth but couldn't find a glass. She knew she must have been drinking out of a glass. She wouldn't have drunk straight from the bottle. At least she didn't think so. Then she noticed a piece of paper lying on the floor near the overturned brandy bottle and picked it up. The paper had holes gouged in it and there was one partial sentence written on it in her handwriting. It said: *I called this press conference to tell you . . .* And that was all. She remembered then that she had thought about calling a press conference just as Orson Mulray had and giving her side of the story. And she remembered crying and stabbing the paper with her pen when she couldn't think of anything to say that wouldn't make her look like a fool, or a liar, or both.

The foundation had been her life—literally, her entire life. She had no husband, no children, and no other interests. She had devoted 100 percent of her time, her energy, and her fortune to her work. When she wasn't in the field tending to victims, she was raising money for victims. But who would give Lizzie Warwick money now?

I didn't know. It wasn't my fault. What do I do?

And then she knew the answer.

Daddy's Bulldog.

She rose from where she was sitting by the fireplace and began walking, slowly, in the direction of her parents' bedroom, which like hers was on the second floor of the house. She passed a mirror as she walked, and caught sight of her reflection. Her bathrobe was open and she could see her thin, pale legs, a small, woolly red patch of pubic hair, and her small breasts. Her hair—which had always been naturally curly—hung in tangled, wild strands down to her shoulders. It looked as if she'd washed her hair but hadn't bothered to comb it out afterward.

But she couldn't remember taking a shower.

It seemed to take forever to walk from her bedroom to her parents' bedroom. The house was enormous—four floors, eight full bathrooms, three half-baths, God only knew how many square feet. She hated the house because it was her father's house and the place where her mother killed herself, but she inherited it after her father died and she moved back in as a practical matter, thinking it would be a good place for holding fund-raisers. And it had been. The table in the main dining room seated twenty-four and she had hosted parties attended by more than a hundred people.

She couldn't sleep in her parents' bedroom, however, and when she moved back into the house after her father's death, she moved back into her old room. She had her father's clothes removed after he died, but a lot of his other possessions were still in the house—golf clubs, fishing poles, skis, and all of his weapons and hunting equipment. The guns were all down in the basement in a big steel gun safe, and she didn't know its combination, but she knew he kept the Bulldog in his bedroom.

She found the Bulldog where she expected to find it, in the nightstand on her father's side of the bed. It had been manufactured by a company called Charter Arms and used .44-caliber ammunition, and she remembered her father saying it would blow a hole in a man the size of a baseball.

She sat down on the floor at the foot of her parents' bed. It took her a while to figure out how to open the part where the bullets were kept, but she finally did and saw that the gun contained five bullets. She pulled one out and saw that it was a shiny, stubby, ugly thing. She studied it for a moment, surprised something so small could have such destructive powers, then put the bullet back in the cylinder, the chamber, whatever it was called. Then she just sat there for the longest time, holding the gun in her lap. It was a heavy weapon and for some strange reason, the weight of it was comforting.

She had always expected to work in the field until she was too old for such strenuous work, and then she'd raise money for the needy until she was too old to do that. When she died, her funeral would be held at the Philadelphia Episcopal Cathedral, the bishop would celebrate the funeral Mass, and the cathedral would be full of people: the rich and famous, the poor and unknown, all the people who had admired her and her work. She would be eulogized by someone important, maybe even the vice president.

But that wouldn't happen now. Now her obituary would read: *Lizzie Warwick, head of the infamous Warwick Foundation, the organization that helped Orson Mulray test drugs on starving Africans, died yesterday.* Aside from her good friend Miriam Fullerton, whom she'd gone to grade school with, she wondered if anyone else would even attend her funeral. She should call Miriam, but . . .

She put the barrel of the Bulldog in her mouth—but she didn't like the oily, metallic taste, the feel of the steel against her teeth. And then she imagined someone finding her, the back of her head blown open, blood and brains splattered all over the wall. That was just too . . . too messy. She removed the barrel from her mouth and placed it beneath one of her little breasts, against her heart.

That was better.

She begin to apply pressure to the trigger—she was surprised how much force it took—but then she caught sight of her reflection in the full-length mirror on the door of the walk-in closet. She looked like Medusa, with her uncombed, frizzy red hair springing out from her head in all directions. And her body, which was visible as the robe was still open . . . Well, it looked just . . . *pathetic*. She'd always been thin, but she'd hardly eaten a thing since she met that terrible reporter in Africa, and now she looked positively emaciated. Her rib bones were starkly outlined beneath her white, white skin, her legs were sticks, and her small breasts were droopy little sacks.

No, this wasn't right.

This just wouldn't do.

She stood up, closed her robe, and walked back to her bedroom. She was moving now like a woman with a purpose. The first thing she did was change the bed. She knew the tangled, sweat-soaked sheets must be terribly smelly. After the bed was made up with clean linens, she stepped into the bathroom attached to her bedroom.

She took a long shower and shampooed her hair. She dried her hair, combed it carefully—she even used a bit of gel to give it some style—then applied pale pink lipstick and just a touch of eyeliner. She put on her underwear—a plain white bra and white panties—then stepped into her closet to find something appropriate to wear. She finally decided on a dark skirt, a dark red sweater-blouse that was really too hot for the weather, and a pair of low-heeled pumps. She looked at herself in the mirror and said, "Good."

She looked around the bedroom to make sure everything was as it should be, and saw the brandy bottles on the fireplace hearth. Now, that wouldn't do at all. She picked up the bottles and took them to the kitchen and placed them in the recycle container beneath the sink. Moving even more quickly now, she walked back to her father's bedroom, picked up the Bulldog, and carried it to the den. She placed the gun on the desk, walked to the front door, unlocked it, then returned to the den and took a seat in the plush red leather chair behind the desk. The chair had been her father's and she'd never liked either its size or its color—but she liked it now.

She picked up the phone and when she didn't get a signal, she laughed. She'd forgotten she'd unplugged all the phones in the house. She rose from her chair, plugged the phone cord into the jack, and made the phone call. She concluded with, "And thank you so much for your help."

Phone call finished, she opened the drawer where she kept her best stationery and took out a single sheet of heavy bond paper manufactured by Crane & Co. She searched the leather cup on the desk for a good pen but could find only ballpoints—and ballpoint wasn't acceptable. She knew she had a fountain pen somewhere and opened drawers in the desk until she found a blue box with a red velvet liner that contained an ivory-colored fountain pen given to her by a dictator—a man who had thanked her for all the work she did in his country as he starved his own people to death.

She took the pen and wrote: *I didn't do anything wrong* and signed her name: *Elizabeth Allison Warwick.*

Then she placed the Bulldog once again against her chest.

35

Emma read the article in the *Washington Post* about Lizzie Warwick's suicide.

It stated that before she shot herself, Lizzie called 911 and told the dispatcher the front door to her home was unlocked so the medics wouldn't have to break it down, and she would really appreciate it if someone could come to her house right away. Lizzie apparently didn't want to shock anyone with the sight of her decomposing corpse if she was found at some future date. Naturally, the article discussed all the good, generous things Lizzie had done since she formed her foundation—and quoted a number of prominent people lauding her commitment to the poor and helpless—but also noted that speculation persisted as to whether she had been a willing participant in Mulray Pharma's clinical trials.

Emma felt horrible. She was the one who had sicced the press on Lizzie. Her intentions had been honorable—to get some law enforcement agency to investigate Mulray Pharma—and she'd believed at the time that Lizzie Warwick had been helping Orson Mulray. But Celia Montoya had told her—and now Emma believed her—that Lizzie had no idea what Mulray was doing. So now Lizzie Warwick—a fragile, gentle, good-hearted person—was dead, and it was Emma's fault as much as it was Orson Mulray's.

Now, more than ever, she had to make Mulray pay for what he had done.

The problem was that in the days following Mulray's press conference it became apparent that no one in the U.S. government—the FDA, the Justice Department, or the FBI—felt compelled to investigate what had happened at the Warwick Care Centers. Whatever Mulray had done fell outside their jurisdictions, there appeared to be no imminent threat to the American public, and there was nothing to indicate that Mulray had committed any crimes. As for the politicians, they made stern faces and said that if Orson Mulray had indeed taken advantage of disaster victims, he may have done something *unethical* but, as far as they knew, he hadn't done anything *illegal*. To a politician, there is a wide, wide gap between an unethical action and an indictable offense. What the politicians were really saying, but not saying out loud, was that the pharmaceutical industry was a major force both economically and politically, and that *somebody* had to be the guinea pigs so the industry could develop cures for diseases—and it was certainly better to use foreign guinea pigs than homegrown ones. If a dozen American grandmas had died to develop Mulray's latest product, then the politicians might have chosen to take a harder look—but it wasn't American grandmas who'd died.

Emma sat there thinking about Lizzie Warwick—and what her death meant in terms of all the people she might have helped in the future—until it was time for her appointment with the Alzheimer's doctor. Emma had decided that she needed to know more about the disease, so she'd called a few friends—her network was vast—and they'd steered her to a physician at Georgetown University Hospital.

The doctor, a man named Reynolds, was a handsome man in his forties with an abundance of curly dark hair and Cupid's bow lips. He *reeked* of arrogance. Emma imagined that all his life he'd been told what a fine-looking, brilliant fellow he was.

"I want to know," Emma said, "if Mulray Pharma needed autopsy results to establish the efficacy of the drug they developed."

"Probably," Reynolds said, but before Emma could ask him to explain himself, he added, "All I know for sure is that Orson Mulray is going to become a very, very wealthy man. For the next five years other companies won't be able to infringe on whatever patents he has and won't be able to make a generic version of the drug, and during that period he'll be able to set the price at any amount he desires." Emma started to tell him that she didn't care about how rich Mulray was going to become, but the doctor pulled a calculator from his desk.

"Let's say he sets the initial price for treatments at, oh, three hundred dollars a month."

"You think people would pay that much?"

The doctor laughed. "At one time, men were willing to pay more than four hundred dollars for thirty Levitra capsules."

"Levitra?"

"A drug for erectile dysfunction," Reynolds said. "Anyway, let's say Mulray charges three hundred for a month's supply of the drug. I think three hundred is a good number because although that amount seems high it won't be out of reach for a lot of people, and maybe their health insurance will help with the cost. Let's also assume he's able to prevent other companies from producing a similar drug for at least five years so no one else shares in the profits. Now, there are approximately one hundred and twenty million people in the United States over the age of fifty, and let's assume that just one *fifth* of them can afford the drug either on their own or with the help of their insurance companies." The doctor's long fingers began tapping the buttons on his calculator. "One hundred twenty million divided by five times three hundred dollars times twelve months times five years that's . . . four hundred and thirty *billion* dollars. Just in this country. The worldwide population is over six billion people and, just for the sake of argument, let's assume that only *one percent* of them can afford the drug." He tapped again on his calculator. "That gives you over a *trillion* dollars in a five-year period. And, of course, people who are fifty today could take the drug for as many as twenty or thirty years if it's effective or if they even *think* it's effective."

"Don't you have to take into account the amount it costs to manufacture the drug, marketing costs, those sorts of things?" Emma said.

Reynolds waved the question away. "Those costs will be a fraction of the selling price."

Emma hadn't thought about how much money Orson Mulray could make, but it had never occurred to her the amount could be so much. *A trillion dollars.* The number was mind-boggling. And Reynolds was right. Middle-class, middle-aged people who had seen parents and grandparents afflicted with Alzheimer's would be willing to pay three hundred dollars a month to keep that from happening to themselves. Emma certainly would.

"And I think," the doctor said, "that the number of people who will pay for this drug worldwide will be much higher than one percent. For people over fifty it will be like having a personal computer; everyone that age will want it. And unlike computers and software, you can't share a pill with other people, so what I'm saying is, if you think Bill Gates is a rich man . . ."

"We're getting off the subject," Emma said. "Tell me about the disease and if autopsy results would be needed to determine if the drug is effective."

"Alzheimer's," Reynolds said, "is named for Alois Alzheimer, a German physician who identified the disease in 1906. It is a progressive disease—meaning that the symptoms grow worse over time—and it's ultimately fatal. Recent studies indicate that over five million Americans have the disease today and that fifty to eighty percent of the people described as having dementia actually have Alzheimer's. It is the seventh-leading cause of death in this country."

"Yeah, yeah," Emma said, "but what causes it?"

"I'll keep this simple," the doctor said—a comment which made Emma grit her teeth. "There are two abnormal protein structures called plaques and tangles which damage and kill nerve cells in the brain. The plaques build up between nerve cells and contain deposits of a protein fragment called beta-amyloid. Tangles are twisted fibers of another protein called tau, and the tangles form inside dying cells. Now, most people develop some plaques and tangles as they age—which is what will make Mulray's drug so appealing—but those with Alzheimer's tend to develop far more of them, and they form in areas affecting learning and memory, block communication among nerve cells, and disrupt activities that cells need to survive."

"I see," Emma said, "but you still haven't answered my question. Would Mulray need autopsy results?"

"I'm sure Dr. Ballard would," Reynolds said. "He'd want to look directly at the brain to determine if his drug was inhibiting the growth of the proteins I mentioned. But he obviously has some noninvasive way of telling if the drug is working."

"Why *obviously*?"

"If looking directly at the brain was the only way to determine the efficacy of the drug then Ballard would need a baseline, if you will. What I mean is, he'd have to slice the brain open before he administered the drug, then slice it open again after a few months of treatment to study progress, and he clearly didn't do that. The people in these Warwick Care Centers weren't operated on, as far as I know. So Ballard has some way of telling if the drug was working via the biological samples and tests he performed during the clinical trials, and he later used autopsy results to validate his conclusions."

Emma shook her head. "It sounds to me like you don't really know what Ballard did."

Reynolds looked irritated; he didn't like Emma pointing out that he wasn't omniscient. "You're right, I don't—and neither does anyone else. My colleagues and I are all playing catch-up. I learned about this new drug the same day the public did and, of course, I don't have access to Ballard's research. So, you're right. I don't know exactly what Ballard did to prove the effectiveness of the drug and I'm sure he was anxious to get autopsy results, but there's no reason to believe anyone was murdered to provide test data."

What planet do you live on? Emma wondered. There were a trillion reasons to believe people may have been murdered. And she recalled reading that in the 1940s, black soldiers in the United States were intentionally given syphilis to prove that penicillin was an effective cure. It wasn't all that hard to imagine a drug company killing a few elderly people to test a drug that would make some people billionaires.

"But if people were murdered, is there any way we can prove it?" Emma asked.

"Well, I don't think *you* can," the doctor said, making sure Emma understood that he had no intention of being part of her investigation. "I'm sure the doctor in Thailand who administered the clinical trials will have paperwork from certified pathologists showing that people died of natural causes. If a pathologist *suspected* homicide, then he might test for exotic poisons, but why would he be suspicious? As Orson Mulray said, there's nothing abnormal about an old person dying.

"So, Emma, if Mulray Pharma killed people to provide data to support Ballard's research, the only way you're ever going to know for sure is if someone confesses."

DeMarco was standing on the top rung of a six-foot stepladder, cleaning gunk out of his rain gutters, when Emma arrived at his house. It had rained the night before and when he noticed water cascading down onto his front porch like a miniature Niagara Falls, it occurred to him that he hadn't cleaned out the gutters in quite some time and the downspouts were probably blocked with leaves. And they were—but the leaves were no longer leaves. They were a smelly, bug-infested, decomposing mass.

"I guess you heard about Lizzie Warwick," he said. He could imagine how she must be feeling about Lizzie's death.

"Yes, and I don't want to talk about it," Emma said. She then told him she had just come from seeing a doctor who was an expert on Alzheimer's and relayed to DeMarco what the doctor had told her. As she was talking, he continued to drop handfuls of nasty plant matter onto the ground below him. She finally said, "Get down off that damn ladder before you kill yourself and pay attention."

They went into the house, and after he washed his hands, he said, "So we gotta squeeze a confession out of somebody."

"Yes," Emma said—and from her tone he could tell that she hadn't excluded waterboarding. "Are you going to help me?"

"You know I am." There was no point reminding Emma that this was his case and not hers. "And I'm still going to get Brian Kincaid out of prison." DeMarco paused for a beat, then said, "The way I see it, there are two guys we can squeeze. Hobson or Nelson."

"How would we squeeze Hobson?"

"We can threaten to report him for income tax evasion like Neil said, then offer him a deal to admit he framed Kincaid and conspired to kill Downing, then use him to go after Mulray Pharma."

"Tax evasion. Big deal," Emma said. "He'd probably just get a fine and be ordered to pay back taxes. He's not going to confess to murder to avoid a slap on the wrist. Forget Hobson. The person to go after is Nelson. He's a paraplegic facing a prison sentence and he may be willing to trade information for a deal to stay out of jail. But that means we need someone to influence the person prosecuting Nelson. Someone who can make the prosecutor promise Nelson a deal if he talks about Mulray Pharma or can promise to make his life as miserable as possible if he refuses to talk. In other words—and I can't believe I'm saying this—we need Mahoney."

Mahoney was three sheets to the wind when DeMarco met with him.

A congressman had died, a fellow Democrat from Massachusetts named Callahan. While Callahan was alive, Mahoney rarely had a kind thing to say about the man. He had called Callahan a "righteous, mealymouthed little turd" and said he should have been a priest instead of a politician. DeMarco judged from these comments that Callahan had ethical qualms about some of the things that Mahoney did or wanted him to do. Whatever their past relationship, Mahoney went to Callahan's wake, which was being held at an Irish pub on Capitol Hill, and DeMarco had no doubt that Mahoney gave an eloquent eulogy and lied about how much he had admired the man.

When DeMarco entered the pub, Mahoney had one thick arm around the shoulders of Callahan's chief of staff, a woman named Allison Bridge. Bridge was in her forties, had short blonde hair, a pleasant face, and a marvelous figure for a mother of three. The few times DeMarco had encountered Bridge in the past, she'd come across as cold, calculating, and manipulative—in other words, a perfect political chief of staff. Tonight, however, it looked as if she had had more than a few drinks to help her cope with the passing of her employer—and probably the loss of her job; her cheeks were flushed and she seemed unsteady on her feet. And naturally, Mahoney—being Mahoney—was trying to take advantage of the situation.

As DeMarco approached Mahoney, he heard him say to Bridge, "Yeah, I loved Dick, loved him like a brother. I'm gonna miss him like a, like a . . . like a brother."

DeMarco rolled his eyes, then tapped Mahoney on the shoulder and said, "I need to talk to you. It's important."

Mahoney scowled and said, "Well, whatever it is, it'll wait until tomorrow. I'm busy now."

"Mavis said you're going out of town tomorrow."

"Oh, yeah, that's right," Mahoney said. "Then whatever it is will have to wait until I get back." Mahoney pulled Allison Bridge closer and said, "Did I ever tell you about the time Dick and I—"

"Sir," DeMarco said, "it's about the thing with Brian Kincaid. It's a big deal."

"Aw, for Christ's sake," Mahoney grumped. To Bridge, he said, "Stay here, sweetheart. I'll be right back." To DeMarco he said, "Let's go outside. And, goddamnit, this had better be good."

DeMarco knew Mahoney wanted to go outside so he could smoke a cigar. He about went nuts when the District passed laws outlawing smoking inside restaurants and bars and—in an under-the-table way—had tried his best to get the laws rescinded. It wasn't Mahoney's only political failure but, because it affected him personally, it bothered him more than some other battles he'd lost.

Once they were out on the sidewalk in front of the pub, Mahoney handed DeMarco the shot glass of Jameson's he'd been holding so he could ignite his cigar. When the tip of the stogie was blazing, he took the glass back from DeMarco and drained it. "So now what is it?" he said.

Knowing how short Mahoney's attention span could be, particularly when there was a semidrunk and vulnerable woman to pursue, DeMarco quickly told Mahoney how he needed his help to squeeze a confession out of Nelson.

When he finished, Mahoney muttered, "I could have made a ton of money if I'd bought Mulray stock when this whole thing started." DeMarco didn't know what to say to that and before he could think of anything, Mahoney said, "Okay. I'll call the guy tomorrow, before I leave."

DeMarco wanted to say, *Are you sure you'll remember to call?* But he didn't. He did wonder, however, if Simon Ballard could invent a pill to reduce the number of Mahoney's brain cells that died each time he attended a wake.

36

DeMarco met with the Arlington County prosecutor in the cafeteria of the hospital where Nelson was being treated—and held captive. To DeMarco's amazement, Mahoney had remembered to call the man.

Charles Erhart was a short, chunky guy who compensated for his lack of stature with an aggressive chin and an even more aggressive attitude. As there was no reason to hold anything back from Erhart, DeMarco told him the whole story, concluding with, "So we think Mulray Pharma killed some people to test this new drug, that Brian Kincaid was framed, and that Nelson was in that liquor store to kill me. The only reason he didn't was because an off-duty cop couldn't make up his mind on what kind of wine to buy."

"Can you prove any of this?" Erhart said.

"Nope, I can't prove a thing," DeMarco admitted. "But if you can offer Nelson a deal and get him to talk . . . Well, I'm guessing you can imagine the kind of headline that would generate."

What DeMarco meant was a headline that read: ARLINGTON PROSECUTOR EXPOSES PHARMACEUTICAL GIANT.

Erhart waved the headline comment away as if his career prospects had nothing to do with his willingness to cooperate. He sipped his coffee and pretended to think things over a bit. "Well, if John Mahoney hadn't called me, I'd probably find all this a bit, uh, unorthodox, but since he's the one who asked me to help—"

"Good," DeMarco said, cutting Erhart off. "Let's go talk to Nelson."

DeMarco wondered what Mahoney had promised Erhart. Help getting elected to Congress? Financial support for his next campaign? Whatever he promised, it was enough.

Nelson was lying in bed when DeMarco and the prosecutor entered the room, and DeMarco noticed there was a chin-up bar above the bed and next to the bed was a wheelchair. Nelson had been in the hospital for almost a month and, at least from the waist up, looked okay. He wasn't connected to an oxygen tank and they weren't dripping fluids into him from a bag. The angle of the bed was tilted so Nelson was in a half-sitting position and the television was on with the volume turned down low. Nelson was watching a bass fishing show.

DeMarco had seen Nelson only briefly that day in the liquor store and he didn't know if Nelson had weighed more before he was shot, but the man lying in the bed was a powerful-looking man—broad shoulders, ropy muscles in his neck and arms. His dark hair was cut short on the top and shaved down to stubble on the sides; his face was hard and unforgiving. DeMarco had a mental image of what a Delta Force soldier should look like—and Nelson fit the image. Even lying in a hospital bed, he gave off an aura of lethal competence.

DeMarco could tell that Nelson recognized him, but he didn't ask what DeMarco was doing there. He just glanced at his two visitors briefly, then swiveled his head back to the fishing show.

"Mr. Nelson," Erhart said, "my name is Charles Erhart and I'm the Arlington County prosecutor. You've been dealing with people on my staff until this point. I'm the boss, in other words, and I'm the man who will decide your fate."

Without looking at Erhart, Nelson said, "Get out of here."

"I'm willing to make you a deal," Erhart said. "If you'll confess to your role in Phil Downing's death and tell me everything you did to help Mulray Pharma develop this new Alzheimer's drug, I'll keep you from going to jail. The fact is, no matter what you may have done, you're a small fish and the people I really want are the executives at the Warwick Foundation and Mulray Pharma. But if you don't confess, I'm going to see to it that you're incarcerated in the worst hellhole in Virginia and the one that has the least accommodations for cripples."

Nelson's jaw clenched when Erhart said *cripples.*

"And I'll make sure," Erhart said, "that you get the maximum possible sentence under the sentencing guidelines, which means you'll spend fifteen years in prison. Remember—you tried to kill a cop. So think about that, Nelson. Think about spending fifteen years in a cage and what the animals will do to a man in your condition."

Nelson didn't respond. He just turned up the volume on the television and continued to watch the fishing show, acting as if DeMarco and Erhart weren't in the room. After a moment, Erhart looked over at DeMarco and shrugged and they turned to leave. As they were leaving, they heard: "Bobby Ray, can you believe the size of that fish? My Lord, buddy, that baby must weigh seven pounds."

———◆◆◆———

Standing in the corridor outside Nelson's room, Erhart said, "That didn't go so well, but maybe he'll change his mind after he's had some time to think things over."

"Yeah, maybe," DeMarco said, but he didn't think Nelson was going to change his mind.

"Anyway," Erhart said, "please tell the Speak . . . Congressman Mahoney I tried and I'll call you if anything happens."

"I'll let Mahoney know what you did, and I'm sure he'll be grateful, but you have to do what you said. You gotta make sure that guy gets the max if he doesn't talk."

DeMarco decided to go talk to Bill Hobson next.

37

Bill Hobson sat in his office, thinking about his future.

The fact that Lizzie Warwick had killed herself didn't mean the Warwick Foundation had ceased to exist. The foundation was a legal entity, a nonprofit corporation with money in the bank and assets in various parts of the world. And Lizzie's team—minus Lizzie and Lambert—was still at the refugee camp in Uganda, and Hobson needed to get supplies to them. More important, Hobson needed to make sure that the Warwick Care Centers had everything they needed to continue to operate.

Hobson's primary job had always been related to testing Ballard's drug: shipping drugs to the care centers, getting biological samples sent to the lab in Delaware, delivering corpses to Thailand for autopsy. He also had to make sure the care centers had adequate food and fuel and everything else needed to house forty or fifty elderly people—but the only reason the welfare of the old folk mattered was because they were the petri dishes for testing Simon Ballard's drug.

The original plan had been to close the care centers as soon as the Thai drug trials were complete. They wouldn't need the centers after that—or the people in them. But now, because of the article in the *Washington Post,* they couldn't simply walk away from the centers, leaving a bunch of old people stumbling about with no one to tend to them. That wouldn't look good.

So Fiona had told him to keep the centers running normally for a while, maybe six more months. Then, after the media had settled down a bit and turned their attention to other matters, Hobson would send a letter to appropriate officials in Peru, Pakistan, Indonesia, and Africa saying: *We're making you a gift of those facilities—the Quonset huts, the generators, the beds—but all those old coots are your problem from this point forward.*

After Fiona told him this, he asked her, "Uh, what happens to me after all this is over? Are you going to have another job for me?"

Fiona paused before she answered. "Don't worry, Bill. You're a good man and we owe you. We'll find something for you."

A good man? In the time he had known her, Fiona had never been the least bit complimentary, nor had she ever been friendly toward him. Whenever she'd spoken to him in the past, she'd been pissed off, swearing at him about some minor fuckup, threatening to fire him if he didn't fix whatever the problem was.

But now he was *a good man*—and it was those three words that made up his mind.

Had Hobson been a naïve optimist, he might have thought that he could indeed have a future with Mulray Pharma, that maybe they needed a guy like him to deal with some legitimate logistical issue, like building drug-manufacturing facilities overseas. During his army career, he'd set up bases for entire brigades in parts of the world where they didn't have running water or electricity. Building a facility in China to manufacture drugs would be a piece of cake.

But Bill Hobson wasn't an optimist. He was a pessimist and a realist. And from Mulray Pharma's perspective, he was now one thing and one thing only: he was a *liability*. He knew what they had done in Peru and those other places. He knew what they had done to keep Phil Downing from exposing them prematurely. And he knew—he was absolutely positive—that as soon as Fiona no longer needed him, she was going to have someone put a bullet through his head. Why was he so certain? Because he was *a good man.*

He had six months, however, because Fiona needed him for six months. That would give him plenty of time to develop a getaway plan. Then he thought, *Why wait?* This was the perfect time to run. Nelson was in the hospital and Kelly had disappeared. In six months, Fiona would hire a new pair of killers and Hobson would be at the top of her list—and she wouldn't need guys as good as Kelly and Nelson to dispose of him; any garden-variety hit man would do. Yeah, this was the time for a good man to get out of Dodge.

In the five years he'd worked for Mulray Pharma, Hobson had lived frugally because he'd always known that his future was uncertain. He didn't have any kind of pension plan—he wasn't even eligible for social security since he'd worked for the army for thirty years—so he lived in a cheap apartment, drove an economical car, and saved 30 percent of his annual salary; he was able to save so much because he didn't pay taxes on the money. As a result of all this, he currently had three hundred and seventy five thousand dollars in the bank. With that much money he could buy a trailer—a fuckin' double-wide, like every other broke-dick old man—and then maybe find some kind of job to supplement his savings. And if he moved to someplace down South, like Alabama or Arkansas or Mississippi—someplace where the cost of living wasn't too high—he might be able to get by. But wherever he moved to, it had to be in the South. He hated the cold. He would have preferred Florida, someplace like Fort Myers or Naples, but it was too expensive there.

He finally decided on Little Rock. The city wasn't too big, but big enough that there were employment opportunities. And when he was in the army, he'd visited the Pine Bluff Arsenal near Little Rock and found the city charming in its own way. And except for the occasional tornado, the weather was usually fairly decent.

So that was his plan: run for Little Rock before Fiona sent someone to kill him.

———◆◆◆———

As Mulray Pharma's chief attorney, Fiona was up to her neck dealing with the various legal issues arising from the new drug. None of these issues, however, were unexpected or insurmountable, and it looked as if the two-hundred-person outside law firm that Mulray had retained was doing a better-than-average job of fending off anyone who might cause the company trouble. Yes, it looked like she and Orson had pulled it off. Mulray Pharma's stock continued to rise, and Orson was betting that within a year the drug would be approved for use in the United States and Europe.

As for Orson, he was on a whirlwind media tour. He was appearing on television and radio talk shows saying virtually the same thing he said at his press conference. In part, he was reinforcing the fact that Mulray Pharma had done nothing illegal—but what he was *really* doing was promoting his new drug. Instead of paying a few million dollars a minute to advertise on television, he was being given ten- and fifteen-minute blocks of time to talk about the wonders of his new drug on prime-time shows like *60 Minutes*.

Fiona's cell phone rang—not her BlackBerry. The BlackBerry was her corporate phone and the number she gave out to everybody who might need to talk to her. The cell phone was untraceable and disposable, and was used only to communicate with Kelly, Nelson, Lambert, and Hobson. And now Earl Lee.

"Yes?" she said.

"It's Kelly."

"Where are you, goddamnit! I've got things I need you to do." Actually, she didn't have anything for him to do.

"You don't need to know where I am," Kelly said, "and fuck whatever you need me to do. The only thing I care about right now is Nelson."

"I told you, Nelson's going to be all right. If he pleads guilty they'll give him three or four years, then parole him in a few months because of his condition. He just needs to be patient."

"Yeah, well, there's something you don't know. The Arlington County DA and DeMarco met with Nelson and—"

"DeMarco?"

"Yeah. I don't know why the hell he's involved in Nelson's prosecution, but he is. Anyway, the prosecutor told Nelson that if he didn't give up everything he knows about Mulray, they're going to throw the book at him. He's going to get fifteen years unless he rats you out."

"They're bluffing."

"I don't think so, Fiona, but it doesn't matter if they are or not. I'm going to get Nelson out of the country."

"How will you do that?"

"Never mind how. And that's not the reason I called. I want the rest of what you owe us, the last installment, which is one point six million."

"Well, I don't know about that, since you're no longer working for us."

"Fiona, if you don't give me the money, I'll get a good rifle with a good scope and shoot you in the head from three hundred yards away. Now Nelson and me, we upheld our end of the bargain. You got your drug tested and we did our part, and now I want the rest of the money. If you don't wire it to our account by tomorrow afternoon, I'm going gun shopping."

Maybe this was okay, Fiona thought. Kelly and Nelson had no reason to talk. They'd go to jail if they did. And if Nelson was out of the country, the chance of them talking was even less—and she could always kill them later. As for the money, who gave a shit? Mulray

Pharma was going to make so much money off Ballard's new drug that a million six was pocket change. Hell, it was *less* than pocket change.

"Okay," she said, making it sound as if she was reluctantly giving in. "You'll have the money tomorrow. But you better do what you say, Kelly, and you better keep your mouths shut. You think you're a hard guy, but there are a lot of hard guys like you out there."

After she hung up, she thought about the situation some more. She assumed Kelly was going to try to spring Nelson from the hospital and then fly him out of the country, and, being Kelly, he'd most likely pull it off. But if he didn't pull it off and he was caught . . . well, that could be a major problem.

One option she had was to have Earl Lee kill Kelly and Nelson. She would tell Lee to stake out the hospital, kill Kelly when he showed up to free Nelson, then whack Nelson while he was drooling in his wheelchair. But as much as she liked that idea, she wasn't sure Lee was good enough to kill Kelly, and if he didn't kill him, Kelly would very likely kill her.

The best thing to do at this point was let Kelly do what he wanted. But again she thought: What if he's caught? Would he make a deal with the government for a reduced sentence? No, he wouldn't do that. Kelly and Nelson were serial killers, mass murderers, whatever the correct term was. They'd killed a bunch of helpless old people. There was no way the government would give them a get-out-of-jail deal even if they testified against her and Orson. They might get reduced sentences, like maybe life in prison instead of the needle, but they'd still end up doing years and years in prison if they confessed to what they did. She didn't know what sort of prison sentence Kelly could get for helping Nelson escape, but whatever it was, it would be substantially less than if he confessed to what he had done for Mulray Pharma.

Let's see what happens, she thought. If Kelly succeeded, great. Then she'd find him and Nelson later and send in a fucking *team* to take them out. And if Kelly failed to escape with Nelson then she'd come up with Plan B. Fiona had always been able to develop a Plan B.

Then another thought occurred to her: Why was DeMarco still mixed up in this? Did he still think he could get Brian Kincaid out of jail? And why would the Arlington County prosecutor permit DeMarco to be there when he met with Nelson? She had always thought that DeMarco was just a low-level congressional flunky, but now she was beginning to wonder if that was really the case. It looked like he had some clout—or had someone behind him with some clout—and that wasn't good.

She and Orson had been hoping that what they had done with the Warwick Foundation would never come to light. They didn't want to have to face all the issues they were now facing in the media, the main issue being that they had taken advantage of the downtrodden folk that Lizzie had been trying to help. But after DeMarco and Emma sicced the press on them, Orson dealt with the issue head-on: he admitted what they did with the Warwick people and took the stance that everything they had done was legal—which it was, except for killing a few folks and those killings would never come to light unless Lambert, Hobson, Kelly, or Nelson talked.

So for now there was no reason to kill DeMarco and Emma—the cat was fully out of the bag. Yet it bothered her that DeMarco was still poking into things, and it looked like his latest maneuver had been to convince the prosecutor to threaten Nelson with the maximum sentence. But that gambit would be neutralized when Kelly sprung Nelson.

She paced her office, unconsciously scratching her left forearm, as she mulled everything over. She stopped once to touch the yellowing leaves of a dying fica plant that sat near a window. She had her secretary water the stupid thing and it was in a place where it got sun, but it seemed as if it just *wanted* to die. It was like the plant was committing suicide to spite her.

Her biggest problem, she thought, wasn't DeMarco, nor was it Kelly or Nelson. And she wasn't worried about René Lambert, either. There was no evidence that Lambert had done anything illegal and, even if he had, the United States had no jurisdiction in the countries where he had operated. If the U.S. government could prove that Lambert had broken some U.S. law—although she couldn't imagine what law that would be—he'd have to be extradited from France, and the French, being the contrary pricks they were, would most likely refuse to extradite him. Yeah, René was okay; he wasn't a problem.

Hobson was her problem. That potbellied pencil pusher—he was the weak link. He hadn't committed a major crime—he'd mostly just shipped things to and fro—and although he was an accomplice in Phil Downing's murder, he hadn't pulled the trigger. Yeah, the government would definitely give Hobson a deal if he talked.

Hobson had to go—no matter what Orson said.

She had told Hobson that she needed him to maintain the care centers for six more months, but the more she thought about it, the more she realized she didn't really need him—she just needed someone *like* him. And now that Mulray's role with the care centers was out in the open, some manager at Mulray Pharma could do Hobson's job. Yes, she should get rid of Hobson now, particularly since DeMarco was still poking into things, because when Nelson escaped, DeMarco might decide to squeeze Bill Hobson next.

But no more tricky stuff. She was going to keep it simple with Hobson.

She called Earl Lee. "I want you to take care of Hobson. Break into his house, shoot him in the head, and steal some shit. Do it right away."

"Roger that," Lee said.

Roger that. What an asshole.

The first thing Hobson did after leaving his office was drive to the day care center to pick up Brad.

General Omar Bradley was a purebred black cairn terrier—the cutest little four-legged, button-eyed critter you've ever seen—and he was named after the great World War II general, whom Hobson had always admired. And just as Patton had called the human Omar Bradley *Brad,* that's what Hobson called his pet most of the time.

When it came to spending money on himself, Hobson was miserly. General Omar Bradley, however, was a different matter. The doggie day care center was a four-star facility: Brad ate nothing but the finest, most nutritious foods; he had quarterly checkups at the vet's to make sure he was healthy and free of fleas and worms. The reason Hobson was so generous when it came to his pet was that Omar Bradley was the only creature on the planet who loved him and whom Bill Hobson loved in return. When he walked into the day care center to pick him up, Brad yipped with delight, wagged his stubby tail, and licked his face—which he did every time he saw Hobson.

He would have gone crazy with loneliness had it not been for his little dog.

With Brad sitting on the seat next to him, he drove back to his shitty apartment. He took the dog for a short walk so he could do his business and gave him his medicine (mixed in with a snack), then stood in his small living room, looking at the few things he possessed. There were a couple of pictures on the wall, a sofa and a reclining chair, two end tables, three lamps, and an IKEA bookshelf that held about fifty paperbacks. All his furniture had been purchased at the same yard sale. His laptop, television, and DVD player were the most expensive things he owned, and they were all bottom-of-the-line. He'd keep the laptop but would leave the television and DVD player; he didn't want to lug them around. All his cooking utensils he'd bought at a Goodwill store, and when he needed more, he'd go to another Goodwill.

He packed as many clothes as he could get into a large duffel-bag type suitcase, leaving most of his heavy winter clothes. Then—so he wouldn't even be tempted to use them—he chopped up all his credit cards with scissors, and fed the pieces down the garbage disposal. He kept his AAA card, however, because he might need it if his car broke down—but he hoped he wouldn't.

He grabbed Brad's travel cage and all the dog food he had, and crammed everything—duffel bag, laptop, dog cage, and dog food—into the trunk of his car. He wished he had a pistol for protection, but he didn't, and he'd never tried to buy one when he got of out of prison, figuring it would be too much of a hassle.

He opened the passenger-side door of his Ford Taurus and Omar Bradley hopped into the car and sat down on his haunches. His tail was wagging frantically; Brad loved going for a ride. As they were driving, Hobson tossed his cell phone out the window. If his car broke down, he wouldn't be able to call AAA, but that was okay. Better to be stuck on the highway than have someone track him using his phone.

His next problem was money. He had almost four hundred thousand in a bank in the Caymans, but if he transferred it to another bank he'd leave an electronic trail. So what he couldn't do was transfer the money when he reached Little Rock. He called the Caymans bank from a pay phone, went through all the security rigmarole, had them wire the money to his Philadelphia bank, and then had the Philadelphia bank give him cash. He hated to do it, but he put all the money into a black plastic garbage bag and shoved it into the trunk of his car, where it was going to have to stay until he could find someplace safer to put it.

The final issue was his car. He couldn't fly to Little Rock, because there'd be an electronic record if he flew. He didn't know if you had to show ID these days to take a train or a bus—he hadn't taken either one in years—but traveling by train or bus didn't appeal to him. He wanted the flexibility a car would give him; he could set his own schedule and go wherever he wanted.

But his car was a problem. It had license plates and was registered to him.

What he really needed was a new identity—a driver's license and credit cards in some other name. He knew there were folks out there who made false IDs but he didn't know anyone personally, and he didn't intend to stay in Philadelphia long enough to find somebody. When he got to Little Rock that would be his first priority: to become someone else. But right now what he had to do was get a new, untraceable car.

He drove to an area in South Philly where there were a number of used car lots, found the sort of place he was looking for, and parked his car half a block away but close enough to keep it in sight.

Hamilton Motors had about thirty junkers in its inventory, the prices soaped onto the windows. An overweight man wearing a pork-pie hat and a yellow golf shirt was sitting on a plastic chair outside the sales office, and while Hobson walked around the lot—looking at the cars, checking the mileage—the guy remained where he was seated. He obviously wasn't the high-pressure-salesman type.

Hobson finally settled on a 1999 Toyota Camry. It had a few small dents on the doors—like it had been playing bumper cars with supermarket shopping carts—a couple rust spots on the hood, and a hundred and forty-five thousand miles on the odometer. It was selling for thirty-five hundred. He walked up to the salesman and said, "I want to test-drive that gray Camry."

The salesman let out a sigh—like getting off his butt and getting the keys for the Camry was a major inconvenience. As he handed Hobson the keys, he said, "If you're not back in fifteen minutes, I'll call the cops."

Hobson drove the car around the block a couple of times. He was afraid to go too far because he'd left Brad—and his money—in the

Taurus. The Camry sounded fine, the acceleration was good, and the brakes worked. But he didn't really know anything about cars, which was why he'd kept his AAA card. He drove back to the car lot and said to the salesman, "I'll give you three thousand. Cash."

"Okay," the salesman said, surprising Hobson. "Come into the office and we'll fill out the paperwork."

"No," Hobson said. "No paperwork."

"I can't do that. I gotta transfer the title to you so the car gets registered in your name—but for another hundred I won't ask to see your ID and I don't care what name you give me."

Hobson thought for a second and gave the salesman the name of a man who worked for the Warwick Foundation and who was still in Uganda, then drove his new-used Toyota Camry back to his Ford. He transferred all his and Brad's belongings to the trunk of the Camry, and then used a screwdriver to remove the license plates from the Ford; he'd toss the plates out on the highway on his way out of town. He took one last look around the Taurus—checked the console and the glove compartment to make sure he hadn't left anything with his name on it—then put the key in the ignition so someone could steal it easily.

It was too late in the day to start out for Arkansas so he found a cheap motel not too far from Hamilton Motors and spent the night. The next morning at five A.M., with all his worldly possessions in the trunk of his new car, West Point graduate William Benedict Hobson gave the finger to the City of Brotherly Love and headed south.

His future looked grim—but it was better than no future at all.

<hr />

Kelly forced Nelson's lawyer to go see Nelson in the hospital again so they could use the lawyer's cell phone to communicate.

"How are you doing?" Kelly asked.

"Okay," Nelson said.

He didn't sound okay. He sounded depressed.

Nelson had fully recovered from the gunshot wounds—except for being paralyzed—and had been getting physical therapy every day so he'd be able to operate a wheelchair. During the therapy sessions he made it appear that he was in considerable pain and still as weak as a kitten; Kelly had told him to do this because as soon as he was fully recovered they were going to arraign him and move him to a prison cell.

"How you doing with the wheelchair?" Kelly asked.

"I can operate it fine—the other day I was doing wheelies in the hallway when the nurses weren't looking. And I've been working out two, three hours a day on the chin-up bar over my bed. The only problem is I can't get out of this bed and into the wheelchair by myself unless I just fall out of the bed and onto the floor."

"Don't worry about getting out of bed. I'll get you out of bed."

"So when do we move?"

"Wednesday, two A.M."

While Nelson had been recovering, Kelly had been making all the preparations for their escape. He bought a Taser and a semiauto 9mm with a silencer. He bought a van that had a hydraulic ramp to accommodate wheelchairs. He made arrangements with a pilot—an Iraq War vet he knew—to fly them to Costa Rica without filing a flight plan. He leased a temporary apartment for them in Costa Rica, making sure the apartment was wheelchair-accessible. He'd selected Costa Rica because he and Nelson had been there and liked the place. He also bought them two new sets of IDs—passports, credit cards, driver's licenses. Getting the IDs had taken the most time, but now the IDs were ready—and so was Nelson.

Although he had yet to see Nelson, Kelly had reconnoitered the hospital several times, and during one of those trips he'd stolen a lab coat and a medical technician's ID badge so he could roam freely throughout the hospital. There were only two nurses on Nelson's floor on the graveyard shift, and they couldn't see Nelson's room or the elevator doors from the nurses' station. There was a cop who sat outside Nelson's door, bored out of his skull, and, when he wasn't sleeping, he was bullshitting with the nurses.

Kelly's plan was to park the van near the hospital emergency room entrance and lower the wheelchair ramp. He didn't think it likely that the van would get towed during the short time he planned to be in the hospital. He'd take the elevator up to Nelson's floor, Taser the cop, drag him into Nelson's room, put Nelson in his wheelchair, and roll him to the elevator and then into the van. He didn't want to kill the cop or the nurses because if he did, the cops would make a greater effort to catch him.

"We're going to enjoy Costa Rica, amigo," Kelly said.

"I'm sure," Nelson said, but his response was halfhearted.

"I mean it," Kelly said. "We got a lot of money in the bank and I've rented us a place on the beach. We'll hire a maid and a cook, and we'll buy a fishing boat. Then we'll drink a lot of rum and catch a lot of fish. They got marlin down there—sailfish, too. We're rich men, Nelson. We're gonna be just fine."

"But what about the place in Montana?"

Kelly hesitated. "We're gonna have to walk away from that. Maybe sometime in the future when things settle down we can figure out a way to sell it without having the money traced back to us, but I'm thinking the place in Montana is just . . . Well, it's gone."

"Aw, Jesus, Kelly."

"Yeah, I know, but that's the way it goes."

"I can't believe you're doing this for me."

"What did you think I was going to do? Let you rot in prison?"

"Kelly, there's one more thing."

"What's that?"

Nelson didn't respond.

"Nelson, what's the other thing?"

"I have to wear a diaper."

Aw, jeez. That had to be the worst thing he'd ever heard in his life. And for Nelson that had to be almost as bad as being crippled, thinking about the indignity of Kelly helping him change his diapers.

"So what?" Kelly said. "We can deal with that. You just be ready to go on Wednesday. Hooah."

Nelson was too choked up to give him a hooah back.

As DeMarco drove toward Philadelphia he went over in his head exactly what he was going to say to Bill Hobson. His first lie was going to be that he was a congressional lawyer with a *boatload* of federal clout, and he was going to use all that clout to make sure Hobson spent the remainder of his life in a federal prison. *If you thought Leavenworth was bad,* DeMarco would say, *wait until you see the cage I'm gonna put you in.* His next lie would be—contrary to what was being reported in the media—that the Justice Department was secretly working with law enforcement agencies in four other countries to prove Mulray Pharma had tested their new drug in an illegal manner and killed a few poor souls along the way. *This means,* he'd tell Hobson, *that you just might get the needle. Hell, we'll extradite your ass to Pakistan, where they still hang people.* Finally, he'd tell Hobson the one thing he knew to be true: that Neil had gathered enough information to make sure Hobson was convicted of tax evasion, and where Hobson might normally get a fine, DeMarco—the guy with that boatload of federal clout—was going to make sure he served at least ten years in prison for that particular crime. After he'd told all these lies, he'd tell Hobson the only way out was to testify against Mulray Pharma and, in particular, to testify that he'd helped frame Brian Kincaid for murder. By the time he arrived in Philly, DeMarco had worked up a full head of steam and had his speech down pat.

Fifteen minutes later, he found out that all his mental preparations were for naught. Hobson's secretary told him that Hobson had not shown up for work and wasn't answering his cell phone. The woman was practically in tears because she had no idea what to do with him gone.

Pissed off that Hobson wasn't where he was supposed to be, DeMarco called Neil and had him look up Hobson's address, which turned out to be an apartment building on the east side of town. When Hobson didn't answer his door, DeMarco's nerves began to tingle. He knocked on the apartment manager's door next and asked if she'd seen Hobson, and she told him she saw him putting a suitcase in the trunk of his car, along with the travel cage for his little dog. She thought maybe he was taking a vacation. DeMarco didn't think so.

"Hobson's gone," Earl Lee said.

"Gone where?" Fiona said.

"I don't know, but he's split. I broke into his apartment and it looks like a lot of his clothes are missing—you know, empty drawers and a whole bunch of bare hangers in the closet. And I couldn't find a suitcase in the place, either."

"Goddamnit all to hell," Fiona muttered. To Lee she said, "Okay. I've got some guys who can track him down, and I'll call you when they find him."

"Roger that," Lee said.

If he didn't quit saying that, Fiona was going to rip his tongue right out of his head.

Fiona called her headhunters—those guys had been invaluable—and told them she'd give them a bonus if they found Hobson fast.

One of them called her back a couple hours later and said Hobson had cleaned out his bank accounts and had stopped using his credit cards and his cell phone. He definitely hadn't caught a plane but he could be on a train or a bus. Or he could be driving.

"But don't worry, we'll find him," the headhunter said. "We're good at this."

38

"Hobson's disappeared," DeMarco said, "and I'm guessing he's running from Mulray Pharma. He's afraid they're going to kill him because they think he might talk."

"This is good news," Emma said. "We can offer him protection if he'll testify."

"Only if we can find him first."

"I'll get Neil looking for him."

"In case we can't find him, I have another idea," DeMarco said. "I want Nelson out of that hospital and in a jail cell. It's going to be months before his case goes to trial, and I want to give him a taste of his future. Maybe then he'll feel like talking."

"Can you make that happen?"

"I think so. I don't know what Mahoney promised the Arlington prosecutor, but I think he'll do what I want, and I'm gonna make him move Nelson to the shittiest prison they got."

Nelson was doing one-arm pull-ups on the bar above his bed when the group walked into his room.

There were four of them: Charles Erhart, the Arlington County prosecutor; DeMarco; an older man Nelson had never seen before, an overweight, gray-haired guy who had the watery eyes of a major booze hound; and a pencil-necked little geek wearing a bowtie and holding a TV tray in one hand and what looked like an old-fashioned adding machine under his arm. The geek immediately walked over to an electrical outlet, set up the TV tray near it, pulled over a chair, and plugged the machine into a wall socket.

"What's going on?" Nelson said.

"You're being arraigned today," the prosecutor said.

"What?" Nelson said. Jesus, he hoped whatever was happening didn't fuck up Kelly's plan.

"We're just waiting for your lawyer to get here."

Dennis Conroy, Nelson's lawyer, burst into the room a minute later and immediately said to the old boozer, "Your Honor, I object to this. My client is in no condition to participate in this procedure, and he should be arraigned in a courtroom like any other citizen."

"Arlington County can't afford to keep him here," the prosecutor said. "We're not only paying for a hospital bed, we're paying cops overtime to guard him. And as for your client's health, he's in better shape than half the people in this hospital. When we walked in here, he was doing chin-ups."

"Let's get on with this," the judge said. "I got things to do today."

It turned out the geek with the bowtie was a court reporter, and he began tapping furiously on his machine as the prosecutor explained that Nelson had been arrested for armed robbery and attempted murder, and the fact that he'd tried to kill a cop made his crimes particularly "heinous." He also noted that there were three eyewitnesses who would testify against Nelson, including Mr. DeMarco, who was in attendance and willing to answer any questions the judge might ask.

"How does your client plead, Mr. Conroy?" the judge said to Nelson's lawyer.

"He pleads not guilty, and we request bail. My client is a decorated military veteran and, as you can see, clearly not a flight risk. If he's granted bail, he'll remain here in this hospital so he can continue to receive the physical therapy he desperately needs."

"As Your Honor knows," the prosecutor said, "Mr. Nelson was employed by the Warwick Foundation, and Warwick has links to the suspicious activities of a pharmaceutical company that has billons of dollars at its disposal. This makes him a flight risk."

"That's utter nonsense!" Conroy shouted. "There's no proof whatsoever that my client has any connection to Mulray Pharma. Mr. Nelson has spent most of his life defending this country, and has spent the last five years working for a charitable organization."

"Yeah, yeah," the judge said, "I've heard enough. No bail. The defendant is remanded to Wallens Ridge until his trial."

"Wallens Ridge!" Conroy shrieked. "You can't do that, Your Honor. If my client is removed from this hospital, he should be placed in the Arlington County Detention Center like any other defendant awaiting trial in this county."

"I was told the detention center isn't equipped to deal with people in Mr. Nelson's condition, but Wallens Ridge is. They got a dispensary there, or something."

"Or something! Your Honor—"

"Wallens Ridge," the judge said—and the court reporter unplugged his machine and began to fold up his TV tray.

Nelson couldn't believe this was happening to him. A month ago, he could have killed the men standing around his hospital bed with his bare hands; all he could do now was pray—pray that they didn't plan to move him out of the hospital until tomorrow morning.

DeMarco waited until everyone else had filed out of Nelson's room, then walked over to his bed. "This is just the beginning, Nelson. The only way you're getting out of this without spending the next fifteen years in jail is to testify against Orson Mulray and admit that Brian Kincaid was framed for Downing's murder."

Nelson thought about smashing his fist into DeMarco's face, but he just turned his head away and stared at the wall until DeMarco left the room.

Kelly parked the van in the curved driveway near the Emergency Room entrance, then opened the sliding door on the passenger side of the van and lowered the wheelchair ramp. He figured if anyone noticed the van, they'd think that somebody was there to pick up or drop off a patient. It wouldn't get towed, because he didn't plan to be in the hospital more than ten minutes.

He was wearing the white lab coat and hospital ID badge he'd stolen on one of his previous trips to the hospital. The ID belonged to a black man, but other than his skin color, he looked nothing like Kelly. Kelly wasn't worried about that, however; he knew that no one ever looked closely at the pictures on ID badges.

He took the elevator up to Nelson's floor and glanced down the hallway as soon as the elevator door opened. The nurses' station was to his right, around a corner and not visible to him, but he could hear the two graveyard-shift nurses talking to each other. He turned to his left and proceeded down the hallway. As he walked, he pulled the Taser from the pocket of the lab coat. His plan was to walk toward the cop sitting outside Nelson's door, nod to him in a friendly way—then jam the Taser into his chest and zap him until he was unconscious. After that, he'd drag the cop into the room, tie him up and gag him, then take Nelson from the hospital. Overcoming the cop would be easy compared with what he'd done when he was with Delta Force, but he was still energized and completely focused, the way he always was during a mission.

He turned the corner and looked down the hallway—but the cop wasn't at his station. At first he thought that maybe the cop had gone to the restroom or was bullshitting with the nurses. Then he noticed that the chair where the cop sat wasn't in the hallway. *What the hell?* He continued up the hallway and pushed open the door to Nelson's room. The lights were out in the room, but the hallway lighting provided enough illumination that he could see someone lying in bed and could hear him snoring. Kelly smiled. Nelson had always been calm before a mission, but Kelly figured he would have been wide awake tonight.

He walked over to the bed and poked Nelson, and the man turned his head and opened his eyes—and Kelly realized it wasn't Nelson. The guy in the bed looked about eighty years old—and for just a moment, Kelly thought he was looking at one of the old men he'd killed in Peru. He recovered from the shock immediately and realized they must have moved Nelson to a different room, maybe to a different floor. *Son of a bitch!*

He walked out of the room and directly to the nurses' station. One of the nurses was a young gal who looked like she might be Filipino. The other nurse was a fat, tough-looking black woman. The Filipino was saying, "So I go see his teacher, and I ask her how come—"

Kelly interrupted her. "Where's the guy who was in Room 526? The guy with the gunshot wounds who was being guarded by the cops?"

The black woman frowned, probably not liking Kelly's tone of voice or maybe the wild-eyed way he looked. "Who are you?" she said. But the Filipino said, "He's gone. They discharged him today."

"Discharged him?" Kelly said.

"Yeah, I heard they took him to prison," the Filipino nurse said.

"Why are you asking about the patient?" the older nurse said, but Kelly turned and walked back to the elevator without responding.

What the hell was going on? What did she mean they took him to prison?

———◆———

Kelly was livid. He was going to give Nelson's lawyer a beat-down when he saw him, he was gonna beat him like he'd never beaten anyone in his life. He realized then that he didn't know where Conroy lived; he always met the lawyer in the underground parking garage in the building where the lawyer worked. He pulled out his cell phone, planning to call directory assistance to get Conroy's address, then stopped. *Slow down,* he told himself. He didn't know if Conroy had a wife and kids who lived with him, and if he went to the lawyer's house he'd have to deal with them, too. It was two-thirty in the morning. The lawyer would show up at his office in a few hours—and Kelly would be there when he did.

———◆———

As soon as Conroy stepped from his car, Kelly exited the van—the van that he'd bought to transport Nelson. There was no one else in the parking garage when Conroy arrived, but Kelly wouldn't have cared if there had been. He strode toward Conroy aggressively, and Conroy must have seen the simmering rage in his face because he said, "Wait, wait, wait a minute." Kelly didn't wait. He grabbed Conroy by the throat and slammed him up against his Lexus. Then, because he was so pissed, he slammed him again, practically breaking Conroy's back.

"What happened to Nelson?" Kelly said. "A nurse at the hospital said he was taken to prison."

Conroy tried to talk but all that came out of his mouth was a squawk, and Kelly realized he was squeezing the man's throat so hard he couldn't speak. He relaxed his grip and the lawyer croaked, "They arraigned him yesterday."

"Arraigned him?"

"Yeah," Conroy said. "The county prosecutor said they couldn't afford the expense of continuing to guard Nelson in the hospital, so he brought a judge to his hospital room and they arraigned him and the judge refused to give him bail."

"Why the fuck didn't you call me yesterday and tell me this?"

"I didn't know about the arraignment until a half an hour before it happened. They sprung it on me. It was an ambush. And I did call you. I left a message on your cell."

"Bullshit," Kelly said, and he pulled his cell phone off his belt and saw he had a voice mail waiting. The lawyer must have called when he was in the shower or maybe he just didn't hear the phone ring. He'd suffered some hearing loss on a mission in Iran. "Where's Nelson now?" he asked.

"Wallens Ridge. The prison at Big Stone Gap."

"Ah, Jesus," Kelly muttered. "So what happens next?"

"He'll go to trial. The court hasn't set a date yet but it'll be at least four or five months from now." He saw the anger flare in Kelly's eyes and quickly added, "Look, I'm sorry, but the prosecutor is being completely unreasonable. I called him yesterday to see what kind of a deal I could get for Nelson, and he said he wouldn't make a deal. He said he has no doubt he'll win at trial and that the judge—the same asshole who refused to give him bail—will throw the book at him. And there's something else."

"What?" Kelly said. What more bad news could there possibly be?

"There was a guy at Nelson's arraignment yesterday, a guy named DeMarco, and—"

"Shit," Kelly said.

"Do you know who he is?"

"Yeah. He's a lawyer who works for Congress."

"Congress? Well, I don't know what Congress has to do with this, but yesterday I saw DeMarco talking to the judge and the prosecutor, shaking their hands and patting them on the back, like he was telling them they'd done a good job. The prosecutor was definitely kissing his ass."

Goddamnit, Kelly thought. It looked like somebody had decided that Nelson was the guy to squeeze to find out what Mulray Pharma had done—and it looked like DeMarco was the one applying the pressure. DeMarco had started off as a guy halfheartedly poking into Phil Downing's death and had somehow ended up exposing everything. And now he was trying to fuck up Nelson's life. It was time to kill DeMarco.

His first priority, however, was to see if he could come up with a way to get Nelson out of Wallens Ridge—but he knew freeing him from a prison was going to be a thousand times harder than springing him from a hospital.

His jabbed two fingers into Conroy's chest. "You get your ass down to Wallens Ridge today and see how Nelson's being treated, see if they're taking care of him the way they're supposed to. And if they're not, you fuckin' well better do something about it. Call me this afternoon."

39

Bernie Poole placed his small feet up on his desk, laced his small hands behind his balding head, and asked himself a question: What did he know about Bill Hobson?

He knew Hobson had a dog and spent a lot of money on it. He had an ex-wife in Dayton, Ohio, a son in Toledo, Ohio, and a daughter in Lexington, Kentucky, but he hadn't phoned any of them in years. He rented movies from Netflix, shopped at Safeway, and bought pizzas from a place called Tacconelli's.

He had almost four hundred grand in cash. The money had been transferred from an account in the Caymans to a Philadelphia checking account and then Hobson had cleaned out the Philadelphia account. He wasn't using his credit cards or his cell phone, and he hadn't bought an airline ticket. Not much to go on, Bernie had to admit—but he'd found people knowing a whole lot less than he did about Bill Hobson.

While employed at the CIA, Bernie had spent most of his time in front of a computer. He never operated in the field, never carried a weapon, and, except for a couple of classes he attended, never left Langley. At Langley, he started out as an intelligence analyst, but following 9/11, he found terrorists—and people who knew terrorists and sent money to terrorists. Bernie suspected that half the people he tracked down weren't terrorists at all but just guys unlucky enough to be stuck with names like Ali or Mohammad. Whatever the case, Bernie spent ten years finding people who didn't want to be found—and he was good at it.

Upon retiring from the agency, he and two other guys from Langley decided to set up their own shop. They weren't private detectives, and they weren't licensed as such. They didn't advertise—you had to have connections in the right places to know about them—and on their tax returns they listed their occupations as *corporate consultants*. And, depending on your definition of the word *corporate,* that was somewhat true. But *headhunters,* as Fiona thought of them, was a more accurate job description, although even that word didn't capture the total scope of Bernie's services or the nature of his clients, or the depths he'd go to satisfy them.

Some of what Bernie and his pals did was rather mundane. For example, if a company was planning to hire an executive for several hundred thousand dollars a year, Bernie and his associates would make sure the executive's resume matched reality; too many guys claimed to have graduated from Harvard when they really hadn't. Or if you were a party boss and wanted to be sure the candidate you were backing was as squeaky-clean as he claimed to be, Bernie was the man to assist you; it was better to learn of your candidate's past transgressions from Bernie than from an article in the *New York Times.* Then there were clients like Mulray Phama. When Fiona needed to locate a charismatic, debt-ridden, foreign-born physician to help test drugs in an unorthodox manner, and an ex-convict capable of managing a relief organization—Bernie was the man she came to.

But Bernie's services went beyond simply researching people's backgrounds. He and his pals were literally headhunters. They had found crooked accountants who had dipped their sticky fingers into the till, drug mules who'd absconded with bags of white powder that didn't belong to them, and bigmouthed mobsters who ratted out their pals and thought they were safe in the arms of the Witness Protection Program. It didn't matter how far they ran, how deep and dark the hole in which they tried to hide, Bernie and his buddies found them all. Eventually.

What made Bernie so good at his job was that when he was at Langley he developed contacts in a lot of organizations, both private and public—organizations like credit card companies and telephone companies and law enforcement agencies. People in these organizations helped either because the government forced them to or out of a sense of patriotism. Now that he was retired from the CIA, he discovered that these same people would still help. It just took cash—and a client like Mulray Pharma had buckets of that.

The way Bernie found folks most often was by tracking banking transactions, credit card charges, and cell phone calls. A credit card and cell phone were, from Bernie's perspective, almost as good as a GPS device strapped to a sex offender's ankle. And the first thing he did to find Hobson was look at his credit card and cell phone records, which was how he knew about Hobson's dog and his preference for Tacconelli's pizzas. The other thing people invariably did, even when they were on the run, was call friends and relatives, and Bernie would monitor the friends' and relatives' phone records.

The problem with Hobson was that he didn't seem to have any friends and he never called his relatives, and when he saw that Hobson wasn't using his credit cards or cell phone, he knew that finding the guy was going to take some time and effort—and Fiona had indicated that she didn't have a lot of time. Actually, Fiona had screamed at him that he'd better find Hobson in a hurry or she was never going to use his useless ass again. Fiona was not the ideal client. He'd worked for drug dealers who were more civil.

Bernie figured his best chance for finding Hobson was through his dog. According to his credit card records, a veterinarian on Girard

Avenue in Philly cared for Hobson's mutt, and every three months he paid the vet about a hundred bucks. And every month there was a sixteen-dollar credit card charge to PetMeds.com. So it looked like Hobson bought some sort of medication for his dog, though Bernie couldn't understand why he paid the vet every three months. Quarterly checkups? That seemed kind of excessive.

Finally he just called the Philadelphia vet. He told the young lady who answered the phone that he was Bill Hobson's neighbor and that Hobson had left his dog with him.

"Bill was called away," Bernie said, trying to sound flustered. "Some kind of big emergency. But he was so rattled by whatever was going on, he didn't explain very well about the medicine I'm supposed to give the dog, and he said if he was gone very long, I had to take it to your clinic. I don't know what to do."

Bernie figured animal doctors wouldn't be superconcerned about patient confidentiality since the patient was a four-legged critter—and he was right. The young lady told him all about Hobson's pet. She said the animal suffered from a mild form of epilepsy and took phenobarbital to control seizures, and you just mixed a pill in with the dog's food.

"The thing is," the young lady said, "phenobarbital can cause liver problems and Mr. Hobson insists that we test the General's liver function every three months, which really isn't necessary, but he's a real mother hen when it comes to his pet."

The general? Bernie thanked the lady—and figured she'd just given him what he needed to catch Bill Hobson. At some point, Hobson would contact his Philadelphia vet and have his dog's medical records sent to wherever he was staying. Or maybe he'd have to contact the vet to get authorization to refill his dog's prescription and, since he wasn't using his credit cards, wouldn't be able to get the medication online. What Bernie would do was start watching the veterinarian's phone records—he could get those—and start looking for calls coming from and going to out-of-state pharmacies and out-of-state vets, and he'd eventually figure out where Hobson was staying and track him down.

Hmmm. Yeah, that would work, but it was going to take *way* too long. The dog—The General?—wasn't due for a liver test for another fifty days. No way would Fiona stand for that. He had to come up with a faster way to locate Hobson.

And then Bernie got lucky.

———◆◆◆———

Hobson got a speeding ticket in Morristown, Tennessee, for going thirty-two in a twenty-five-mile-per-hour zone. A small-town revenue generator in the form of a speed trap, and Bill Hobson put his foot right in it. And for some reason, the cop who stopped Hobson contacted the police in Philadelphia, the Pennsylvania Highway Patrol, and the Pennsylvania DMV to see if Hobson had any outstanding warrants. When the cop contacted the Pennsylvania DMV Bernie was notified, because one of the first things he had done to find Hobson was talk to a source there to get information about Hobson's car—and his source told him about the inquiry from the Tennessee cop. The great news about the speeding ticket was that Bernie now knew the general direction Hobson was traveling. He also knew that Hobson wasn't driving the Taurus that was registered to him but instead had a Toyota Camry.

Bernie pulled out a United States road map and found Morristown, Tennessee. It appeared that Hobson was heading in a southwesterly direction—not due south toward Florida or due west—and this made Bernie wonder if Hobson might be going to Texas and was planning to cross into Mexico. If he crossed the border, it would be harder to find him, because Bernie didn't have contacts in Mexico like he had in the U.S. He did, however, have numerous contacts in Homeland

Security from his days at the CIA, and U.S. Customs and Border Protection worked for Homeland. Maybe, Bernie thought, he could convince his pals in Homeland that Hobson was a fugitive and get them looking for him at the Mexican border crossings—assuming Hobson was planning to cross the border, which was a big assumption. And then Bernie had what he considered to be a brilliant idea, the word *fugitive* having given him the idea.

He called Fiona and said, "I've got a way to track Hobson down in a hurry, but it's going to cost a bundle and it'll involve the cops."

"What's your definition of a bundle?" Fiona said.

"Fifty K."

"Shit, is that all? What's your plan?"

Bernie told her.

One of Bernie's contacts from his days at Langley was a guy who worked at the Hoover Building in D.C. The guy wasn't an agent—he was an IT weenie—and he helped Bernie by looking things up in the FBI's databases, and Bernie repaid these favors with a case of single malt or good seats at a Redskins game. What Bernie wanted this time, however, was going to cost a whole lot more than a case of Glenfiddich.

"Jesus, Bernie! I'll lose my job if it's traced back to me," the guy said when Bernie told him what he wanted. "Hell, I could go to jail."

"Can't you think of a way to do it without having it traced back to you?"

"Maybe, but I'm not gonna take the chance."

"Twenty-five thousand," Bernie said.

His FBI pal didn't say anything for a long time. "Give me a couple of hours to think about this and I'll get back to you."

Bernie thanked him, then spent a few minutes thinking about how he would spend the twenty-five thousand dollars *he'd* just made.

———◆◆◆———

Two hours later Bernie called Fiona and gave her an update.

"We're all set. The FBI is going to e-mail a bulletin to all law enforcement agencies located in the direction I think Hobson is traveling, which is southwest, toward Texas. The bulletin will say that Hobson was last seen in Morristown, Tennessee, is a convicted child molester, and is suspected of kidnapping a five-year-old girl in Pennsylvania. The bulletin will include Hobson's DMV photo and the make and license plate number for his car and will say that he's traveling with a dog. Now if the cops spot him, he'll be detained and questioned, but at some point the cops will notify the FBI and, when they do, my guy at the Bureau will know and he'll call me. But the thing is, the call won't go directly to my guy. It'll go to an FBI hotline number and whoever is on the hotline will pass the information on to the Bureau's kidnapping guys and somebody will eventually figure out the bulletin's a fake and the FBI will tell the cops to let Hobson go. What this means is that you'll have maybe an hour—two at the most—from the time Hobson is picked up until he's released."

"Then how in the hell are we going to be able to get to him before he's released?" Fiona asked.

"Does your company have a jet?"

"Of course."

"Then what I'd do," Bernie said, "is fly a guy to Memphis right away and tell him to charter a fast plane that can land at small airports."

"Why Memphis?"

"Like I said, Hobson is headed southwest. If my plan works, Hobson will get picked up someplace between Knoxville and Dallas, and Memphis is about halfway between those two cities. So if your guy is in Memphis and has a small, fast plane at his disposal, he might be able to get to wherever Hobson is before he's released by the cops."

———◆———

"Somebody else is looking for Hobson," Neil said.

"How do you know?" Emma said.

"Because whoever's looking is using some of the same sources I use. And one more thing. The FBI just issued the equivalent of an Amber Alert for Hobson."

"An Amber Alert?"

"Yeah. A bulletin that says Hobson kidnapped a five-year-old girl. I'm assuming the bulletin's a phony, but it's going to cause a lot of people to start looking for him."

"It's gotta be Mulray Pharma," Emma said. "They're hoping the cops will pick him up and, when they do, they'll be there to kill him."

"So what do you want me to do?" Neil said.

"I want you to find him before Mulray does."

"I don't know if I can do that, Emma. I don't have ten thousand cops helping me."

"Will you know if Hobson gets picked up?"

"Yeah. But if the cops do pick him up, they'll have to release him when they find out the bulletin's a fake. And that means that once the cops notify the FBI, you're gonna be in a footrace with Mulray Pharma."

"Call me as soon as you hear something," Emma said.

40

Hobson couldn't believe his luck—or, to be accurate, the fact that the only luck he had was *bad* luck.

The Camry he bought from Hamilton Motors overheated four hours after he left Philadelphia. No wonder the goddamn salesman hadn't haggled over the price. Then, because he didn't have a cell phone, he and General Bradley had to walk for thirty-five minutes—him holding Brad's leash in one hand and the garbage bag filled with his money in the other—until he could find a pay phone.

The closest town to where his car broke down was Harrisonburg, Virginia, and he had the car towed there—thank God he'd kept his AAA card—but the garage had to order him a new thermostat from Richmond. By the time the car was fixed, it was almost seven P.M. and because he and Brad were tired, he decided to spend the night in Harrisonburg.

The next morning at five A.M., he set off again for Little Rock, but at ten he got hungry and pulled off the interstate into Morristown, Tennessee, for some breakfast—and got pulled over by a cop, who happened to be a six-foot-three-inch female. She looked like LeBron James's mean big sister. The lady cop told him that he was going thirty-two in a twenty-five-mile-per-hour zone, and when he asked where in the hell the fucking speed limit sign was, she pointed back up the road to a sign that was almost totally hidden by the branches of a tree—and then told him that if he didn't want to get arrested, he'd better watch his foul mouth.

The other thing was, the car wasn't registered in his name because he'd given Hamilton Motors a phony name when he bought it. The good news was that he'd picked the name of a guy who he knew was in Uganda working for the Warwick Foundation. He told the cop he'd borrowed the car from a friend and all she had to do to confirm he was telling the truth was call the man—knowing that if she called, the guy wouldn't be at home. But being a cop, she was skeptical, and he'd pissed her off by swearing at her, so she got on the computer in her patrol car and spent half an hour checking to see if he had any warrants out for his arrest—and this wasn't good since he was trying to stay completely off the grid. She finally decided he wasn't a wanted criminal or a car thief, but she made him follow her to the city treasurer's office to pay his fine, which he had to do before he could leave Morristown.

After he paid the speeding ticket, he decided to skip breakfast and headed out of Morristown as fast as he could—meaning twenty-five miles per hour. He figured the chance of somebody seeing that he'd gotten the ticket was small, but these days, with everything on computers, everything connected to the Net, he was nervous. He had a decision to make. Should he ditch the Camry at the next town he came to and buy another car, or just keep on going to Little Rock? He finally decided that since Morristown was almost six hundred miles from his destination, the fact that he'd gotten the ticket shouldn't be a problem. How would anybody know he was headed to Little Rock?

Five hours later, about four in the afternoon, he pulled into a truck stop near Waverly, Tennessee, for an early dinner. When he saw the two police cars parked in front of the restaurant, he didn't give them any thought at all. He took a seat at the counter and ordered a cheese-burger for himself with everything on it and a cheeseburger without a bun for General Omar Bradley; Brad liked a good cheeseburger now and then. While he was eating, he glanced over at the two cops sit-ting at a table off to his right—and noticed they were staring at him.

The cops looked like brothers, both of them beefy blond guys with buzz cuts. He glanced at them again—they were still staring at him. They were starting to make him really nervous. He finished his cheeseburger in four big bites and paid the bill.

The cook put Brad's cheeseburger into a square Styrofoam box. Hobson had planned to feed the burger to him in the parking lot and then let him walk around for a while until he did his business. But, because of the cops, he decided he'd drive a few miles farther down the road and see if he could find a park or rest area where he could feed and walk his dog. He could practically hear Brad's little tummy growling.

He was unlocking his car when a voice called out, "Hey, hold it right there."

He turned around and, sure enough, it was the two cops. What the hell did they think he'd done? When they got closer he saw that one's name tag said J. Johnson and the other one was R. Johnson—brothers just like he'd thought, or maybe inbred cousins.

"Sir, what's your name?" J. Johnson asked him.

"Uh, Bill Hobson," Hobson said. By then the cops were standing next to him—and as soon as he said his name, R. Johnson grabbed his arm, spun him around, and slammed him up against the side of his car. The cheeseburger that he'd bought for Omar Bradley fell to the ground.

"Where is she, you son of a bitch?" R. Johnson said.

"What?" Hobson said. "What are you talking about?"

R. Johnson pulled his arm up behind his back so hard that Hob-son screamed in pain, and he wondered if the guy had dislocated his shoulder.

"Sir, do we have permission to look in your trunk?" R. Johnson said as he continued to apply pressure to Hobson's arm.

"Yeah, yeah, just let go of my arm. You're hurting me."

R. Johnson ignored Hobson's plea and said to his partner, "Open the trunk."

"We should get a warrant," J. Johnson said.

"She could be suffocating in there. Open it."

"Who could be suffocating?" Hobson said—then he thought: *Oh, shit, the money. Please, please, God, don't let them see the money.*

A moment later, J. Johnson said, "She's not in the trunk."

"She who?" Hobson screamed. "What do you think I've done?"

"We know what you've done," R. Johnson said. "You're a goddamn baby-rapin' pervert and we're gonna make you tell us what you did to that little girl."

"I haven't done—"

"Shut the fuck up!"

R. Johnson cuffed his hands behind his back, grabbed him by the nape of his neck, and walked him over to one of the patrol cars. As he opened the back door of the car, he said, "Watch your head"—and then rammed Hobson's head into the roof of the car. Hobson was almost knocked unconscious, but he heard R. Johnson say, "I told you to watch your head."

"What about my dog and my car?" Hobson said, his vision still blurred from the blow to his forehead.

"Fuck your dog and your car," R. Johnson said.

But J. Johnson said, "Your car will be towed to the station for our crime scene guy to look at, and we'll have Ray here at the truck stop look after your dog until we figure out what to do with it."

From the backseat of the patrol car, Hobson watched J. Johnson put Brad in his travel cage and take him into the restaurant. While that was happening, R. Johnson got on the radio and said, "Marge, I need to talk to the chief. It's important." A moment later, he said,

"Chief, we got that guy they issued the Amber Alert for. We found him out at Ray's eatin' his dinner like he didn't have a worry in the world. The little girl wasn't with him."

Amber Alert! What the hell was going on? Then he knew: Mulray Pharma. They did this to catch him. His biggest worry had been that the cops would find the cash in the garbage bag in his trunk, but now that was the least of his worries.

"You guys are making a big mistake," Hobson said to the back of R. Johnson's thick neck. "That Amber Alert's a phony."

"I told you to shut your mouth," R. Johnson said.

———◆◆◆———

"Got him," Bernie told Fiona. "He's being held by the cops in Waverly, Tennessee."

———◆◆◆———

When Fiona called and told him the cops in Waverly were holding Hobson, Earl Lee was sitting in the Millington Regional Jetport outside Memphis, bullshitting with the charter pilot he'd hired. The hunting rifle he'd purchased at a sporting goods store in Memphis was in an unmarked box next to his duffel bag.

"How far are we from Waverly?" Lee asked the pilot.

"About a hundred and fifty miles."

"Is there an airport near Waverly?"

"Yeah," the pilot said, and explained that the Humphreys County Airport was located just outside of Waverly.

"Can I rent a car there?"

"Sure. Call ahead and they'll have one waiting for you."

An hour later, Earl Lee was parked in his rental car across from the Waverly Department of Public Safety waiting for Bill Hobson to be released.

"He was picked up by the cops in Waverly, Tennessee," Neil said.

"Shit," Emma said, and hung up. She turned on her computer, found out where Waverly was located, and saw that the nearest major city was Nashville. She checked flights from Dulles and Reagan National and saw there was a nonstop leaving for Nashville from Dulles in an hour and the flight would take two hours; then she'd have to rent a car and drive to Waverly, which would take *another* hour. Not good. It would be close to five hours by the time she got to Waverly, and by then Hobson would be gone—or dead. She wondered if Mulray's people had a way to get to Waverly faster than she did, but realized that if they did, there wasn't anything she could do about it.

She thought about the situation for a moment, then used the Internet to find private detectives located in Waverly, and found a female detective in McEwen, only fifteen minutes from Waverly. She called the detective.

"I'm going to e-mail you a photograph of a man named William Hobson. He's being held at the jail in Waverly for kidnapping a little girl." She heard the detective inhale sharply when she said this. "I need you to get over to the jail and wait for Hobson to be released, which he will be shortly. He didn't kidnap anyone, but he is involved in a number of other crimes, and I need you to follow him when he leaves the jail and stick with him until I can meet you. But you need to be careful. There are some people who may try to kill Hobson when he's released from jail and I don't want you to get hurt. Believe me when I tell you that he isn't worth dying for."

The detective asked a couple of questions—good questions. She sounded bright, but Emma really had no idea how capable she was. The only basis for picking her was that she lived near Waverly and was female. It had been Emma's experience that women tended to be more competent than men. She didn't think she was being biased in favor of her sex; it was just an opinion formed by experience.

And speaking of a man who wasn't always competent, she called DeMarco and told him where things stood. "Meet me at Dulles. We're going to Nashville."

The Johnson brothers read Hobson his rights and asked him if he wanted a lawyer, to which he responded he didn't need a lawyer because he hadn't done anything wrong. They spent the next hour screaming at him, asking him where a five-year-old girl named Julie Templeton was, even though he kept telling them that he hadn't kidnapped anyone and the Amber Alert was some kind of mistake. At one point R. Johnson left the interrogation room, and when he came back he said, "Where'd you get all that money in your car? Did you sell that little girl, you useless piece of shit?"

It just kept getting worse and worse.

Then R. Johnson said to his partner, "Maybe I oughta get a phone book." Looking at Hobson, he said, "If I smack you in the back of the head with a big thick phone book a dozen times, it won't leave any marks, but your brain will bounce from one end of your skull to the other and you'll be a drooling idiot by the time I'm done."

J. Johnson, who appeared to be slightly brighter than R. Johnson, said, "No, we can't do that. But there is something we can do." He took out his cell phone, but before he dialed, he said to Hobson, "You know that little dog of yours?"

"Yeah," Hobson said, not liking J. Johnson's tone.

"If you don't tell us what we want to know, I'm gonna call the truck stop and tell the cook to let that little mutt out of its cage. That's a real busy highway down there."

"You can't do that!" Hobson screamed.

"Just watch me," J. Johnson said, and punched a number into his phone and spoke to someone named Ray, telling Ray to let Hobson's dog take a walk. Then he said something that chilled Hobson to the bone.

"Wait a minute, Ray," J. Johnson said, "I just thought of something. Does your cousin Henry still have that pit bull, the one that's blind in one eye? Oh, good. Well, on second thought, why don't you take that little mutt over to play with Henry's dog."

"You can't do that!" Hobson screamed again, and he was just about to tell them everything when the interrogation room door opened and the chief of police walked in. Or at least Hobson thought he was the chief, because he had three stars on the shoulders of his uniform shirt. He was older than the Johnson brothers/cousins by twenty years but he resembled them: the same big build, the same buzz cut—now more gray than blond—and the same small, mean blue eyes. Hobson wondered if the whole damn police department was related to one another.

"It seems we've made a mistake, Mr. Hobson," the chief said. "The FBI just told me that somebody hacked into their computers and that that kidnapping bulletin was a prank or something. Now, I'm sorry you were detained, sir, but I'm sure you can understand that when we get what appears to be a legitimate bulletin from the Federal Bureau of Investigation, one that says a little girl's life is in danger . . . Well, we had to act on the information we had."

Had Bill Hobson not been on the run, he would have told the chief that he was going to sue his ass off—a lawsuit large enough to bankrupt the jerkwater town of Waverly, Tennessee. But as he had no intention of doing that and just wanted to get out of jail, all he said was, "My dog better be all right."

"Your dog's fine," the chief said. "But would you mind explaining why you have all that cash in your car?"

"Because I don't trust banks," Hobson said. "And I'm going to count my money as soon as I leave here."

Betty Ann Farmer had three children, all girls, but they were married now and had moved away. She and her husband had both retired from the post office four years ago and her husband spent all day in the garage building bird feeders and doghouses that nobody bought. She volunteered at the hospital and the church, and made bridesmaids' dresses whenever there was a wedding within fifty miles of her home-town. She could sew a purple bridesmaid's dress faster than anyone else in Humphreys County. But she still had too much time on her hands, and her husband was driving her nuts talking about the bird feeder market, so she got a private detective's license, over the objections of everyone in her family.

Since she had gotten her license, she'd only had two cases before this one. Her cousin had hired her to figure out who was stealing tires from his gas station in Clarksville, and she'd been hired by a woman in Franklin to prove her husband was cheating on her with a cocktail waitress. She'd solved both cases and was proud she had, but she sure wished her business would pick up a little. She'd barely made enough to pay for her Web site.

She put Hobson's photo and her .38 LadySmith in her purse, walked out to the garage, and, screaming over the noise of the band saw, told her husband she had a case and he might have to make his own dinner. Forty-five minutes later, she watched Bill Hobson leave the Waverly police station and walk over to a Camry. For some rea-son, the first thing he did was open the trunk of the Camry and stick his head inside a black plastic garbage bag, like he was sniffing glue in industrial quantities. Then he closed the trunk and drove away.

———————◆◆◆———————

Hobson drove to the truck stop as fast as he could. There was no way the cops would give him a speeding ticket after what they'd just pulled. He found Omar Bradley in the kitchen, inside his travel cage, and he looked just fine; fortunately, that asshole cop had been bluffing about letting him play with a pit bull. Brad, as usual, yipped in delight and wagged his short tail when he saw Hobson, and when he let him out of the travel cage, he licked Hobson's face like they'd been separated for a month. God, he loved that little mutt.

He carried Brad back to the car, talking inane baby talk to him as he walked. He wanted to get in the car and peel out of the parking lot as fast as he could, but decided he needed to think, so he put Brad on his leash and they walked around the lot. Brad peed on the tires of two long-haul rigs, then crapped near some bushes on the edge of the parking lot. Normally, Hobson would have picked up the poop, but since he was more than just a little pissed at the town of Waverly, he didn't bother.

"Now what are we going to do, Brad?" he asked the dog. Brad ignored him while he sniffed an enormous beetle that had been crushed by a tire.

He had no doubt that Mulray Pharma knew right where he was—that Amber Alert had been no prank—and he suspected that someone was watching him right now. And maybe while he was inside the jail they'd put a tracking device on his car.

It would be dark in about an hour, and he recalled seeing a muffler shop when he drove into town. He'd take his car there, have them put it up on the rack, and see if he could spot a tracking device. Then, when it was dark, he'd take off and hope he'd be able to see the headlights of anyone tailing him, and if he did, he'd try to lose whoever it was.

Then another thought occurred to him. Why run at all? Why not just go back to the police station and tell the cops—who would tell the FBI—that he was willing to be the star witness against Mulray Pharma.

Yeah, the more he thought about it, the more he liked that idea. If he stayed on his own, Fiona was going to kill him, no doubt about it. And since she now knew where he was, his chances of staying alive were between slim and none. But if he could get the feds to take him into protective custody, he might make it. And with what he knew about Mulray Pharma, he would definitely get a deal that would keep him out of prison. The other thing about going into Witness Protection was that the feds would do for him the things he had been planning to do for himself: get him a new identity and a job someplace where nobody knew him.

He couldn't believe it had come down to this: either run for his life or become a federal witness.

He remembered the day he graduated from the Point with his beaming parents and his bride-to-be in the audience. And he remembered the day they pinned a colonel's eagles on his shoulders at the Pentagon, his wife and kids proudly watching; well, his kids had been bored, but at least they had come to the ceremony. But after that it all went downhill at an incredible rate—arrested for embezzlement, six years in a cage at Leavenworth surrounded by animals, the things he'd done for Mulray Pharma. His wife was gone, his kids hated him, and the only one who loved him was a four-legged critter who, quite frankly, would love anyone who fed him.

"Brad," he said to his dog, "it's like the old saying goes: Life's a bitch and then you die."

And then Bill Hobson died.

Betty Ann Farmer watched Hobson walk around the truck stop parking lot with his little dog, which was cuter than a bug's ear.

And then she saw him collapse.

One minute he was just standing there, talking to his dog, and the next minute he was sprawled out on the ground and the dog was licking his face—and she didn't know what to do. If he'd just fainted and she helped him, she might blow her cover. But what if he'd had a heart attack? No, she couldn't just sit there—she was a Christian woman. No matter what Hobson may have done, she had an obligation to help.

Betty Ann jumped out of her car and ran over to Hobson—and saw all the blood on the ground. She'd never seen a gunshot wound before but she was pretty sure that's what the hole in his forehead was. She knelt down, shooed the little dog away—he had blood all over his paws—and felt for a pulse in Hobson's throat. She couldn't find one.

The windows in her car had been rolled up and the radio was playing when Hobson fell, and she hadn't heard a shot. She looked around and could see four or five places within two hundred yards where a sniper could hide—and suddenly realized that the sniper could be aiming at her, right at that moment. As she was thinking this, four guys came out of the restaurant and ran over to her, and she heard one of them say, "Jesus, this guy's been shot."

Betty Ann suddenly felt queasy—she could actually smell all the blood on the ground—and she knew she had to sit down before she fainted. She walked on unsteady legs over to her car and sat there with the driver's-side door open, taking deep breaths. Then she said in a firm voice, "Betty Ann, you just get a grip on yourself! You're a licensed private detective." She took out her cell phone and dialed the lady who'd hired her, but the call went to voice mail.

After she left a message for the woman, she noticed the dead man's little black dog sniffing at the corpse, looking forlorn, wondering what had happened to his master. Betty Ann pushed through the crowd of men standing around Hobson's body and scooped up the dog—God, he was a cutie. She noticed he had two tags on his collar. One had his name on it and his master's address; the other one was some sort of medical tag. Hmmm. She'd have to check that out. She figured she'd hang on to the dog until someone claimed him, and if nobody did, she'd give him to one of her granddaughters.

The chief walked out of the Public Safety Building and over to where the Johnson brothers were standing. They were in the parking lot next to their patrol cars, bullshitting with another one of his officers, a plump, sexy gal named Donna Tremont who was married to a dentist. The chief suspected that both Johnsons were screwing Donna.

"Dispatch just got a call from the truck stop," he said. "And right after that we got another call."

"Yeah?" R. Johnson said, not sure what the chief was getting at.

"That guy, Hobson? Well, someone just shot him, put a bullet right between his eyes."

"Jesus!" J. Johnson said.

"The other call we got was from a man saying that he took care of that motherfuckin' child molester we turned loose. Excuse my language, Donna. Did you boys tell anyone about Hobson?"

"Well, yeah," J. Johnson said. "I mentioned the Amber Alert to Ray when I took Hobson's dog into the restaurant, and the other cook heard me."

"How many people were in the diner?"

"Hell, I don't know. Three truckers, maybe four. I didn't know any of them. Karl from the hardware store was there. So was Tim McIntyre and—"

"McIntyre?" the chief said. "His grandson in Kansas City was molested by a soccer coach a few years ago."

"And he's a hunter," J. Johnson said.

"Tim McIntyre wouldn't hurt a fly," Donna Tremont said.

"Well, you guys get down to the truck stop and get the names of everybody who was in there today. Donna, you call the weigh stations on the interstate and tell 'em to e-mail you the license plate of every truck that passes through in the next hour, and I'm gonna call the FBI and tell them this hacker-prankster they got just got a man murdered."

As Emma and DeMarco walked down the jetway at Nashville, Emma turned her cell phone back on and saw she had a voice mail. She listened to the message, muttered "Goddamnit," and hung up. "That was a message from the detective I hired to follow Hobson. She said Hobson was shot. He's dead."

"Good work with Hobson," Fiona said to Earl Lee when he told her the Hobson problem had been taken care of.

"Piece o' cake," Lee said.

Fiona sat at her desk, pleased that Hobson was no longer a problem, but then her thoughts turned to Kelly and Nelson. When Kelly had been planning to free Nelson from the hospital, she hadn't seen a whole lot of downside with that idea. But now that Nelson was in Wallens Ridge, the situation had changed dramatically, because Nelson was now getting a taste of what his future was going to be like—and maybe he'd get desperate enough to talk about what he'd done for Mulray Pharma. And there was no way Kelly was going to be able to spring Nelson from a maximum security prison. She called Earl Lee back.

"I want you to take care of Kelly."

"Oh," was all Lee said. He didn't say, "Piece o' cake."

"He was planning to break Nelson out of the hospital where they were keeping him," Fiona said, "but Nelson's been moved to Wallens Ridge State Prison in Big Stone Gap, Virginia. So I'm not sure what Kelly will do next, but he'll have a hard time getting Nelson out of Wallens Ridge. On the other hand, I can get to Nelson *in* Wallens Ridge. But I want Kelly gone before I do that, because if Nelson dies, even of natural causes, Kelly will cut my head off."

"I can protect you," Lee said.

"Yeah, right. You just get Kelly, and get him right away."

"How do I find him?"

"He's probably scoping out the prison where they're keeping Nelson, but I don't know that for a fact."

"So what do you want me to do? Drive around the prison hoping to spot him?"

"I want you to get to Virginia as fast as you can. I've got a guy who specializes in finding people, and I'm going to call him and get him looking for Kelly. And, Lee . . ."

"Yeah?"

"When you catch up with Kelly, just kill him. Nothing tricky, nothing fancy. Just blow his brains out."

"Roger that," Lee said.

Fiona sighed, and hung up.

Since Bernie had researched Kelly before Fiona recruited him in Afghanistan, Bernie already had Kelly's military ID photo and a lot of other information about the man. Now, Fiona gave him Kelly's cell phone number, but she said she doubted Kelly was still using the phone because she'd called him on it several times after he got back from Peru and he never answered it; she figured Kelly had most likely dumped his old cell phone as part of his preparations for Nelson's escape. "Your best bet," Fiona said, "would be to throw a net around Wallens Ridge. He's most likely checking out the place to see if he can spring Nelson from there."

Bernie started to tell Fiona that he didn't want the assignment. His contact at the Hoover Building had called half an hour earlier, hysterical, saying that Hobson had been killed and the FBI was on a witch hunt trying to find out who had issued the phony bulletin. And if the bulletin was traced back to his contact, his contact would give up Bernie in a heartbeat. So it was time to sever his relationship with Fiona; working for her was just too dangerous. But before Bernie could say it was time for Fiona to find another team of headhunters, Fiona said, "If you can find Kelly in the next forty-eight hours, you'll get a bonus. Twenty-five K."

Bernie took the assignment.

41

DeMarco and Emma were sitting at a bar in the Nashville airport waiting for their flight back to D.C. DeMarco was drinking a beer; Emma was having orange juice. He knew Emma liked a martini now and then, and he wondered if her medical condition no longer allowed her to drink alcohol. For DeMarco, that would be a tragedy of epic proportions.

"So now what?" he said.

"I don't know," Emma said, "but I'm not giving up."

"I'm not talking about giving up. I'm just saying that we're running out of options. Do you know anyone at the Bureau?"

"The only senior people I know are all in counterterrorism. Why?"

"Well, maybe one of those guys can steer you to someone in OPR—"

OPR was the Office of Professional Responsibility, the FBI's version of Internal Affairs—"and tell them that if they can find out who issued that phony Amber Alert they might eventually trace it back to Mulray."

"I doubt they'll find any connection to Mulray," Emma said, "but tomorrow I'll call a guy I know."

Neither of them said anything for a while, until Emma said, "With Hobson dead, we have to make Nelson talk. We *have* to. He's the only one that can give us Mulray. But we're going to have to wait a while—at least a couple weeks, maybe a month."

"Why wait so long?"

"Because he's a tough guy. I mean, putting him in Wallens Ridge like you did was a good idea." Now that was rare: for her to give him credit for a good idea. "But it's going to take more than just a couple of days for him to appreciate what it's going to be like spending fifteen years in the place."

"Maybe while we're waiting we can work on Linger," DeMarco said.

"Linger?"

"Congressman Talbot's chief of staff. If he's willing to talk about the conference call that was used to frame Kincaid, maybe that'll give us something to grab on to."

"Like what?

"Hell, Emma, I don't know. But I can't think of anything else to do."

"Do you think Linger will talk to you?"

"No, but he'll talk to Mahoney."

———————

Mahoney decided to talk to Stephen Linger like DeMarco wanted because if he succeeded he might be able to cause Republican congressman Edward Talbot a major problem. Causing any Republican a problem always made Mahoney's day, but with Talbot it was personal. Talbot was an annoying, grandstanding little asshole, and he took cheap shots at Mahoney every chance he got. (The fact that Mahoney took cheap shots at Talbot every chance *he* got was beside the point.) He called Linger and politely asked him to come to his office.

Linger was a tall, slim, dark-haired, dark-complexioned guy in his thirties with eyebrows that turned up at the end. Mahoney thought he looked like the Devil dressed in a Brooks Brothers suit. He had been involved in Republican Party politics in one capacity or another since graduating from college, and had been Talbot's chief of staff for five years. He probably danced in the streets the day Mahoney lost his job as Speaker.

"Would you like a drink?" Mahoney asked.

"I don't drink . . . *Congressman*," Linger said, emphasizing the word to make the unnecessary point that Mahoney was no longer the Speaker.

"Well, good for you." Mahoney poured himself a shot of Wild Turkey over ice, then settled into the chair behind his desk with a grunt. "You remember a lobbyist named Phil Downing who was killed a couple years ago?"

"Vaguely," Linger said.

"Son, now is not the time to get cute with me. I'm trying to help you."

"Help me? I don't understand."

"You see, Steve, I know how it happened. Your boss got a call from Mulray Pharma and they asked for a little favor—they asked for you to be in on a conference call at a certain time with some Warwick people. And Mulray, being a big supporter . . . I can understand why Ed would want to be helpful."

"Sir, I don't know what you're . . ."

"But then Downing is killed and his partner, an unlucky bastard named Kincaid, gets convicted for murdering him—and the conviction is based primarily on the time of the conference call, a time *you* basically established."

"I didn't—"

"Listen to me, Steve. I'm sure you've been reading all this stuff about Mulray and Warwick and how some poor refugees may have been killed to test Mulray's new drug. Well, that stuff's all true, and there're a lot of things going on behind the scenes right now that you don't know anything about. The bottom line is the government *knows* Phil Downing was murdered because he knew what Mulray Pharma was doing in Peru, and they know that Brian Kincaid was framed for his murder. And when the FBI puts all the pieces together, you're going to be convicted as an accomplice to Downing's murder unless you help yourself. You see, I know how your boss's mind works. He'll say he didn't have anything to do with that conference call, that it was all your idea. He'll leave you out there high and dry, son. He'll leave you out there to hang."

Linger just shook his head, as if everything Mahoney was saying was total nonsense.

"Now, the smart thing for you to do is to step forward right now, before things get too far downstream and—"

"Step forward how?" Linger said.

"All I want you to do is talk to a guy. Tell him everything you know about how the call was set up, who talked to who, that sort of thing. If you don't do that . . . Well, there's no point repeating myself."

Linger sat there a moment staring at Mahoney with no expression on his face, then he stood up and said, "I'm late for a meeting, *Congressman*. I haven't done anything wrong, Congressman Talbot hasn't done anything wrong, and nobody can prove otherwise. Good day, sir."

"Well, poop," Mahoney said to himself after Linger left his office. He took another sip of bourbon and called DeMarco. "He didn't go for it."

"Shit," DeMarco said—but he wasn't really surprised.

This had been DeMarco's plan: Step One—convince Stephen Linger that the government knew more than it really did and convince him that he could be convicted as an accomplice in Phil Downing's murder. Step Two—get Linger to talk about who at Mulray Pharma had contacted him or his boss and then, maybe, Step Three—stick a wire on Linger and have him go talk to this person and see if he or she would admit to something they could use to get Orson Mulray.

It hadn't been much of a plan to begin with, and Stephen Linger was smart enough—or arrogant enough—not to fall for it.

When DeMarco called Emma and told her that Mahoney had struck out with Linger, she said, "All we can do now is wait a while and go talk to Nelson."

"I just hope Mulray doesn't make a run at him while we're waiting," DeMarco said.

Emma hung up.

42

Dick Younger ran the largest detective agency in Richmond, and he could supplement his operatives with off-duty cops if he needed to—and for this job he needed a lot of people. A client had e-mailed him a picture of a hard-looking black guy and told him to send a dozen people over to Big Stone Gap. The black guy, according to the client, was scoping out Wallens Ridge so he could help a prisoner escape, and the client wanted Younger to find the man but not apprehend him.

So Younger did as he was told and sent a dozen people—eleven men and one woman, and he was betting it was the woman who would find the guy. Anita Gomez was the only female operative he employed on a full-time basis. She was a short Puerto Rican in her fifties, built like a fireplug, who knitted sweaters for her grandkids when she was on stakeouts. She was also the most observant person he had ever met. And sure enough . . .

Younger's secretary called out from her desk, "Dick, Anita is on line two."

"Dick," Anita said, "I'm watching the guy right now."

Wallens Ridge State Prison in Big Stone Gap, Virginia, is a Security Level Five facility—a super max built to contain the worst of the worst. There was no way a disabled, first-time offender like Nelson should have been incarcerated in the place, and Kelly knew the only reason he had been was because that bastard DeMarco had used his political clout to pressure the Arlington County prosecutor. If anything happened to Nelson in Wallens Ridge, Kelly was going to kill DeMarco in the most painful way he could devise.

The prison reminded Kelly of pictures of medieval castles he'd seen. It was surrounded by a high white wall, perched on a hilltop, and could only be approached by a single, winding road. Being a student of military history, Kelly knew castles were usually taken in three ways. The first was by brutal frontal assault using war machines—catapults, and later cannons—to batter down the walls and gates. If the attackers took this approach, however, they had to be willing to accept casualties in large numbers. The second way was by laying siege—surrounding the castle, cutting off all contact with the outside world, and starving the occupants into submission. The best way to take a castle, however, was from the *inside*—by bribing a traitor to open the gates.

Kelly would need a traitor to free Nelson from Wallens Ridge.

He had studied the place for hours, writing down his observations in a small, spiral-bound notebook. He drew a map marking the placement of guard towers and cameras; he observed the procedure for admitting people into the facility; he identified areas along the outside walls that were not fully illuminated by the lights at night. Earlier in the day he observed, through binoculars, a produce truck exiting the prison and how the guards did a sloppy job of searching the underside of the vehicle. He'd been looking at his notes for the last hour, going over them again and again, looking for some weakness in the prison's security procedures—and then he slammed his hand down on the notebook, making the coffee cup on the table jump.

He was sitting in a diner, and several people looked over at him—and he knew what he had just done was foolish and undisciplined. He didn't need to call attention to himself.

He also knew he was wasting his time.

Even if he could bribe a guard willing to help Nelson escape, how would the guard get a man in a wheelchair past all the other security measures inside the prison? To free Nelson, his only choice was to wait until Nelson was moved from Wallens Ridge to Arlington for his trial—and, before he was moved, to learn everything there was to know about how the guards transported prisoners. He'd know how many guards accompanied the prisoners, how they were armed, and whether they used a regular car or an armored vehicle. He'd study the likely route from Big Stone Gap to Arlington and identify the best place for an ambush. And it wouldn't really matter what type of vehicle they used and whether it was armored or not. He would acquire whatever weapons he needed—maybe a rifle with a grenade launcher like he'd used in Africa—then he'd disable the vehicle, kill the guards, and free Nelson. Yeah, he could do that easily—but again he realized he was deluding himself.

He was deluding himself because he knew Fiona West. He knew Fiona would have Nelson killed long before he went to trial.

Before the trial, Fiona would bribe a guard—she'd offer the guard more damn money than he could count—and the guard would get some murderous psycho to stick a shiv into Nelson. It would just be one of those things that happens in prisons all the time.

So Kelly couldn't wait until Nelson's trial. Nelson was a dead man if he didn't spring him from the prison in the next few days. And Kelly knew—he knew as soon as he saw the prison—that there was only one way he could save Nelson's life.

What he didn't know was if he had the courage to do what needed to be done.

Earl Lee was in his motel room in Big Stone Gap, lying on the bed, drinking a beer, and watching a rerun of a reality show about a bunch of Playboy bunnies who lived together. All the women were blonde, had big fake tits, big foul mouths, and were dumber than a box of rocks—but, boy, were they an eyeful. He was so absorbed in the show his cell phone rang three times before he heard it.

"Yeah?" he said.

"I was told to call this number," a woman said. She had an accent of some kind, like she might be Mexican or something. "I'm watching a man named Kelly. He's at a restaurant called the Huddle House on Wildcat Road, just off Route 23."

"I'm on my way," Lee said. "Stick with him until I get there."

"I'll be across the street from the restaurant, standing outside my car, and the hood of my car will be up like I had a breakdown. I'm wearing a pink blouse and blue jeans."

"Okay, but if Kelly takes off before I get there, you follow him and call me again."

Lee glanced back at the television. One of the Playmates was taking off her top, about to jump into a swimming pool. Damn, he thought, but he grabbed his duffel bag and headed out the door.

Earl Lee wondered where Kelly was headed.

When Kelly left the restaurant, he drove northeast, toward Roanoke, on I-81. He was about a half-mile ahead of Lee now and there were three cars between his car and Kelly's van. Lee also wondered why Kelly was driving a clunky-looking van, but it sure made it easy to follow him. Three hours later, Kelly drove through Roanoke, continued traveling northeast, and Lee saw a sign that said he was two hundred miles from Washington, D.C.

Kelly exited the freeway near Waynesboro. Lee stayed behind him, hanging back as far as he could while still keeping Kelly in sight, and watched Kelly pull into one of those minimart gas stations. Lee drove past the gas station, made a u-turn a block later, and parked. Kelly was just starting to fill up his gas tank.

Lee exited his car and opened the trunk, but didn't immediately pick up his new rifle. It had been necessary to leave the rifle he'd used to kill Hobson behind when he flew from Tennessee to Virginia, but the first thing he did when he arrived in Virginia—a state with some of the most user-friendly gun laws in the nation—was buy a new rifle with a good scope, a .45 semiauto, and a Kevlar bullet-proof vest. The vest seemed like a good idea since he was going up against Kelly.

With the trunk lid still open, Lee looked at Kelly again; Kelly was still standing by the gas pump. It was getting dark, but it wasn't dark yet, and it would be risky to shoot Kelly from where he was because if someone drove up the street they were bound to see him. Then he noticed the espresso stand.

The espresso stand—a shack made of plywood and decorated with pink, plastic flamingos—was closed for the day. If he positioned himself on the side of the stand that wasn't visible from the street, killing Kelly would be like shooting fish in a barrel. He glanced around to make sure no cars were coming, pulled his rifle from the trunk, jogged over to the espresso stand, and dropped to a prone position.

He raised the rifle and looked through the scope. Kelly's face appeared as if it was two inches away. He put the crosshairs right in the middle of Kelly's forehead, let out a breath, and began to apply pressure to the trigger—then stopped.

Nah, he didn't want to do it this way. Kelly had always looked down his nose at him, had always thought he was smarter—and tougher—than him. Maybe it was because Kelly had been Delta and he hadn't, but whatever the case, it had always pissed him off that whenever he saw Kelly, Kelly would give him this little I-can-kick-your-ass-any-time-I-want-to smile. And his fuckin' buddy, Nelson, was the same way.

No, he didn't want to snipe Kelly. He wanted Kelly to know who killed him.

———◆◆◆———

Lee was worried he was going to lose Kelly.

Kelly had just crossed the Key Bridge and was now on M Street in Georgetown, and even though it was after ten P.M., the traffic was heavy with college kids cruising the M Street strip. And every time he was stopped by a red light, more cars got between him and Kelly's van, and Kelly was now two blocks ahead of him. If he lost Kelly, Fiona was gonna ream him a new asshole.

Then Kelly made a left-hand turn off M Street, and Lee almost did lose him. By the time he was able to make the turn himself, Kelly was almost out of sight and he could just barely see his taillights. He stomped down on the gas pedal to catch up, now worried that Kelly might notice he was being followed. Then he laughed off that idea. Delta Force guys were trained to attack—not to evade.

Kelly turned onto P Street, with Lee a block behind him. Kelly was driving slowly now, like he was looking for an address, and he finally pulled over to the curb and parked. Lee drove past him, turning his head to the left so Kelly wouldn't see his face, and continued down the block. He turned at the next corner, parked his car in front of a fire hydrant as there was no place else to park, then, staying in the shadows, crept back to where he'd last seen Kelly.

As he hid behind a tree, he watched Kelly ring the doorbell of a narrow, two-story town house. He stood there a while, rang it again, and when no one answered, bent down, and it looked to Lee like he was picking the lock. Three minutes later, Kelly entered the town house, and when he was inside he didn't turn on any lights.

Lee didn't know what the hell Kelly was doing—or whom he was visiting—but this looked like the best opportunity he was going to get. He'd wait until Kelly left the house, and once he did Lee would kill him when he returned to his car. Then Lee remembered something. He wanted to prove something to Kelly—and to himself—but there was no point being a total idiot. He jogged back to his car, took the Kevlar vest from the trunk, and put it on.

43

DeMarco enjoyed a late dinner in Georgetown and after dinner went to a movie to get his mind off Brian Kincaid and everything associated with Mulray Pharma. He saw a movie starring Leonardo DiCaprio where Leo somehow managed to invade people's dreams and make them do whatever he wanted. The movie didn't make a whole lot of sense to him, but he heard two women talking as he was leaving the theater, the women going on and on and on about Leo. DeMarco concluded that if you looked like Leonardo DiCaprio you didn't have to make movies that made any sense.

As he walked back to his place, he passed a drugstore, and his mind unwillingly drifted back to Orson Mulray. He'd come to the conclusion that no matter what he and Emma did, Mulray was most likely going to get away with what he had done and Brian Kincaid was going to spend his life in prison. The papers were filled with editorials discussing the ambiguous morality of Mulray testing his drugs on uneducated, impoverished disaster victims—but no law enforcement agency appeared to be making any attempt to prove that Mulray had done anything illegal. Meanwhile, the scientific and medical communities were coming to the conclusion that Dr. Ballard's drug was a wonder drug—and it was selling like hotcakes in Asia.

DeMarco unlocked his front door and stepped into his house, then stood in the foyer for a moment trying to decide if he should go straight to bed or watch the news first. He decided on the news. He walked into his den, flipped on a light, and saw a large black man sitting in the room, holding a gun.

DeMarco immediately recognized the man as Kelly, Nelson's partner, because he'd seen Kelly's photo in the passports Emma had brought back from Peru. Emma said she'd killed him. She obviously hadn't. And now it looked like Kelly was going to kill *him*.

DeMarco had always wondered how he would act when confronted with the possibility of—or in this case, the certainty of—his own death. Would he go out groveling and begging, or would he face his last moments with some semblance of dignity? Would he be the guy who stands there calmly, refusing the blindfold when they put him in front of the firing squad, or would he be the one they'd have to tie to a stake to keep him upright as he wailed for mercy? DeMarco decided there was no way in hell he was going to beg this guy.

"You're Kelly, right?" DeMarco said, surprised at how calm he sounded.

"Yeah. Sit down."

"If you don't mind, I'm gonna get a drink," DeMarco said. "You want one?"

"No."

DeMarco walked over to his liquor cabinet and pulled out the best cognac he had, the bottle he saved for special occasions—in this case, the special occasion being his untimely death. His hand shook as he poured a large shot into a snifter, thankful that Kelly couldn't see his hand, then took a seat facing him.

"I feel like killing you for what you did to Nelson," Kelly said.

DeMarco took a large pull on the brandy, but the words *I feel like* suddenly gave him hope. "What did I do to Nelson?" he said.

"You're the one who stuck him in Wallens Ridge."

"I didn't have anything to do with that," DeMarco lied. "That was the prosecutor's idea. Anyway, what do you want?"

"A deal."

"A deal? What kind of deal?"

"The first thing I want is Nelson moved out of Wallens Ridge and placed under the protection of federal marshals. And I want that done right away, like tomorrow morning—Mulray will have Nelson killed if he stays in that prison. Then I want Nelson given a suspended sentence. I don't care what you have to do legally but you just let him go. And finally, Nelson and I have a lot of money, and Nelson gets to keep the money. He's going to need it to take care of himself."

"And if I can do all this, what do I get in return?"

"I'm not finished telling you what I want. The last thing I want is a deal for me. I know I'll end up doing some time, but I want a sentence that's commensurate with what I'll give you. I won't do a long stretch or life without parole."

"Maybe I can make all that happen," DeMarco said, "but you still haven't told me what the government gets in return."

The fact was, DeMarco had no authority to make a deal of any kind, but there was no point telling Kelly that.

"I'll give you Fiona West," Kelly said, "and she'll give you Orson Mulray. Fiona would roll over on her own mother to save her skin."

"Who's Fiona West?"

"Officially, she's Mulray Pharma's lawyer. Unofficially, she's Orson Mulray's attack dog. She's the one who organized everything."

"I need specifics," DeMarco said.

"Okay. Fiona ordered me to kill Phil Downing because Downing found out what Mulray Pharma was doing in Peru. And I framed Kincaid just like his lawyer said at his trial—and I'll testify to that."

"So what was Mulray doing in Peru?"

"Testing the Alzheimer's drug on disaster victims and killing some of them to provide autopsy results."

"Who killed the people?"

"I did."

Just like that: *I did.*

"How many people did you kill?"

Kelly hesitated. "I'll testify that in June I killed three people in Peru."

"You only killed three? What about at the Warwick Care Centers in Africa and Pakistan?"

"Like I said, I'll testify that I killed three people. That's all. And I'll testify that Fiona ordered me to do the killings and that René Lambert gave me the drug I sprayed into those old folks to kill them."

"Sprayed?"

"Yeah. I used a poison in the form of a nasal spray."

"Do you have any proof? Any kind of physical evidence?"

"Like what?" Kelly said.

"Hell, I don't know. Do you have the poison you used? Did you record any of the conversations you had with Fiona West? Do you have a document from West to you that corroborates what you're saying? Something other than just your word against Mulray Pharma."

Kelly shook his head. "No, I don't have anything like that. But Nelson will back up my testimony, so it won't just be my word alone. And there's gotta be a way to trace the money from my account back to Mulray."

DeMarco wasn't too sure about that. Neil hadn't been able to do so, but maybe the U.S. government could.

"Would you be willing to wear a wire? You know, meet with West and get her to admit that she ordered you to do these things?"

"Yeah. And Fiona will talk, and when you take her she'll give you all the proof you need to get Orson Mulray."

"Why are you doing this?" DeMarco asked.

"Because if I don't, Nelson's going to die. If he wasn't crippled it would be a different story, but in the condition he's in now he'll never survive in prison. But I can survive inside."

"I still don't get it. Why are you willing to go to prison for Nelson?"

"Because he's taken bullets meant for me and now I'm paying him back."

DeMarco sensed that it was more than Kelly paying Nelson back, but he didn't press the issue. Instead he said, "I kinda doubt you're gonna get everything you want even if you are willing to testify."

"Who do you think the government would rather throw in jail?" Kelly countered. "From a political standpoint, I mean. Me and Nelson —a couple of hired guns—or a rich son of a bitch like Orson Mulray? And the government does this all the time with Mafia and drug guys. I've read about Mafia hit men who've killed dozens of people getting into Witness Protection because the government would rather have the bosses."

"You got a point there," DeMarco said. In fact, DeMarco personally knew a couple of Mafia killers who were now leading seminormal lives under the protection of federal marshals.

They sat there in silence for a moment, then DeMarco said, "Why did you do it, Kelly? I've seen your military record. How'd you go from what you once were to . . . I mean, Jesus! You killed a bunch of old people."

Kelly didn't say anything for a moment, then said, "Have you ever wanted anything so badly that you'd do anything to get it?"

"No," DeMarco said—and he wasn't being self-righteous. That was the truth.

DeMarco thought for a moment that Kelly was going to explain himself—make some attempt to rationalize what he'd done—but he didn't. All he said was, "Well, good for you."

Kelly stood up. "Give me a number where I can call you tomorrow. I'll give you until noon to talk to the right people and set everything up. If you can't do what I want and if Nelson gets killed in Wallens Ridge, I'm gonna kill you, DeMarco. And that's a promise."

And DeMarco believed him.

———◆◆◆———

Earl Lee was standing behind a tree in front of DeMarco's house holding his weapon in his hand, wondering how long Kelly was going to be inside the house. Fifteen minutes later, he smiled as Kelly walked out the door.

He waited until Kelly was halfway down DeMarco's sidewalk before he stepped out from behind the tree, and as soon as he showed himself, Kelly reached for his gun. Lee couldn't believe how *fast* Kelly was—the son of a bitch was so fast that he almost shot Lee before Lee could shoot him, and Lee already had his gun in his hand. But he beat him. He shot Kelly in the chest.

He walked over and looked down at Kelly and smiled. It had worked out just the way he wanted it: Kelly was still alive—but just barely—and his eyes were open.

"Surprise, ol' buddy," Lee said. That's all he had wanted: for Kelly to know who had beat him. He had just raised his weapon to shoot Kelly in the head and end it, when Kelly shot him. Lee felt the bullet smack into the vest he was wearing—and he almost smiled again—but Kelly's next shot hit him in the throat and the bullet blew through the side of his neck, taking out a chunk of his carotid artery.

———◆◆◆———

DeMarco was on the phone with Emma, telling her about Kelly's visit, when he heard the gunshots. "I'll call you back," he said, and ran to the window that was next to his front door and saw Kelly and another man lying on the sidewalk. Neither man was moving.

He opened the door and saw that the other man was still alive. He was making a horrible, choking sound and blood was spurting out of his neck with each pump of his heart. DeMarco ignored him, though, and ran to Kelly. He needed Kelly alive.

And Kelly was still alive, but just barely. His eyes were shut, and he was taking shallow, rapid breaths, and the front of his shirt was dark with blood.

"Hang in there," DeMarco said. "I'm calling an ambulance."

He moved over to the second man, a big guy with short blond hair. Blood was no longer pumping from his throat. The man was dead. DeMarco ran into the house, called 911, and came back out with a dish towel to press against the wound on Kelly's chest.

But by then, Kelly was dead, too.

DeMarco spent the next four hours telling policemen of increasing rank the same story. He told the story so often that after a while he almost believed his own lies. He told the cops he had never met Kelly—which was *almost* true; he hadn't met him until that night. He told them that he had been inside his house and when he heard gunshots, he looked out his window and saw two men lying on the sidewalk. Like a good citizen, he checked to see if the men were alive and called 911. He had no idea, he said, why these men came to his house and shot each other.

He didn't tell the cops that he and Kelly had talked before Kelly was shot, because then he'd have to tell them *what* they'd talked about. He didn't want to do that because as soon as Orson Mulray found out he'd talked to Kelly, he'd become worried that Kelly had told

DeMarco something that could harm him—and then there was a good chance that Mulray would try to have DeMarco killed. Again. Why paint a bull's-eye on his back?

The cops didn't believe him, of course. They found it rather implausible that two men had coincidentally decided to kill each other four feet from DeMarco's front door. But DeMarco stuck to his story, and they eventually let him go. Fortunately, the case was not a who-done-it; the forensic evidence made it clear that Kelly and Lee had shot each other. Their motives may have been unknown but there was no doubt about what had happened, so although DeMarco may have been an uncooperative witness, he wasn't a murder suspect.

44

The waiter saw that René Lambert's glass was empty, so he picked up the wine bottle to refill the glass, then realized the bottle was empty, too.

"Would monsieur like another bottle?" the waiter asked.

Lambert had chosen the restaurant because though the food was good, the wine list excellent, and the view of the Alps incredible, it was the sort of place where one could dress casually. He'd driven from Paris to Grenoble in casual clothes and hadn't felt like driving up the mountain to the chalet and changing before dinner. And right now he was feeling so mellow he didn't feel like leaving—but should he order another whole bottle of wine?

"Can I buy just a glass?" he asked the waiter.

"Not the Louis Jadot 2004, monsieur. We have a 2008 Maison Champy and a 2007 Meursault Rouge we sell by the glass."

"I don't think so," Lambert said, his tone making it clear what he thought of the waiter's suggestions. "Just bring me another bottle of the Jadot."

It was such a relief to be out of Paris, the main reason being that his wife had discovered he was having an affair with his agent. She'd caught him in other affairs, and when she had she wasn't happy about his infidelity, but she hadn't gone crazy, either. This time she went crazy. He wondered if it was because she'd just turned forty and was feeling insecure. Whatever the case, she went berserk, throwing things, crying and screaming, and, of course, threatening to divorce him, which he was sure she would never do. And his daughters, who'd just turned eleven and twelve, and who were miniature versions of their mother both physically and emotionally, naturally took her side. So finally he'd just said, "Enough!" and that morning threw a suitcase into his car and left for Grenoble.

Since Mulray Pharma had repurchased the family chalet in Grenoble for him when he signed on with the company in 2006, he'd only used the place twice. His small-minded wife and ungrateful daughters had been there many times, but he'd been too busy running around the world with Lizzie Warwick. Poor Lizzie. He still couldn't believe the silly woman had committed suicide. But his globe-trotting days were over, thank God. No more hellholes like Uganda. No more living in tents, showering once a week, eating food that wasn't fit for animals. He'd endured five years of absolute misery, but, in hindsight, it had been worth it. He was out of debt, had a substantial amount of money in the bank, owned a hundred thousand shares of Mulray stock that was increasing in value daily, and was about to start writing his memoirs—which was how he met the agent.

He'd been approached by a publisher to write about his experiences with the Warwick Foundation and Mulray Pharma. The publisher said the book would be controversial—and controversial was always good. Some would see him as a humanitarian who sacrificed five years of his life aiding disaster victims while at the same time helping develop a drug that was going to be the salvation of millions. Others, of course, would take the view of that diabolical reporter from the *Washington Post* and accuse him of taking advantage of poor, ignorant people. Yes, it would be controversial, and controversial was good.

And that's when he'd contacted the agent. A friend had recommended her, and he'd had no idea how young and good-looking she was until he met her. The affair was inevitable. And not only was she lovely, she was bright. She was the one who suggested that in addition to writing the book, he needed to hit the lecture circuit while his name was still in the news. She was thinking at least five thousand euros a lecture, maybe ten, with the lectures drawing both critics and admirers. Appearances on television shows would certainly be in his future, and he'd probably be asked to debate softhearted liberals who wanted to rail about the evils of greedy pharmaceutical companies performing clinical trials in third world countries.

But he didn't want to think about any of that right now. He wanted to spend a few days at the chalet, taking walks in the woods, sitting in the hot tub, simply relaxing without his wife's shrill voice in his ear.

The waiter brought the bottle of wine to his table, and as he was uncorking it, Lambert heard a peal of laughter from a young lady at the bar. He looked over and saw two blondes in their early twenties. They were wearing snug-fitting T-shirts, shorts, and hiking boots. He thought they might be Germans, although he couldn't have said why he thought so, other than the fact that they were blonde and Germans liked to hike in the mountains near Grenoble. The short one was a few kilos too heavy but had magnificent breasts. The tall one was almost too skinny but her legs were wonderful. He couldn't help but think that if God had done His job properly, He would have made one girl out of the parts of these two. Nonetheless, they were young, attractive, and lively. And they weren't his wife. He wondered if he might be able to talk them into joining him in the hot tub at the chalet, and if they chose not to . . . well, having a drink or two with them would still be fun.

He picked up the wine bottle and walked over to the bar.

45

Fiona was out of control—and Orson Mulray didn't know what to do about the situation.

He didn't disagree with her decision to have Hobson eliminated after he fled his post at the Warwick Foundation, but once again she had acted without his authorization. And now Kelly and Lee were dead, and he was certain she was behind that, too, although he couldn't imagine how she got them to kill each other. What he didn't like was that an investigation into the deaths of the two men might somehow lead back to Fiona, and from her to him. He didn't see how that could happen, but the possibility certainly existed.

He also couldn't understand why the two men shot each other outside DeMarco's house. What were they both doing there? Had Fiona ordered Lee to kill DeMarco, and did Kelly for some reason—maybe some reason related to his efforts to free Nelson—try to stop Lee and that's how they ended up shooting each other? Or maybe Lee had been ordered to kill Kelly and they'd killed each other, and it was just a coincidence the shooting took place at DeMarco's house. That seemed unlikely, but he couldn't come up with another explanation. All he knew for sure was that if Fiona didn't stop killing people she was going to ruin everything. Maybe it was time to hire his own killer.

He called Fiona, ordered her to come to his office, and hung up before she could debate the directive.

———◆◆◆———

When Fiona entered his office, Orson was on the phone talking to someone about actions needed to get Ballard's drug approved in Europe. Based on Orson's end of the conversation, it sounded to Fiona like the British were balking about something and Orson wanted the balkers out of the way. Whatever the problem, she was certain he'd deal with it. This was the sort of thing he was good at.

Orson hung up, grumbled a bit about government bureaucrats, foreign and domestic, then just sat there glaring at her. What the hell was his problem? Mulray Pharma's stock had doubled in value, and Hobson and Kelly were out of their hair. He should have been doing cartwheels, but instead he was sitting there scowling at her.

"What were Kelly and Lee doing at DeMarco's house?" he asked, making the question sound like an accusation.

"I don't know. I told Lee to take care of Kelly the first chance he got and I know Lee was following him, so I'm guessing he followed him to DeMarco's place. But I don't know why Kelly went to DeMarco's. I would assume he went there because of Nelson, that maybe Kelly was planning to kill DeMarco since it was DeMarco who put Nelson in Wallens Ridge. But I don't know for sure. And what difference does it make, Orson? This worked out perfectly. I was trying to figure out what to do with Lee when all this was over, but now I don't have to worry about that. And all the cops seem to know is that Kelly and Lee both worked for Lizzie Warwick—but they don't have a clue as to why they shot each other."

"Hmmm," Orson said.

It just *infuriated* her when he did that, like he was fucking Yoda, pondering everything she told him, looking for flaws, when the truth was he rarely had an original idea to contribute.

"What are you planning to do about Nelson?" Orson asked.

"He's going to die in prison before he goes to trial. I'm having Bernie—"

"Who's Bernie?"

"My headhunter, the guy who does my research for me. Right now he's looking into prison guards at Wallens Ridge to find one who needs money, then Nelson will shortly run afoul of some prison gang, and that will be that."

Orson shook his head. "No, Fiona, I don't want Nelson killed. At least not until we're sure he poses a threat. Have his lawyer talk to him. Have the lawyer find out his state of mind."

"He already poses a threat!" Fiona said. "He's a cripple looking at a long prison sentence. I'm *not* going to take the chance of him making a deal."

"But killing him poses a risk, too. You could make a mistake. This Bernie person or the guard might talk. And if you attempt to kill Nelson and fail, he'll definitely talk. Just offer Nelson more money to keep his mouth shut. Promise him anything."

That was enough of this shit! "Let's get something straight here, Orson. Your job is selling Ballard's drug to every senile old coot on the planet. My job is making sure that what we did doesn't come back and bite us on the ass. So if I decide it's necessary to get rid of Nelson, that's what I'm going to do." Then, before Orson could make an objection, she added, "And one other thing. As near as I can tell, Nelson's the last problem I have to deal with, so I'm going to be quitting pretty soon, and I want the money you promised me five years ago when we started all this. Now, I realize it's going to take a little time and it's going to be complicated, so I want you to lay out a payment plan and show it to me this week."

Complicated was an understatement. Orson didn't have a billion dollars in cash on hand to pay her, but because Mulray Pharma's stock had doubled in value since the day he told the world about Ballard's drug, his net worth had also doubled. Furthermore, his bonus as CEO, which was tied to the company's stock price, was going to be enormous this year—well over a hundred million—so what Orson had to do to pay her was either transfer some of his stock to her or sell some of his stock, and she wanted him to get moving on that. And she didn't care what hoops he had to jump through with the SEC and the board; she was going to make sure that within a month, she had what he owed her.

She expected him to give her an argument about asking to be paid so soon, but he didn't. She also expected that he might say how much he was going to miss her or maybe praise her for the fine job she'd done. She thought he might even beg her not to quit because he couldn't operate the company without her. But he didn't say any of those things. Instead he said, "What on earth are you going to do with yourself after you quit, Fiona?"

The question caught her by surprise, and it took a moment for her to respond, "I really don't know."

And she didn't. She had worked her whole life to reach this point— she'd killed to reach this point—and now she was finally there, about to become one of the richest women in America—and she didn't have a clue as to what she was going to do with all the money.

But that was such a nice problem to have.

———◆———

Fiona stepped into her car, a 2011 Jaguar, which still had that new-car smell. She figured that from this point forward, every car she owned would have that smell, because she'd buy a new one as soon as the odor faded from the current one. She turned on the radio, a device so complicated she still hadn't figured out all its functions. It was tuned to a news-only channel, because Fiona had no interest in music or talk shows. The newscaster was going on about a typhoon in the Philippines that had killed a few hundred people, which made her think for a moment about Lizzie Warwick. She really couldn't understand why the ditzy bitch had killed herself, but it was nice that she had, because now she didn't have to worry about Lizzie suing Mulray Pharma.

Then the newscaster said, "Prominent French physician René Lambert died yesterday in a traffic accident near Grenoble, France. Alcohol was believed to have been a factor. Lambert was known internationally for his charitable work with the Warwick Foundation, but his reputation was somewhat tarnished by his role in testing the new Alzheimer's drug developed by Mulray Pharma. He is survived by his wife and two daughters."

Fiona turned off the radio, amazed at the news. She had given some thought to eliminating René sometime in the future, but she hadn't considered him to be a major threat like Hobson or Nelson. Now, however, without her having to lift a finger, he was gone.

Just as she was reflecting on her good fortune, she noticed a billboard that said the Powerball lottery was up to three hundred forty million, which made her feel like stopping at the next convenience store and buying a thousand dollars' worth of lotto tickets. The way her luck had been running lately, she was bound to win.

Looking back on her life, she couldn't believe how far she'd come—and luck had had very little to do with it. She had been christened Eunice Beatrice West, named after an aunt her parents hoped would leave them money in her will—which she never did. Her childhood was a wide-awake nightmare. Her mother was grossly overweight, superstitious, religious, and incredibly stupid; most of the time she seemed barely aware that Eunice—who became Fiona—even existed.

Her father was a pathetic loser, bouncing from one menial job to the next, and he began molesting her when she was twelve. When she was fourteen, her brother, who was two years older than her and crazier than a shithouse rat, began to molest her, too, and that's when she left home.

She lived on the streets for a year, panhandling for money, and when she almost froze one night, she moved in with a tattooed mechanic who was twice her age and she traded sex for food and a warm place to live. At sixteen, she could easily pass for eighteen, and she moved out of the mechanic's house and turned to exotic dancing. She was a horrible dancer but had such a good body that the customers didn't care, and she made enough in tips to survive. Barely.

That year, she had an epiphany: she realized she had to take some drastic action to change her life. While she still had her looks, she could continue to dance in strip joints, or even become a prostitute, though she knew she'd commit suicide before she ever became a hooker. But once her looks began to fade, what options would she have? With no education, the best she could hope for was waitressing until she was old enough to collect social security. She thought long and hard about the best way to extract herself from the sinkhole that was her life, and finally decided that religion was the answer—or, to be more specific, that religious do-gooders were the answer.

She presented herself at a church one Sunday—a church attended by wealthy Christians, not poor Holy Rollers—and proclaimed to the Jesus freaks that she was a wretched sinner and needed the Lord's help—meaning *their* help. She told them about her background and said that if her prayers went unanswered, she'd have to go back to living with a man who raped her every night and who would soon become her pimp.

Her experience that Sunday was what convinced her to become a lawyer. She made a reasoned yet emotional plea, one which wasn't the least bit unrehearsed, and was successful in convincing a skeptical jury—or in this case, an entire congregation. The result was that a good Christian couple took pity on her. They never formally adopted her but they took her into their home until she graduated from high school, and thanks to their continued support and a few hard-earned scholarships, she was able to get her law degree. And while she was attending college, she pretended to be a dutiful daughter: she called home, baked cookies with her new "mother," attended mind-numbingly boring family affairs. The day she had her degree in hand, she legally changed her name to Fiona West and stopped speaking to the couple, and she never saw them again.

She vectored into corporate law because she figured the best way to get rich was to become associated with a company that was already rich. Now, twenty years after taking her clothes off for drunks trying to shove dollar bills into her G-string, she was on top of the world. She would soon have mansions in idyllic spots and servants to wait on her hand and foot. She'd never want for anything again—and she'd never be forced to have sex again. But Orson had a point. What *would* she do with herself? She couldn't imagine sitting around all day doing nothing.

She'd never had any sort of hobby. She wasn't particularly interested in decorating a fabulous home or attending high-toned cultural events. She certainly had no interest in philanthropic causes. Her life had always been about scheming and plotting to ascend the next step up the ladder.

So, she asked herself, what could a person like her do that would be *fun*? A person who was brilliant and knew how to wield power. And then the answer came to her.

Politics.

Senator West. Yes, she liked the sound of that.

46

"There's a guard at Wallens Ridge," Bernie said, "who's in debt to the tune of three hundred and thirty grand. His wife's got some weird disease and their insurance won't cover all her medical expenses and the doctors have just bled this guy dry. He's got two mortgages on his house and he's having a hard time meeting the payments since his wife can't work anymore, and I'd say there's about an eighty percent chance he's going to lose his home. And, if that's not bad enough—this poor bastard has the luck of Job—his daughter was just arrested for using meth and he's going to need money for a lawyer and a drug treatment center, and drug treatment isn't covered by his insurance, either."

"That all sounds good," Fiona said—but she had a problem. With Earl Lee dead, she didn't have anyone to approach the guard and make him an offer.

"I need you to go see the guard, Bernie," Fiona said.

"Why?" Bernie asked.

Fiona hesitated as she tried to find an indirect way to tell Bernie what she wanted, and when she couldn't think of one, she said, "I want Nelson dead. I want this guard to talk to some psycho—and Wallens Ridge probably has a couple thousand—and have the psycho take out Nelson."

"Are you insane!" Bernie said. "I'm not going to be an accomplice to murder. I'm already worried the FBI's going to trace that phony kidnapping bulletin on Hobson back to me. I find people, Ms. West. What happens to those people after I find them is something I don't concern myself with."

"Well, you're gonna have to concern yourself this time, pal. It's time to get your hands dirty."

"No way," Bernie said. "And this is the last job I'm doing for you. I'll e-mail you the information I have on the guard."

"Half a million, Bernie. Do you think you can man up for half a million?"

She knew what Bernie was now thinking: half a million tax-free dollars wasn't a bonus—it was a whole new lifestyle. A second home, a sailboat, whatever his heart desired.

She heard Bernie inhale sharply. "All right," he said after a long pause. "And what do I offer the guard?"

"Hell, you can offer him half a million, too," Fiona said. "It sounds like he'll need that much to get out of debt. Money, at this point, is the least of my problems."

Bernie had spent his whole career at the CIA in an office, in front of a computer, and he had no idea how he was supposed to approach a guard at a state prison and offer him a bribe to kill a man. CIA operatives—real spies—did that sort of thing. They bribed people to betray their country or to defect or to commit assassinations on the agency's behalf. They were trained for that sort of thing, or maybe it just came naturally to them.

Being a party to killing Nelson didn't bother Bernie; he could live with that. What bothered him was the possibility of being sent to jail for trying to bribe the guard; he could end up in the same prison as Nelson.

Then he thought again about what he could do with half a million dollars.

Man up, Bernie, he told himself.

The guard's name was Albert Morehouse, and Bernie figured the safest thing would be to contact him by phone. If he met with the man, the guard might slap cuffs on his wrists and call the cops. He knew from his research that Morehouse worked the day shift at the prison, so he waited until six P.M. before he called Morehouse's home phone. A young girl answered—Morehouse's meth-addicted daughter, he assumed.

"Is Mr. Morehouse available?" Bernie said.

"He's takin' a nap. He was up all last night with my mother."

"This is very important," Bernie said.

"Well, okay, but he's gonna be pissed."

Great, Bernie thought, but the fact that Morehouse had been up all night taking care of his sick, uninsurable wife could be a good thing.

"Who is this?" Morehouse said when he came to the phone. He had a voice like a guy who'd sing bass in a barbershop quartet.

"My name isn't important," Bernie said, "but I happen to know that you're over three hundred thousand dollars in debt and—"

"Is this one of those debt consolidation companies? And how the fuck did you get this number? This number's unlisted."

"I'm not from a debt—"

"Don't you ever call my house again, you bloodsucking son of a bitch," Albert Morehouse shouted, and slammed down the phone.

That didn't go so well, Bernie said to himself. Now what?

He decided to write Morehouse a letter. Yes, that was the way to approach him. He'd lay out his offer in writing and that way Morehouse would never see him and couldn't hang up on him while he made his pitch.

Bernie went to a public library to type the letter, because he didn't want there to be any evidence on his computer. In the letter, he said he knew that Morehouse was over three hundred thousand dollars in debt because of his wife's medical expenses, that his daughter needed drug treatment and a lawyer, and that Morehouse was about to lose his house. He said if Morehouse was willing to do him a favor that involved an inmate at Wallens Ridge, Bernie would pay him half a million dollars, half the money up front and the remainder upon satisfactory completion of the job.

Now had it been his money, Bernie would have been worried that Morehouse might take the two hundred and fifty grand and then do nothing further. But since it was Fiona's money, Bernie wasn't too concerned about that.

The last sentence of Bernie's letter said that if Morehouse was interested, he should call him at _____. He left the space for the number blank and printed off his letter, then purchased a prepaid cell phone and filled the phone number in by hand. He wiped the letter down with a Kleenex to remove his fingerprints, put on latex gloves, and stuck the letter in a self-sticking envelope so he wouldn't leave DNA. Next he went to a FedEx place, put the envelope into a FedEx envelope, and addressed it to Morehouse, printing out the address in block letters and using his left hand instead of his right. Morehouse would receive the letter the following day.

Bernie figured his tradecraft was excellent, about as good as any real spy could have done.

———◆◆◆———

Morehouse called him the next day. "How do I know this isn't some kind of sting operation?" Morehouse said.

"Well, I guess you don't," Bernie said. "But think about it. Would the cops put up half a million dollars to set up a prison guard? I don't think so. Maybe five or ten thousand, but not half a million. I mean, it's not like you're a major drug dealer or something."

"If it wasn't for my wife, I wouldn't even be talking to you," Morehouse said.

"I'm sure that's true," Bernie said.

"And how did you even know about my wife and daughter?"

"Mr. Morehouse, we don't have time to get into all that. Are you interested?"

"What do you want me to do?"

"I want a prisoner killed."

"I'm not going to kill anyone."

"I don't expect you to. But I suspect you know inmates inside the prison who would be willing to kill other inmates."

Morehouse didn't say anything for a moment. "Maybe," he said. "Who do you want taken care of?"

"A man named Nelson."

"What's his first name?"

"He's the new inmate in a wheelchair."

"Oh, him. And you're going to send me half the money?"

"Yes. I'll FedEx you two hundred and fifty thousand as soon as you tell me you know a way to get the job done."

"I already know a way. But what makes you think I won't take the money and not do anything?"

"Mr. Morehouse, my problem is killing somebody *inside* Wallens Ridge. Killing someone who works there isn't really a problem."

47

———◆———

Although he had no desire to do so, DeMarco drove to Hazelton, West Virginia, to talk to Brian Kincaid. He didn't want to see Kincaid because he didn't have good news for him, but he figured the decent thing to do was let him know where things stood.

When Kincaid entered the conference room, accompanied by a guard, DeMarco was shocked by his appearance. The first time DeMarco saw him, Kincaid had looked tired and defeated, but otherwise okay; the man who entered the conference room today didn't look okay. He had a black eye that was almost swollen shut, a yellow-purple bruise on his left cheek, more bruises on his throat, and he moved like there was something wrong with his back.

DeMarco waited until the guard left the room, then asked, "What happened to you, Brian? Who beat you up?"

Kincaid didn't look at DeMarco. He pulled out a cigarette and tried to light it, but his hands were shaking so badly DeMarco finally took the matches and lit the cigarette for him.

"Brian, tell me what's going on," DeMarco said.

Kincaid took a puff on the cigarette, exhaled, then finally focused his eyes on DeMarco. "I'd heard all those stories about guys getting raped in prison, and when I first got here I was terrified that—"

"Aw, Jesus. Did someone rape you?" DeMarco asked.

"No. I'm just saying that's what scared me. But it never happened. And the whole time I've been here, I've gone out of my way not to make enemies. I get along with everyone. I write letters for illiterate guys. I look up shit for them in law books. But two weeks ago, I'm having lunch with four, five guys and this one guy starts talking about how his mother used to make spaghetti and he says something about his mother dumping the spaghetti into a *calendar* and rinsing it off. Well, without thinking about it, I said, 'You mean a *colander*.' The guy gives me this funny look and I'm thinking maybe he doesn't understand, so I say, 'The strainer thing you rinse the spaghetti in is called a *colander*, not a *calendar*.' No big deal. Right? Wrong. That's the kind of shit that gets you killed in this place."

"What?" DeMarco said.

"The guy walks up to me a couple hours after lunch, hits me in the gut, and tells me I embarrassed him in front of his friends. So I apologize, of course, but it doesn't matter. A few days later, he catches me alone and beats the shit out of me. Two days after that, he comes up behind me and chokes me until I almost pass out. I figure he's going to kill me eventually, so I tell the guards and they put him in isolation for a couple days, and when he gets out, he says, 'Now I'm gonna kill you.'"

Kincaid laughed at the irony of his situation and said, "Anyway, I hope you've got good news for me, DeMarco, because I'm gonna die in here pretty soon because I was dumb enough to tell some psycho he mispronounced a word."

DeMarco told him he did have some good news, and then went on to explain everything they'd learned about Mulray Pharma. He concluded by saying, "So you were right, Brian. They framed you for Downing's death."

"Thank God," Kincaid said. "So when can I get out of here?"

"It's not gonna be that easy," DeMarco said. "I mean, I know all these things but I can't prove anything."

"But—"

DeMarco held up a hand to silence him. "Brian, tomorrow I'm going to see one of the guys who helped kill Downing. He's in prison right now, and I'm gonna offer him a deal to testify against Mulray Pharma and admit what he did."

DeMarco didn't tell Kincaid that he'd already offered Nelson this deal, but he was hoping that with Kelly dead, Nelson might change his mind.

"What if he won't take the deal?" Kincaid asked.

DeMarco wanted to say: *Then you're screwed.* But he didn't. Instead he said, "He's going to, Brian; he doesn't have any other options. So just hang in here a little longer. And I'm going to talk to the warden about this guy who's bothering you. What's his name?"

Before DeMarco left the prison, he pulled out his congressional ID badge and forced the warden to meet with him. He told the warden that Brian Kincaid was a friend of the ex–Speaker of the House and that if anything happened to him the warden should start looking for a new job. Maybe he shouldn't have said *ex*-Speaker. If the warden was intimidated, he didn't act like it.

———◆———

It occurred to DeMarco afterward that he could have broken the news about Kelly's death to Nelson in a more compassionate manner.

A guard held the door to the meeting room open, and Nelson wheeled himself in. The wheelchair he was using was a lightweight model, like the type wheelchair athletes use. There was a small table and two chairs in the room, and the normal procedure was for the prisoner to sit in one of the chairs and the guard to handcuff him to an eyebolt in the table so he'd be restrained. However, to follow the normal procedure, Nelson would have to be transferred from his wheelchair to the prisoner's chair, which was a minor hassle, so the guard decided to let Nelson remain seated in his wheelchair. How much of a threat could a guy in a wheelchair be?

As soon as the guard left the room, DeMarco scooted his chair around the table so he could sit closer to Nelson and face him. Nelson looked good, DeMarco thought, and he looked strong. Other than being partially paralyzed, he appeared to have fully recovered from being shot and his upper body seemed even bigger than the last time DeMarco had seen him. It was apparent he'd been working out to stay in shape.

Before DeMarco could say anything, Nelson said, "Why are you here? I've already told you I'm not going to testify against anybody."

"Kelly came to see me," DeMarco said.

"Bullshit," Nelson said.

"He told me everything. He told me how the two of you killed Phil Downing and framed Brian Kincaid, and how you killed a bunch of old people to test Mulray Pharma's new drug. He said he was the one who did all the killing and you didn't kill anyone. I figure he was probably lying about that, but at this point it doesn't matter. He also said a woman named Fiona West was the one who gave the orders."

"Bullshit," Nelson said again.

"What's bullshit?" DeMarco asked.

"There's no way Kelly came to see you and told you all that."

"Well, he did, Nelson, and the reason he did was to get you out of this place. He said Mulray is going to have you killed while you're here at Wallens Ridge and the only way he could stop that from happening was to testify. So he wanted a deal. He said he'd give up Mulray if the government would let you walk."

Maybe he shouldn't have said *walk*.

It took a moment for Nelson to absorb all that, and although he was still skeptical, he said, "So is that why you're here, to tell me they're going to let me go?"

"No. I'm here because Kelly's dead. A guy named Earl Lee killed him. Lee's dead too—Kelly shot him. So you've got one chance, Nelson. Assuming you don't get shanked by some nut here at Wallens Ridge, you're going to—"

Nelson let out a roar—the roar of an animal in pain—and before DeMarco could react, Nelson, using only his massive arms, launched himself at him. He knocked DeMarco out of his chair and onto the floor, placed his hands around his throat, and began to choke him.

DeMarco wasn't a small man—he was five foot eleven, weighed a hundred and eighty pounds—and he had good upper body strength. Nelson, however, was six foot four, weighed two twenty, and had *incredible* upper body strength. He didn't need his legs to choke a man.

DeMarco tried to pull Nelson's hands apart, and when he couldn't, he began to strike Nelson's head with his fists, which was like hitting a cinder block—but Nelson seemed oblivious to whatever pain he might be feeling. In less than a minute, DeMarco's vision began to blur. He was going to die; he was going to be strangled to death by a man who used a wheelchair.

DeMarco didn't hear the guard throw open the door to the room, because he was unconscious by then. Fortunately for DeMarco, the guard had heard Nelson's wheelchair slam against the wall. The guard jumped on Nelson's back and tried to pull him off DeMarco, but he couldn't break Nelson's grip, either. He stood up and kicked Nelson in the ribs with his boot, tried to break his grip again, then kicked him again, screaming for help as he did. Another guard rushed into the room. He kicked Nelson in the face, then both guards tugged at Nelson's arms until they finally pulled him off DeMarco.

DeMarco came to in the prison infirmary. A woman—he didn't know if she was a doctor or a nurse—told him he was going to be all right and to just lie there for a few minutes and not stand up right away. DeMarco's throat felt like it had been kicked by a mule wearing jackboots, but he sat up and said he needed to talk to the warden immediately. His voice sounded like Louie Armstrong's.

The warden was short and broad, dressed in an ill-fitting gray suit. The suit coat came down too far on his legs, as if it was made for a taller man; most likely the warden couldn't find an off the rack coat that would simultaneously accommodate his stubby legs and his wide shoulders. He also looked like a worrier. He had four or five lines running across his forehead like deep furrows in a freshly plowed field. At the moment, he was probably worried that DeMarco might sue the prison for having almost been killed by Nelson. He began by apologizing for what had happened, but DeMarco interrupted him.

"I'm fine, Warden," DeMarco said, "and it was my fault Nelson attacked me. The reason I'm talking to you is I'm concerned Nelson's going to get killed. He's a key witness against a powerful pharmaceutical company, and they're going to find some way to get to him while he's in this prison."

"I never wanted him here in the first place," the warden grumped. "Some judge in Arlington rammed him down my throat."

"Yeah, well, I'm sorry about that," DeMarco said, "but you need to find some way to protect him until I can get him out of here." DeMarco saw no reason to tell the warden that it was his idea to put Nelson in Wallens Ridge in the first place.

The warden said he'd do his best but couldn't make any guarantees, and DeMarco left Wallens Ridge rubbing his throat and wondering how long Nelson had to live.

48

"We have to get Nelson out of Wallens Ridge," DeMarco told Charles Erhart, the Arlington County prosecutor.

"What's wrong with your voice?" Erhart asked.

DeMarco ignored the question. "I made a mistake having you put him down there. Maybe he'll change his mind about testifying later, but right now you have to get him out of there and put him someplace where he can be protected."

"I can't move him," Erhart said. "It was the judge who sent him there."

"So talk to the judge."

"He's out of town. He's fishing someplace in Canada, one of those places you fly into by floatplane."

"So talk to another judge."

"Another judge won't move him. Another judge will just say wait a week until Judge Harris gets back from his fishing trip."

DeMarco then did the only thing he could do: he invoked his boss's name. "Mr. Mahoney's not going to be happy to hear this," he said.

"Look, I'll try," Erhart said, "but I'm just telling you the way it is."

"We have to get Nelson out of Wallens Ridge," DeMarco said.

"What's wrong with your voice?" Mahoney asked. "If you're sick, don't go breathin' on me."

"I'm not sick," DeMarco said, and explained how Nelson almost choked him to death when he told Nelson that Kelly was dead. To this, Mahoney responded by laughing. "You almost got killed by a guy in a wheelchair?"

DeMarco didn't bother to explain that Nelson wasn't your average disabled person. Instead, he said, "I need you to call somebody and get him out of there."

"But it was your bright idea to put him there."

"Yeah, I know. But if we leave him there—"

"We? What's this *we* shit?"

"Boss, he's gonna get killed. Right now the guy's upset about Kelly's death, but maybe after a little time has passed, maybe then I can get him to testify. His big concern with testifying before was giving up Kelly, but with Kelly gone, maybe he'll come to his senses. Plus now he knows Mulray killed Kelly, and if he wants to avenge Kelly's death, he has to testify. So I need your help. I need you to get him moved to someplace where Mulray can't get to him."

The State of Virginia is politically schizophrenic, unable to make up its mind if it wants to be red or blue. The majority of Virginians voted for a Democrat in the last presidential election, elected two Democrats to the Senate, then immediately turned around and elected a Republican governor—which for Mahoney wasn't good, because he needed the governor's help.

Had the governor been a Democrat, Mahoney would have just leaned on the man to get his way—and Mahoney's weight was still considerable within his own party. But with a Republican, he needed either leverage or something to trade. He mulled this problem over, and when he couldn't think of any way to coerce the governor or of any political favor to trade, he finally did the simple thing and just called the guy and asked for his help.

For once, Mahoney's instincts about the nature of politicians—that they only did something when they got something in return—turned out to be wrong. He told the governor the story—that he suspected that Mulray Pharma had killed a bunch of old people to develop their latest drug and that the next person they were going to kill was Nelson.

"If Nelson's killed," Mahoney said, "there won't be anybody to testify against Orson Mulray."

"But what do you want from me?" the governor asked.

"I want you to get him out of that prison and stash him somewhere with guys that can't be bribed. The problem is, Mulray's got so fuckin' much money he could probably bribe the Pope."

The governor didn't say anything, and Mahoney wondered if he'd offended the man with his language or his reference to the Pope. More likely, though, he was just trying to come up with a diplomatic way to tell Mahoney to shove his request up his ass. But he didn't.

"Okay, Congressman, I'll take care of it. And don't worry, I know men who can't be bought."

"Well, uh, thanks," Mahoney said, flabbergasted the guy was being so cooperative. "One of these days we'll have to get together and have a drink."

"I don't drink, sir," the governor said.

So the guy wasn't perfect—but he was all right.

49

Albert Morehouse couldn't believe what he was about to do.

He was being crushed by the weight of his debts, and if he lost his house . . . Well, he could just see himself living out of his car, his wife lying in the backseat moaning, her wheelchair in the trunk, and his meth-head daughter becoming a hooker before she killed herself with drugs. There were days he felt like getting in his car and just driving away. Most days, however, he felt like taking a gun and shooting everyone who worked at the HMO that wouldn't pay for his wife's treatments.

"Clancy," he yelled, "get your dumb ass over here. I want to talk to you."

Ike Clancy raised the three hundred pounds he was bench-pressing like it was a ten-pound sack of sugar, set the bar down on the rack above him, and slowly got to his feet.

Ike Clancy was six foot six, and because he couldn't think of anything better to do, he spent about six hours a day lifting weights or doing push-ups and sit-ups in his cell. He looked like the Incredible Hulk on steroids—or the way the Hulk might have looked if he had a shaved head, a thrice-broken nose, and swastika tattoos on his chest, his back, and both arms. He also had an IQ that Morehouse suspected was about the same as the ambient temperature on a warm day—not a hot day.

Clancy had been sentenced to twenty years in Wallens Ridge, although he might be paroled after serving half that amount. Clancy had committed murder—but not cold-blooded, premeditated, first-degree murder. Clancy's crime was a crime of passion. He had beat his common-law wife to death when he found her in bed with their landlord. Clancy claimed at his trial that he wouldn't have killed the woman if she'd been screwing the guy to pay the rent, but as he'd paid the rent just that week, he knew that wasn't the case.

"What did I do?" Clancy asked.

"You didn't do anything," Morehouse said. "But I want you to do something for me."

"What?"

Morehouse didn't answer immediately. He looked over at a group of prisoners who were laughing their asses off about something and he thought, as he always did, that prison administration in the United States needed to be drastically changed. Half these people were living better than they'd ever lived on the outside. They were given three squares a day, clothes, a warm place to sleep, exercise facilities, television and library privileges. Wallens Ridge was like a fucking low-class resort. He figured prisons would be more of a deterrent if these thugs were forced to do hard labor the way they did in Russia, or the way he heard they did in Russia. They should feed them table scraps once a day, make them dig canals through snake-infested swamps, and use horsewhips on them when they misbehaved. Then he thought that maybe it was a good thing prisons weren't so hard, because with what he was about to do, he might end up in one.

Answering Clancy's question, he said, "I want a prisoner named Nelson to stop breathing."

"Who's Nelson?"

"The new guy in the wheelchair."

Morehouse knew—but couldn't prove—that Clancy had shanked two inmates since he'd been at Wallens Ridge. One of the men died; the one who lived was afraid to testify that Clancy was the one who put out his eye with a jagged piece of sheet metal.

"What's in it for me?" Clancy asked.

"I'll put Carly Mendez in your cell for a week."

Carlos Mendez, who called himself Carly, was twenty-seven but looked eighteen. He shaved his legs and his armpits and let his hair grow down to his shoulders, and when he wore lipstick and eye shadow he looked like a young Jennifer Lopez—or so most of the other prisoners thought. He was arguably the most sought-after he-she in the prison, but Carly liked handsome black men, not redneck grotesques like Ike Clancy.

"For a week?" Clancy said.

God forgive me, Morehouse thought. "Yeah, for a whole week," he said.

50

He found a Coke can that one of the guards had carelessly left sitting on a window ledge—a guard could lose his job for a mistake like that—and was delighted to see that the pull tab that opened the can was still attached. He shoved the can into his underpants, and when he returned to his cell he pulled the pull tab off the can and spent three hours grinding the end of the tab against the cement floor in his cell until it was pointed at one end. When he was finished, he had a crude but effective can opener. He punched the pointed pull tab/can opener into the top of the Coke can and begin to gouge and tug and rip to remove the top. It took him an hour, and he cut his hand a couple of times, but he was eventually able to remove the top of the can. He spent another two hours grinding the pull tab to reestablish a point on it and then repeated the procedure with the bottom of the can.

Six hours after he began, his hands and fingers ached and were cut in a dozen places, but he now had a Coke can with no top or bottom. He flattened the can with his foot, then doubled it over, flattened it again by hitting it with a rock he'd found in the exercise yard, doubled it over a second time, and beat on it with the rock to flatten it more. When he was finished he had a piece of metal approximately one inch wide, five inches long, and less than a quarter-inch thick.

Then came the hard part. He took one corner of the rectangle, wedged it into a crack in the cinder-block wall in his cell, and began flexing it back and forth—which wasn't easy, but fortunately his hands were strong. It took him two hours, bending the corner back and forth, until finally the metal weakened and the corner broke off, leaving him with a shaft about four inches long and a triangular point on the end of the shaft about an inch long. Then he spent four more hours grinding the point against the floor.

Twelve hours after finding the Coke can, he had a weapon that was pointed if not exactly razor-sharp. But it was sharp enough. He would wrap a rag around the shaft to protect his hands and drive the pointed part of the flattened can into soft flesh, then rip downward. Then he'd repeat the procedure—stab, rip, stab, rip, stab, rip—until the asshole was dead.

He waited until the guy went to the library.

He was at a table, his back to the door, but he wasn't reading or writing like he usually did. He was just sitting there. Maybe he liked that the library was quiet. Or maybe he figured he was safe because he was in plain sight of the trustee who checked out the books.

He turned to his buddy and said, "Get the old guy away from the desk. Tell him to show you where they keep the law books."

His buddy did as he was told, and as soon as the librarian was out of sight, he walked up behind the bastard and plunged the Coke can shiv into his neck a dozen times. He must have hit an artery, because blood started spraying out like the guy's neck was some kind of fountain.

He dropped the shiv on the floor—he hated to leave it after all the work he'd put into it—and walked out of the library.

As he walked away he could hear Brian Kincaid choking on his own blood.

That'll teach you, you cocksucker, to make fun of how people talk.

"Is he going to die?" Mahoney asked.

"No," DeMarco said, "but he lost a lot of blood. And his neck's a mess; he may not be able to move his head right because of all the muscle and nerve damage."

"Aw, geez," Mahoney said. "Mary Pat's gonna be pissed."

This was typical of Mahoney: instead of being concerned for Brian Kincaid, he was worried about his wife being mad at him.

"And I suppose you still haven't figured out a way to get him out of prison."

"No," DeMarco said. "He's going to serve the time unless you can get him a presidential pardon."

"Well, that ain't gonna happen," Mahoney said.

"If I could just convince that damn Nelson to testify."

"So go talk to him again."

"He almost killed me the last time I tried," DeMarco said.

"Yeah, well, be more careful next time."

51

Ike Clancy walked over to the table where he normally sat for chow, but ignored the guys around him as he thought about Nelson. Killing the guy wasn't really a problem. He was a cripple in a wheelchair and all Clancy had to do was walk up behind him and shank him or put a choke hold on him. The problem he had was that he didn't want to get caught for killing the guy. He'd be out in ten years if he didn't get in any more trouble, but if they pinned Nelson's murder on him, he'd never get out.

He'd been thinking that maybe he should tell Morehouse that he'd changed his mind and that Morehouse should get someone else to do the job—but then he'd start thinking about spending a week with Carly Mendez, the little bitch suckin' his dick four, five times a day, him jamming it to her until she screamed, and then smacking her around because that was almost as much fun as screwing her. (It never occurred to him to think of Carly as anything but *her*; to do otherwise would make him queer, and anyway, Carly thought of himself, herself, whatever, as a her.) Oh, yeah, it was gonna be a great week, the most fun he'd had since being stuck in Wallens Ridge. He just couldn't pass that up.

Yesterday, just like the day before, he saw the crip in his wheelchair, sitting on the edge of the exercise yard, his back to the other inmates, staring off into space. When he'd first arrived at Wallens Ridge, he did laps around the yard in his chair like he was training for something, and then he'd lift weights like everybody else. But the last couple of days . . . well, he just sat there like he was moping about something.

Okay. If the guy did the same thing today, Clancy was going to take him out—and he thought he had a way to do it so he wouldn't get caught. He'd tell two of his short friends to start a fight with the niggers over by the weight-lifting area. While the fight was going on and everybody, guards included, was watching it, he'd get four of his tallest friends to walk out with him to where the crip was sitting. They'd form a half-circle around him, their backs to the guard up in the tower, and while his friends stood there, blocking the tower guard's view, he'd choke Nelson and then just leave him sitting there in his wheelchair.

Yeah, that would work, but he still had a problem: he'd have to give his friends something to make them help him, because they weren't really friends, just assholes he hung with for his own protection. Shit, what could he give them? Hell, the only thing he could think to give them was Carly. Goddamnit, he'd have to let each of them spend a couple hours with her if he wanted their help. Well, there was nothing that could be done about that.

———◆◆◆———

Albert Morehouse watched as Clancy talked to a group of his Aryan Nations asshole buddies, then saw two of the men Clancy had been speaking to walk in the direction of the weight-lifting benches. Clancy and four other guys, guys almost as tall as Clancy, started walking in Nelson's direction—and Morehouse knew exactly what was going to happen next. Any minute now, a fight would break out in the weight-lifting area, and while everybody was watching the fight,

Clancy, surrounded by his buddies, would kill Nelson. For a moment, Morehouse thought about stopping Clancy—he still could. Then he thought again about his wife's medical bills.

And that's when the warden stepped into the exercise yard—and with him were two tall Virginia State Police troopers. The troopers were in uniform—blue short-sleeved shirts, gray pants, and those black Smokey the Bear hats that added three inches to their height. They had on their equipment belts, which contained radios and Mace and handcuffs, but they weren't wearing their sidearms, as no one was allowed to bring a gun into the prison. What the hell were troopers doing here? Morehouse wondered. For that matter, what the hell was the warden doing in the exercise yard? He hardly ever left his office—he was terrified of being taken hostage.

The warden stood there for a moment looking at the cons like he was searching for somebody—the troopers standing next to him were so tall they made him look like a dwarf—and then the warden walked right up to him, Morehouse being the nearest guard.

"Where's the prisoner in the wheelchair?" the warden asked.

Before Morehouse could answer, one of the troopers said, "I see him."

The troopers started to walk toward Nelson, but before they took two steps, a con in the weight-lifting area roared out in pain or anger, and Morehouse glanced over in that direction. Two guys, one black, one white, were whaling the shit out of each other. Then another white guy jumped in, and then another black guy joined the fray. Morehouse glanced over to see where Clancy was and could see that he and his four buddies had formed a semicircle around Nelson's wheelchair and that Nelson was no longer visible. And that's when the two troopers started running.

The troopers ignored the fight going on near the bench presses and ran as fast as they could toward Nelson, then plowed right into all the convicts surrounding him, flinging prisoners out of their way until they reached Nelson, who was lying on the ground with Ike Clancy on top of him. Morehouse couldn't see what Clancy was doing to Nelson; what he did see was one of the troopers take a leather sap out of his back pocket and swing it at Clancy's head. Morehouse, standing two hundred feet away, actually heard the sap hit Clancy. It sounded like a bat smacking a watermelon.

The exercise yard was bedlam. The fight in the weight-lifting area had turned into a gang fight—with twenty black and white inmates throwing punches at one another—and prison guards had joined the melee, trying to pull them apart. And both state troopers now had saps in their hands, and they were swinging them at Clancy's friends, who were throwing punches at them in return. In two minutes, two of Clancy's buddies had joined Nelson and Clancy on the ground.

Morehouse realized that the warden was yelling at him. "Go help them!" the warden shouted, pointing his finger at the troopers, who didn't appear to really need any help. But Morehouse jogged over to join the troopers, not in any hurry, and by the time he got there, Clancy's two remaining friends—the ones not on the ground—were backing away from the sap-swinging troopers. One of the troopers was missing his hat and bleeding from the mouth, but the other man appeared untouched, his Smokey the Bear hat still on his head.

"Are you guys okay?" Morehouse asked the troopers, but they ignored him. The trooper with the bloody mouth knelt down next to Nelson and felt for a pulse in his throat.

"Is he alive?" Morehouse asked. *Please, Lord, let him be dead.*

The trooper again ignored him. He stood up, looked around for his hat, found it, and put it back on. "Give me a hand," he said to his partner, and they picked Nelson up and carried him away from the exercise yard.

"Is he dead?" Morehouse asked again, speaking to the troopers' backs.

52

Mahoney called while DeMarco was beating up his punching bag.

The eighty-pound bag was on the second floor of DeMarco's house and it hung from an exposed rafter like a headless fat man. The only other thing on the second floor of his home was a second-hand upright piano that he'd bought on impulse at an estate sale and now rarely played. At one time his second floor had contained chairs, beds, rugs, and paintings—but all those things had disappeared when his wife divorced him and took practically everything he owned. He often thought of his ex-wife as he hit the bag, and pretended he was pounding on the asshole she'd had an affair with before she divorced him. An asshole who also happened to be his cousin.

DeMarco was punching the heavy bag because after Nelson—a paraplegic confined to a wheelchair—nearly killed him, he figured he should get back in shape. He had put on a little weight—his pants were becoming noticeably harder to button—and pounding on the bag was a great workout. When Mahoney called, he and the bag had gone six rounds and DeMarco figured he was ahead on points, but he was drenched with sweat and his hands felt like two bags of concrete mix at the end of his arms.

Mahoney told him how Nelson had almost been killed by another inmate at Wallens Ridge and that he was now being protected by Virginia staties. "You need to get this fuckin' thing wrapped up," Mahoney said.

"Well, if you could get somebody with a badge investigating it would be a hell of a lot easier," DeMarco shot back. If Mahoney had been there he would have hit him instead of his punching bag.

"The FBI isn't going to investigate," Mahoney said, "unless they think Mulray's committed a crime, and right now you can't prove he's done anything illegal. But if you can get Nelson to talk, then maybe I can convince them to wade in on this thing."

DeMarco hated to admit it, but he knew Mahoney was right.

He called Emma and told her what had happened to Nelson. "I'm gonna go see him again."

"I'm going with you," Emma said.

"Good," DeMarco said.

<hr />

While waiting for DeMarco, Emma called Celia Montoya at the *Washington Post*. "I'd like you to do me a favor."

"What sort of favor?" Montoya said. She sounded guarded, and not all that happy to hear from Emma. The articles she'd written about Mulray Pharma hadn't turned out at all the way she'd hoped. No one in the U.S. government—or any other government—was trying to find out if Mulray Pharma had done anything illegal and, of course, Mulray had decided to sue the *Washington Post*. The *Post*'s lawyers said that Mulray couldn't possibly win his lawsuit, but since he had a two-hundred-person law firm at his disposal and money to burn, he was going to make life miserable for the *Post*'s lawyers for months, if not years, to come—and the *Post*'s lawyers were all blaming Celia Montoya for this increase in their workload.

"I want you to print an article that says that Nelson's dead," Emma said.

"Is he?"

"No."

Emma then gave Montoya the most recent news about Nelson. She concluded by saying, "He's in hiding now and being protected, but as soon as Mulray learns Nelson's still alive he'll try again, and maybe succeed next time."

"And you expect me," Montoya said, "to put my credibility on the line by writing a story I know to be false?"

"You can leave yourself some wiggle room," Emma said. "Say you got the story from an anonymous source at Wallens Ridge and—"

"I don't think so," Montoya said.

"Celia, listen to me. Nelson is the only witness we have against Mulray. Right now his head is messed up because of Kelly's death and he's not thinking straight, and I need some time to work on him. And maybe since they tried to kill him he'll cooperate, and if he does, you may still have a shot at that Pulitzer."

"Pulitzer! Right now I'll be happy just to keep my job."

"Will you help? Please. You know what Mulray's done. You know we can't let him get away with this. And we owe it to Lizzie Warwick to make this right."

"All right," Montoya finally said. "But the story won't have my byline on it. I'll feed it to the crime beat guy, the one who reported Kelly's death."

"Thank you," Emma said.

———◆———

Before going to see Nelson, Emma wanted to learn more about him and his relationship to Kelly. She found it odd that a cold-blooded killer like Kelly would be willing to sacrifice himself for another person. She knew that Nelson had saved Kelly's life—Kelly had told DeMarco this—and she wouldn't have been surprised to learn that Kelly had saved Nelson's life, too. And she knew about the bonds formed between men who were in combat together, bonds that were sometimes stronger than blood. But Kelly's willingness to sacrifice himself—considering what Kelly had done—still puzzled her.

Then there was the fact that they owned a home together in Montana. That was somewhat odd, but maybe not too odd. For all she knew, they bought the place together as a business opportunity and were planning to flip it. Or maybe the simple answer was that they could stand each other and couldn't stand a lot of other people and simply preferred to live together in a beautiful, isolated setting. And there was, of course, a third possibility.

From Neil's research, she had the basic facts about the two men. That is, she'd seen their military files and knew where they'd served and knew they'd performed in an exceptional manner. But the files didn't really give her a sense of either man's personality and certainly didn't give her any sense of the relationship they had with each other. She wanted to talk to someone who had served with them, and preferably someone who served with them in Delta Force.

Because she'd worked for the Defense Intelligence Agency—and worked at a very high level—Emma knew several officers who'd been in Delta Force. She had, in fact, helped plan some of Delta's missions. It took her half an hour to get to the right general—a man who owed her politically and personally—and she told him, "I want to talk to a guy who was on the ground with them on some of their missions. Someone who went into combat with them."

The general called back half an hour later and said the man she wanted to talk to was in Afghanistan and he'd call her in a couple of hours.

"Ma'am, this is Major John Howard. General Curtis told me to call you."

"Thank you for calling, Major."

"It's a privilege to be talking to you, ma'am. I know who you are. I'm sure you don't remember me—I was just a butter-bar lieutenant at the time—but you briefed my team once on a job we did in Iran. I can't say anything about the job on an unsecure line but—"

"I remember the mission, Major. Your team did well on that one."

"Yes, ma'am. Thanks to the plan you put together. Anyway, what can I do for you?"

"The general may have told you, but I want to talk to you about two guys you served with."

"Yes, ma'am. Kelly and Nelson. What would you like to know?"

"I want to know what you thought about them, what they were like, that sort of thing. I want more than the dry facts I can get from personnel files."

"The first thing I'll say is that they were two of the finest soldiers I've ever known. There was no one I'd rather have with me if we were going into a hot zone. Having said that, they were strange."

"Strange how?"

"Well, it's not unusual to have a loner in the unit, some guy who just keeps apart from the rest of the guys. You know, the guy who stays in the barracks when everybody else heads for the bar to let off some steam. The loner can be a perfectly good guy to go with on a mission, but he's just not a mixer, not a social animal."

"I know what you mean, Major," Emma said. Emma had been that loner in every unit she served with.

"But what was unusual about Kelly and Nelson was that they were this loner *couple*. They always hung together; they even took leave together. They were both fly-fishing fanatics and when they got some time off, that's what they'd do. One time they took a fishing trip to New Zealand together."

"But *why* were they a couple, Major?"

"I heard a story that when they were in basic training, Nelson was in some bar and some black guys—gang guys—started hassling him and Kelly came to his aid and they wiped up the bar with the guys. I don't know if the story's true but that was the rumor about how they met." The captain paused, then said, "I always had the impression that neither of them ever had a close friend growing up, and I know they weren't close to their families; I don't remember them ever getting a letter or a package from home. I think they became friends in boot camp and from that point forward figured they never needed another friend. All I know is that they were tight. They always had each other's back, they stuck together, and they didn't mingle with the rest of the unit."

"Were they gay?"

"Don't ask, don't tell, ma'am."

"Don't give me that crap, Major. Soldiers always know when they're serving with someone gay. And in a unit as tight as a Delta team, you'd know."

"Well, ma'am, the fact is I wondered about that but I *don't* know. And that's the God's honest truth. Like I said, they stuck together, but they didn't act . . . well, they didn't act gay. And frankly, I didn't care, because they were two of the toughest bastards you ever saw in a firefight."

"Is there anything else you can think of?"

"Just that they were, I don't know, *cold*. What I mean is, these weren't the kind of guys you see on TV passing out chocolate bars to kids. If someone in the unit got shipped out, they didn't usually attend the going-away thing. If someone got hurt, they didn't visit him in the hospital."

"Why'd they quit the army?"

"All they told me was that it was time to move on and they decided to go private because that's where the money was. In case I'm not being clear here, these guys didn't open up to anybody but each other. They just turned in their papers and mustered out. Can you tell me why you're asking about them, ma'am?"

"Major, Kelly's dead and Nelson's in prison."

"Jesus."

"And they did some very bad things that I don't have the time to go into. I'm going to be meeting with Nelson pretty soon to see if I can convince him to talk about something, and I'm just trying to get a handle on him."

"Well, good luck with that, ma'am. I never could."

53

Nelson was being kept in a cabin in the Blue Ridge Mountains, protected around the clock by four Virginia state troopers. DeMarco and Emma met him in the great room of the cabin, a room dominated by the head of a twelve-point buck mounted over the fireplace mantel. Because of the mid-July heat, Nelson was wearing only a T-shirt and shorts, and DeMarco was again impressed by how powerful Nelson looked—and realized he was lucky to have survived his last encounter with the man.

Nelson had changed since DeMarco first met him. In those early meetings in the hospital, Nelson refused to even look at DeMarco and had remained completely aloof and unwavering in his commitment not to cooperate. And the last time he'd seen Nelson, all he'd seen was the fury on his face as Nelson did his best to strangle him. The man was different today. He seemed calm, almost peaceful, as if he'd come to terms with his condition and his situation. But maybe not.

"I was wondering when you'd be back," he said to DeMarco, but before DeMarco could respond he turned to Emma. "You're the lady who almost killed Kelly in Peru."

"Yes," Emma said.

Nelson made a hat-tipping gesture. "Well, you must be something else."

Emma ignored what she assumed was a compliment. "Mr. Nelson," she said, "first, let me say that I'm sorry your friend Kelly was killed."

Nelson nodded, accepting the lie.

"But we need your help. We need you to testify against Mulray Pharma. If you don't, you're going to prison and someone will kill you eventually."

"I'm not sure dying bothers me all that much," Nelson said. "Spending the rest of my life in this chair isn't my idea of living."

"A lot of people in this world are in much worse shape than you are," Emma said scornfully. "You'll adjust and most likely have a long life. And Kelly told DeMarco you have money, so that should make your life even better."

"What sort of deal will I get?" Nelson said.

From the way he said this, DeMarco got the impression Nelson didn't really care about a deal, but Emma answered his question. "If you cooperate and give us the information we need to convict Mulray, you'll be released from prison."

DeMarco looked over at Emma. She had no authority to make any sort of deal, particularly one that generous, and she knew it. But Nelson didn't question her authority or her generosity. Instead he shook his head and said, "I might be able to help you get Fiona, but me testifying won't be enough to get Mulray. Kelly and I officially worked for Lizzie Warwick. There's no documented connection between us and Mulray's company, and you're not going to be able to trace the money we were paid back to Mulray. And I never met Mulray. I only met Fiona, I only met her four times, and the only people who can confirm that those meetings took place are Kelly and Hobson, and they're both dead. Now, I'm not a lawyer, but I'm pretty sure if I testify that I helped kill a bunch of people because Fiona told me to, it'd just be my word against hers, and the only one that will go to jail for murder will be me. And even if you could find enough evidence to convict Fiona, Mulray will just say that she was an overzealous employee and he didn't have anything to do with the things she did."

"But if you're willing to testify," DeMarco said, "we can get the FBI to start digging, and they have the smarts and the resources to find the evidence we need."

"Maybe," Nelson said, "but I've got a better idea."

"What's that?" DeMarco said.

"Let me tell you something about Fiona," Nelson said. "When she thinks people are a threat, she kills them. She ordered me and Kelly to kill Phil Downing when he discovered what was going on in Peru, but when you think about Downing, you'll realize that killing him wasn't really necessary. All Fiona had to do was pay him off and he would have cooperated. She also ordered us to kill you two when you started poking into things, and she did this before she even knew if you'd found out anything that could harm her. And then there was Hobson. Hobson was definitely a guy she could have simply paid to keep his mouth shut. What I'm telling you is, the way Fiona solves problems is by killing people. It's like she can't think of any other solution."

"I don't understand," Emma said. "How does knowing this help us?"

Nelson smiled. "If you're able to convince Fiona that Orson Mulray's a threat, she'll kill him."

DeMarco said, "We're not going to do that." But at the same time, Emma said, "How would we do that?"

"I don't know," Nelson said, addressing Emma. "But if you can figure out a way, I guarantee you Fiona will have someone take Mulray out."

Neither Emma nor DeMarco said anything for a moment, until DeMarco repeated what he'd previously said. "We're not going to do that. We need to do this the legal way. You testify, the FBI gathers up evidence to support your testimony, and Fiona and Mulray go to jail."

Nelson laughed. "DeMarco, do you really believe that a rich son of a bitch like Orson Mulray will ever see the inside of a prison?" Before DeMarco could answer, Nelson said, "No, if you want my help, we're gonna do this my way. You're going to convince Fiona that Mulray's a threat—and after he's dead, come back and see me. Then I'll do anything you want. I'll testify to everything. I'll tell you what I did to help test Mulray's drug and how Kelly and I set up Kincaid for Downing's death. I'll give you whatever you want—after Mulray's dead."

They wasted the next half hour trying to get Nelson to change his mind. They told him if he didn't help them, he was going to be put back in Wallens Ridge where somebody would eventually kill him. And if he wasn't killed, he was going to spend fifteen years in a cell and when he got out—*if* he got out—he'd be nothing more than a penniless cripple, because they'd make sure he never got the money Mulray Pharma paid him. Their strongest argument was that if he didn't cooperate, Kelly's death would never be avenged.

But Nelson turned to stone on them.

———◆———

"So now what?" DeMarco said.

They had left Nelson in the cabin and gone outside to talk. They were sitting on a fallen log next to a burbling brook shaded by old trees. The setting was incredibly tranquil—and completely at odds with the subject matter of their conversation.

"The first thing we have to do is decide if Nelson is right," Emma said.

"Right about what? That Fiona is willing to kill people to protect herself?"

"No—I think he's right about that. What we have to decide is if Nelson went to court and testified, could the government convict Orson Mulray. And I think Nelson's right about that, too. The government wouldn't have a chance, because there's no evidence that Mulray ever ordered Nelson to do anything."

"Yeah, but how 'bout all the other stuff?" DeMarco said. "The fact that Hobson was killed and that Lee killed Kelly, and the attempt on Nelson's life at Wallens Ridge? That's a lot of circumstantial evidence."

"Those events all make for an interesting tale, but again, there's nothing to positively connect Mulray to them. If Mulray's indicted—and right now I can't imagine why he would be—he'll hire a battalion of lawyers, they'll delay the trial forever, and while they're delaying, he or Fiona will try to kill Nelson again and maybe succeed this time. And when the case finally does go to trial, with or without Nelson testifying, Orson Mulray will walk."

"So what do you want to do?" DeMarco asked again.

Emma picked up a rock and flung it into the stream. "I want to do what Nelson said. I want to figure out a way to make Fiona believe that Mulray poses a threat to her."

"You'd be willing to do that? You'd be willing to let her kill him?"

Emma answered immediately. "Yes. Think about Orson Mulray, Joe. Think about who he is and what he did. He was already a rich man before this drug was developed. He was richer than most people can ever imagine being. I read he inherited over a billion dollars from his father. A billion! The Ugandans who died to develop his new drug would have felt rich if they had a *thousand* dollars. And the worst thing is that he didn't have to kill anyone. He could have developed his drug in the normal, legal manner; it would have just taken longer if he'd followed the rules. But Mulray couldn't wait. He couldn't wait a few years to go from being merely rich to obscenely rich. And for people like Mulray, I don't think it's really about money at all. I mean, how much money can one person possibly spend on himself? No, it's not about money. It's about ego. Orson Mulray doesn't want to be richer—he wants to be a financial *icon*. And it appears right now that there's nothing that can be done to bring him to justice, and as his wealth and influence grows it will become even harder. So will it weigh heavily on my conscience if we do something that causes Fiona to kill him? I don't think so."

"Yeah, but—"

"And another thing," Emma said. "If we push Fiona, maybe she won't kill him but maybe she'll do something else, something we can use to get more evidence against her and Mulray. I'd rather push her than do nothing."

"But how do we push her?"

"I haven't the slightest idea."

The drive from the Blue Ridge Mountains back to Washington took three hours, and while they were driving they barely spoke. They were about a mile from Emma's house in McLean when DeMarco said, "I have an idea."

"What is it?" Emma said, sounding skeptical.

"At his press conference, Mulray said the people who died during the clinical trials were given funerals in accordance with their religions and customs. He wouldn't have said that publicly if it wasn't true; he wouldn't want to be caught in a lie."

"So?"

"So that means there are bodies out there, bodies that can be exhumed and autopsied again."

"And you think if a second autopsy was performed, a pathologist could figure out that some people were poisoned like Kelly said?"

"I think—"

Before DeMarco could complete the sentence, Emma said, "It would never work. First, we'd have to figure out which corpses we need to exhume. Second, the corpses are in Thailand, and I can't even imagine what hoops we'd have to jump through to get one out of the ground. But the main thing is, Orson Mulray runs a pharmaceutical company. Don't you think if he poisoned somebody he'd make sure he used a poison that couldn't be detected during an autopsy?"

"Emma," DeMarco said, "I'm not talking about exhuming and autopsying anyone. I'm talking about making Fiona *believe* we can do it."

"But she already knows the government isn't willing to investigate what Mulray did in Peru and those other places."

"Who says the government has to be involved?" Before Emma could interrupt him again, DeMarco said, "Who has the greatest motive for getting Orson Mulray in legal hot water over this new drug of his?"

It took Emma less than a second to answer. "Another pharmaceutical company."

"That's right. Some competitor that has pockets just as deep as Mulray's and who has just as much influence would *want* to cause him problems, because that might give them an edge. So here's what I think we should do."

After he explained his plan, and when Emma couldn't think of any substantial objection to it—other than the fact that it was his plan and not hers—DeMarco said, "I'll go see Fiona the day after tomorrow. That should give us enough time."

"I think I'm the one who should talk to Fiona," Emma said.

"It won't work if you do it. I'm a lawyer and I work for Congress. You don't have any official standing."

Emma shook her head. "You have a law degree, but you're not a real lawyer. You're Mahoney's bagman."

"Hey—"

"And you don't look like a lawyer. You look like a guy some mob lawyer would defend."

How many more times could she insult him?

"It doesn't matter," DeMarco said. "It won't work unless I do it."

54

DeMarco dressed in a white shirt, a dark suit, and a somber tie—he figured he looked pretty lawyerly, in spite of Emma's belief to the contrary—and drove to Fiona West's place in Wilmington. She had a condo in a building on Brandywine Creek where the *cheap* units sold for two million bucks. He parked in the loading zone in front of the building and a uniformed doorman immediately charged out—like a linebacker planning to sack a quarterback—to tell him he couldn't park there.

DeMarco flashed his Congressional ID in the doorman's face and said, "I'm a government lawyer here on official business. If my car is towed, I'll have your ass arrested for interfering in a federal investigation. Now get out of my face."

Fiona's condo was located on the seventh floor—the entire seventh floor. When DeMarco stepped off the elevator, he found himself standing in Fiona's foyer, a room with marble floors and decorative wall sconces. The foyer was separated from the rest of the condo by a massive oak door that had to be nine feet tall. DeMarco rang the doorbell, waited a bit, and rang it again, and when Fiona still didn't respond he began to hammer on the door with his fist. Fiona finally flung open the door.

"Who are you," she screamed, "and what in the *hell* do you think you're doing?"

She was wearing sweatpants and a tank top and there was a sheen of sweat on her arms and face. She had apparently been exercising, and DeMarco was willing to bet there was a fully equipped gym somewhere in the condo.

"I'm Joe DeMarco. The guy you told Nelson to kill."

Fiona's face registered her surprise—she'd never seen DeMarco before—and for a moment she looked fearful. But she quickly regained her composure. "I don't know what you're talking about. Now get out of here or I'll call the police."

"I'll leave if you want, but I think it might be smarter if you listened to what I have to say. I'm here to make you a deal."

"A deal?"

"May I come in?" DeMarco said.

Fiona hesitated, then her curiosity got the best of her. "I'll give you five minutes, but if this is some kind of . . ." She didn't complete whatever threat she was about to make; instead she just turned around, and DeMarco followed her into the living room.

DeMarco had once been in the Asian Art Museum in San Francisco —and that's what Fiona's living room reminded him of. The room was filled with beautiful Japanese screens, paintings, and sculptures. He had no idea what period the artwork came from, but he was willing to bet that the pieces were very old and very expensive. He was sure the Oriental rug on the hardwood floor in Fiona's living room had cost more than his Toyota. The woman may have been a murderer, but she had excellent taste, or an excellent decorator.

Fiona took a seat on a couch that was itself a work of art and pointed DeMarco to a love seat that looked so delicate he was afraid it might collapse under his weight. "All right. What do you want?" she said.

"I don't want anything," DeMarco said. "I'm here to tell you what's going to happen to you if you refuse to testify against Orson Mulray."

Fiona laughed. "Testify? Why would I testify? Orson hasn't done anything illegal, and neither have I."

"Yeah, well, you can keep saying that, but I know what you've done. You see, there's something you don't know. The night Kelly was killed, he talked to me. He told me everything you did. He told me how he killed Phil Downing and framed Brian Kincaid, and how he killed those old folks in Peru with a nasal spray. He told me all these things because he was trying to get Nelson out from under a prison sentence, and because of what he told me, an investigation is under way."

"Bullshit. No government agency is investigating Mulray Pharma. I'd know if one was."

"You're almost right. No *law enforcement* agency is investigating— but a select group of congressmen has decided to investigate themselves. And do you know why?"

Before Fiona could respond, he said, "Because one of Mulray's competitors has decided that if Orson Mulray had a few legal problems, it could be to their advantage."

"Who is it?" Fiona snarled. "Pfizer? Eli Lilly? Which one of those bastards is doing this?"

DeMarco almost laughed. "It doesn't matter who it is. What matters is that a pharmaceutical company with extremely deep pockets has convinced a few congressmen that Mulray should be investigated. And these congressmen, who weren't all that hard to buy, agreed."

DeMarco reached into his suit coat, pulled a folded piece of paper from an inside pocket, and handed it to Fiona.

"What is this?" Fiona said.

Her question was understandable, as the words on the paper were written in Spanish. They'd been written by Emma.

"That's a copy of a letter written by a woman named Mercedes Acorta requesting that the body of Frederico Salas be returned from Thailand to Peru. If you can't read Spanish, I'm sure someone will translate the letter for you."

"Who is—"

"Yeah, I'm sure you don't know who Frederico Salas is—or was. To you he was just a piece of meat with a microchip stuck in his arm. Well, Frederico was one of the people Kelly killed in Peru, and Mercedes Acorta is Frederico's only living relative, a distant, distant cousin. I was able to convince Ms. Acorta that returning her cousin's body to Peru would be in the interests of justice, and since a certain drug company is paying for everything, including a small stipend for Mercedes's suffering, she agreed.

"Now, the Thai government hasn't agreed to allow us to exhume the body yet, but they will eventually, because my friends in Congress are applying pressure to the right people and our friendly pharmaceutical company is spending money to grease the skids. In the meantime, a private security firm has been hired to watch Mr. Salas's grave at the Christian cemetery in Bangkok to make sure the body doesn't disappear. And do you know who is going to perform the autopsy on Mr. Salas?"

Fiona didn't say anything. She was scratching her arm like she was trying to dig ticks out from under her skin as she glared at DeMarco.

"Dr. Jonathan Hayes," DeMarco said. "Dr. Hayes is one of the most highly regarded forensic pathologists in the world, and he specializes in detecting toxins during autopsies. Google him; there are about a million articles on the Internet talking about all the cases he's solved here and overseas."

"You see, Fiona, the problem you and Orson Mulray have is that what you did was enormously complex and involved a lot of people. People in Simon Ballard's lab in Smyrna, Delaware. People associated with Dr. Panyarachun's clinic in Thailand. All we need is a crack in the door and some of these people will be convinced to talk to strengthen our case. You also gave money to a lot of people, including Kelly and Nelson and Hobson. You don't think the money can be traced back to Mulray Pharma, but my buddies in Congress are eventually gonna get the accounting geeks at the FBI involved. You know, the guys who are able to follow money laundering schemes involving Mexican drug cartels—criminals a lot smarter than you and Orson Mulray, in other words. It will take some time, but the guys with the green eyeshades *will* find a money trail leading back to Mulray Pharma."

Fiona finally spoke. "If you can do all this, why are you here?"

"Because it's going to take a lot of time and a lot of money," DeMarco said. "Frankly, I don't really care about the money, since it's coming from a drug company and the U.S. Treasury, but I do care about the time—my time, that is. I don't want to spend the next three or four years of my life working on putting you in a jail cell. But if you cooperate, it will make my job easier, and you'll get a deal from the government—a reduced sentence for sure, if you help."

Before Fiona could say anything, DeMarco raised a hand to silence her. "We have two ways to go here. The hard way is we collect a lot of evidence—autopsy results, statements from scientists in Ballard's lab, phone records, banking transactions—and we use all this evidence to get Orson Mulray . . . and then we get you. And you'll do just as much time as Mulray.

"The other way we can go, and the way I prefer to go, is to give you a deal, because if you'll testify against Mulray it will strengthen the government's case and save everybody a lot of work. You see, it's really Orson Mulray we want, because we know you were just his pawn in all this. But if you don't cooperate, you go from pawn to full-blown accomplice."

He could tell that Fiona didn't like being called Mulray's pawn.

"So, what's it going to be, Fiona? Are you going to help me, or do you want to bet your life that I can't make a case against you and Mulray now that I have people with money and political clout behind me?"

It didn't take two seconds for Fiona to respond. "Get the hell out of here," she said. "I haven't done anything wrong, and you can't prove otherwise."

DeMarco rose from his seat. "All right. But you need to understand something. The government's like a glacier when it goes after a crime as complicated as this one. It takes a long time to get the glacier moving, and then it moves slowly, but in the end it grinds up everything in its path. Well, I've got the glacier moving now, Fiona, and it's gonna run right over you. I'll give you a couple days to make up your mind, but after that you won't see me again until the day I show up here with FBI agents and watch them put handcuffs on you."

DeMarco called Emma after leaving Fiona's building.

"Did you sell it?" Emma asked.

"I have no idea," DeMarco said.

Fiona walked back to her home gym, mounted the stationary bike, and began to pedal.

When she read in the paper that Nelson had been killed at Wallens Ridge, she was delighted. Hell, she was *ecstatic*. René Lambert, Hobson, Kelly, Nelson, and Lee were all gone—meaning there was no one left to testify that she had hired them to do anything. There was that little twit Bernie, of course, and the guard he bribed to have Nelson killed at Wallens Ridge, but there had been nothing in the papers to indicate that anyone was investigating Nelson's death. He'd died in a routine prison *you-lookin'-at-me?* beef. Yes, when she read that Nelson was dead, she'd thought: *It's finally over. I can get on with my life.*

Then DeMarco shows up, like a bad penny that just won't stay lost.

She knew he was lying, of course. She knew this because a) he was a lawyer and b) he worked for Congress. She couldn't think of two more certain criteria to define a liar. But what was he lying about? It did seem plausible that a rival pharmaceutical company would be willing to spread some money around to cause Mulray Pharma problems, and it seemed plausible that a few congressmen could be paid to assist them. It was also possible that they were trying to get a body exhumed to do an autopsy. She wasn't, however, the least bit worried about an autopsy.

The only crime she and Orson had committed to develop the Alzheimer's drug was murdering a few people to provide timely data for Ballard's research. Because of this, they knew it was critical that the old folks be killed in a manner in which murder could not be proven and, for that reason, they contacted a renowned pathologist in Switzerland. They paid the pathologist—through a middleman—to identify a poison that couldn't be detected during an autopsy, and he gave them the name of the aerosol spray. That was step one. Step two came after the first person was killed with the poison, when they had two other pathologists, one a German and one an Israeli, perform independent autopsies on the corpse. They told the two pathologists that it was suspected that poison had been used to kill the person and they should perform every test known to modern science to prove this was the case. The pathologists spent a month trying and, in the end, concluded the person had died from a garden-variety heart attack. So Fiona was confident that no matter what pathologist they used—this Dr. Hayes or anyone else—they wouldn't be able to prove that people had been poisoned.

The problem, however, was that DeMarco was right about one thing: a lot of people had taken part in developing the drug, and Fiona had never been involved in the work done at Ballard's lab or in the clinical trials in Thailand. She had no idea if buried somewhere in all the paperwork was evidence to support the allegation that people had been killed to provide data. She just didn't know.

The other thing DeMarco was right about was the money trail. The government, given enough time and the ability to apply pressure to various offshore banks, might be able to trace money from Mulray Pharma to people like Kelly and Nelson.

The thing was—and DeMarco had basically said this—if the government launched a massive investigation the trail wouldn't lead directly to her. It would lead to the *company*—to Mulray Pharma. And if they could prove the company had done something illegal, then they would go after Orson, because he *was* the company. And if they had enough evidence to convict Orson, would he give her up? What a dumb question. Of course he would. He would blame everything on her. He'd say she was the one who paid Kelly and Nelson and directed all the killings. He'd claim she'd acted without his knowledge, and maybe the government would believe him. But whether the government believed him or not, he'd try his best to lay the blame on her.

Stop it! You're letting DeMarco get inside your head. There was no way the government would ever be able to prove a crime had been committed. And if a case ever went to trial, it would be incredibly complex. It would involve things done in foreign countries where the United States had no jurisdiction; there would be impossible-to-comprehend scientific mumbo jumbo and dueling experts providing conflicting testimony about everything. And Orson's two-hundred-person outside law firm would be throwing up roadblocks every step of the way. There was no chance in hell the government would be able to win in court, assuming it could ever indict anyone for a crime.

But then this voice—the voice that had propelled her from sexually abused trailer trash to a woman with a net worth of a billion dollars—said: *Are you sure? Are you absolutely sure?*

Fiona began to realize that what really bothered her was that she couldn't stand the thought of living in fear for the rest of her life.

But she could see it. It's three, four, five years in the future, and the government eventually finds something they can use to bring her and Orson down. And then she spends years engaged in legal battles—and maybe loses the war. She did *not* want that sword hanging over her head. She *refused* to have it hanging over her head. She wanted to get on with her life—and the only way to do that was to eliminate the person who posed the greatest threat, and that person was Orson Mulray. But how would she get rid of Orson, with Kelly and Nelson no longer around to help her?

And then the answer came to her. It would be risky—she would be risking everything—but it was better to take the risk now than one day wake up and find DeMarco knocking on her door again, this time accompanied by guys with badges.

55

Orson was sitting in his den, wearing a comfortable jogging suit. He was trying to read a report that one of his VPs had sent him, but was having a hard time concentrating because he had a cold. He figured he'd caught the cold because he'd been working so hard and that it would be good to stay home for a couple of days and rest.

The phone on his desk rang.

"Yes?" he said.

"Sir, there's a woman here to see you. A Ms. West."

After the story had come out in the *Washington Post,* Orson began to get a lot of hate mail, and some of the mail came from people living in countries where Lizzie Warwick had established her care centers. One was from some maniac in Uganda who claimed that one of the test subjects who died had been like a mother to him and took care of him after his real mother died. He said if he ever got the chance, he was going to hack Orson to death with a machete.

Orson wasn't too worried about some machete-wielding African killing him, but decided that he really should do more to protect himself. He was a wealthy man and therefore a likely kidnapping target, and there were always dangerous poor people out there who resented people like him who were successful. So now he had a full-time, live-in

bodyguard—an ex-Marine who could shoot a gun with either hand—
and it was the bodyguard who had called to tell him Fiona was there.

"Let her in," Orson said. Then he said, "Wait a minute. Search her
before you let her in. You know, pat her down, check her purse, that
sort of thing. She'll go nuts and swear at you, but fuck her. Tell her
you're just doing your job and you search everyone, and you won't
let her in unless she's searched."

Fiona made him nervous.

"Why did you have that goon frisk me, goddamnit?" Fiona screamed
as soon as she entered Orson's den.

"He frisked you?" Orson said, acting bewildered. "I apologize. I'll
make sure that never happens again."

She didn't believe him; he had told that gorilla to search her. Then
she took a breath, because being angry didn't suit her purpose. "So
how are you feeling? Your secretary said you were sick."

"It's just a cold; I'll be fine in a day or two. And I need to get
back to work, because I'm a little concerned we may not be able
to keep up with demand for the product. They're working around
the clock at the plant in Thailand, but we're going to need more
capacity, and I have to decide if I want to add on to the existing
plant in Bangkok or build a new facility in Africa, where labor
rates are even cheaper."

"Well, that's terrific," Fiona said. And she meant it. The fact that
the drug was selling so well that Orson was concerned about keeping
up with orders was a very good thing indeed, since Fiona owned a lot
of Mulray Pharma stock. "But you need to take care of yourself. You
can't run the company if you're sick. And you look so tense! I think
you need one of my massages."

When she and Orson had been lovers, one of the things she did to avoid having sex with him was give him massages until he fell asleep. She was an excellent amateur masseuse, and Orson knew it. This was going to be even easier than she had imagined.

"Oh, that's all right," Orson said, but Fiona ignored his halfhearted protest and walked behind him and placed her hands on his fat shoulders. "My God! Your muscles are so tight; they're all knotted up." She started to knead his shoulders with her strong fingers and said, "Now, how does that feel?"

"Good," Orson admitted, and gave a little moan of pleasure.

"I thought so," Fiona said, and massaged his shoulders for a couple more minutes. Then she stopped and reached into her pocket.

"Ooh, don't stop," Orson said.

"I'm not," Fiona said—and she brought her right hand around to the front of his face, jammed the nozzle of the nasal spray container into his right nostril, and gave it a good squeeze.

Orson jerked his head away. "What did you do?" he asked.

"I killed you," Fiona said.

Orson tried to stand, but just as he placed his hands on his desk to rise, he clutched his left arm and collapsed back into his chair. Fiona walked around to the front of the desk so she could see his face. She had heard somewhere that having a heart attack was like having an elephant dance on your chest, and judging by the expression on Orson's face, it looked like there might be a whole herd dancing on him. He reached for the phone—to call his bodyguard, she assumed —but before his hand could touch the phone, she moved it a couple of inches until it was just beyond his reach. He looked at her then, his eyes begging for help, then his head fell onto the desk with a loud thump—and he died.

Fiona knew she was taking an incredible risk, because she knew Orson's body was going to be autopsied and that the autopsy was going to be performed by one of the best pathologists in the business.

But Fiona was betting her life on another pathologist, the one who had identified the poison she'd just used and who'd said that an hour after death, no autopsy would be able to detect it.

Fiona sat with Orson's corpse for forty-five minutes, reading a travel magazine she found in his den. She was particularly interested in one article about a man who took select clients out on his two-hundred-foot yacht for cruises around the Mediterranean. The boat had a crew of six, including a Cordon Bleu chef, a masseuse, and a personal trainer, and Fiona just loved the idea of sitting on the deck all by herself, the crew waiting on her hand and foot, as the boat sailed through Grecian islands.

She checked her watch. Enough time had passed, and she rose to leave. She looked at Orson again, his big head lying on the desk blotter, a little drool seeping from his mouth, and tried to think of something appropriate to say. The only thing she could think of was: "Bon voyage."

She opened the door to his office and said loudly, for the benefit of Orson's bodyguard, "I'll call you as soon as I hear from the *Post's* attorneys."

As she was leaving the house, she said to the guard, "Mr. Mulray told me to tell you that he doesn't want to be disturbed for at least two hours. As you know, he's sick, and he said he was going to nap on the couch in his den. And if you ever frisk me again . . ."

56

DeMarco rose from his bed dressed in boxer shorts and a Washington Nationals T-shirt with a hole in one armpit. He brushed his teeth, then went to the kitchen and added water and coffee to his Mr. Coffee. The coffee brewing, he walked to the front door, picked up the newspaper lying on his porch, and saw the headline: ORSON MULRAY DEAD.

"I'll be damned," he muttered.

He sipped his coffee as he read the article. There was no indication that the authorities found Mulray's death suspicious. An autopsy would be performed, of course, but it appeared that Mulray had most likely died from a heart attack. The reporter noted that Orson's mother had died of a heart attack at the age of fifty-six and that Orson was fifty-eight, but added that Orson's father, Clayton Mulray, had lived to the ripe old age of eighty-four. The reporter said it was tragic that Mulray had died on the cusp of his company's greatest achievement and before he could see how profoundly his new drug would benefit mankind.

The last person to see Mulray alive was his lawyer and close friend, Fiona West, and she was quoted as saying: "He'll be remembered forever for his unwavering commitment to rid the world of one of its most terrible diseases."

And maybe he would be remembered that way, DeMarco thought. It was hard to imagine Orson Mulray being placed in the same category with Jonas Salk, but history was quite often distorted. He sat for a moment, probing his conscience, to see if he felt guilty about having pointed Fiona at Orson Mulray like a guided missile—and concluded he didn't feel guilty at all.

It was time to go see Nelson again.

57

Nelson kept his side of the bargain.

He gave the Arlington County prosecutor a videotaped confession, admitting everything he and Kelly had done for Fiona West and Mulray Pharma. He provided dates and places where he met with Fiona, including his first meeting with her in Afghanistan. He said the government should at least be able to verify that Fiona had been to Afghanistan, and because Fiona had used American bodyguards, some of those men could confirm that she visited the prison where Kelly and Nelson had been detained. He also told how he and Kelly had killed Phil Downing and framed Brian Kincaid, and the details he provided gave credence to his story. For example, he told how Kelly had made a wax impression of the secretary's key, and he provided the name of the locksmith in southeast D.C. who made the key Kelly used to enter Downing's office. He admitted that Fiona gave him and Kelly ten million dollars to assist her, and he gave the prosecutor information on all his bank accounts. Certainly, Nelson said, the government should be able to trace some of that money back to its source.

The only thing Nelson would not do was confess to murder. He said Kelly had killed everyone: Downing, seven people in Peru, four in Pakistan, and three in Africa. And DeMarco had to admit that when he met with Kelly, Kelly had said the same thing: that he was the murderer, not Nelson. Nelson did admit that he'd been in the liquor store that day to kill DeMarco.

There were a number of problems with Nelson's testimony, however, the major one being that Fiona had always spoken to Kelly when she wanted something done. For instance, Kelly had told Nelson that Fiona wanted DeMarco killed, but Nelson never spoke directly to Fiona. The government might be able to show that Kelly and Fiona had phoned each other, but there would be no phone records linking Nelson to Fiona.

The prosecutor packed up all of Nelson's testimony and went to see the FBI—like a cat bringing its master a dead, unappealing rat. A meeting was then held, attended by a platoon of lawyers who reached the conclusion that Nelson's testimony against Fiona wasn't going to be good enough. All they really had was Nelson's word against Fiona's. And other than Phil Downing and Bill Hobson, they couldn't even prove that murder had occurred. The FBI wasn't about to start digging up bodies in Thailand on a case that appeared to be going nowhere.

They finally decided the best thing to do was put a wire on Nelson, have him talk to Fiona, and see if he could get her to admit to anything that would strengthen the government's case against her.

Nelson said he'd be happy to wear a wire.

After Orson Mulray died, Nelson had been released back into the hands of Arlington County. He was still under indictment for the liquor store robbery, and the prosecutor decided that since the newspapers had reported that Nelson was dead, it was no longer necessary to keep him isolated in a cabin in the Blue Ridge Mountains protected by

Virginia state troopers. On the other hand, the prosecutor didn't want Nelson placed in the Arlington County lockup with other prisoners awaiting trial: a man in a wheelchair was just too vulnerable and too noticeable. He eventually concluded it would be best for Nelson to be placed in a motel under a phony name and guarded around the clock by Arlington cops.

This arrangement suited Nelson fine.

Nelson asked his jailers if he might be permitted a visitor, a guy he'd served with in Iraq. The prosecutor mulled this over and said, "Sure, why not?" Nelson was cooperating, and if he were being kept in the county lockup, he would have been allowed visitors.

So Nelson called a guy name Dan Ingraham, and asked Ingraham to drop by so they could bullshit about the bad old days. Ingraham was delighted to hear from Nelson. When most of his left leg was blown off by an IED, Nelson was the guy who had dragged him out of the personnel carrier and saved him from being burned to death.

"But I need you to do me a favor," Nelson said.

"Sure, man, anything," Ingraham said.

When Ingraham arrived that evening, the cop guarding Nelson frisked him to make sure he wasn't carrying a weapon. He also looked inside the bag that Ingraham had brought with him. In it were chips and dip—and a half-gallon of Jameson's.

Nelson invited the cop to join him and Ingraham for a couple of drinks. In the time the cop had been guarding Nelson, he had revealed that he was a member of the Virginia National Guard and was an Iraq war vet, too. So Nelson said, "Come on. Have a pop or two with us. Who's gonna know?" "Ah, what the hell," the cop said, and entered the motel room.

The cop, mindful that he was going to be relieved by another cop in five hours, sipped his whiskey slowly, but Nelson and his one-legged friend drank like there was no tomorrow. They didn't talk about combat or guys who died or guys they'd killed. They talked about the funny stuff that happened over there, about the time a sergeant named Riley came back from R&R with a tattoo of a heart on his ass and the name Marlee inside the heart—and how Riley couldn't remember getting the tattoo and didn't know who Marlee was. They talked about an Iraqi kid who had enough pirated DVDs to start a Blockbuster store and a female soldier who kicked the shit out of a Ranger when the Ranger told her she ran like a girl. Nelson started to tell a funny story about Kelly but got too choked up to finish it.

At one point, Ingraham excused himself to go to the bathroom. The cop, still thinking like a cop, went into the bathroom after him and looked around to make sure Ingraham hadn't left anything in there. The cop didn't notice that the bathroom window was cracked open a couple of inches, and if he had noticed he probably wouldn't have cared. The bathroom window wasn't big enough for a guy Nelson's size to crawl through, and if it had been, what would be the point of a guy in a wheelchair crawling out a window, anyway?

———⋅◆⋅———

Getting Nelson into the same room with Fiona so the FBI could record a conversation between them was a problem. If Nelson—a man she thought was dead—showed up at her condo, Fiona probably wouldn't let him in. If he rolled up to her in a restaurant, all Fiona had to do was walk away, or up a flight of stairs, and Nelson would be unable to stop her or follow her. So they needed to find someplace for Fiona and Nelson to meet where Nelson would at least have a chance of keeping her there long enough to make his pitch.

The FBI began following Fiona to learn her habits and see if they could figure out an appropriate meeting place. She was no longer working at Mulray Pharma, so her office was out of the question. She had lunch and dinner at restaurants almost every day, but varied the places where she ate. She spent a lot of time shopping in high-end stores and going to spas, and joined an exclusive country club and began taking golf lessons, but a golf course was not a good venue for Nelson. She also met with a real estate agent and twice flew to Florida to look at homes that were for sale. The last one she looked at was right next door to the place where Tiger Woods used to live.

One thing she did that puzzled the FBI agents following her was spend a lot of time with a high-priced consultant who managed campaigns for various politicians. No one could figure out why Fiona was visiting the consultant unless she was planning to run for office, but it was hard for people to imagine her doing that. Only DeMarco disagreed; he said Fiona would make a perfect politician.

And it was DeMarco who finally came up with the perfect place for Nelson and Fiona to meet—and the reason he came up with the solution, as opposed to all the cops and lawyers, was that his idea was somewhat illegal. DeMarco suggested they simply stick Nelson in Fiona's condo while she was out and, when she came back home, he would be there waiting for her. The lawyers pointed out that this would mean that Nelson would have to break into Fiona's place, to which DeMarco responded a) who gives a shit and b) he wouldn't *really* have to break in. And the FBI found out that DeMarco was right. The maintenance man in Fiona's building, after being told what the FBI was trying to do, said he'd be happy to let Nelson into Fiona's condo. He said the bitch was always threatening to fire him and didn't tip worth shit.

The FBI set up their recording equipment in the condo of a woman who lived on the sixth floor, the floor below Fiona's. The woman was chairman of the condo board and had had a number of disagreeable encounters with Ms. West. Unlike the maintenance man, she was too refined to call Fiona a bitch, but she said she'd be delighted to assist the FBI in any endeavor that might result in Fiona no longer being a tenant.

The FBI coached Nelson extensively on what he was to say to Fiona; they wanted him to focus on Phil Downing's murder and the attempt to kill DeMarco in the liquor store. The lawyers figured if they could make a case against Fiona for those domestic crimes, they might be able to go after her for things she had done for Mulray Pharma overseas. They had Nelson practice for several hours with a female FBI agent who pretended to be Fiona.

Nelson told the agents he liked the way they were going about things —taking their time, thinking things through. It was the way he and Kelly used to operate: lots of surveillance, practice, and preparation. The FBI agents felt a little uncomfortable being complimented by Nelson.

When the FBI guys were satisfied Nelson was ready, two agents drove him in a wheelchair-accessible van from his motel in Arlington to another motel in Wilmington. The following morning, the agents rolled him into Fiona's building and took the elevator to the sixth floor, where two FBI technicians and a Justice Department lawyer were waiting. The technicians taped a microphone to Nelson's chest and made sure all the recording equipment was working, and then the agents took Nelson by elevator to the seventh floor, where the building's maintenance man was waiting. All tenants were required to give the building's management firm a key so they could gain access to the condos in the event of some sort of emergency, and the maintenance guy used that key to open Fiona's door.

Nelson rolled himself into Fiona's lair.

———————◆◆◆———————

While Nelson waited for Fiona to return home, he helped himself to the food in her kitchen. He polished off a whole container of duck liver pâté, which he spread on crackers as thin as Communion wafers. He also found a bottle of Dom Pérignon in the refrigerator. He didn't normally drink champagne, but he did know that Dom was very expensive. So he opened the bottle and sat there sipping the most expensive booze he'd ever had in his life and thought about Kelly and their place in Montana as he waited for Fiona.

Three hours later Fiona opened the door, and when she walked into her living room she immediately saw Nelson sitting in his wheelchair. Naturally, she reacted like a person who was seeing a ghost—because she thought she was indeed seeing one. The first words out of her mouth were an inarticulate stream of babble, consisting of "What? What? What the hell? What are you . . ."

Nelson said, "Yeah, I'm alive, you cunt."

The Justice Department lawyer, one floor below, frowned when she heard this. Nelson was supposed to let Fiona talk—it was imperative that Fiona at least admit that she knew Nelson.

"What are you doing here?" Fiona said.

This was when Nelson was supposed to go into his carefully prepared spiel, saying that he wanted money to remain silent and not testify against her. He would have to tell her how it was that the papers had reported him dead and how he came to be in her apartment, but the FBI had prepared him to deal with those issues. Nelson, however, didn't launch into his spiel.

The next thing the technicians, the lawyer, and the agents on the sixth floor heard was Fiona saying, "No. Wait. No. We can work this out." Then they heard two gunshots. The agents went running out of the sixth-floor condo and up the stairs to Fiona's floor. The technicians manning the recording equipment heard Nelson mutter something, and then heard a third shot.

"What did he say?" the lawyer asked.

"He said hooah or hoo-haw, something like that," one of the technicians said.

"I always *thought* the damn guy was being too cooperative," DeMarco said to Emma. "We should have seen this coming."

"How did he get the gun?"

DeMarco told her what the Arlington prosecutor had told him. The night Nelson's buddy, Ingraham, visited him, Ingraham must have brought the little .32-caliber semiauto with him. While Nelson, his pal, and the cop were all drinking and joking together, Ingraham went into the bathroom and opened the bathroom window, and after he left he drove to the back of the motel and dropped the gun through the window and onto the bathroom floor. Then Nelson hid the gun somewhere—taped it to the bottom of his wheelchair, stuck it in his diaper, or maybe just sat on it. Nobody ever thought to search Nelson for a weapon, and Ingraham—a guy whom Nelson had kept from burning to death—denied knowing anything about a gun, and his fingerprints weren't on it.

"He was planning to kill Fiona all along," DeMarco said. "The guy used us by pretending to cooperate, just hoping he'd have the chance to get close to her. If he hadn't been able to get a gun, he would have found some way to get his hands on her and then he would have snapped her neck or strangled her. I think the reason he really wanted the gun was to kill himself, and the gun just made killing Fiona easier. I guess he thought that life in a wheelchair really wasn't worth living. Or maybe he just couldn't live with the awful things he'd done."

"I don't care why he killed himself," Emma said. "But I think he figured that a life without Kelly wasn't worth living."

Epilogue

The FBI agent read Bernie his Miranda rights and asked if he understood them. Oh, yeah, he understood them, Bernie said—and he also understood that he was screwed.

The Bureau had traced the phony kidnapping bulletin on Hobson back to his IT pal at the FBI—and his pal gave up Bernie in a heartbeat. He admitted that Bernie gave him money to issue the bulletin, and phone records showed that Bernie had called him.

The FBI agents told Bernie that they were going to convict him for being an accomplice to Bill Hobson's murder, but Bernie figured no way in hell would that ever happen. The Bureau didn't have a clue who killed Hobson or any way to connect Bernie to his death, and Bernie wasn't about to tell them anything about Mulray Pharma. He *would* have told them about Mulray and Fiona if that would have helped him, but as Orson Mulray and Fiona were both dead, Bernie figured talking about Mulray would just give the FBI more information they could use against him. There was no point digging his grave any deeper than it already was.

So Bernie's plan—if you could call it a plan—was to stonewall the FBI. He wasn't going to say a damn thing. All they could prove was that he'd called his buddy at the Hoover Building—they couldn't even prove the money the guy received came from him—and then it was just his buddy's word against his. So maybe he'd go to jail for being an accomplice to issuing a phony bulletin—he wasn't even sure what category of crime that was—or maybe not. But one thing he knew for sure. All that money he got from Fiona . . . well, that was gone. His goddamn lawyer was going to get every penny of that trying to keep him out of jail.

———————◆◆◆———————

Albert Morehouse was surprised that after Ike Clancy killed Nelson—or tried to kill Nelson—the guy who sent him the letter sent him the other half of his payment, the two hundred fifty grand he'd promised. He didn't have to do that, because Morehouse had no idea who'd written him the letter.

Morehouse also wasn't sure what happened with Nelson. He heard a rumor coming out of the warden's office that Clancy didn't kill Nelson, that the state troopers just took him away, but the next day he saw an article in the paper that said Nelson was dead. If Clancy had killed Nelson, however, they would have charged Clancy with Nelson's murder—but Clancy was never charged. The warden just tossed him into the hole for ninety days.

And Clancy never told anyone that Morehouse had offered him a week with Carly Mendez to kill Nelson—and Morehouse didn't know why. Maybe Clancy figured the other guards would make his life hell if he gave up Morehouse—or maybe ratting out an accomplice went against whatever personal code of honor an asshole like Ike Clancy had. Whatever the case, Albert Morehouse had half a million dollars to get out of debt and help with his wife's future medical expenses—and the only reason he did was due to the integrity of two criminals.

It was a shame his wife's HMO didn't have that sort of integrity.

———— ◆◆◆ ————

General Omar Bradley loved his new human—a short creature that wore her hair in pigtails. She had a high, squeaky voice and called him Doggie, and she spent a lot more time playing with him than the sad man with the round stomach who had called him Brad.

———— ◆◆◆ ————

Simon Ballard couldn't understand how his life had fallen apart so fast.

One day he had his own private laboratory, a handpicked staff, a phenomenal salary, and his name was being mentioned as a possible— some said *certain*—Nobel laureate. The next day he was unemployed, evicted from his lab like a tenant who couldn't pay the rent, and being hounded by crass reporters.

It all started with a few people having minor strokes in Thailand— people who had been part of the clinical trials in that country. He was certain—well, almost certain—the strokes weren't caused by his drug, but without a laboratory, he couldn't prove it. What he needed, in addition to a lab, was access to people who had been given earlier versions of the drug—the people in Uganda, Pakistan, and Peru—but the Warwick Care Centers had been closed and those people were scattered about in remote places and he didn't even know their names. The RFID chips that had been installed in them had been removed at the same time Mulray Pharma walked away from the care centers.

When the strokes were reported, the FDA decided to withhold approval of the drug until the cause of the strokes could be determined. At that point, he fully expected that Mulray Pharma would ask him to lead the investigation—and that's when he was fired. The new CEO of Mulray Pharma—the one the board hired to replace Orson

Mulray—decided he wanted to distance the company from Simon Ballard. The CEO was concerned about lawsuits and improperly conducted clinical trials and figured that he might be able to lay all the blame on Ballard, as Orson Mulray was no longer alive to blame. And without any financial backing or a place to work, Ballard couldn't do the research he needed to prove the strokes weren't connected to his drug.

And, in the back of his mind, he did wonder if maybe the strokes *could* be related to the drug. He remembered when they got those anomalous results from some of the subjects in Thailand, and he tried to convince Mulray he needed to do a little bit more testing, how Mulray ran roughshod over his concerns in his rush to market the drug. Or at least that's the way he remembered things.

Then along comes Dr. Matthew Reynolds from Georgetown University, a man so arrogant he was insufferable. Reynolds had been hired by Pfizer to develop a version of the drug that was based on his techniques, but sufficiently different that Pfizer might be able to claim they weren't infringing on Mulray Pharma's patents. Well, Reynolds was now claiming—and his claim was backed up by a few other people with MDs and PhDs behind their names—that Ballard's drug prevented Alzheimer's for only a few years and that after that the drug became ineffective, and possibly dangerous. He was sure Reynolds was wrong, but again, without a lab, he couldn't prove otherwise—and between Reynolds' claims and the people who stroked in Thailand, the Nobel Committee was backing away from him like he was the leper with the fewest fingers.

The final straw was the TV movie. It claimed to be fiction, but portrayed characters who were obviously based on him and Orson Mulray, and it showed shadowy figures injecting old people with poison and slicing up their brains so the fictional Simon Ballard could produce his drug and the fictional Orson Mulray could rub his hands in glee as the money poured in. After the movie came out, the tabloid press began to hound him, accusing him of actually killing people to develop his drug, and they gave him idiotic nicknames like the Grim Reaper and Dr. Death. He tried to explain to the reporters that he had nothing to do with Mulray Pharma's clinical trials, but they wouldn't believe him, and the lawyers he hired to sue the tabloids and the movie producers for damaging his reputation . . . Well, all the lawyers did was take his money.

It was so unfair.

***

DeMarco and Brian Kincaid's mother were waiting for him when Kincaid walked out of prison. There were puckered scars on the right side of his neck, and when he looked over at DeMarco he had to move his whole upper body because his neck didn't swivel like it should have.

Because of Nelson's videotaped confession—and a lot of pressure applied by John Mahoney—Kincaid's conviction had been overturned. But the attorney in the District of Columbia who had prosecuted Kincaid for Phil Downing's murder wasn't about to let Brian Kincaid sue the District for ten or twenty million dollars for having been incorrectly imprisoned. As far as the attorney was concerned, his office had acted in good faith based on the evidence it had, and a jury of his peers had convicted Kincaid—and there was no proof that Kelly or Nelson killed Downing, no matter what the late Mr. Nelson said. So the attorney told Kincaid he could either sign papers agreeing not to sue the District, in which case he'd get out of jail immediately, or he could hire a lawyer and see if he could convince some judge to give him a new trial. Kincaid agreed not to sue.

Brian Kincaid was now forty-seven years old, completely broke, and unemployed. Thanks to one pharmaceutical company, he didn't have much of a life to look forward to. Thanks to another one, he was addicted to the medication he was currently taking to alleviate the constant pain in his neck. But Brian Kincaid's mother didn't care. She was just happy to have her son back.

Acknowledgments

Fred Sego for his help in explaining to me how drugs are approved by the FDA and how clinical trials are conducted. Any errors in this novel regarding how this process works are mine and mine alone, and not Mr. Sego's. I also want to thank Linda Kirk for introducing me to Fred.

The late Charles Burton. Charles Burton was, among many other things, a book collector, and I was shocked to learn he died while I was writing this book. He helped me on this particular novel with the Wilmington scenes, but in general he was always a huge fan and promoter of my books. I can recall fondly the last time we had dinner together in San Francisco and will truly miss seeing him at future Bouchercons.

Dara Schultz, Ryan Schultz, and Rich Bennallack. Dara attended a charity auction and won the rights to naming a character in this novel. The character is Rich Bennallack, the young off-duty cop who shot Nelson. The real Mr. Bennallack is Dara's father. I also want to thank Ryan Schultz for all his help in promoting my books to his Rotary Club members.

My good friend Bob Koch for building me a shiv. I called Bob one day and read him the section where the prison inmate builds a shiv out of a Coke can to stab Brian Kincaid and asked Bob if my shiv-construction technique would work. Bob, who is one of the best engineers I know, said he wasn't sure my method would work and then went out to his shop and actually built a shiv from a soda can as described in this novel. (He did use an electric grinder to put an edge on the weapon, as opposed to grinding it on a rock.) Bob made me a gift of the shiv he constructed and I will cherish it, as bizarre as that might sound.

Frank Horton, as always, for reading all my books, and finding tons of typos, before the books go to my editor and copy editor. Readers have e-mailed me about typos they've found in my published novels, and I want to point out that the fault does not lie with Frank or subsequent editors. They do a wonderful job. The fault is mine, because I make so many mistakes in the first draft of my novels that even Frank and two other people can't possibly find them all.

Like DeMarco, I had no desire to go to Peru to research the settings in this book. Fortunately, I know a wonderful, generous man named Russ Lawrence. Russ is the former owner of Chapter One Book Store in Hamilton, Montana. He and his wife, Jean, interrupted their comfortable life in Montana to be Peace Corps volunteers in Peru— God bless 'em—and Russ provided me an eloquent, detailed, written description of the road Emma took from Arequipa to Pinchollo. Any errors in the book regarding Peru are errors I made when I modified and took "literary license" with what Russ sent me.

Nancy Isbell, doctor of veterinary medicine, and the wife of friend and fellow writer Tom Isbell. Nancy generously took the time to educate me on doggie diseases. Once again, any errors with regard to General Omar Bradley's medical condition are those I made.

Dr. Jonathan Hayes, for permitting me to use his name. Dr. Hayes actually is a forensic pathologist in New York City, as well as a fellow writer. He last novel, *A Hard Death,* was a terrific read.

Dr. Robert Yekel for advice on Emma's cancer. Any errors regarding the disease or the cure are mine alone.

My wife, Gail Lawson, for finding a fascinating 2010 article in *Vanity Fair* titled "Deadly Medicine," and written by Donald Bartlett and James Steele. This article discussed in sobering detail the practices of American pharmaceutical companies testing drugs on people in third world countries. It may be legal, but as DeMarco says in the book, it seems a bit slimy.